nickelodeon

THE LOUD HOUSE

3 IN 1 #5

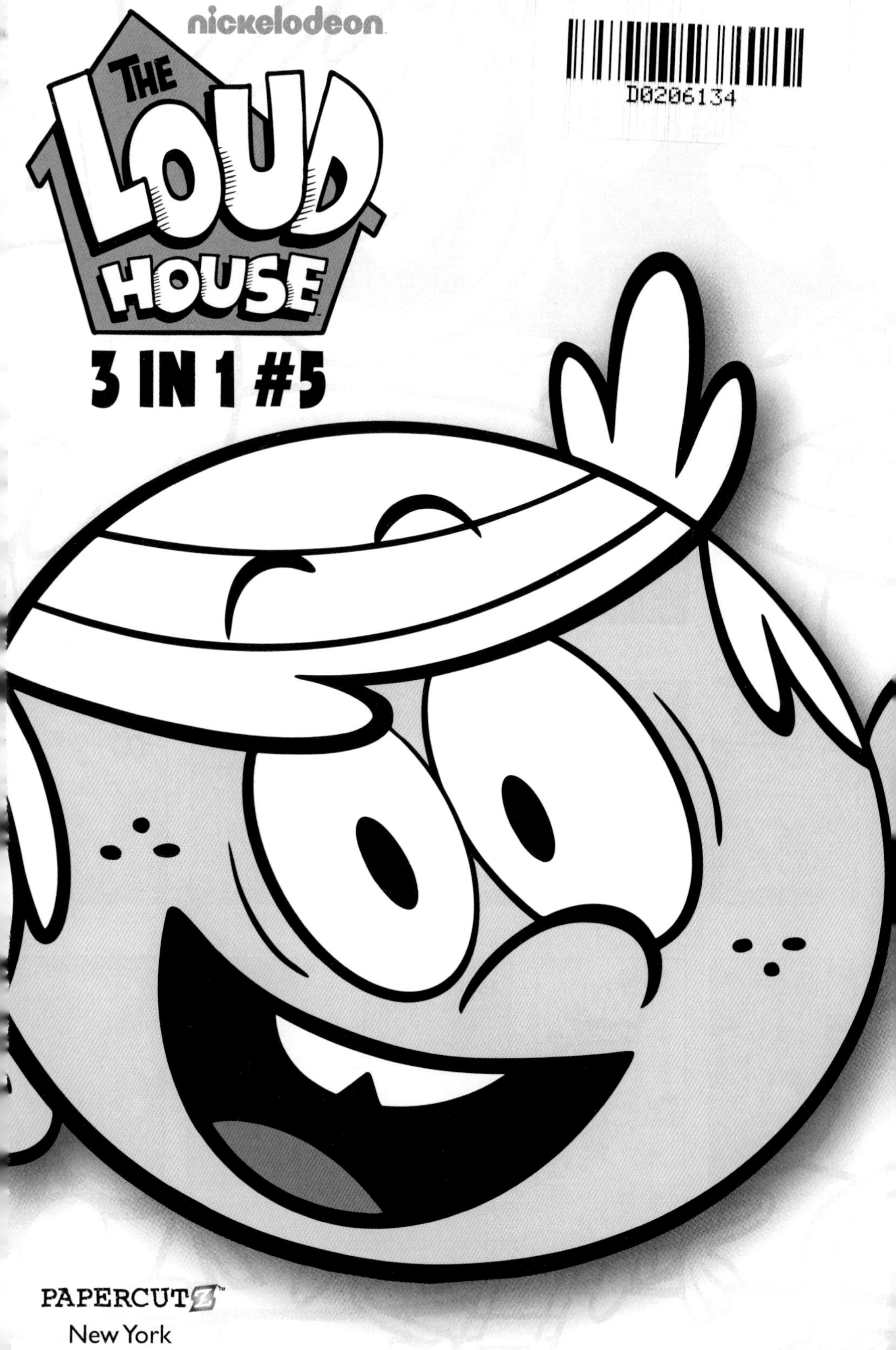

PAPERCUTZ
New York

MORE GREAT GRAPHIC NOVEL SERIES AVAILABLE FROM
PAPERCUTZ™

THE SMURFS TALES

BRINA THE CAT

CAT & CAT

THE SISTERS

ATTACK OF THE STUFF

LOLA'S SUPER CLUB

SCHOOL FOR EXTRATERRESTRIAL GIRLS

GERONIMO STILTON REPORTER

THE MYTHICS

GUMBY

MELOWY

BLUEBEARD

GILLBERT

ASTERIX

FUZZY BASEBALL

THE CASAGRANDES

THE LOUD HOUSE

ASTRO MOUSE AND LIGHT BULB

GEEKY F@B 5

THE ONLY LIVING GIRL

papercutz.com
Also available where ebooks are sold.

Melowy, Geronimo Stilton; © 2018 Atlantyca S.p.A; The Sisters, Cat & Cat © 2018 BAMBOO ÉDITION; Brina the Cat © 2021 TUNUÉ (Tunué s.r.l.); Attack of the Stuff © 2021 Jim Benton; Lola's Super Club © Christine Beigel + Pierre Fouillet, 2010, Bang. Ediciones, 2011, 2013; School for Extraterrestrial Girls © 2021 Jeremy Whitley and Jamie Noguchi; Mythics © 2021 Éditions Delcourt; GUMBY ©2018 Prema Toy Co., Inc.; Bluebeard © 2018 Metaphrog; Gillbert © 2021 Art Baltazar; ASTERIX® - OBELIX® - IDEFIX® -DOGMATIX ®© 2021 HACHETTE LIVRE; Fuzzy Baseball © 2018 by John Steven Gurney; The Loud House and The Casagrandes © 2018 Viacom International Inc.; Manosaurs © 2018 Stuart Fischer and Papercutz; Geeky Fab Five ©2021 Geeky Fab Five LLC.; The Only Living Girl © 2018-2019 Bottled Lightening LLC.

© Peyo - 2021 - Licensed through I.M.P.S. (Brussels) - www.smurf.com

nickelodeon THE LOUD HOUSE

THE LOUD HOUSE 3 IN 1 #5

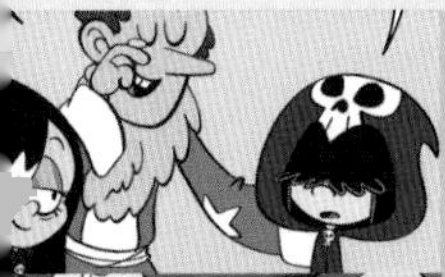

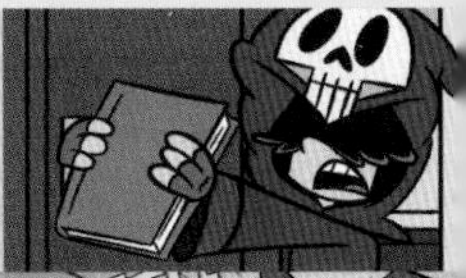

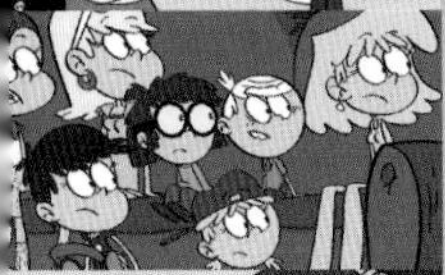

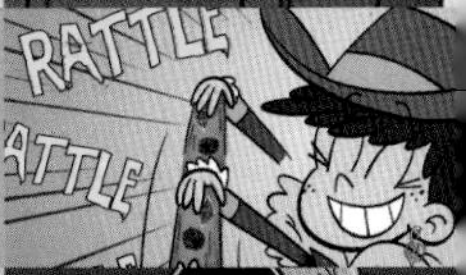
RATTLE

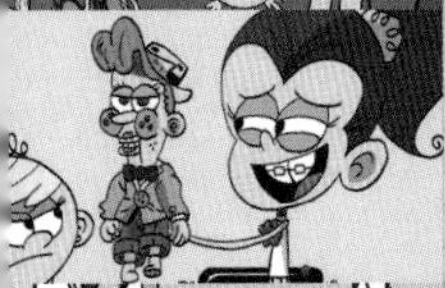

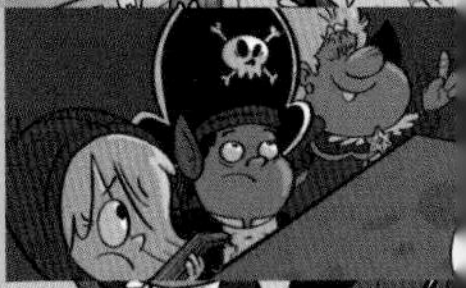

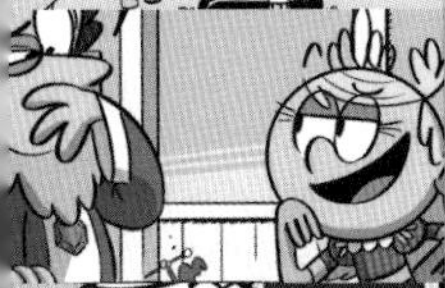

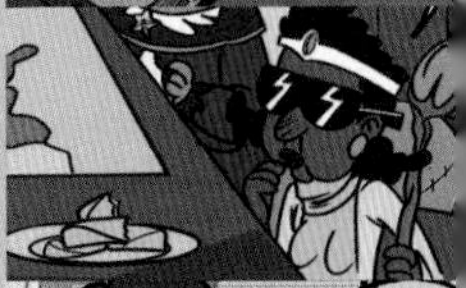

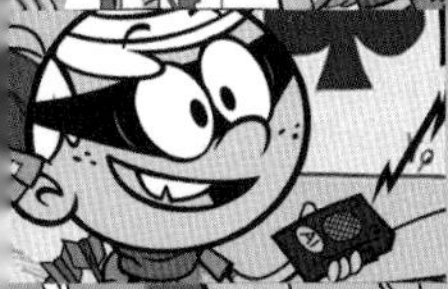

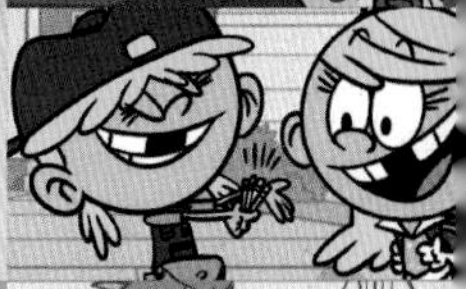

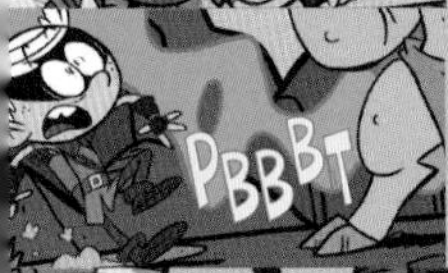
PBBBT

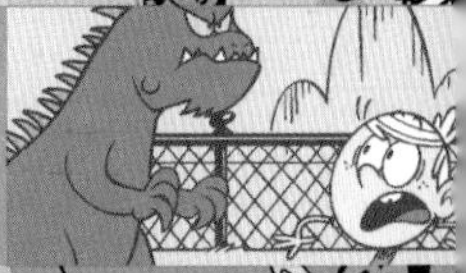

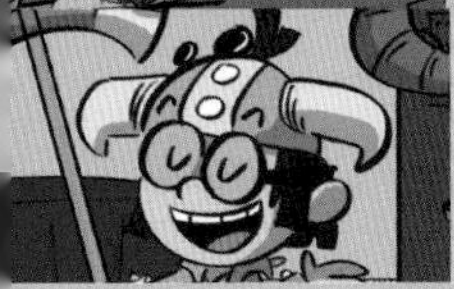

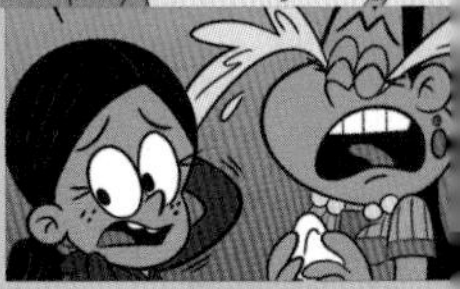

KELSEY WOOLEY — COVER ARTIST
ZAZO AGUIAR, KELSEY WOOLEY, RON BRADLEY — RPG costume designs
MICOL HIATT — Comic Designer/Nickelodeon
JAYJAY JACKSON — Design
EMMA BONE, CAITLIN FEIN, KRISTEN G. SMITH, NEIL WADE, DANA CLUVERIUS, MOLLIE FREILICH, JOAN HILTY, ARTHUR "DJ" DESIN, AND JAMES SALERNO — Special Thanks
KARLO ANTUNES — Editor
STEPHANIE BROOKS — Assistant Managing Editor
JEFF WHITMAN— Comics Editor/Nickelodeon
JIM SALICRUP
Editor-in-Chief

ISBN: 978-1-5458-0892-4

Printed in Turkey
April 2022

Distributed by Macmillan
Second Printing

"I BELIEVE"
Kevin Cannarile—Writer
D.K. Terrell —Artist, Colorist
Wilson Ramos Jr. — Letterer
114

"THE TEAM-UP"
Derek Fridolfs—Writer
Ron Bradley —Artist, Colorist
Wilson Ramos Jr. — Letterer
129

"CLOSING MIME"
Amanda Fein —Writer
Erin Hyde —Artist, Colorist
Wilson Ramos Jr. — Letterer
142

"AN UNDEAD DEBATE"
Kacey Huang-Wooley—Writer
Kiernan Sjursen-Lien —Artist,
Colorist
Wilson Ramos Jr. — Letterer
117

"SISTER NATURE"
Derek Fridolfs—Writer
Angela Zhang —Artist
Erin Rodriguez — Colorist
Wilson Ramos Jr. — Letterer
131

"GONE GNOME"
Jair Holguin—Writer
Jessica Gallaher —Artist
Erin Rodriguez — Colorist
Wilson Ramos Jr. — Letterer
145

"MALL TRIP"
Paloma Uribe —Writer
Erin Hyde —Artist, Colorist
Wilson Ramos Jr. — Letterer
120

"A DIRTY RESCUE"
Kacey Huang-Wooley—Writer
Amanda Lioi —Artist
Erin Rodriguez — Colorist
Wilson Ramos Jr. — Letterer
133

"FRIENDS FUR-EVER"
Caitlin Fein —Writer
D.K. Terrell —Artist, Colorist
Wilson Ramos Jr. — Letterer
147

"PLAYING TO THE CROWD"
Derek Fridolfs—Writer
Marc Stone —Artist
Erin Rodriguez — Colorist
Wilson Ramos Jr. — Letterer
125

"FAN FRENZY"
Jair Holguin —Writer
Joel Zamudio —Artist, Colorist
Wilson Ramos Jr. — Letterer
136

"PURRSONAL HYGIENE"
Kiernan Sjursen-Lien —Writer, Artist,
Colorist
Wilson Ramos Jr. — Letterer
150

"CONSTRUCTION CONUNDRUM"
Kiernan Sjursen-Lien —Writer
Joel Zamudio —Artist, Colorist
Wilson Ramos Jr. — Letterer
126

"LISA'S PAPER VIEW"
Kacey Huang-Wooley—Writer
Kelsey Wooley —Artist, Colorist
Wilson Ramos Jr. — Letterer
139

"ONE GOOD PUSH"
Kevin Cannarile—Writer
Lex Hobson —Artist, Colorist
Wilson Ramos Jr. — Letterer
153

**GUESS WHO?!: Can you identify all THE LOUD HOUSE and THE CASAGRANDES characters
silhouetted on these 2 pages? [Answers on pages 159-160!]**

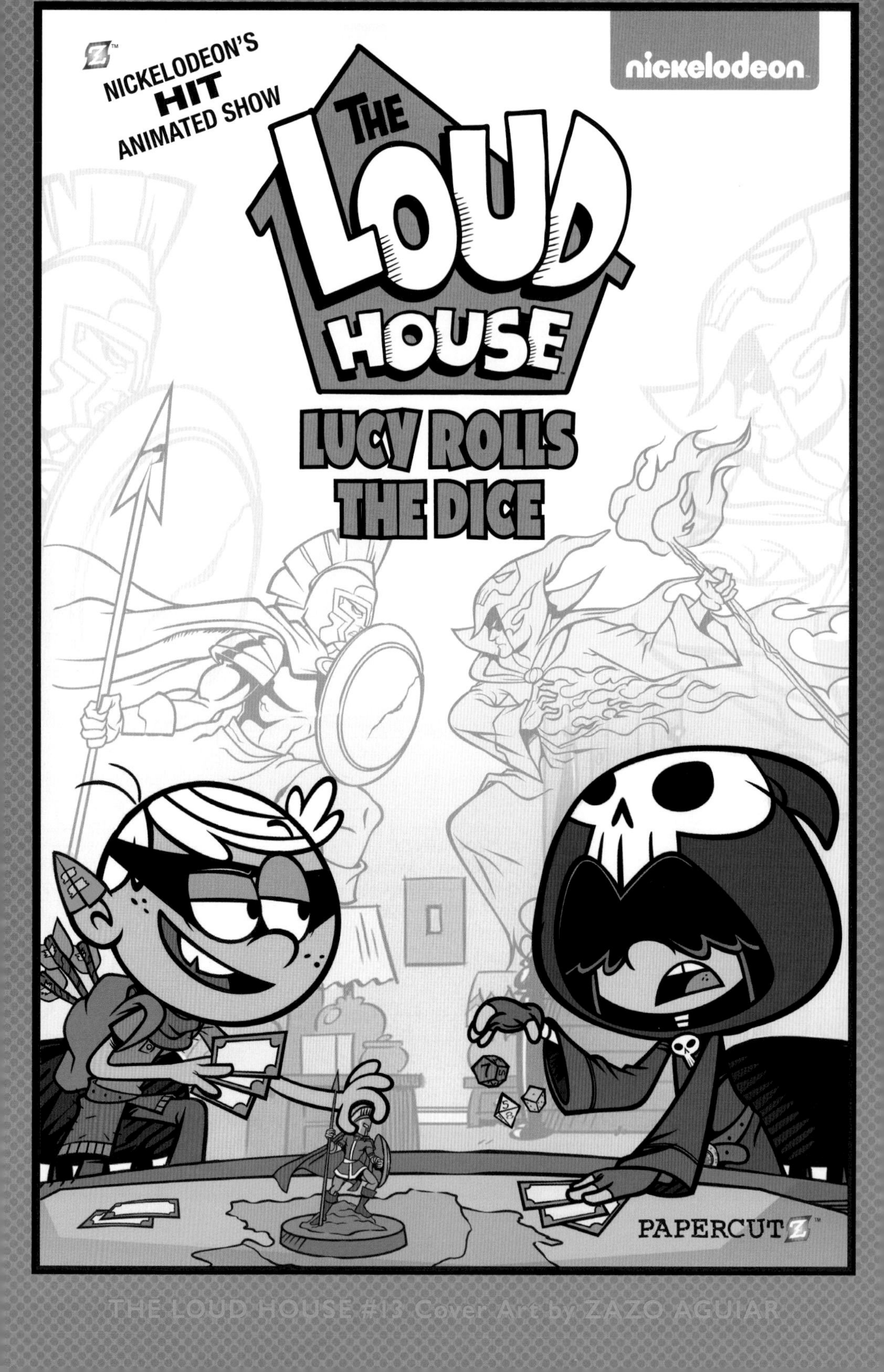
NICKELODEON'S
HIT
ANIMATED SHOW
nickelodeon
THE
LOUD
HOUSE
LUCY ROLLS
THE DICE
PAPERCUT

THE LOUD HOUSE #13 Cover Art by ZAZO AGUIAR

"LUCY ROLLS THE DICE"

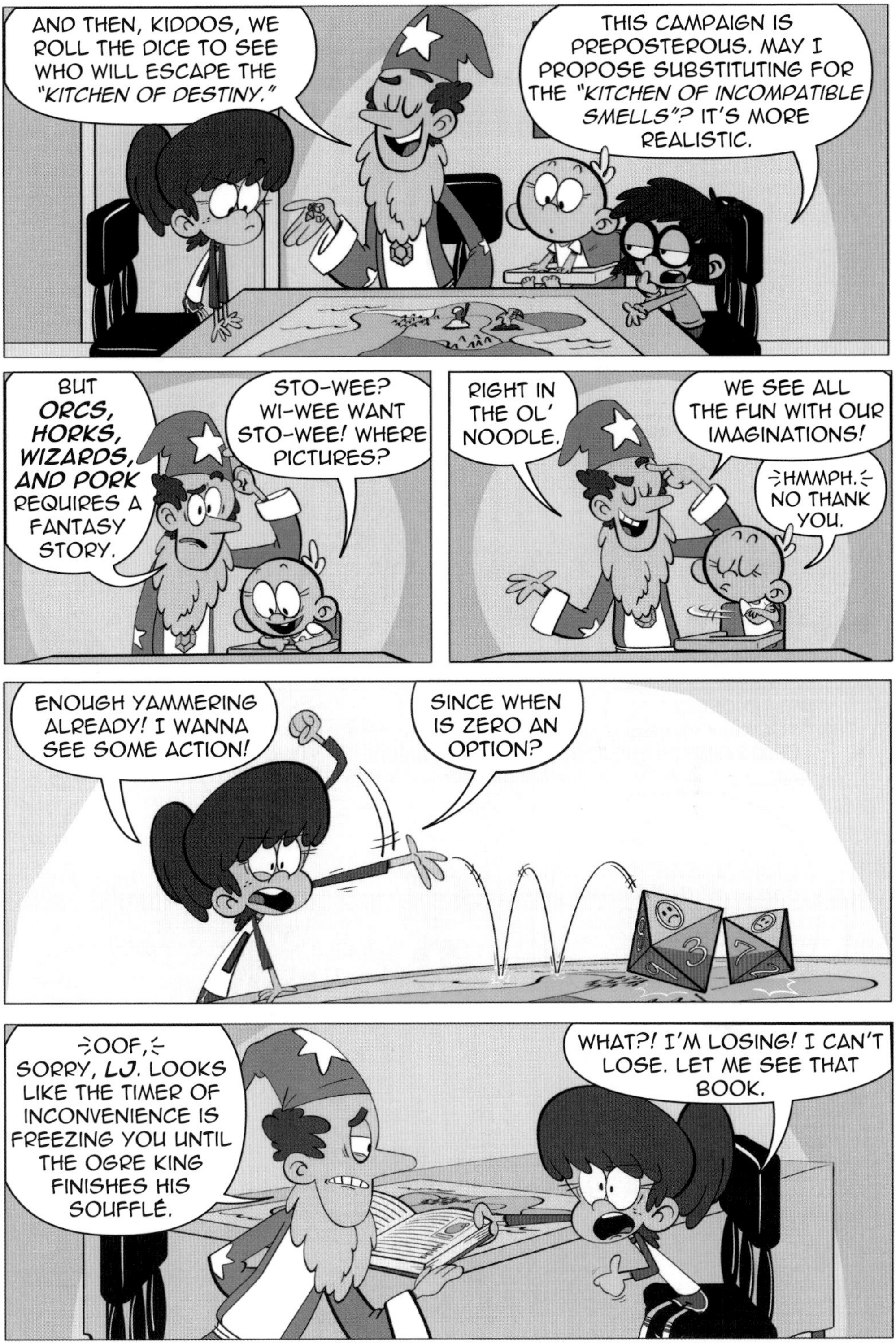
AND THEN, KIDDOS, WE ROLL THE DICE TO SEE WHO WILL ESCAPE THE *"KITCHEN OF DESTINY."*
THIS CAMPAIGN IS PREPOSTEROUS. MAY I PROPOSE SUBSTITUTING FOR THE *"KITCHEN OF INCOMPATIBLE SMELLS"*? IT'S MORE REALISTIC.
BUT ***ORCS, HORKS, WIZARDS, AND PORK*** REQUIRES A FANTASY STORY.
STO-WEE? WI-WEE WANT STO-WEE! WHERE PICTURES?
RIGHT IN THE OL' NOODLE.
WE SEE ALL THE FUN WITH OUR IMAGINATIONS!
HMMPH. NO THANK YOU.
ENOUGH YAMMERING ALREADY! I WANNA SEE SOME ACTION!
SINCE WHEN IS ZERO AN OPTION?
OOF, SORRY, ***LJ***. LOOKS LIKE THE TIMER OF INCONVENIENCE IS FREEZING YOU UNTIL THE OGRE KING FINISHES HIS SOUFFLÉ.
WHAT?! I'M LOSING! I CAN'T LOSE. LET ME SEE THAT BOOK.

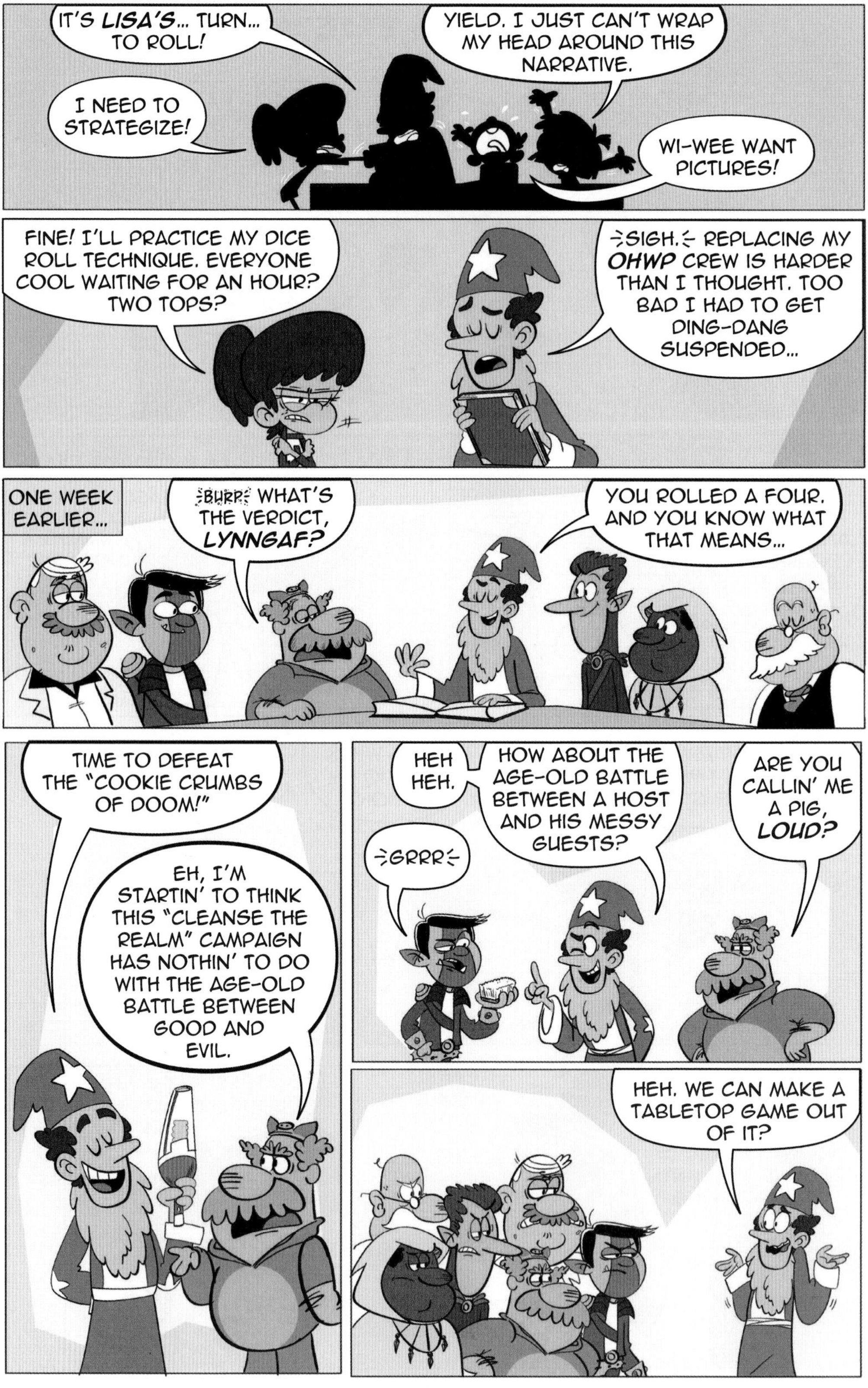
IT'S LISA'S... TURN... TO ROLL!
YIELD. I JUST CAN'T WRAP MY HEAD AROUND THIS NARRATIVE.
I NEED TO STRATEGIZE!
WI-WEE WANT PICTURES!
FINE! I'LL PRACTICE MY DICE ROLL TECHNIQUE. EVERYONE COOL WAITING FOR AN HOUR? TWO TOPS?
SIGH. REPLACING MY OHWP CREW IS HARDER THAN I THOUGHT. TOO BAD I HAD TO GET DING-DANG SUSPENDED...
ONE WEEK EARLIER...
BURP WHAT'S THE VERDICT, LYNNGAF?
YOU ROLLED A FOUR. AND YOU KNOW WHAT THAT MEANS...
TIME TO DEFEAT THE "COOKIE CRUMBS OF DOOM!"
EH, I'M STARTIN' TO THINK THIS "CLEANSE THE REALM" CAMPAIGN HAS NOTHIN' TO DO WITH THE AGE-OLD BATTLE BETWEEN GOOD AND EVIL.
HEH HEH.
HOW ABOUT THE AGE-OLD BATTLE BETWEEN A HOST AND HIS MESSY GUESTS?
ARE YOU CALLIN' ME A PIG, LOUD?
GRRR
HEH. WE CAN MAKE A TABLETOP GAME OUT OF IT?

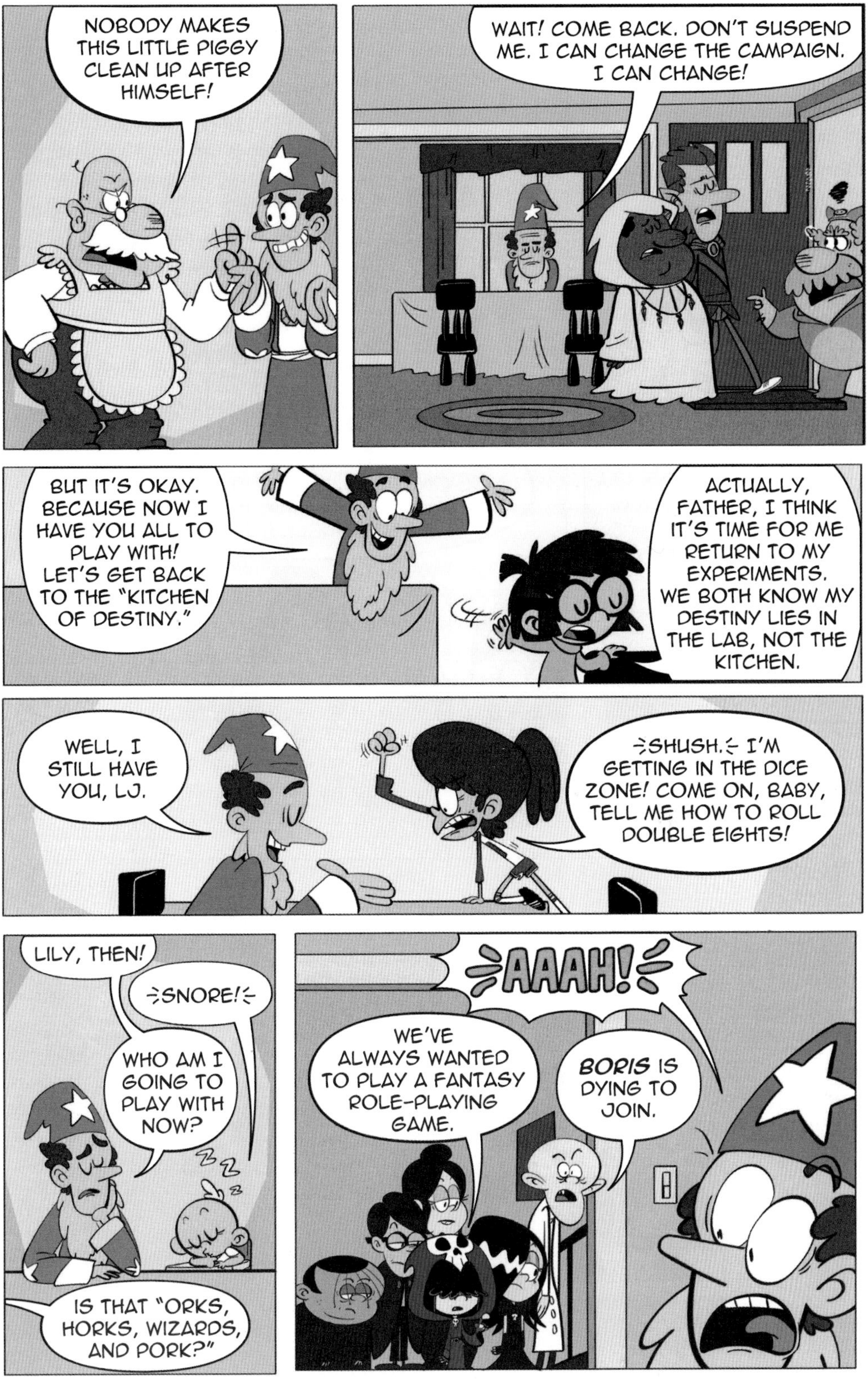
NOBODY MAKES THIS LITTLE PIGGY CLEAN UP AFTER HIMSELF!
WAIT! COME BACK. DON'T SUSPEND ME. I CAN CHANGE THE CAMPAIGN. I CAN CHANGE!
BUT IT'S OKAY. BECAUSE NOW I HAVE YOU ALL TO PLAY WITH! LET'S GET BACK TO THE "KITCHEN OF DESTINY."
ACTUALLY, FATHER, I THINK IT'S TIME FOR ME RETURN TO MY EXPERIMENTS. WE BOTH KNOW MY DESTINY LIES IN THE LAB, NOT THE KITCHEN.
WELL, I STILL HAVE YOU, LJ.
SHUSH. I'M GETTING IN THE DICE ZONE! COME ON, BABY, TELL ME HOW TO ROLL DOUBLE EIGHTS!
LILY, THEN!
SNORE!
WHO AM I GOING TO PLAY WITH NOW?
IS THAT "ORKS, HORKS, WIZARDS, AND PORK?"
AAAH!
WE'VE ALWAYS WANTED TO PLAY A FANTASY ROLE-PLAYING GAME.
BORIS IS DYING TO JOIN.

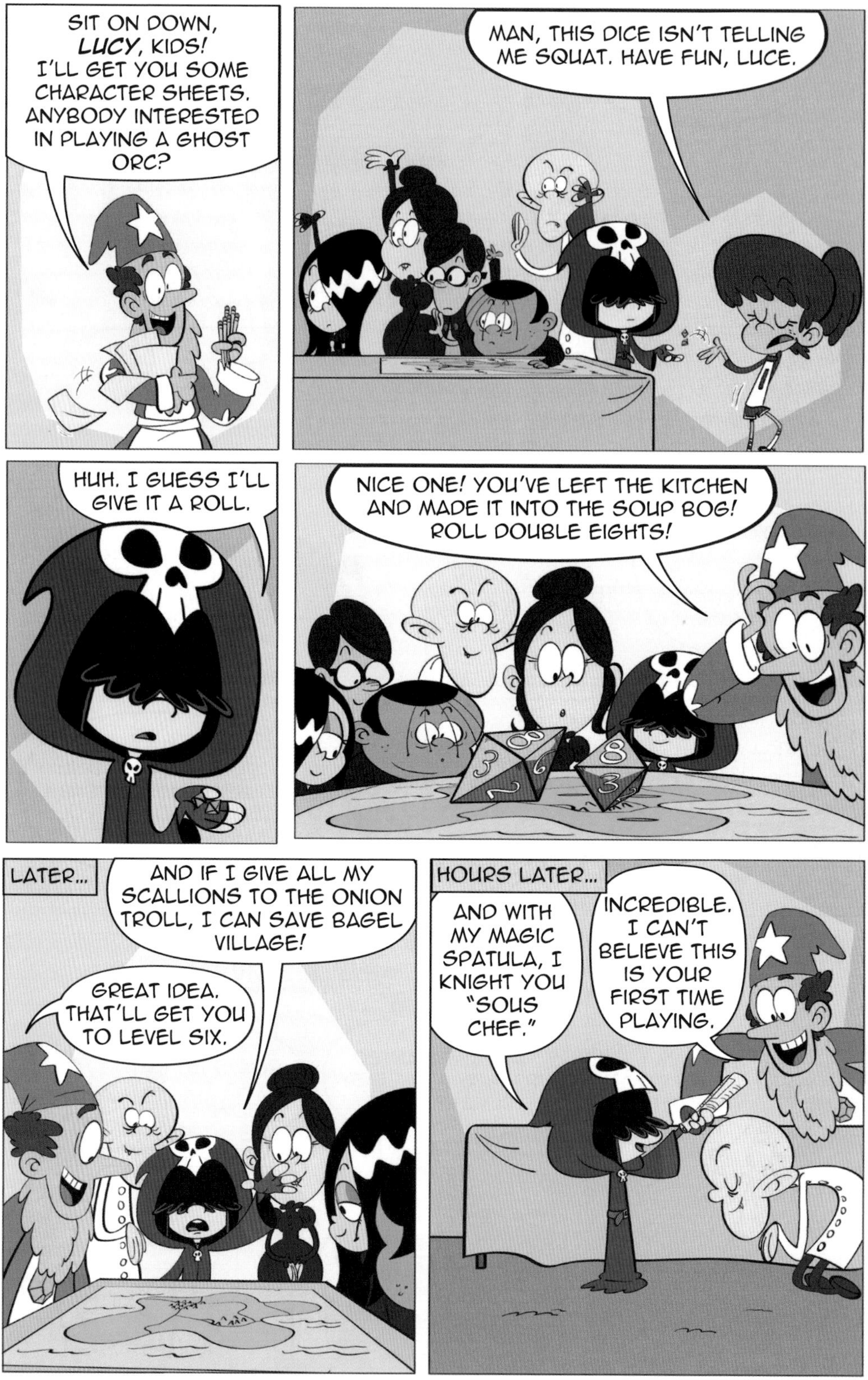
SIT ON DOWN, LUCY, KIDS! I'LL GET YOU SOME CHARACTER SHEETS. ANYBODY INTERESTED IN PLAYING A GHOST ORC?
MAN, THIS DICE ISN'T TELLING ME SQUAT. HAVE FUN, LUCE.
HUH. I GUESS I'LL GIVE IT A ROLL.
NICE ONE! YOU'VE LEFT THE KITCHEN AND MADE IT INTO THE SOUP BOG! ROLL DOUBLE EIGHTS!
LATER...
AND IF I GIVE ALL MY SCALLIONS TO THE ONION TROLL, I CAN SAVE BAGEL VILLAGE!
GREAT IDEA. THAT'LL GET YOU TO LEVEL SIX.
HOURS LATER...
AND WITH MY MAGIC SPATULA, I KNIGHT YOU "SOUS CHEF."
INCREDIBLE. I CAN'T BELIEVE THIS IS YOUR FIRST TIME PLAYING.

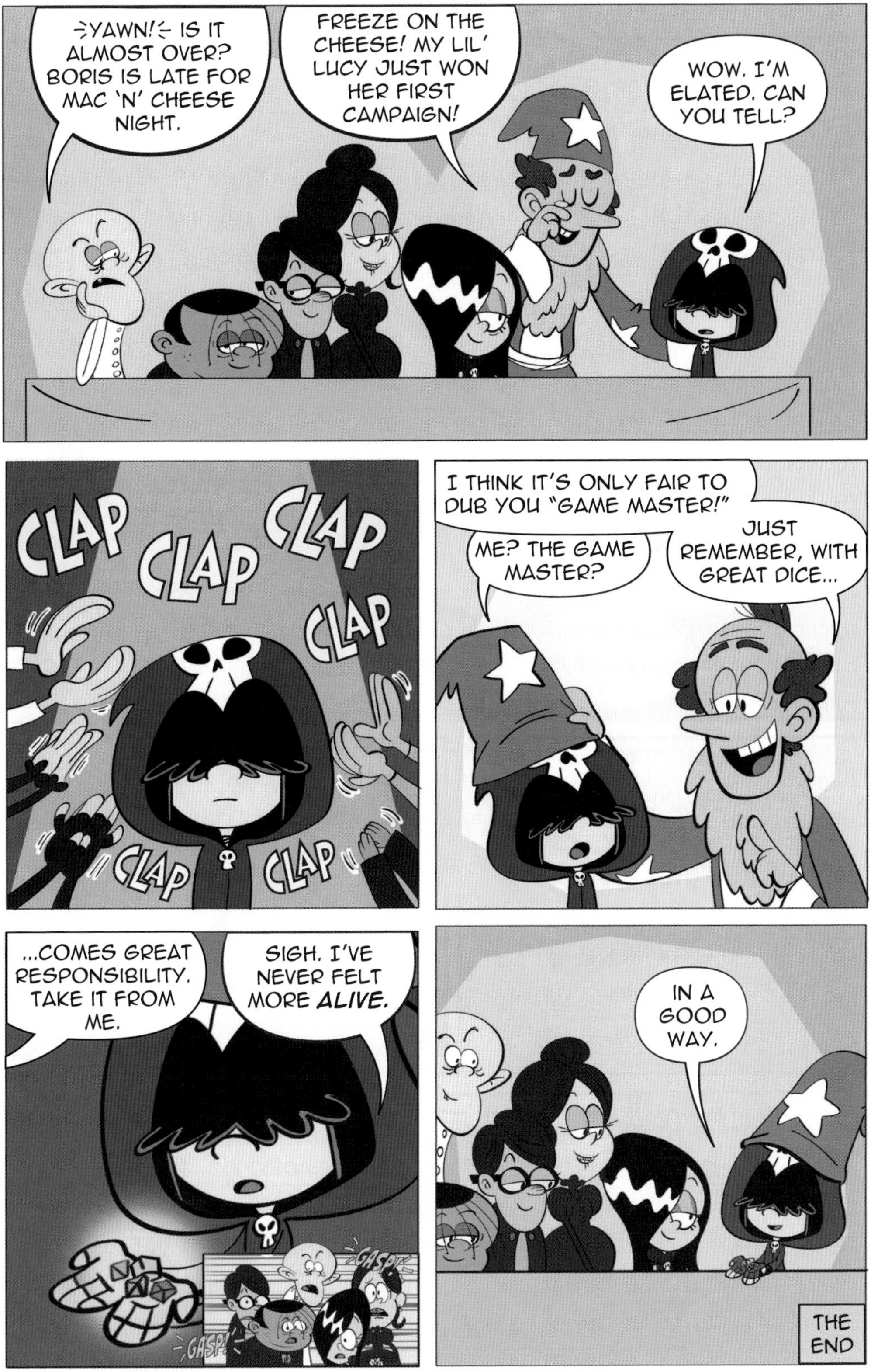

⇒YAWN!⇐ IS IT ALMOST OVER? BORIS IS LATE FOR MAC 'N' CHEESE NIGHT.
FREEZE ON THE CHEESE! MY LIL' LUCY JUST WON HER FIRST CAMPAIGN!
WOW. I'M ELATED. CAN YOU TELL?
CLAP
CLAP
CLAP
CLAP
CLAP
CLAP
I THINK IT'S ONLY FAIR TO DUB YOU "GAME MASTER!"
ME? THE GAME MASTER?
JUST REMEMBER, WITH GREAT DICE...
...COMES GREAT RESPONSIBILITY. TAKE IT FROM ME.
SIGH. I'VE NEVER FELT MORE **ALIVE.**
GASP!
GASP!
IN A GOOD WAY.
THE END

"LARP IT UP"

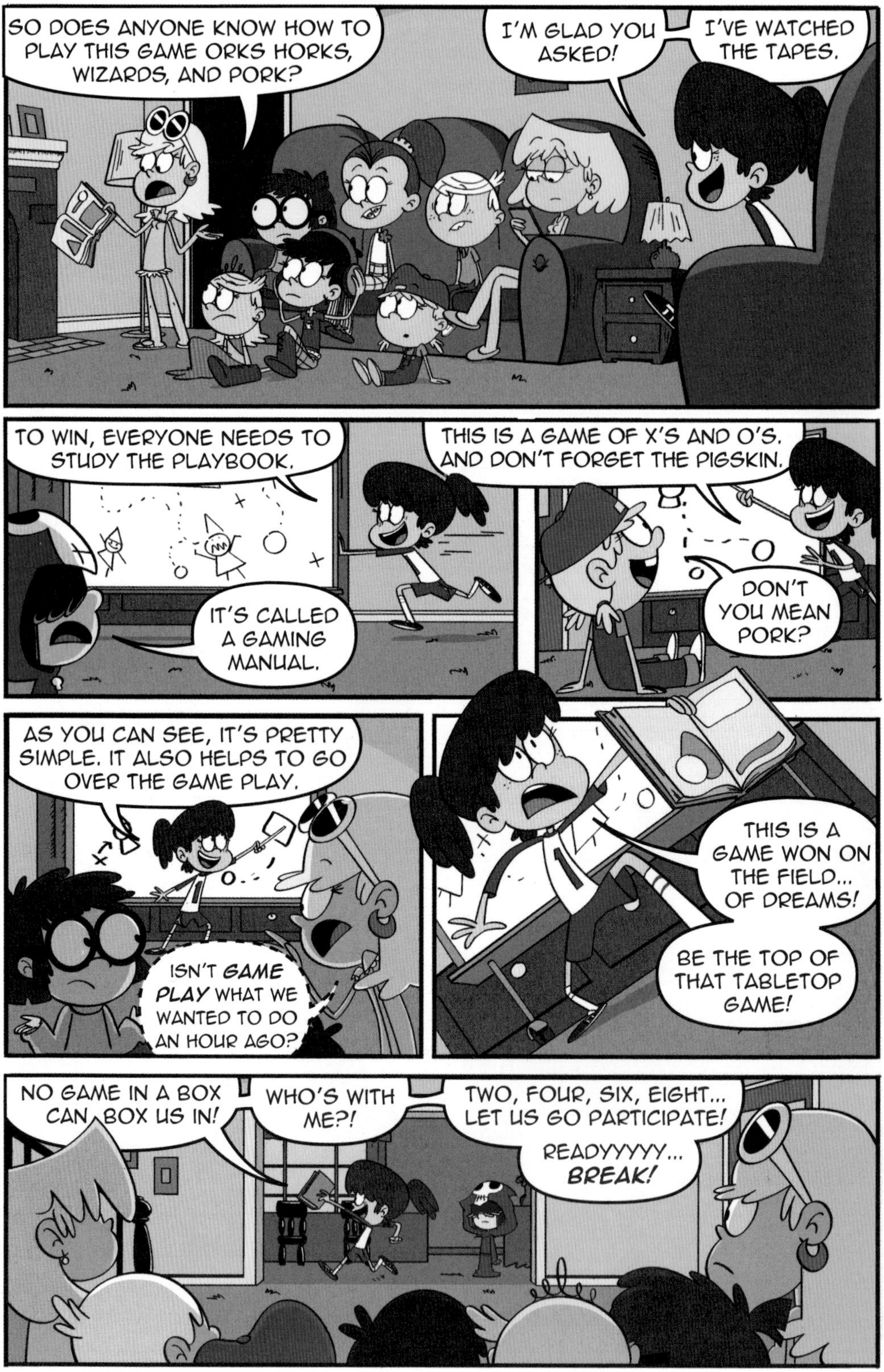
SO DOES ANYONE KNOW HOW TO PLAY THIS GAME ORKS HORKS, WIZARDS, AND PORK?
I'M GLAD YOU ASKED!
I'VE WATCHED THE TAPES.
TO WIN, EVERYONE NEEDS TO STUDY THE PLAYBOOK.
IT'S CALLED A GAMING MANUAL.
THIS IS A GAME OF X'S AND O'S. AND DON'T FORGET THE PIGSKIN.
DON'T YOU MEAN PORK?
AS YOU CAN SEE, IT'S PRETTY SIMPLE. IT ALSO HELPS TO GO OVER THE GAME PLAY.
ISN'T *GAME PLAY* WHAT WE WANTED TO DO AN HOUR AGO?
THIS IS A GAME WON ON THE FIELD... OF DREAMS!
BE THE TOP OF THAT TABLETOP GAME!
NO GAME IN A BOX CAN BOX US IN!
WHO'S WITH ME?!
TWO, FOUR, SIX, EIGHT... LET US GO PARTICIPATE!
READYYYYY... *BREAK!*

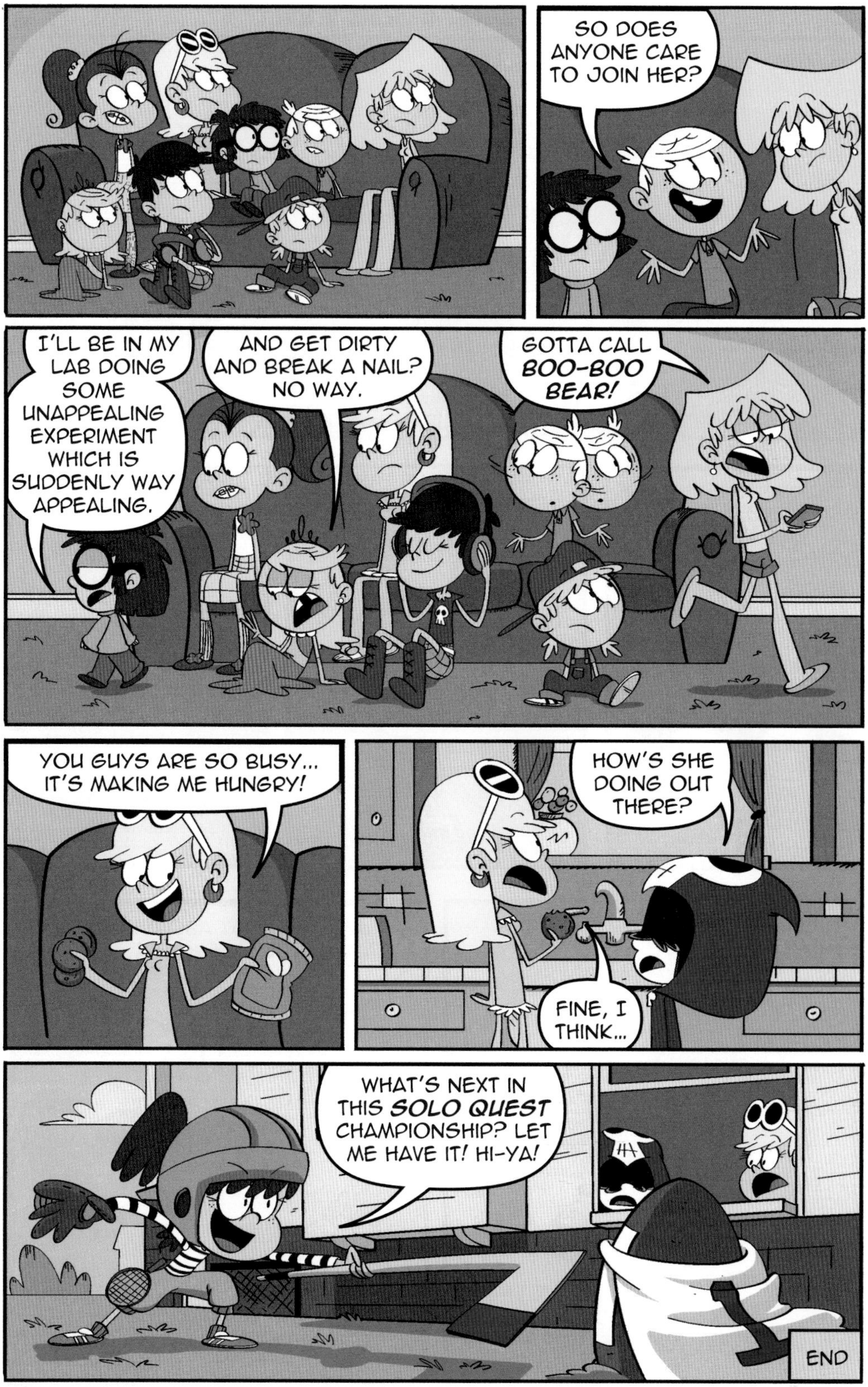
SO DOES ANYONE CARE TO JOIN HER?
I'LL BE IN MY LAB DOING SOME UNAPPEALING EXPERIMENT WHICH IS SUDDENLY WAY APPEALING.
AND GET DIRTY AND BREAK A NAIL? NO WAY.
GOTTA CALL BOO-BOO BEAR!
YOU GUYS ARE SO BUSY... IT'S MAKING ME HUNGRY!
HOW'S SHE DOING OUT THERE?
FINE, I THINK...
WHAT'S NEXT IN THIS SOLO QUEST CHAMPIONSHIP? LET ME HAVE IT! HI-YA!
END

"JEST ME PLAYIN'"

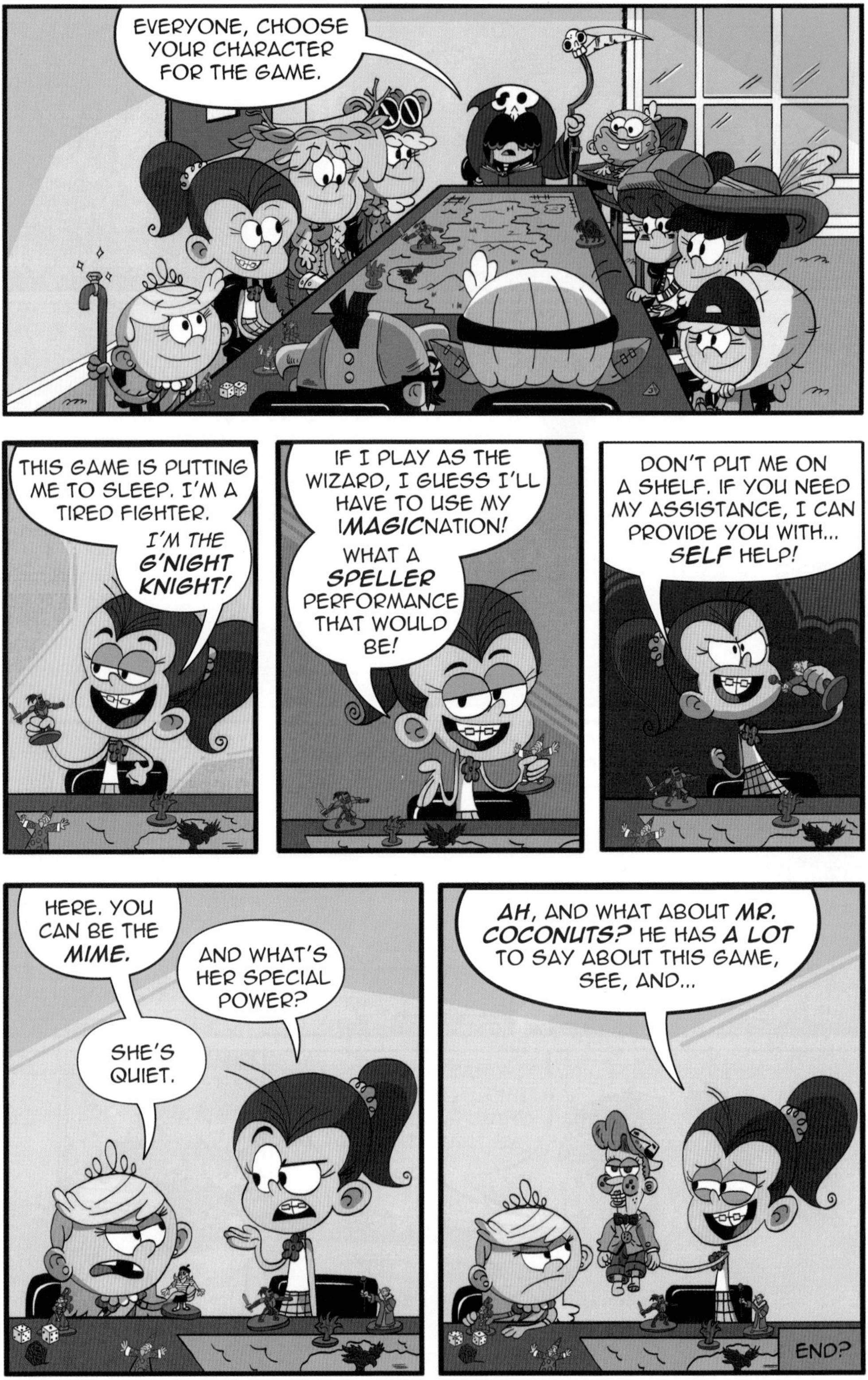

EVERYONE, CHOOSE YOUR CHARACTER FOR THE GAME.
THIS GAME IS PUTTING ME TO SLEEP. I'M A TIRED FIGHTER.
I'M THE G'NIGHT KNIGHT!
IF I PLAY AS THE WIZARD, I GUESS I'LL HAVE TO USE MY IMAGICNATION!
WHAT A SPELLER PERFORMANCE THAT WOULD BE!
DON'T PUT ME ON A SHELF. IF YOU NEED MY ASSISTANCE, I CAN PROVIDE YOU WITH... SELF HELP!
HERE. YOU CAN BE THE MIME.
AND WHAT'S HER SPECIAL POWER?
SHE'S QUIET.
AH, AND WHAT ABOUT MR. COCONUTS? HE HAS A LOT TO SAY ABOUT THIS GAME, SEE, AND...
END?

"BEGINNER'S LUCK"

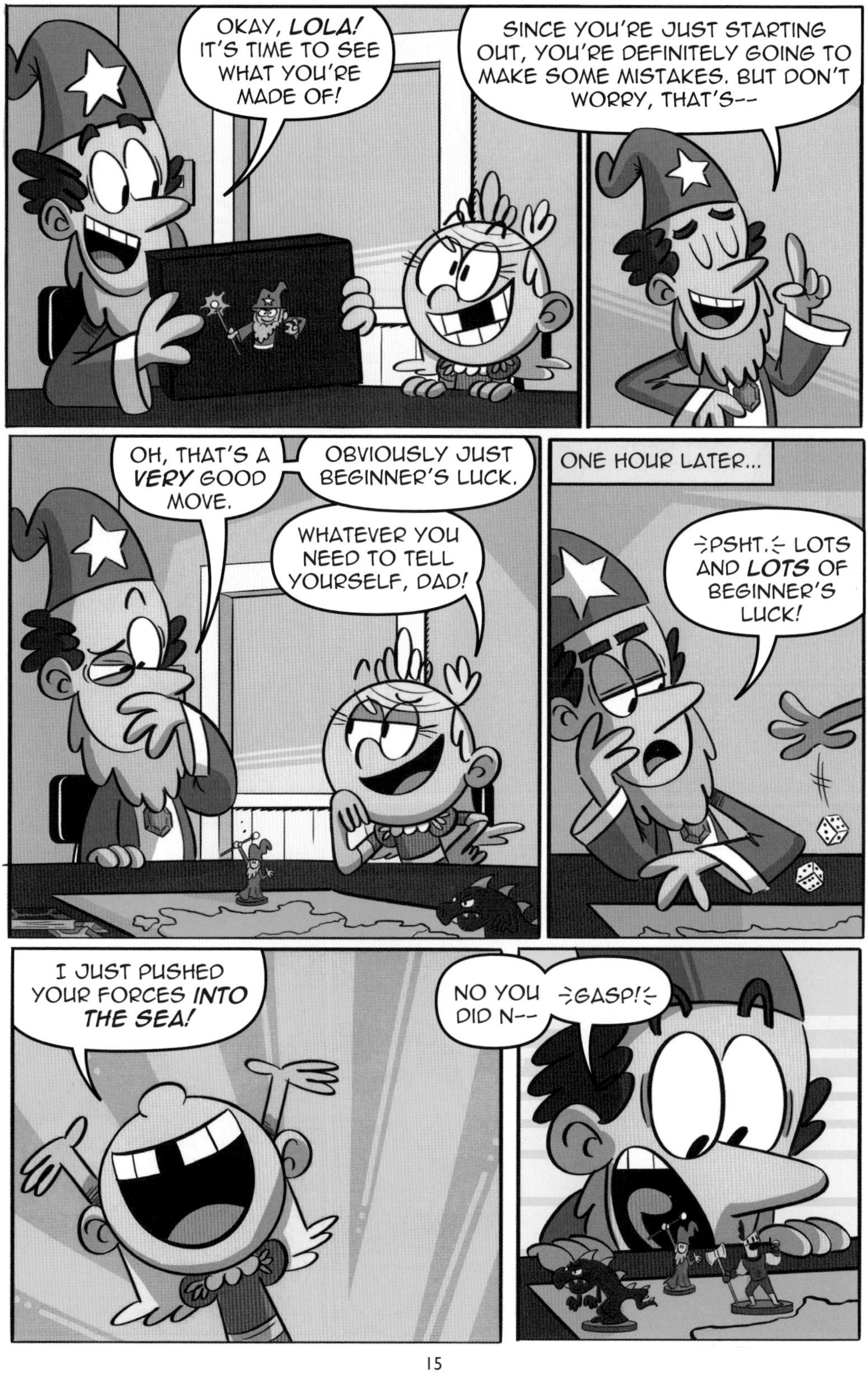
OKAY, LOLA! IT'S TIME TO SEE WHAT YOU'RE MADE OF!
SINCE YOU'RE JUST STARTING OUT, YOU'RE DEFINITELY GOING TO MAKE SOME MISTAKES. BUT DON'T WORRY, THAT'S--
OH, THAT'S A VERY GOOD MOVE.
OBVIOUSLY JUST BEGINNER'S LUCK.
WHATEVER YOU NEED TO TELL YOURSELF, DAD!
ONE HOUR LATER...
PSHT. LOTS AND LOTS OF BEGINNER'S LUCK!
I JUST PUSHED YOUR FORCES INTO THE SEA!
NO YOU DID N--
GASP!

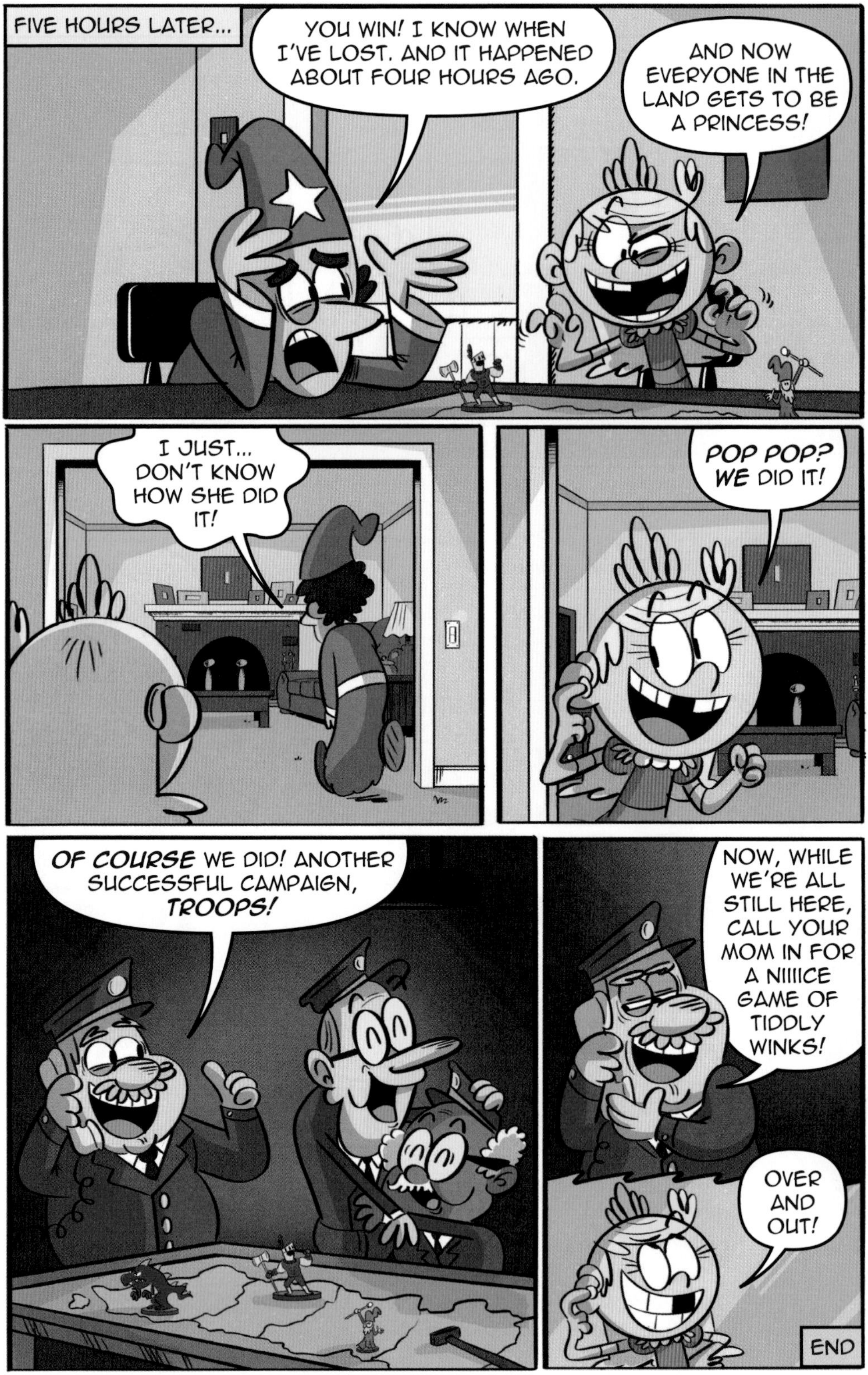
FIVE HOURS LATER...
YOU WIN! I KNOW WHEN I'VE LOST. AND IT HAPPENED ABOUT FOUR HOURS AGO.
AND NOW EVERYONE IN THE LAND GETS TO BE A PRINCESS!
I JUST... DON'T KNOW HOW SHE DID IT!
POP POP? WE DID IT!
OF COURSE WE DID! ANOTHER SUCCESSFUL CAMPAIGN, TROOPS!
NOW, WHILE WE'RE ALL STILL HERE, CALL YOUR MOM IN FOR A NIIIICE GAME OF TIDDLY WINKS!
OVER AND OUT!
END

"LINCOLN'S CHARACTER FLAW"

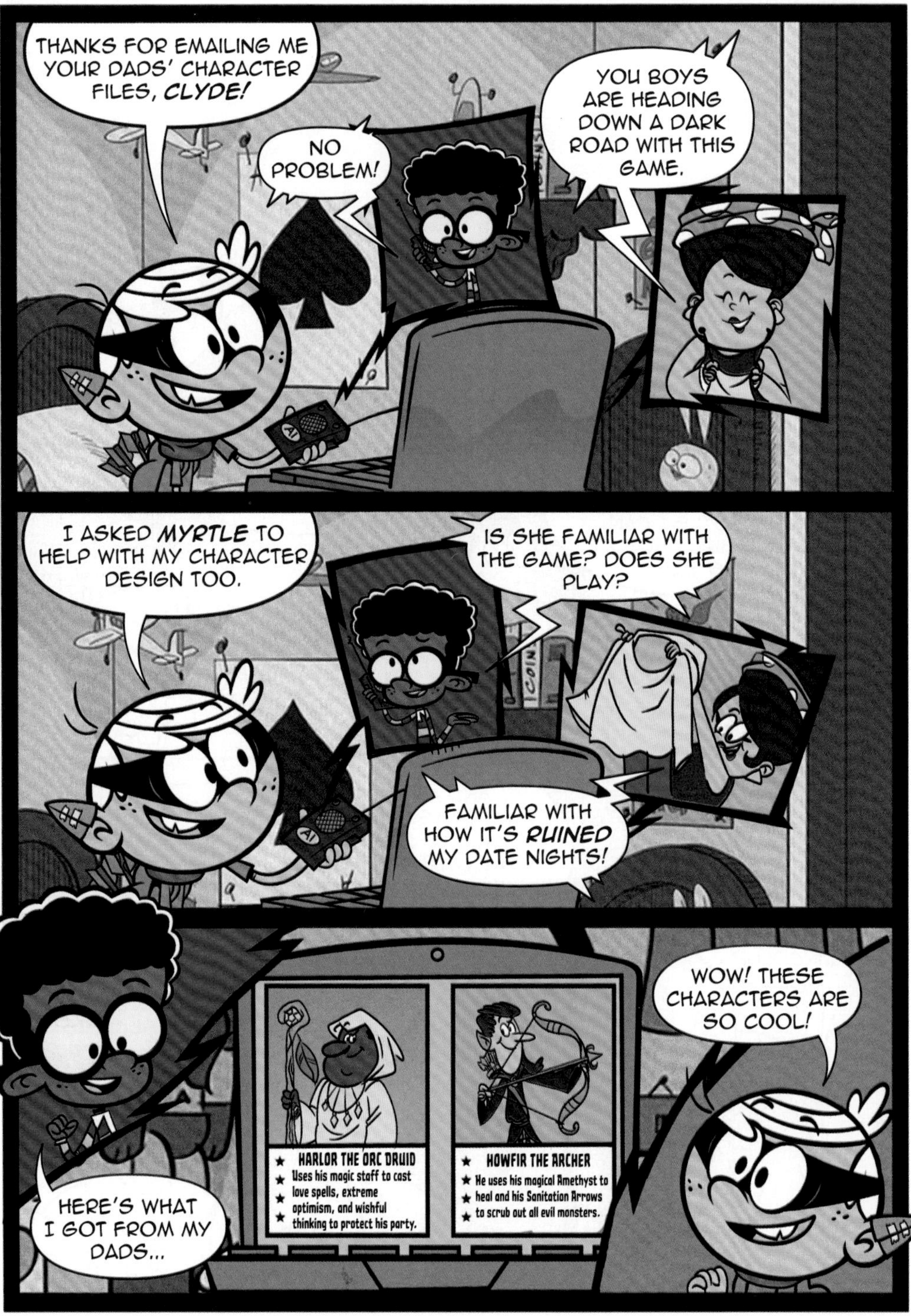

THANKS FOR EMAILING ME YOUR DADS' CHARACTER FILES, *CLYDE!*
NO PROBLEM!
YOU BOYS ARE HEADING DOWN A DARK ROAD WITH THIS GAME.
I ASKED *MYRTLE* TO HELP WITH MY CHARACTER DESIGN TOO.
IS SHE FAMILIAR WITH THE GAME? DOES SHE PLAY?
FAMILIAR WITH HOW IT'S *RUINED* MY DATE NIGHTS!
HERE'S WHAT I GOT FROM MY DADS...
HARLOR THE ORC DRUID
Uses his magic staff to cast love spells, extreme optimism, and wishful thinking to protect his party.
HOWFIR THE ARCHER
He uses his magical Amethyst to heal and his Sanitation Arrows to scrub out all evil monsters.
WOW! THESE CHARACTERS ARE SO COOL!

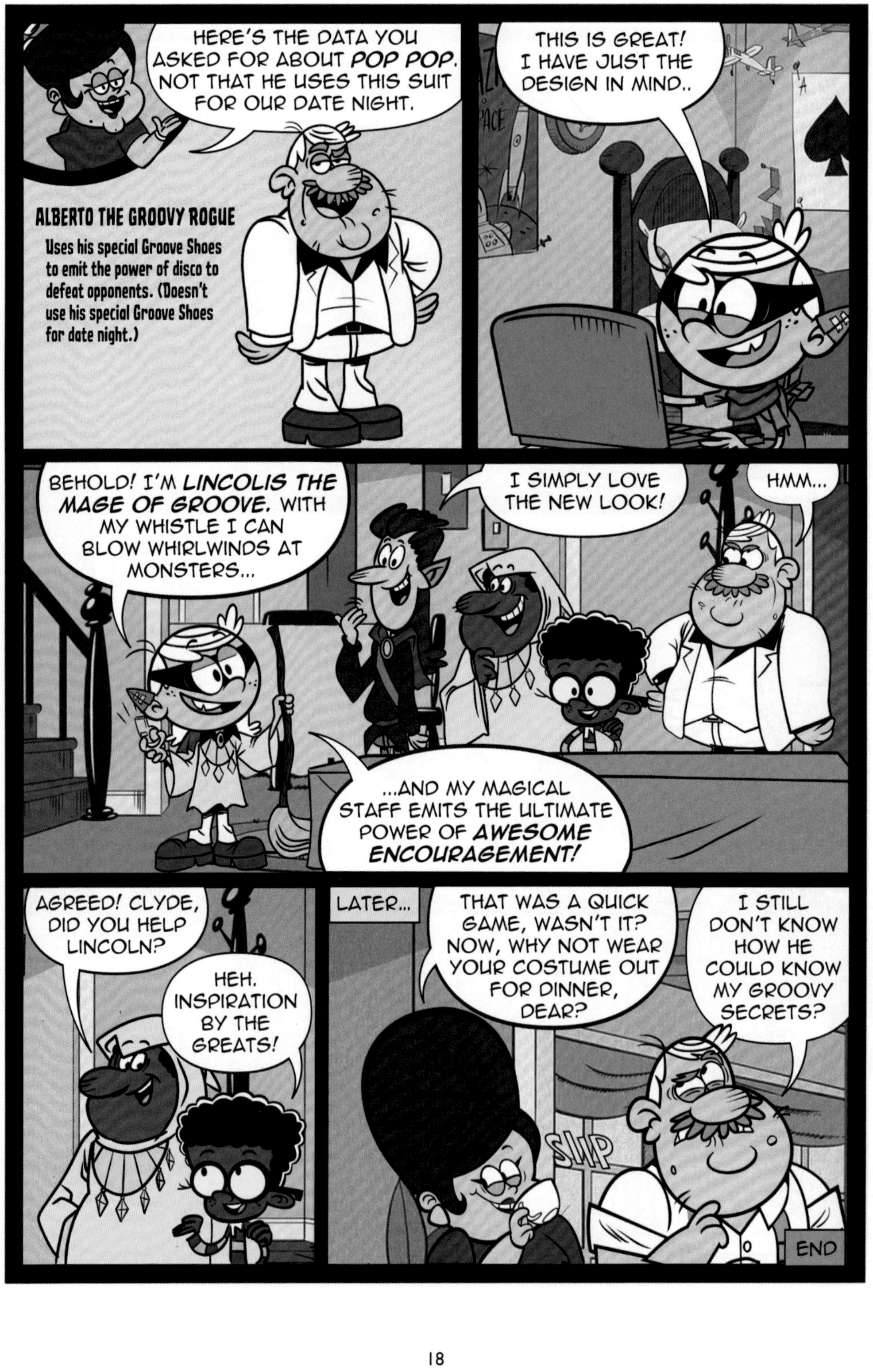
HERE'S THE DATA YOU ASKED FOR ABOUT POP POP. NOT THAT HE USES THIS SUIT FOR OUR DATE NIGHT.
ALBERTO THE GROOVY ROGUE
Uses his special Groove Shoes to emit the power of disco to defeat opponents. (Doesn't use his special Groove Shoes for date night.)
THIS IS GREAT! I HAVE JUST THE DESIGN IN MIND..
BEHOLD! I'M LINCOLIS THE MAGE OF GROOVE. WITH MY WHISTLE I CAN BLOW WHIRLWINDS AT MONSTERS...
I SIMPLY LOVE THE NEW LOOK!
HMM...
...AND MY MAGICAL STAFF EMITS THE ULTIMATE POWER OF AWESOME ENCOURAGEMENT!
AGREED! CLYDE, DID YOU HELP LINCOLN?
HEH. INSPIRATION BY THE GREATS!
LATER...
THAT WAS A QUICK GAME, WASN'T IT? NOW, WHY NOT WEAR YOUR COSTUME OUT FOR DINNER, DEAR?
I STILL DON'T KNOW HOW HE COULD KNOW MY GROOVY SECRETS?
SLIP
END

"LOSE A TURN"

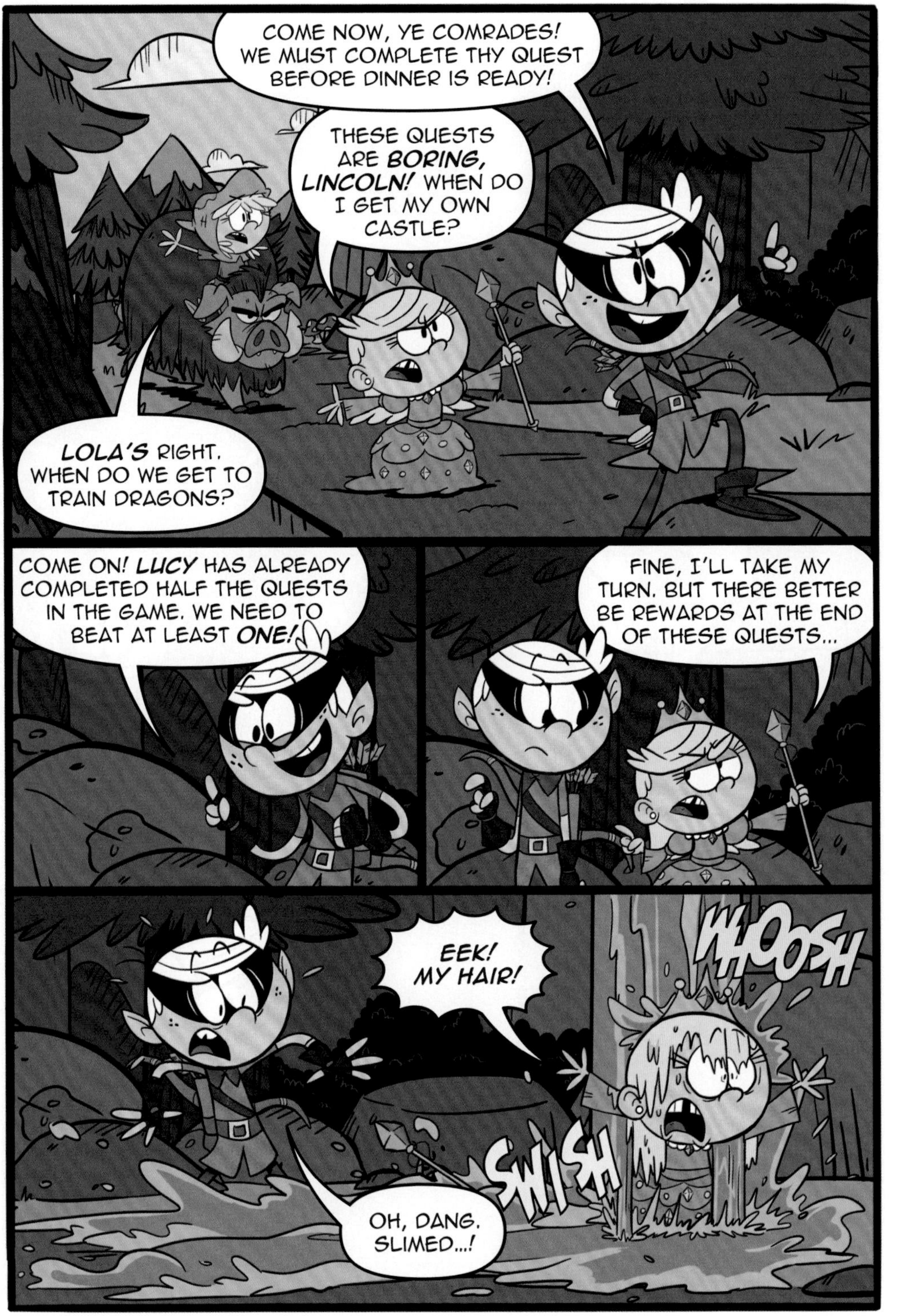
COME NOW, YE COMRADES! WE MUST COMPLETE THY QUEST BEFORE DINNER IS READY!
THESE QUESTS ARE BORING, LINCOLN! WHEN DO I GET MY OWN CASTLE?
LOLA'S RIGHT. WHEN DO WE GET TO TRAIN DRAGONS?
COME ON! LUCY HAS ALREADY COMPLETED HALF THE QUESTS IN THE GAME. WE NEED TO BEAT AT LEAST ONE!
FINE, I'LL TAKE MY TURN. BUT THERE BETTER BE REWARDS AT THE END OF THESE QUESTS...
EEK! MY HAIR!
WHOOSH
SWISH
OH, DANG. SLIMED...!

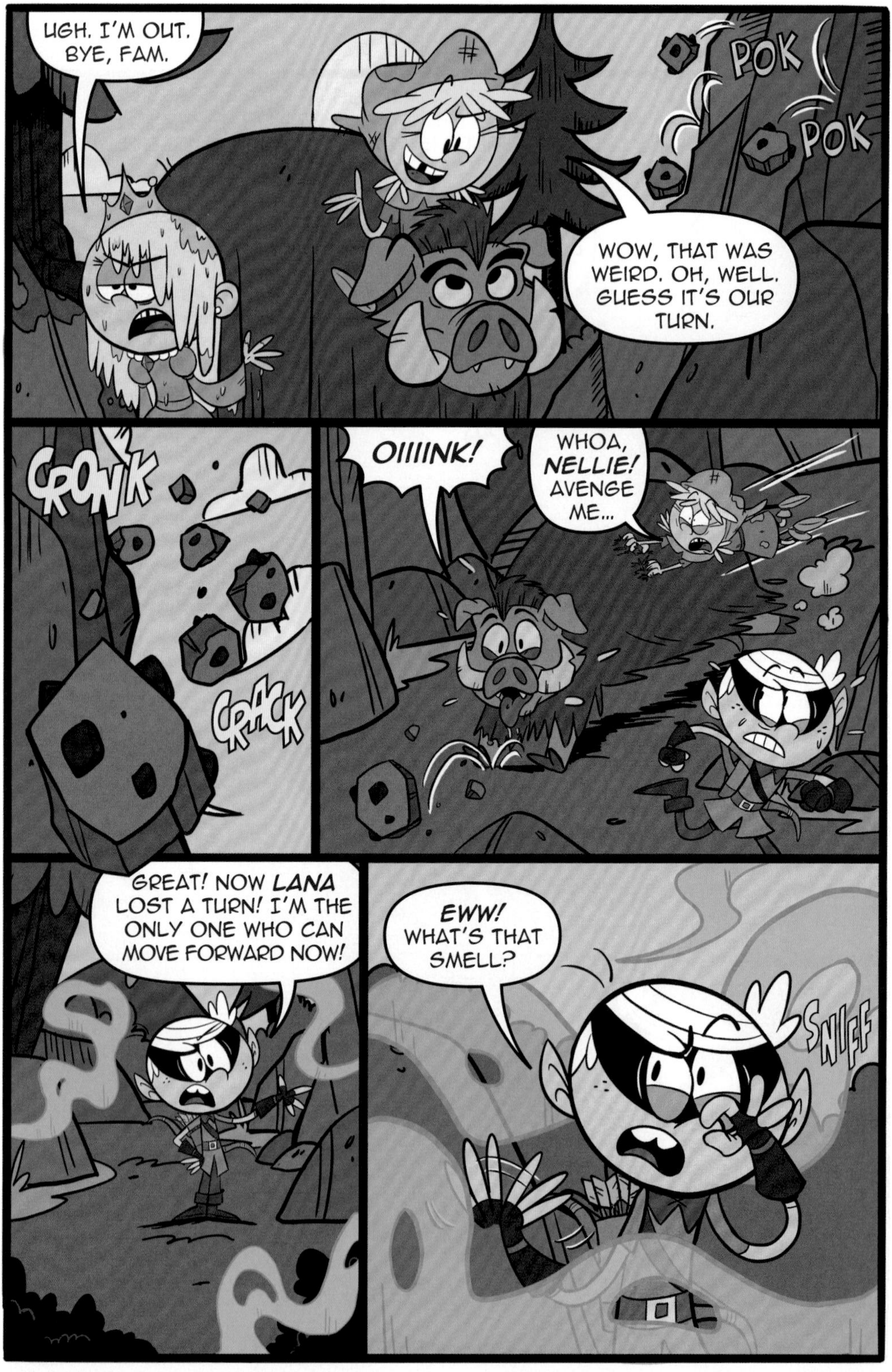
UGH. I'M OUT. BYE, FAM.
POK
POK
WOW, THAT WAS WEIRD. OH, WELL. GUESS IT'S OUR TURN.
CRONK
CRACK
OIIIINK!
WHOA, NELLIE! AVENGE ME...
GREAT! NOW LANA LOST A TURN! I'M THE ONLY ONE WHO CAN MOVE FORWARD NOW!
EWW! WHAT'S THAT SMELL?
SNIFF

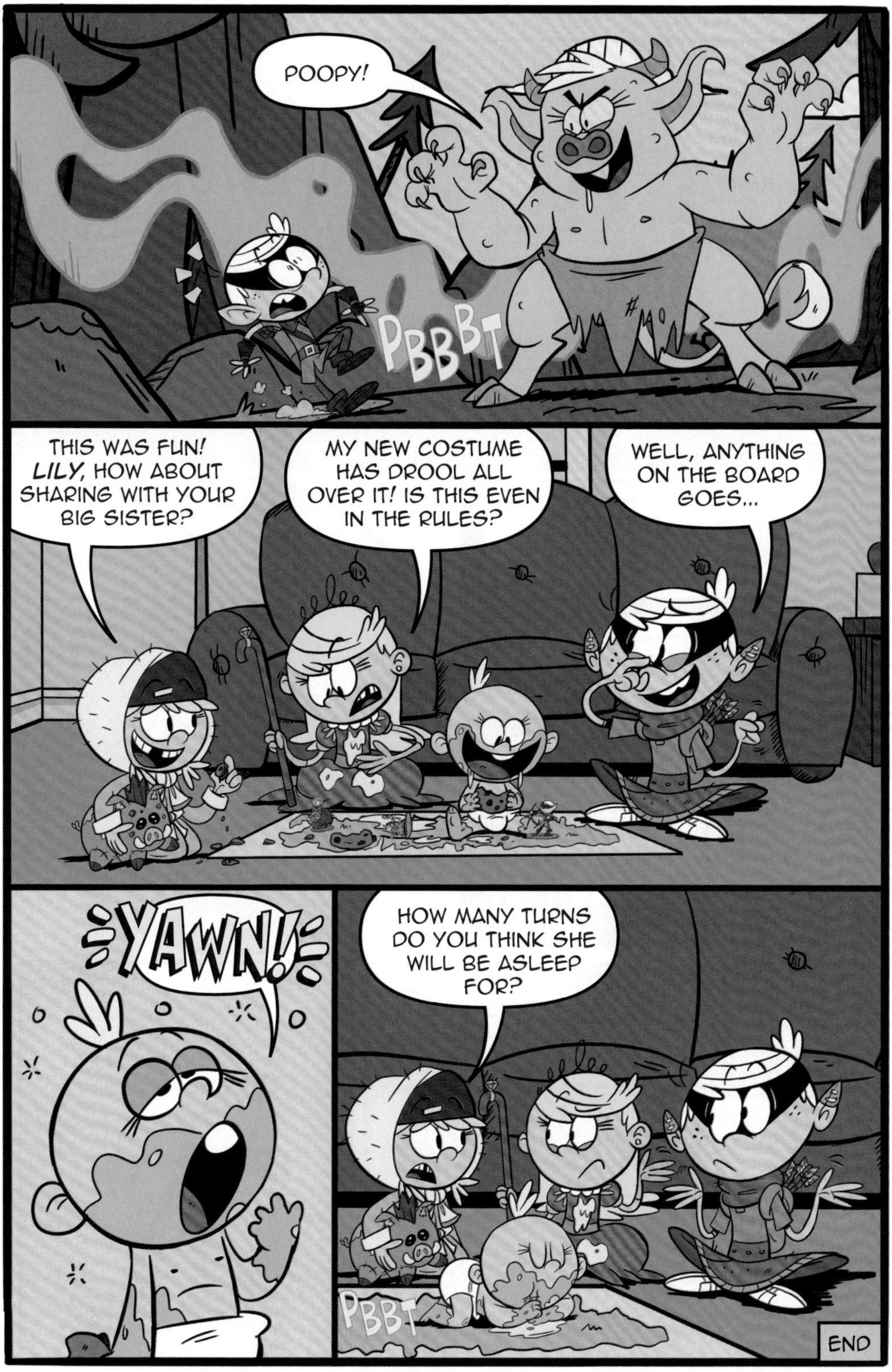

POOPY!
PBBBT
THIS WAS FUN! *LILY*, HOW ABOUT SHARING WITH YOUR BIG SISTER?
MY NEW COSTUME HAS DROOL ALL OVER IT! IS THIS EVEN IN THE RULES?
WELL, ANYTHING ON THE BOARD GOES...
YAWN!
HOW MANY TURNS DO YOU THINK SHE WILL BE ASLEEP FOR?
PBBT
END

"DECISIONS, DECISIONS"

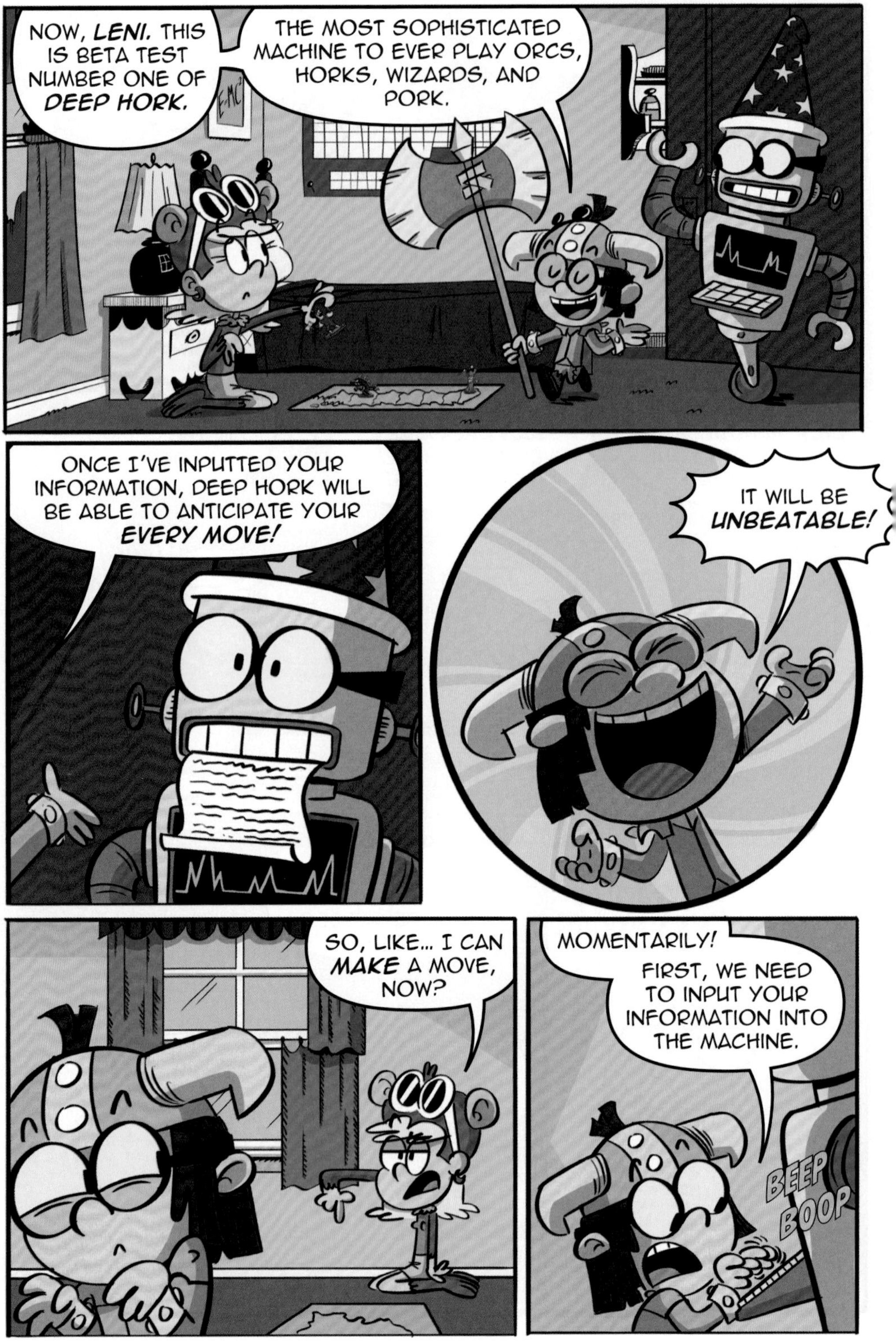

NOW, LENI. THIS IS BETA TEST NUMBER ONE OF DEEP HORK.
THE MOST SOPHISTICATED MACHINE TO EVER PLAY ORCS, HORKS, WIZARDS, AND PORK.
ONCE I'VE INPUTTED YOUR INFORMATION, DEEP HORK WILL BE ABLE TO ANTICIPATE YOUR EVERY MOVE!
IT WILL BE UNBEATABLE!
SO, LIKE... I CAN MAKE A MOVE, NOW?
MOMENTARILY!
FIRST, WE NEED TO INPUT YOUR INFORMATION INTO THE MACHINE.
BEEP BOOP

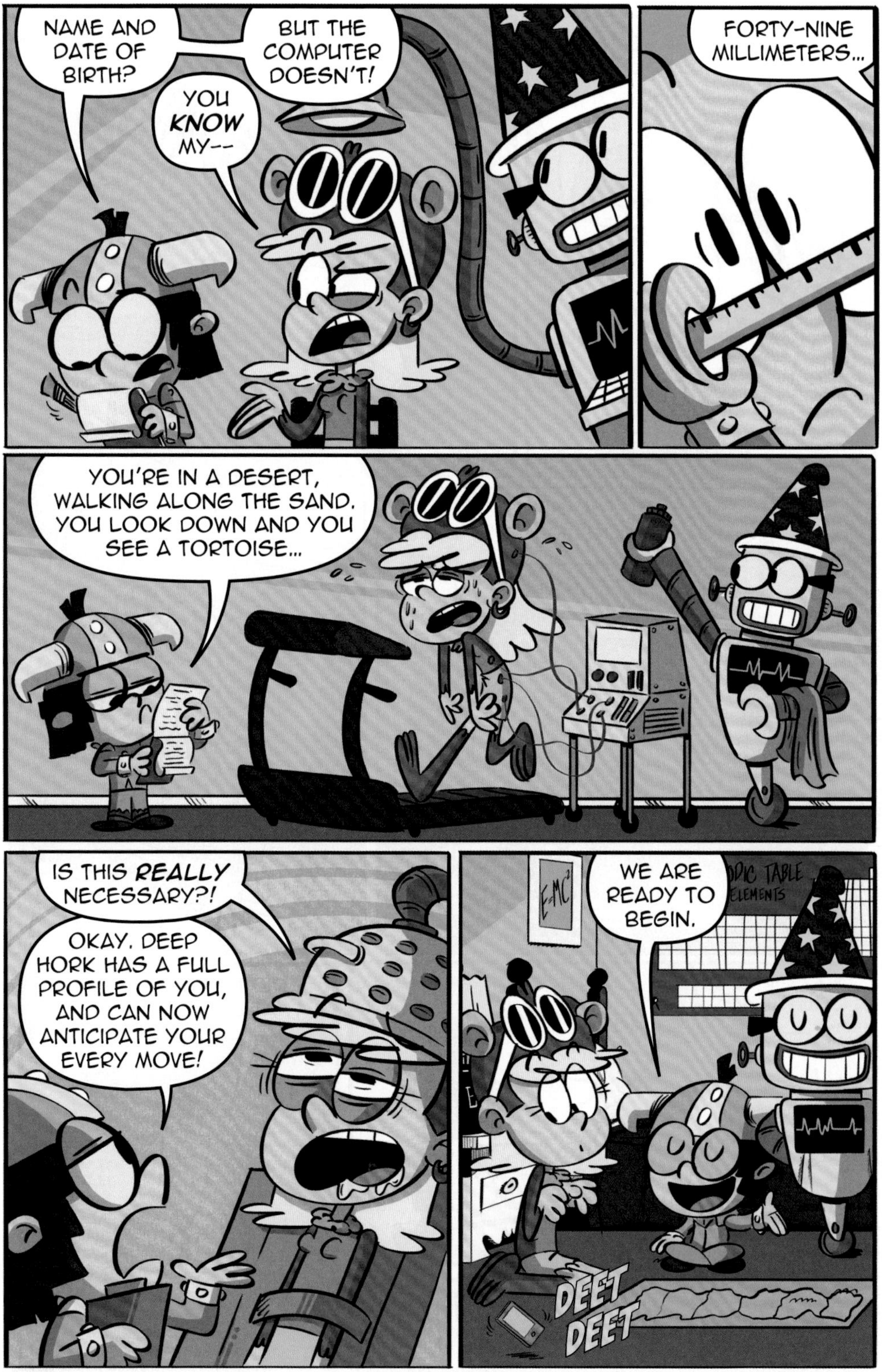
NAME AND DATE OF BIRTH?
YOU KNOW MY--
BUT THE COMPUTER DOESN'T!
FORTY-NINE MILLIMETERS...
YOU'RE IN A DESERT, WALKING ALONG THE SAND. YOU LOOK DOWN AND YOU SEE A TORTOISE...
IS THIS REALLY NECESSARY?!
OKAY. DEEP HORK HAS A FULL PROFILE OF YOU, AND CAN NOW ANTICIPATE YOUR EVERY MOVE!
WE ARE READY TO BEGIN.
DEET DEET

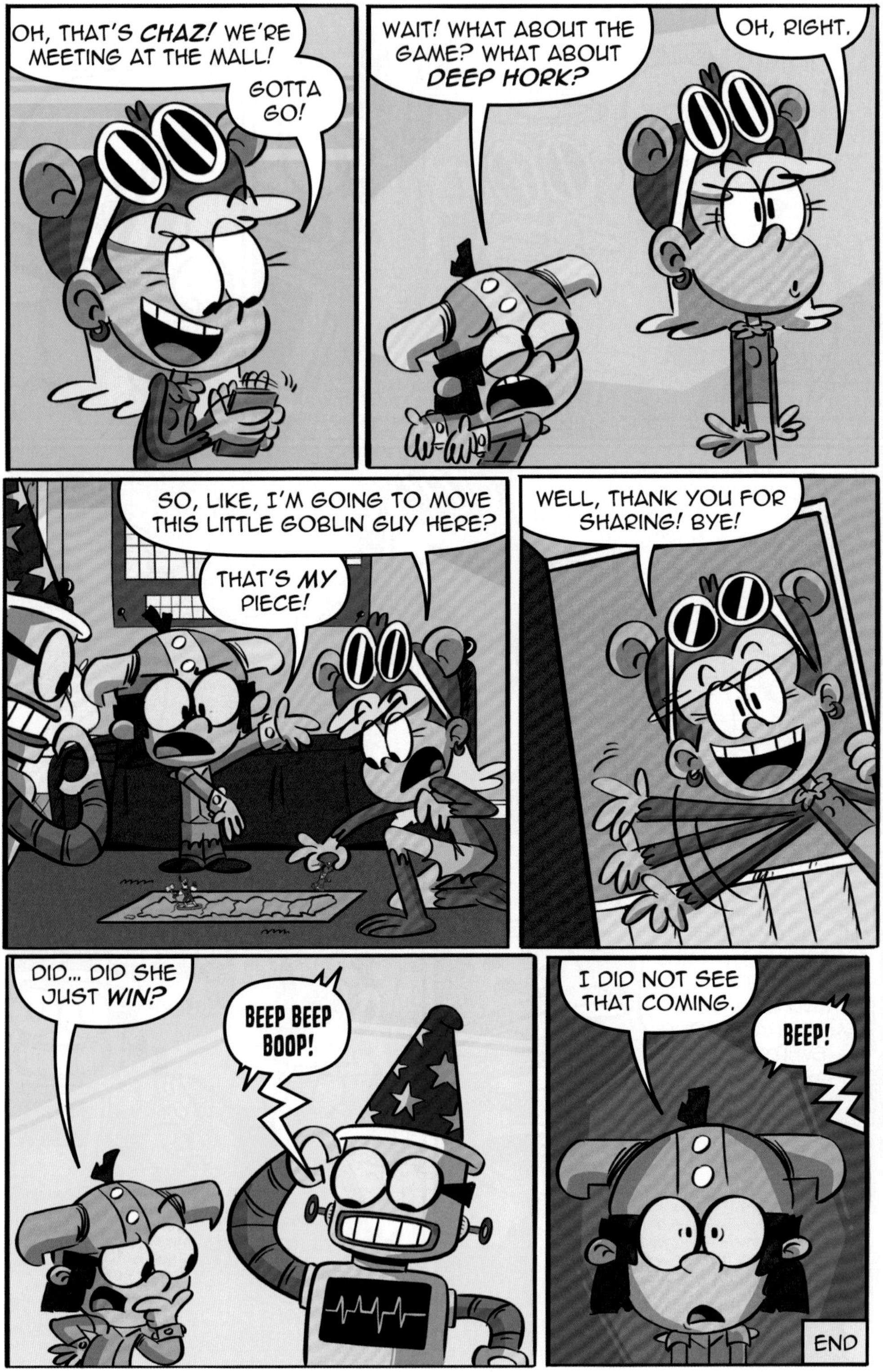

OH, THAT'S CHAZ! WE'RE MEETING AT THE MALL!
GOTTA GO!
WAIT! WHAT ABOUT THE GAME? WHAT ABOUT DEEP HORK?
OH, RIGHT.
SO, LIKE, I'M GOING TO MOVE THIS LITTLE GOBLIN GUY HERE?
THAT'S MY PIECE!
WELL, THANK YOU FOR SHARING! BYE!
DID... DID SHE JUST WIN?
BEEP BEEP BOOP!
I DID NOT SEE THAT COMING.
BEEP!
END

"POWER PLAY"

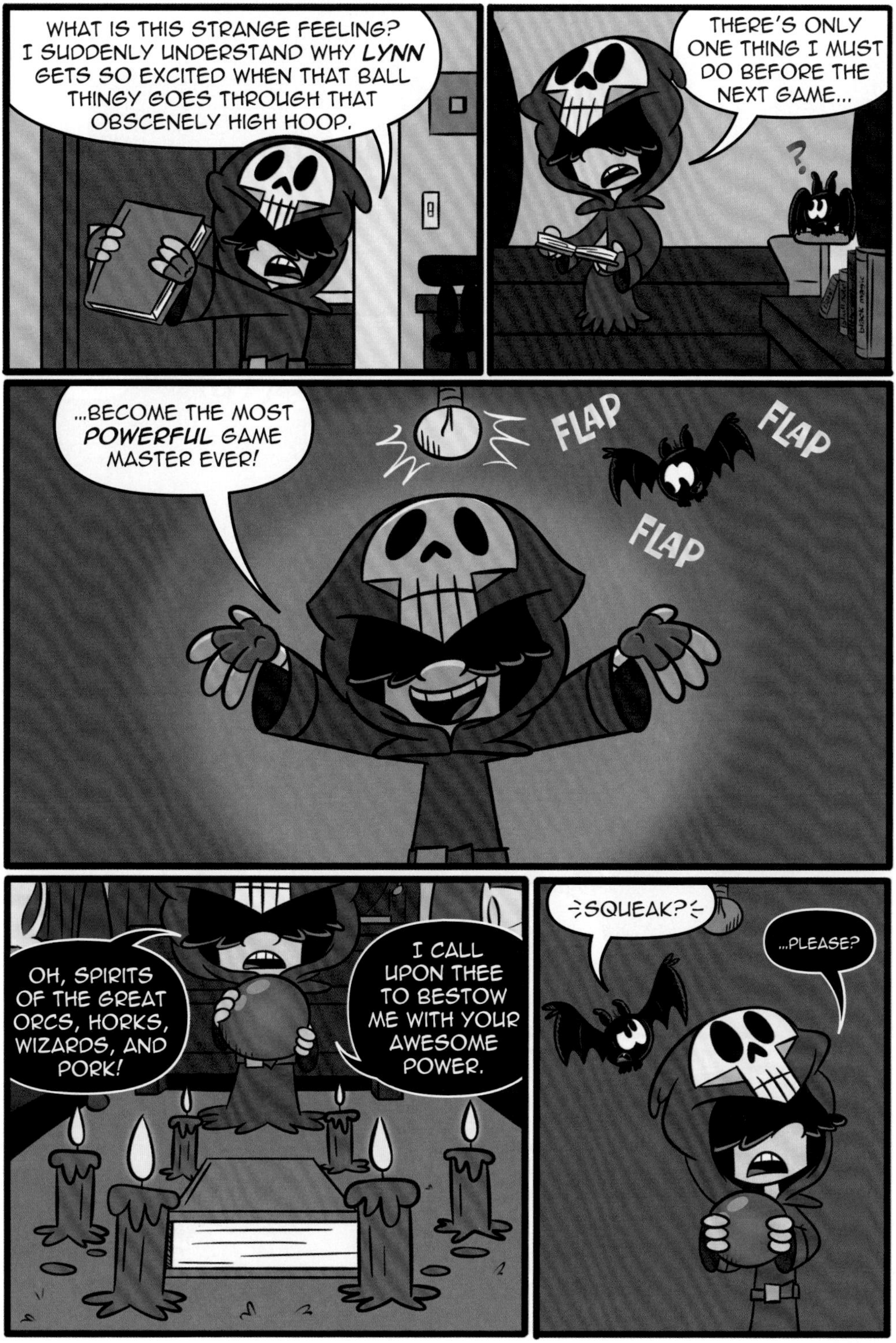
WHAT IS THIS STRANGE FEELING? I SUDDENLY UNDERSTAND WHY LYNN GETS SO EXCITED WHEN THAT BALL THINGY GOES THROUGH THAT OBSCENELY HIGH HOOP.
THERE'S ONLY ONE THING I MUST DO BEFORE THE NEXT GAME...
?
...BECOME THE MOST POWERFUL GAME MASTER EVER!
FLAP
FLAP
FLAP
OH, SPIRITS OF THE GREAT ORCS, HORKS, WIZARDS, AND PORK!
I CALL UPON THEE TO BESTOW ME WITH YOUR AWESOME POWER.
SQUEAK?
...PLEASE?

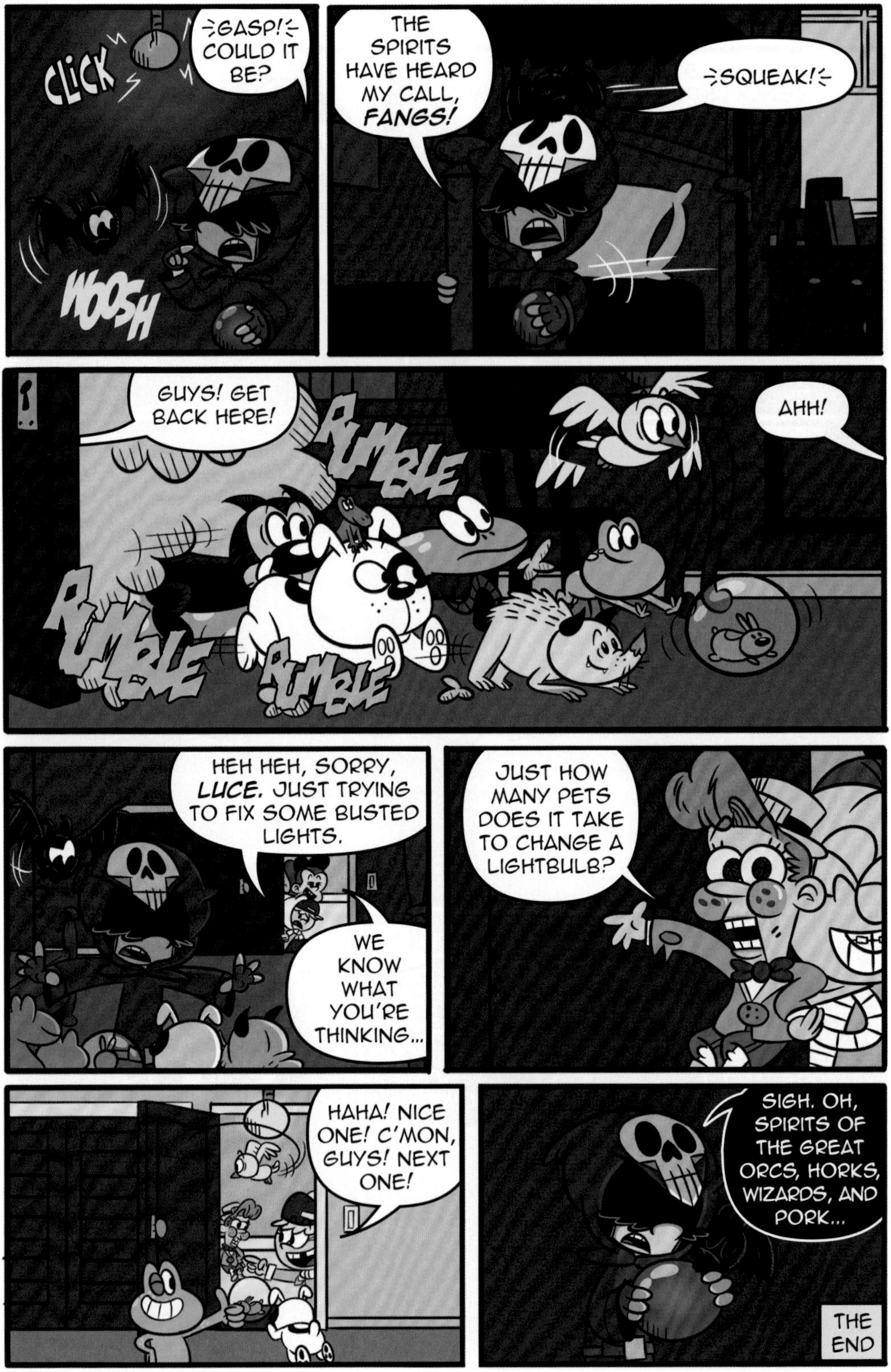
CLICK
⇛GASP!⇚ COULD IT BE?
WOOSH
THE SPIRITS HAVE HEARD MY CALL, FANGS!
⇛SQUEAK!⇚
GUYS! GET BACK HERE!
RUMBLE
AHH!
RUMBLE
RUMBLE
HEH HEH, SORRY, LUCE. JUST TRYING TO FIX SOME BUSTED LIGHTS.
WE KNOW WHAT YOU'RE THINKING...
JUST HOW MANY PETS DOES IT TAKE TO CHANGE A LIGHTBULB?
HAHA! NICE ONE! C'MON, GUYS! NEXT ONE!
SIGH. OH, SPIRITS OF THE GREAT ORCS, HORKS, WIZARDS, AND PORK...
THE END

"ROCK & ROLLED"

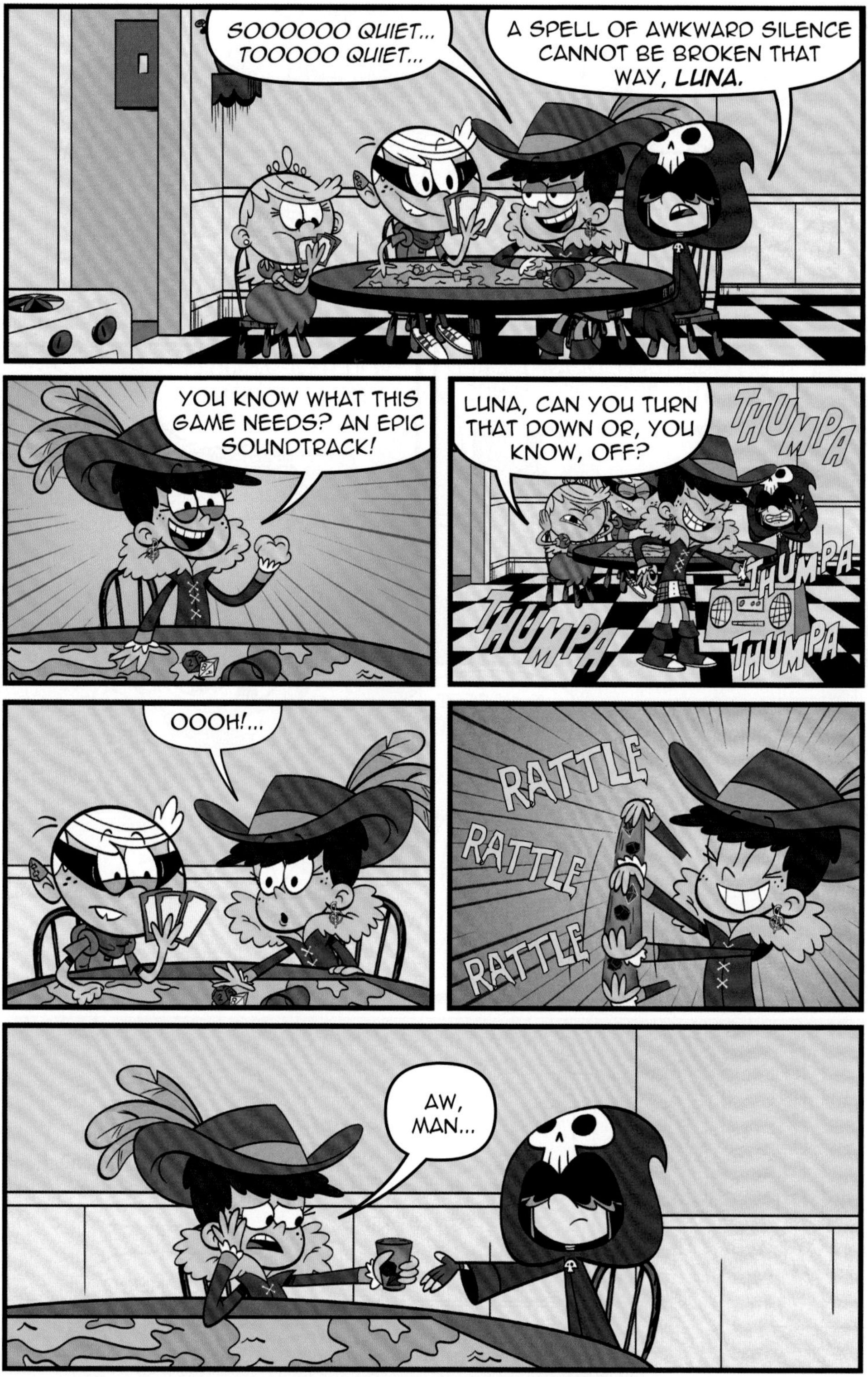

SOOOOOO QUIET... TOOOOO QUIET...
A SPELL OF AWKWARD SILENCE CANNOT BE BROKEN THAT WAY, LUNA.
YOU KNOW WHAT THIS GAME NEEDS? AN EPIC SOUNDTRACK!
LUNA, CAN YOU TURN THAT DOWN OR, YOU KNOW, OFF?
THUMPA
THUMPA
THUMPA
THUMPA
OOOH!...
RATTLE
RATTLE
RATTLE
AW, MAN...

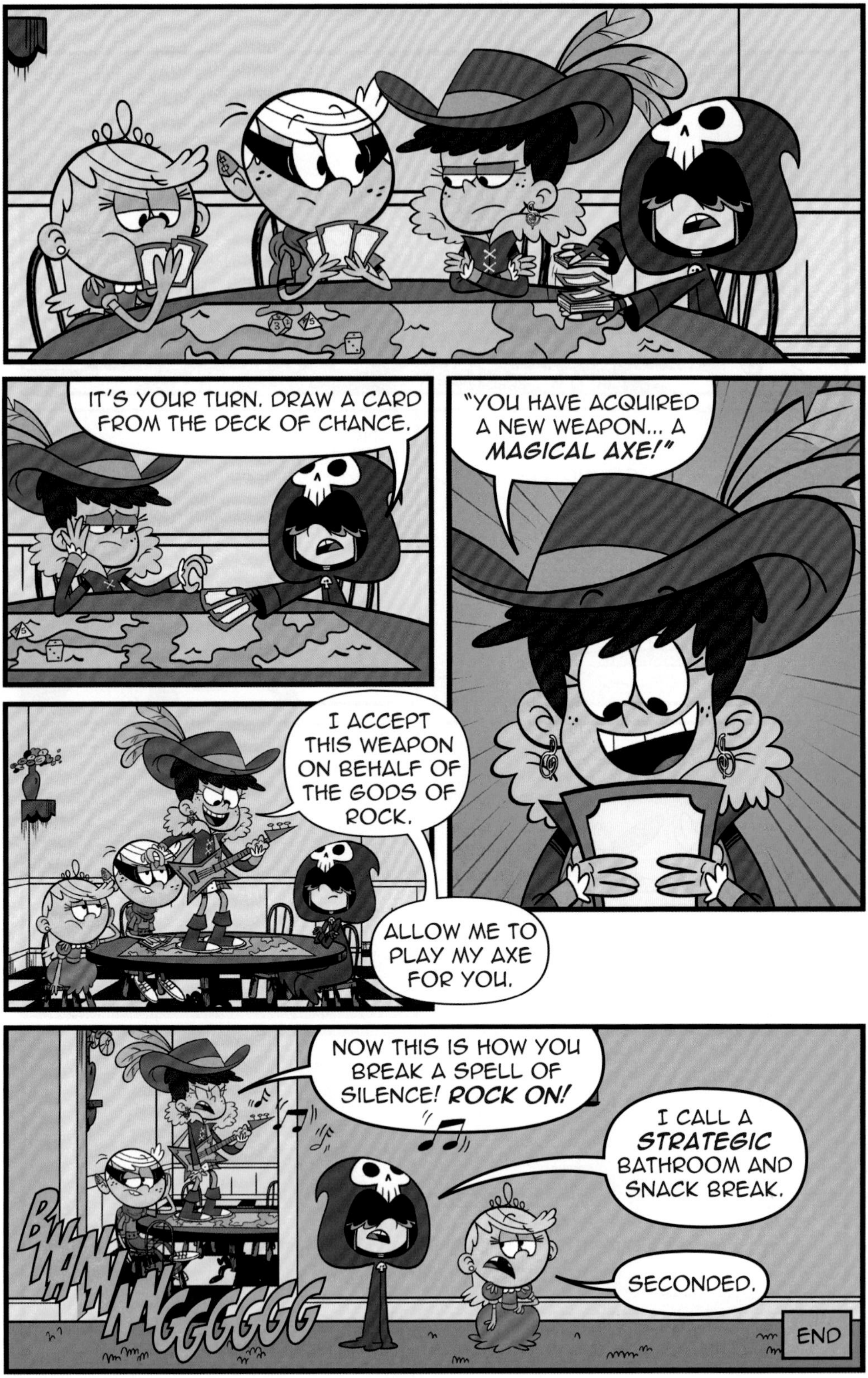
IT'S YOUR TURN. DRAW A CARD FROM THE DECK OF CHANCE.
"YOU HAVE ACQUIRED A NEW WEAPON... A *MAGICAL AXE!*"
I ACCEPT THIS WEAPON ON BEHALF OF THE GODS OF ROCK.
ALLOW ME TO PLAY MY AXE FOR YOU.
NOW THIS IS HOW YOU BREAK A SPELL OF SILENCE! *ROCK ON!*
BWANNNGGGGGG
I CALL A *STRATEGIC* BATHROOM AND SNACK BREAK.
SECONDED.
END

"¡Tu Destino!"

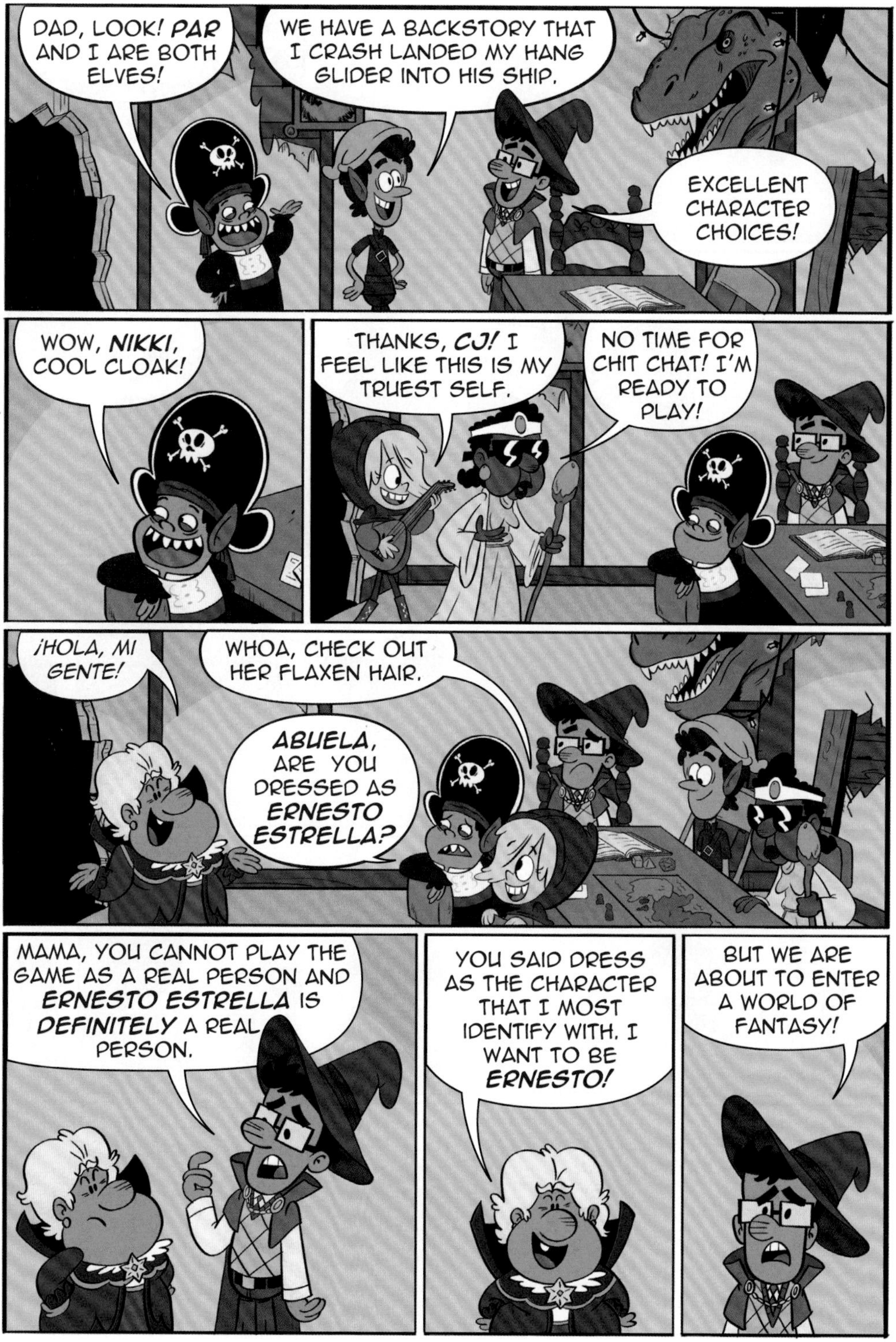
DAD, LOOK! PAR AND I ARE BOTH ELVES!
WE HAVE A BACKSTORY THAT I CRASH LANDED MY HANG GLIDER INTO HIS SHIP.
EXCELLENT CHARACTER CHOICES!
WOW, NIKKI, COOL CLOAK!
THANKS, CJ! I FEEL LIKE THIS IS MY TRUEST SELF.
NO TIME FOR CHIT CHAT! I'M READY TO PLAY!
¡HOLA, MI GENTE!
WHOA, CHECK OUT HER FLAXEN HAIR.
ABUELA, ARE YOU DRESSED AS ERNESTO ESTRELLA?
MAMA, YOU CANNOT PLAY THE GAME AS A REAL PERSON AND ERNESTO ESTRELLA IS DEFINITELY A REAL PERSON.
YOU SAID DRESS AS THE CHARACTER THAT I MOST IDENTIFY WITH. I WANT TO BE ERNESTO!
BUT WE ARE ABOUT TO ENTER A WORLD OF FANTASY!

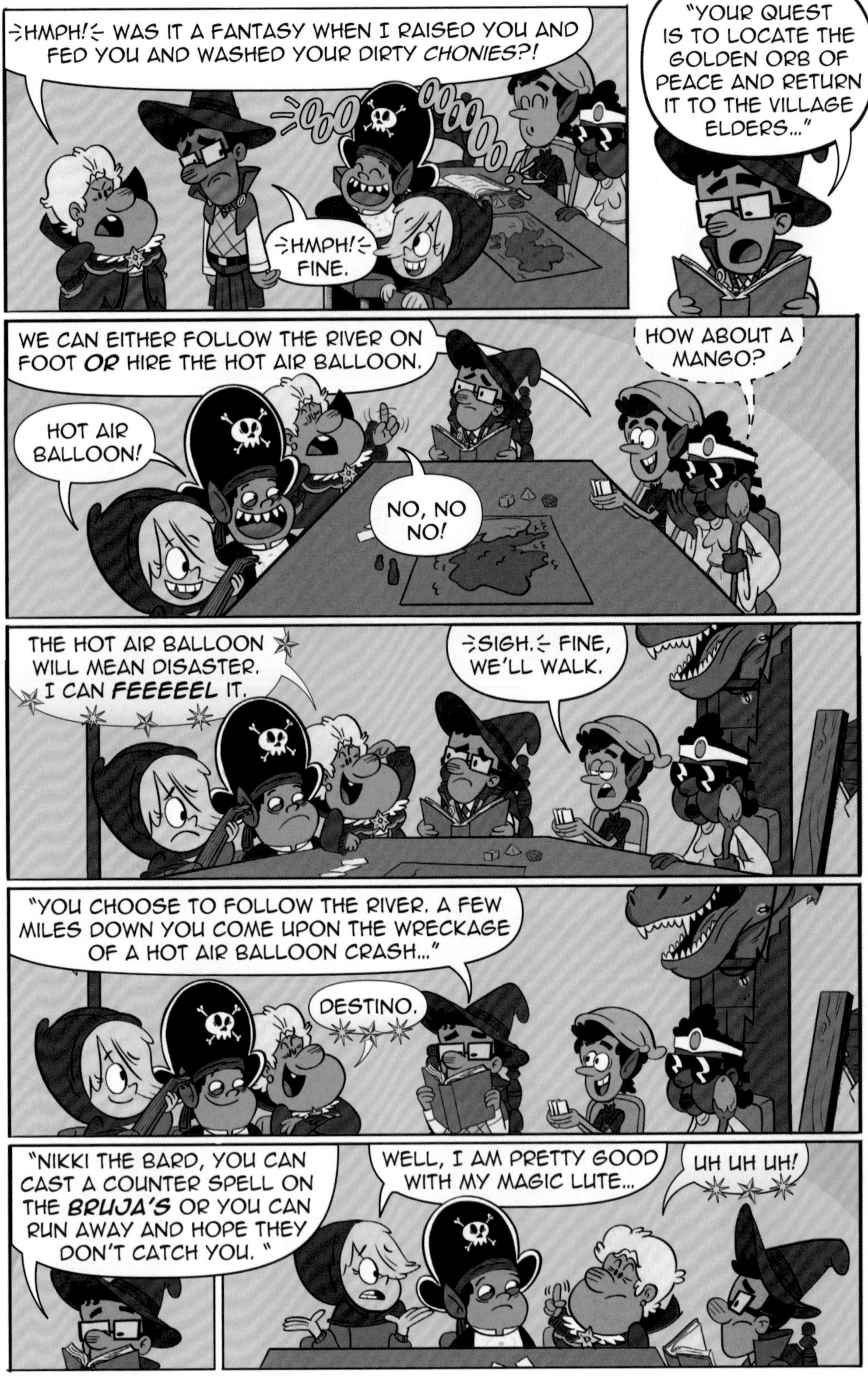

⇒HMPH!⇐ WAS IT A FANTASY WHEN I RAISED YOU AND FED YOU AND WASHED YOUR DIRTY *CHONIES*?!
⇒HMPH!⇐ FINE.
"YOUR QUEST IS TO LOCATE THE GOLDEN ORB OF PEACE AND RETURN IT TO THE VILLAGE ELDERS..."
WE CAN EITHER FOLLOW THE RIVER ON FOOT ***OR*** HIRE THE HOT AIR BALLOON.
HOW ABOUT A MANGO?
HOT AIR BALLOON!
NO, NO NO!
THE HOT AIR BALLOON WILL MEAN DISASTER. I CAN ***FEEEEEL*** IT.
⇒SIGH.⇐ FINE, WE'LL WALK.
"YOU CHOOSE TO FOLLOW THE RIVER. A FEW MILES DOWN YOU COME UPON THE WRECKAGE OF A HOT AIR BALLOON CRASH..."
DESTINO.
"NIKKI THE BARD, YOU CAN CAST A COUNTER SPELL ON THE ***BRUJA'S*** OR YOU CAN RUN AWAY AND HOPE THEY DON'T CATCH YOU."
WELL, I AM PRETTY GOOD WITH MY MAGIC LUTE...
UH UH UH!

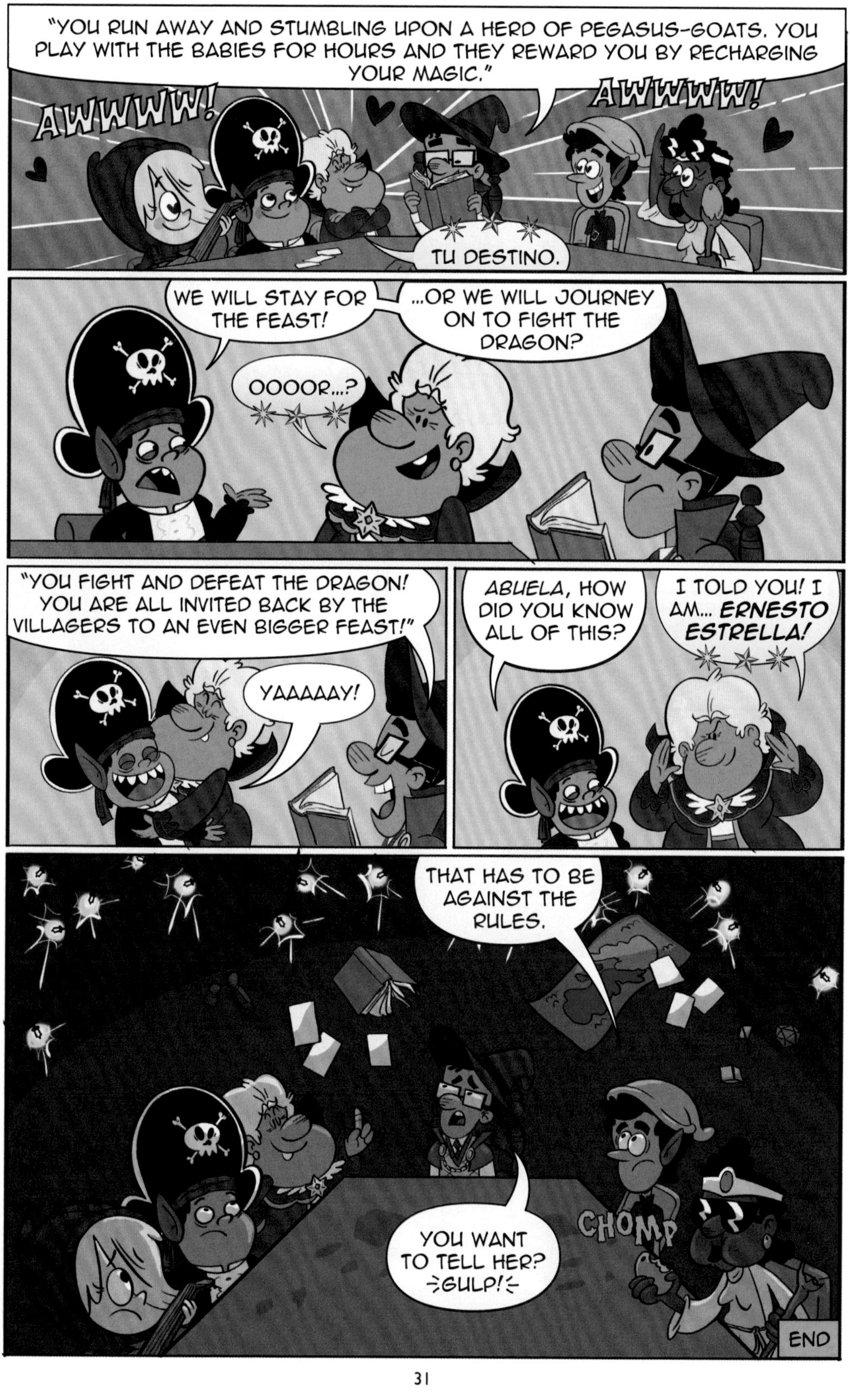
"YOU RUN AWAY AND STUMBLING UPON A HERD OF PEGASUS-GOATS. YOU PLAY WITH THE BABIES FOR HOURS AND THEY REWARD YOU BY RECHARGING YOUR MAGIC."
AWWWW!
AWWWW!
TU DESTINO.
WE WILL STAY FOR THE FEAST!
...OR WE WILL JOURNEY ON TO FIGHT THE DRAGON?
OOOOR...?
"YOU FIGHT AND DEFEAT THE DRAGON! YOU ARE ALL INVITED BACK BY THE VILLAGERS TO AN EVEN BIGGER FEAST!"
YAAAAAY!
ABUELA, HOW DID YOU KNOW ALL OF THIS?
I TOLD YOU! I AM... ***ERNESTO ESTRELLA!***
THAT HAS TO BE AGAINST THE RULES.
CHOMP
YOU WANT TO TELL HER?
GULP!
END

"TROPICAL PUNCH"

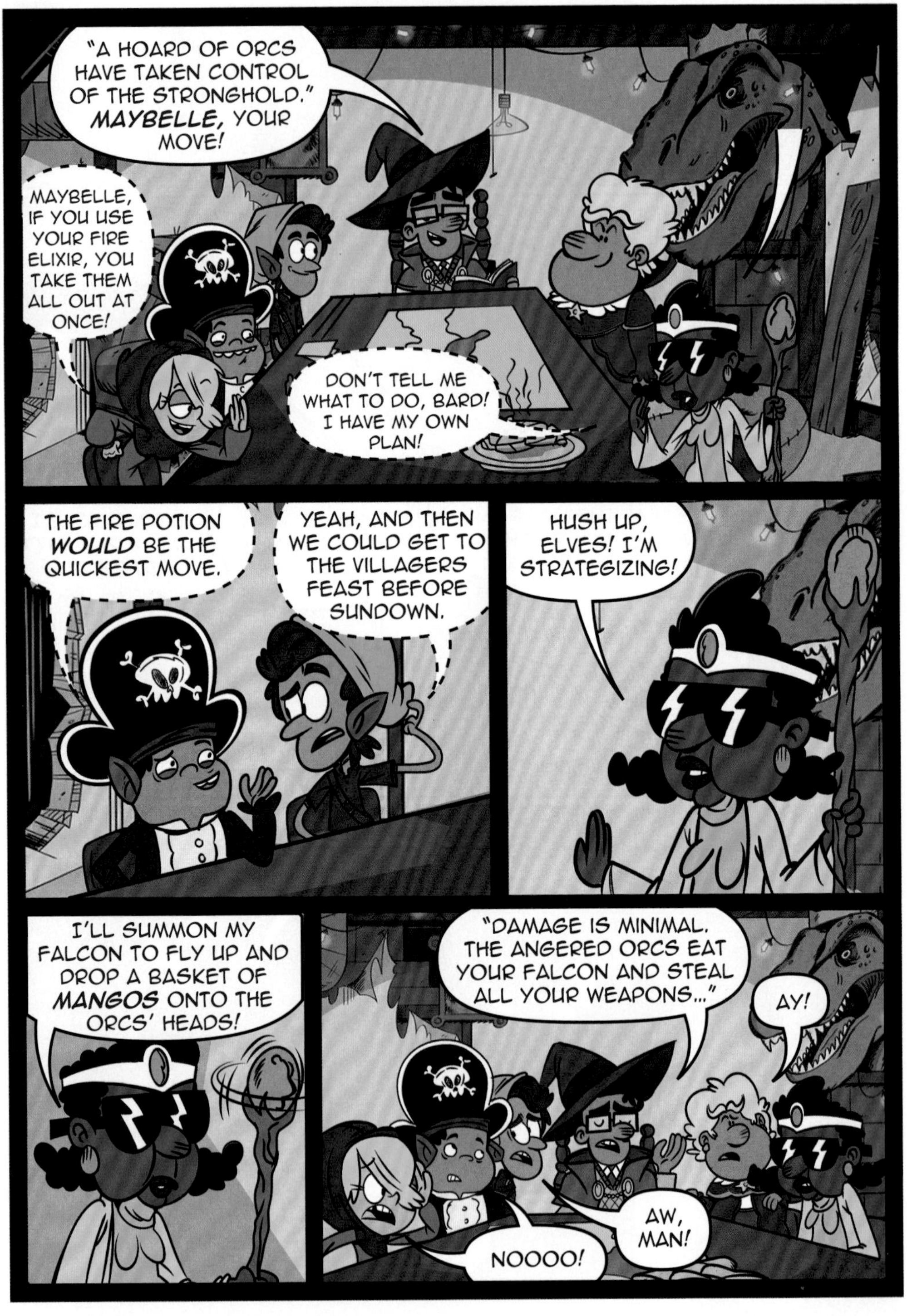

"A HOARD OF ORCS HAVE TAKEN CONTROL OF THE STRONGHOLD." MAYBELLE, YOUR MOVE!
MAYBELLE, IF YOU USE YOUR FIRE ELIXIR, YOU TAKE THEM ALL OUT AT ONCE!
DON'T TELL ME WHAT TO DO, BARD! I HAVE MY OWN PLAN!
THE FIRE POTION WOULD BE THE QUICKEST MOVE.
YEAH, AND THEN WE COULD GET TO THE VILLAGERS FEAST BEFORE SUNDOWN.
HUSH UP, ELVES! I'M STRATEGIZING!
I'LL SUMMON MY FALCON TO FLY UP AND DROP A BASKET OF MANGOS ONTO THE ORCS' HEADS!
"DAMAGE IS MINIMAL. THE ANGERED ORCS EAT YOUR FALCON AND STEAL ALL YOUR WEAPONS..."
AY!
AW, MAN!
NOOOO!

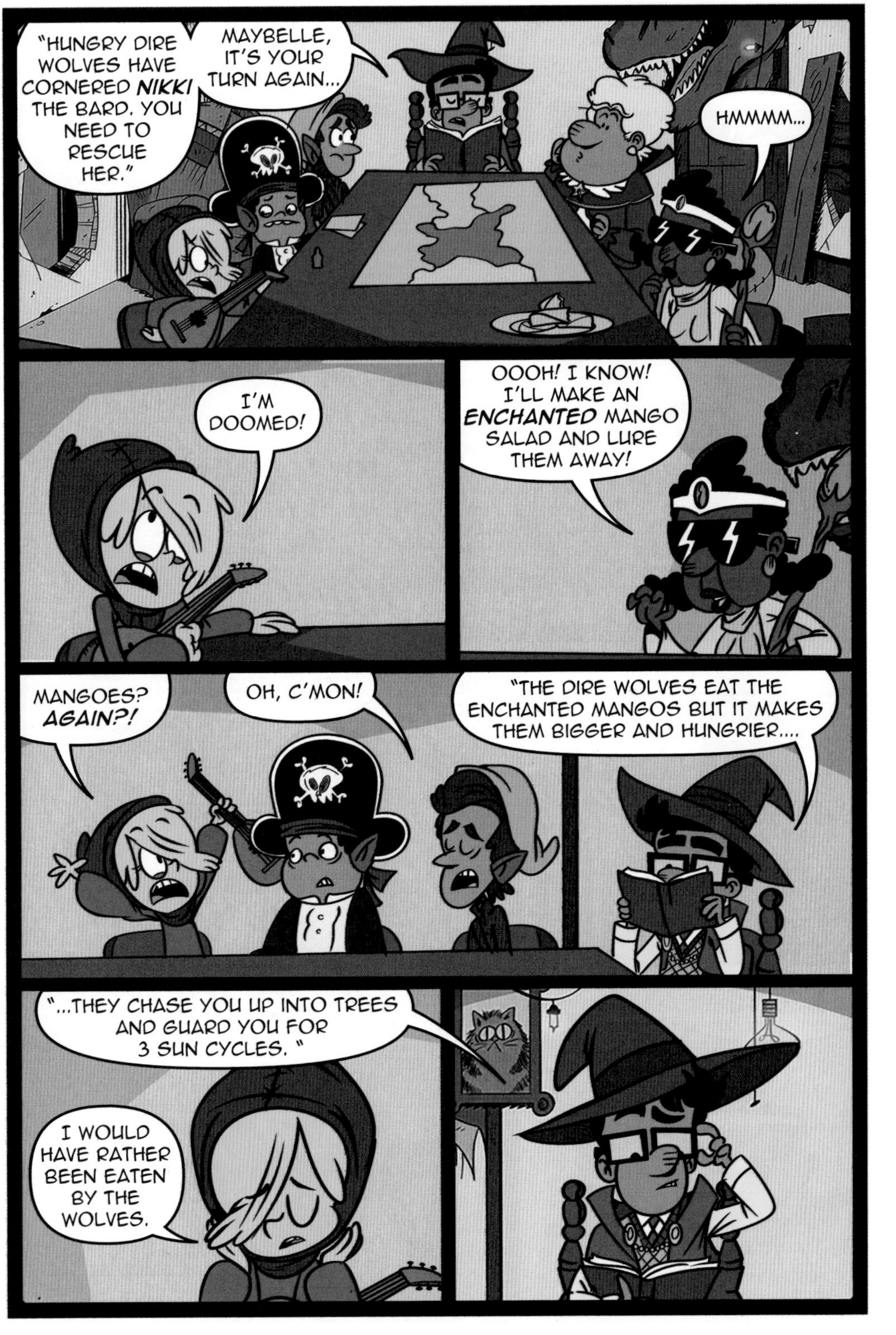
"HUNGRY DIRE WOLVES HAVE CORNERED NIKKI THE BARD. YOU NEED TO RESCUE HER."
MAYBELLE, IT'S YOUR TURN AGAIN...
HMMMM...
I'M DOOMED!
OOOH! I KNOW! I'LL MAKE AN ENCHANTED MANGO SALAD AND LURE THEM AWAY!
MANGOES? AGAIN?!
OH, C'MON!
"THE DIRE WOLVES EAT THE ENCHANTED MANGOS BUT IT MAKES THEM BIGGER AND HUNGRIER....
"...THEY CHASE YOU UP INTO TREES AND GUARD YOU FOR 3 SUN CYCLES."
I WOULD HAVE RATHER BEEN EATEN BY THE WOLVES.

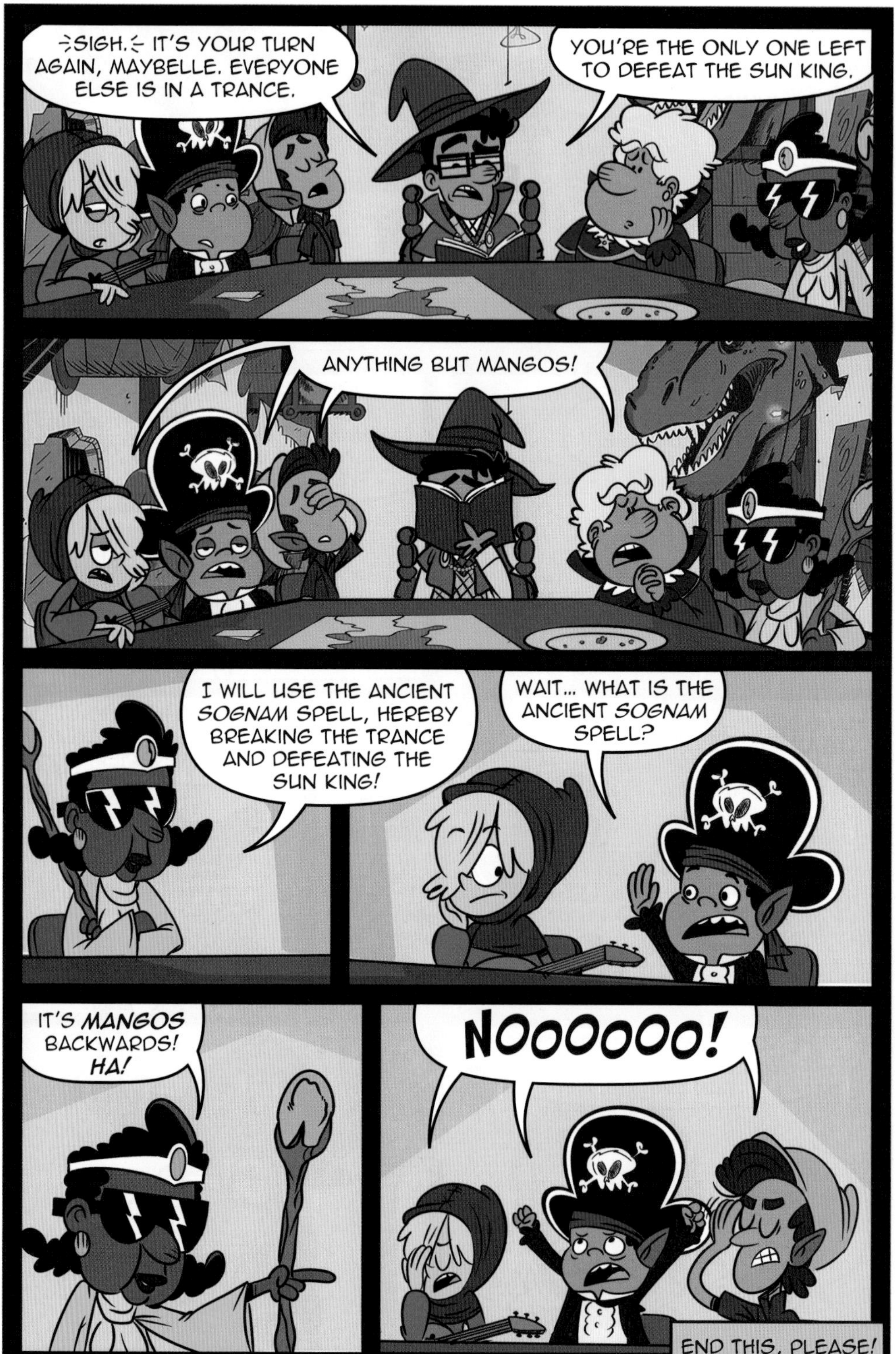

⇢SIGH.⇠ IT'S YOUR TURN AGAIN, MAYBELLE. EVERYONE ELSE IS IN A TRANCE.
YOU'RE THE ONLY ONE LEFT TO DEFEAT THE SUN KING.
ANYTHING BUT MANGOS!
I WILL USE THE ANCIENT *SOGNAM* SPELL, HEREBY BREAKING THE TRANCE AND DEFEATING THE SUN KING!
WAIT... WHAT IS THE ANCIENT *SOGNAM* SPELL?
IT'S *MANGOS* BACKWARDS! *HA!*
NOOOOOO!
END THIS, PLEASE!

"INFINITE FANNY"

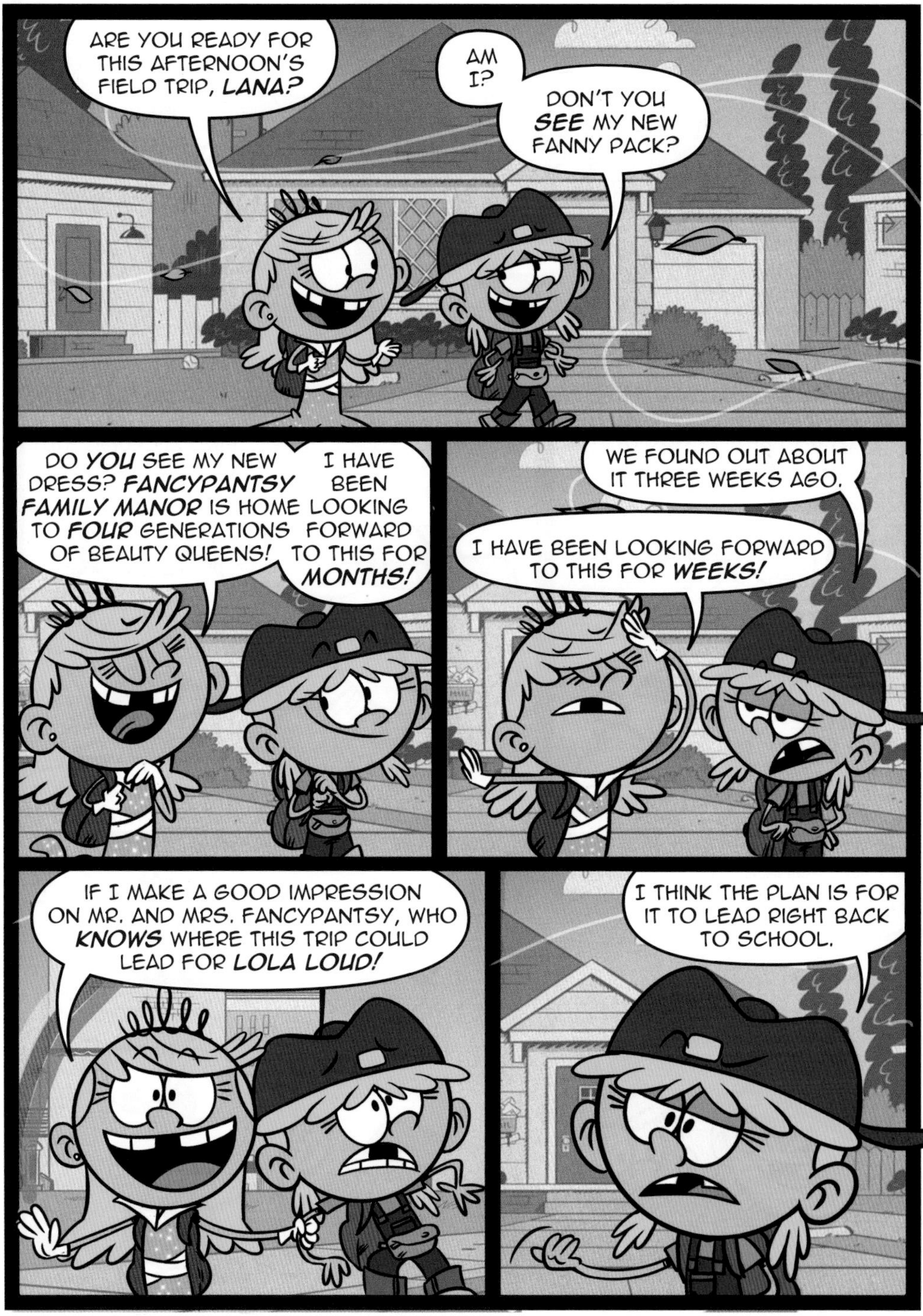
ARE YOU READY FOR THIS AFTERNOON'S FIELD TRIP, LANA?
AM I?
DON'T YOU SEE MY NEW FANNY PACK?
DO YOU SEE MY NEW DRESS? FANCYPANTSY FAMILY MANOR IS HOME TO FOUR GENERATIONS OF BEAUTY QUEENS!
I HAVE BEEN LOOKING FORWARD TO THIS FOR MONTHS!
WE FOUND OUT ABOUT IT THREE WEEKS AGO.
I HAVE BEEN LOOKING FORWARD TO THIS FOR WEEKS!
IF I MAKE A GOOD IMPRESSION ON MR. AND MRS. FANCYPANTSY, WHO KNOWS WHERE THIS TRIP COULD LEAD FOR LOLA LOUD!
I THINK THE PLAN IS FOR IT TO LEAD RIGHT BACK TO SCHOOL.

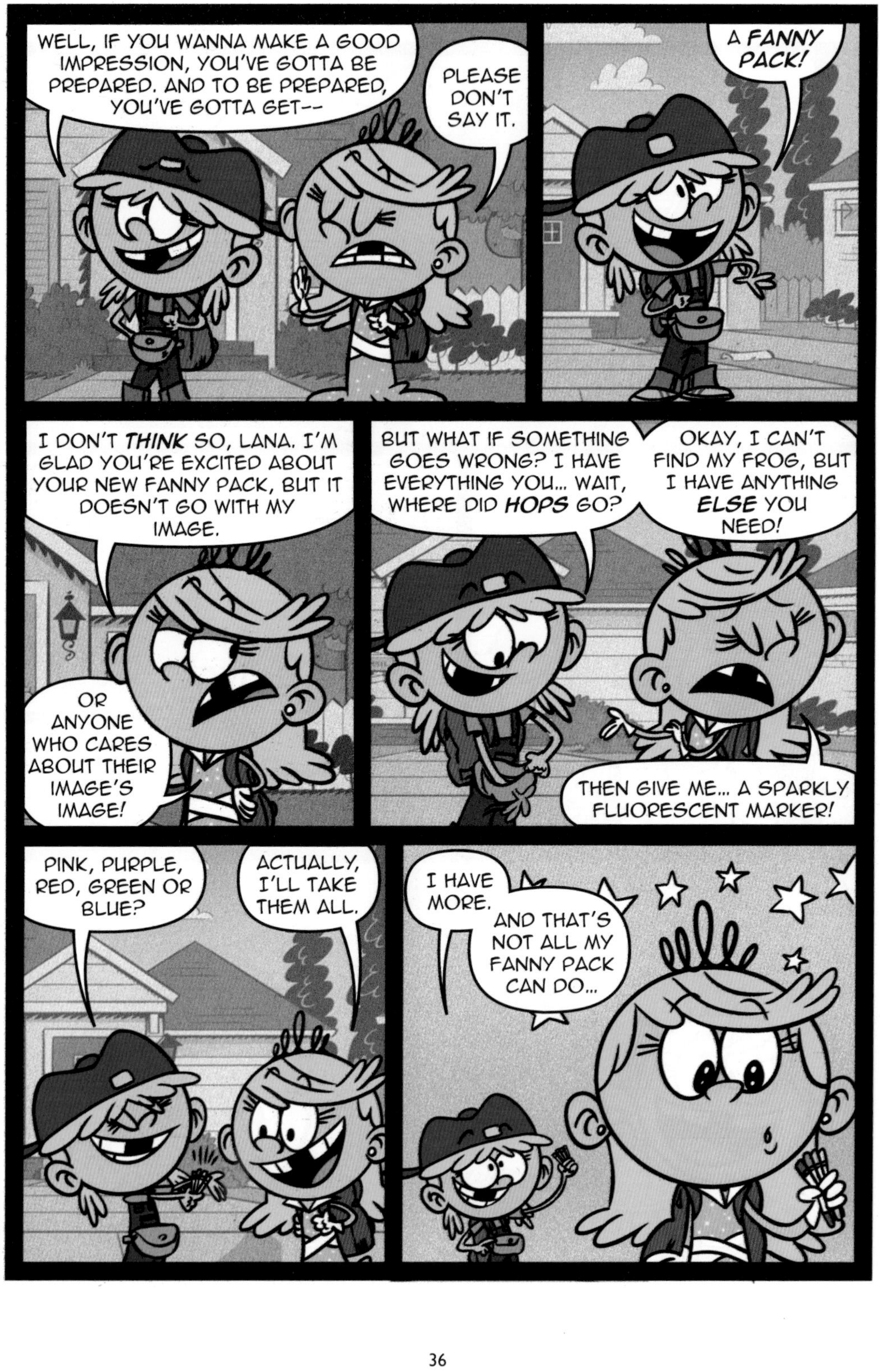
WELL, IF YOU WANNA MAKE A GOOD IMPRESSION, YOU'VE GOTTA BE PREPARED. AND TO BE PREPARED, YOU'VE GOTTA GET--
PLEASE DON'T SAY IT.
A *FANNY PACK!*
I DON'T *THINK* SO, LANA. I'M GLAD YOU'RE EXCITED ABOUT YOUR NEW FANNY PACK, BUT IT DOESN'T GO WITH MY IMAGE.
OR ANYONE WHO CARES ABOUT THEIR IMAGE'S IMAGE!
BUT WHAT IF SOMETHING GOES WRONG? I HAVE EVERYTHING YOU... WAIT, WHERE DID *HOPS* GO?
OKAY, I CAN'T FIND MY FROG, BUT I HAVE ANYTHING *ELSE* YOU NEED!
THEN GIVE ME... A SPARKLY FLUORESCENT MARKER!
PINK, PURPLE, RED, GREEN OR BLUE?
ACTUALLY, I'LL TAKE THEM ALL.
I HAVE MORE.
AND THAT'S NOT ALL MY FANNY PACK CAN DO...

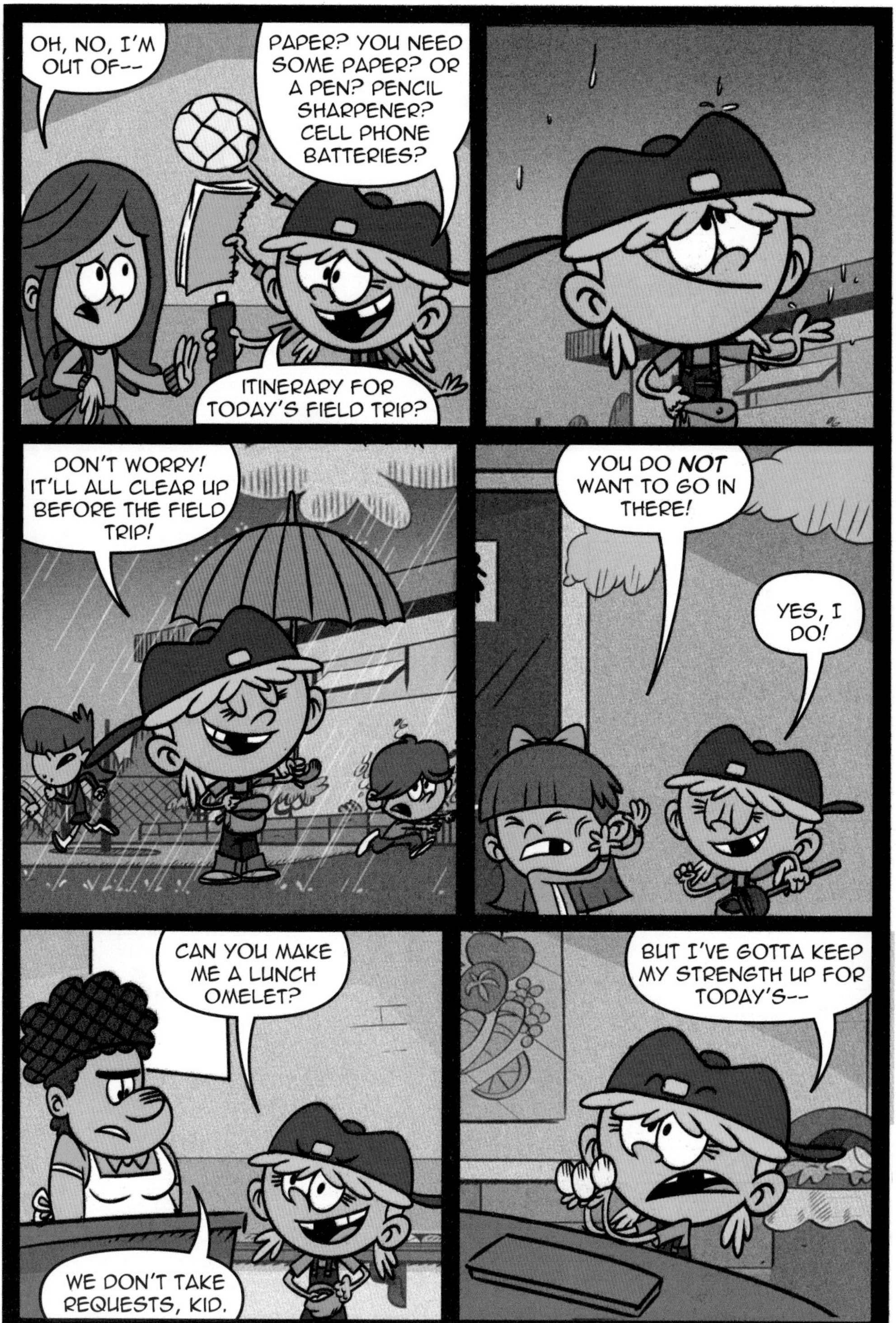
OH, NO, I'M OUT OF--
PAPER? YOU NEED SOME PAPER? OR A PEN? PENCIL SHARPENER? CELL PHONE BATTERIES?
ITINERARY FOR TODAY'S FIELD TRIP?
DON'T WORRY! IT'LL ALL CLEAR UP BEFORE THE FIELD TRIP!
YOU DO *NOT* WANT TO GO IN THERE!
YES, I DO!
CAN YOU MAKE ME A LUNCH OMELET?
WE DON'T TAKE REQUESTS, KID.
BUT I'VE GOTTA KEEP MY STRENGTH UP FOR TODAY'S--

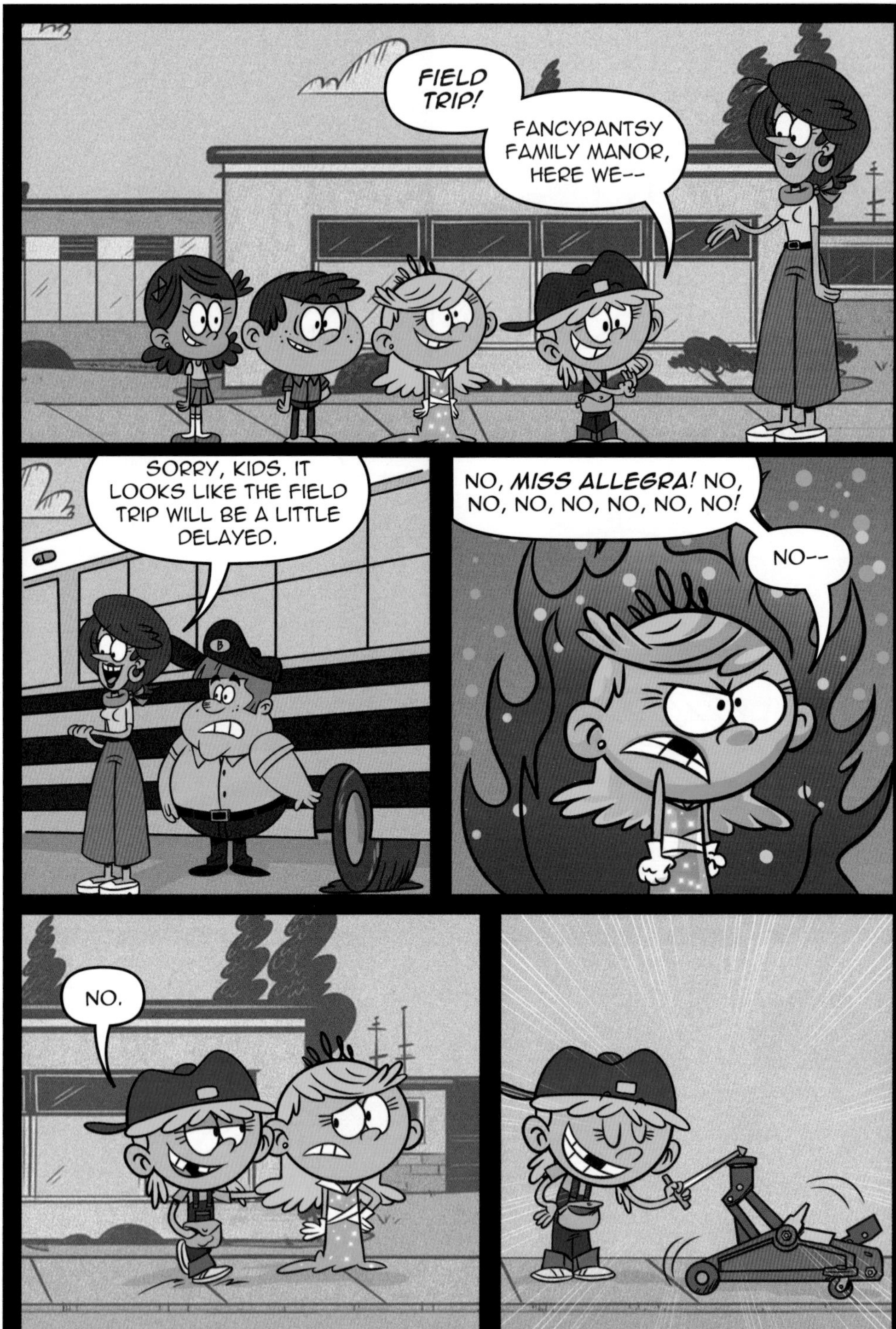
FIELD TRIP!
FANCYPANTSY FAMILY MANOR, HERE WE--
SORRY, KIDS. IT LOOKS LIKE THE FIELD TRIP WILL BE A LITTLE DELAYED.
NO, *MISS ALLEGRA!* NO, NO, NO, NO, NO, NO, NO!
NO--
NO.

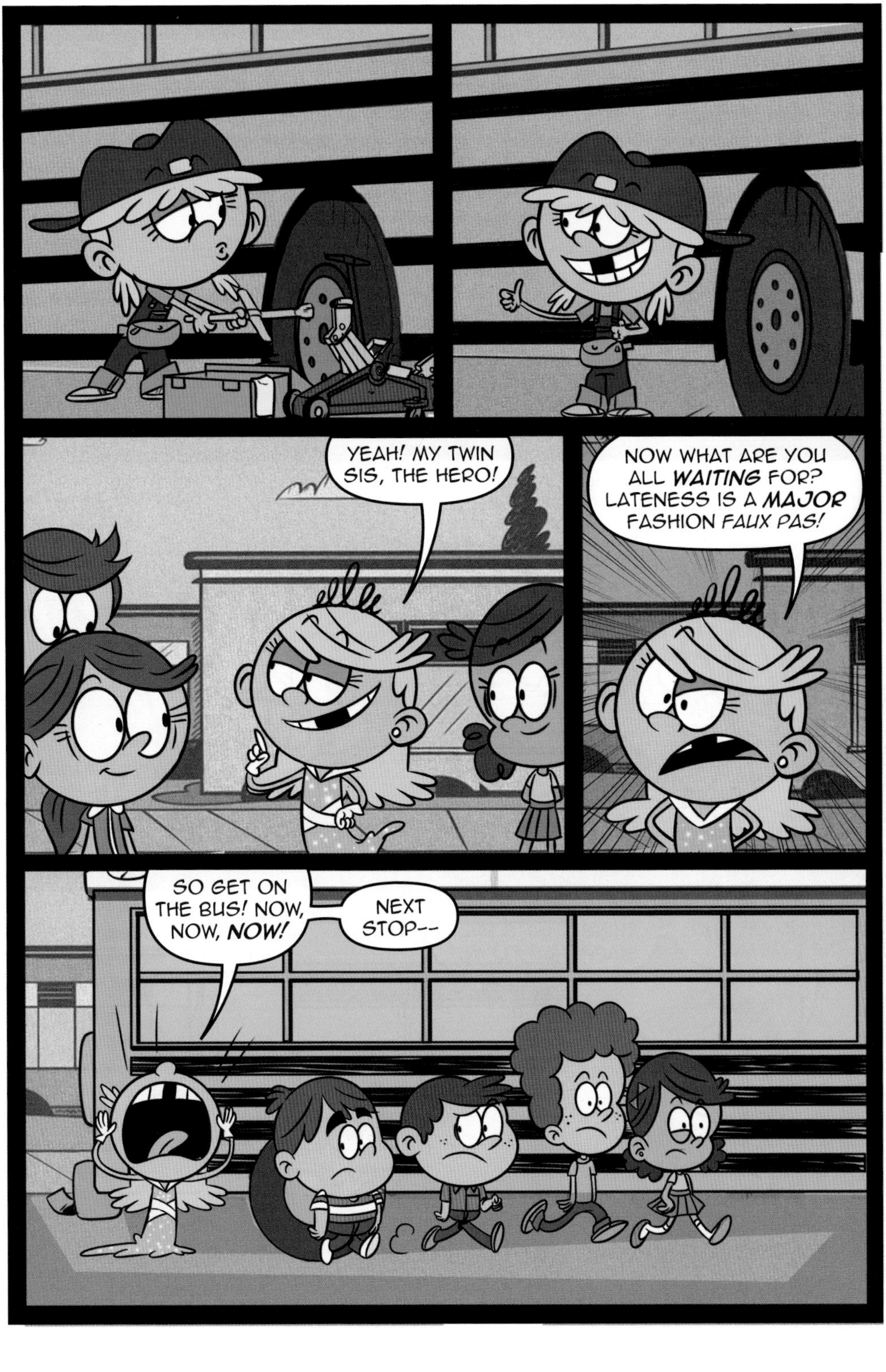
YEAH! MY TWIN SIS, THE HERO!
NOW WHAT ARE YOU ALL *WAITING* FOR? LATENESS IS A ***MAJOR*** FASHION *FAUX PAS!*
SO GET ON THE BUS! NOW, NOW, ***NOW!***
NEXT STOP--

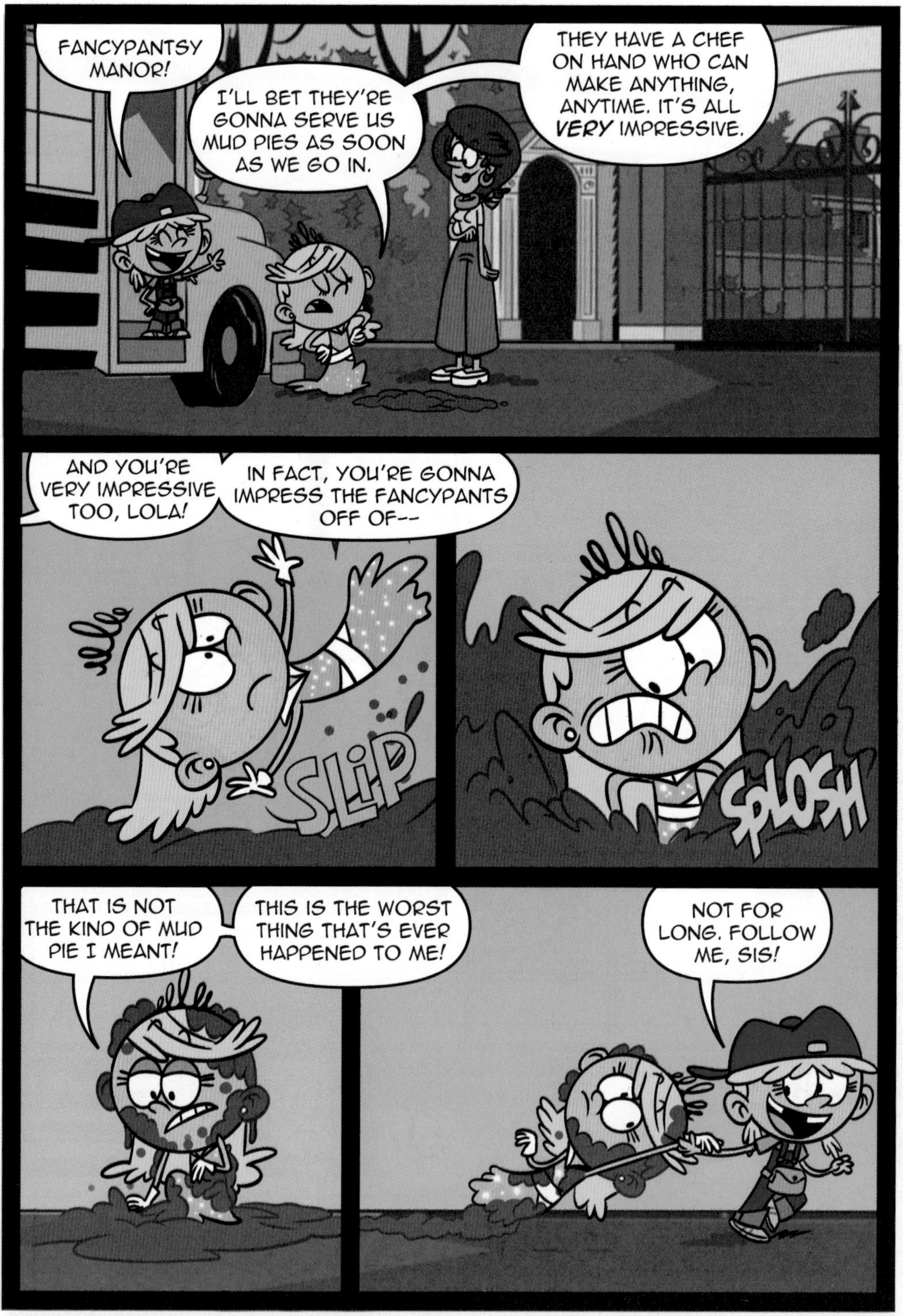
FANCYPANTSY MANOR!
I'LL BET THEY'RE GONNA SERVE US MUD PIES AS SOON AS WE GO IN.
THEY HAVE A CHEF ON HAND WHO CAN MAKE ANYTHING, ANYTIME. IT'S ALL *VERY* IMPRESSIVE.
AND YOU'RE VERY IMPRESSIVE TOO, LOLA!
IN FACT, YOU'RE GONNA IMPRESS THE FANCYPANTS OFF OF--
SLIP
SPLOSH
THAT IS NOT THE KIND OF MUD PIE I MEANT!
THIS IS THE WORST THING THAT'S EVER HAPPENED TO ME!
NOT FOR LONG. FOLLOW ME, SIS!

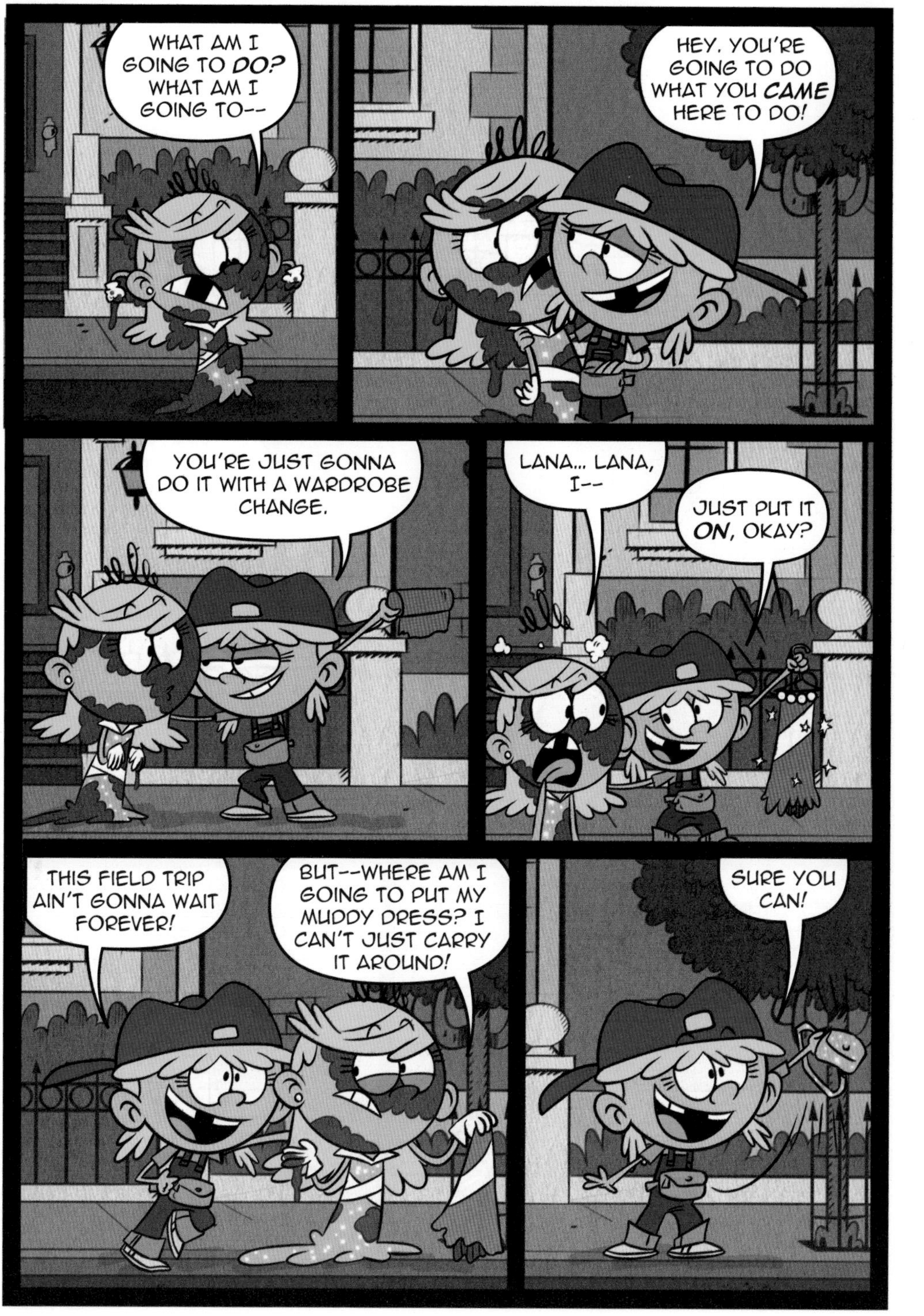
WHAT AM I GOING TO *DO?* WHAT AM I GOING TO--
HEY. YOU'RE GOING TO DO WHAT YOU *CAME* HERE TO DO!
YOU'RE JUST GONNA DO IT WITH A WARDROBE CHANGE.
LANA... LANA, I--
JUST PUT IT *ON*, OKAY?
THIS FIELD TRIP AIN'T GONNA WAIT FOREVER!
BUT--WHERE AM I GOING TO PUT MY MUDDY DRESS? I CAN'T JUST CARRY IT AROUND!
SURE YOU CAN!

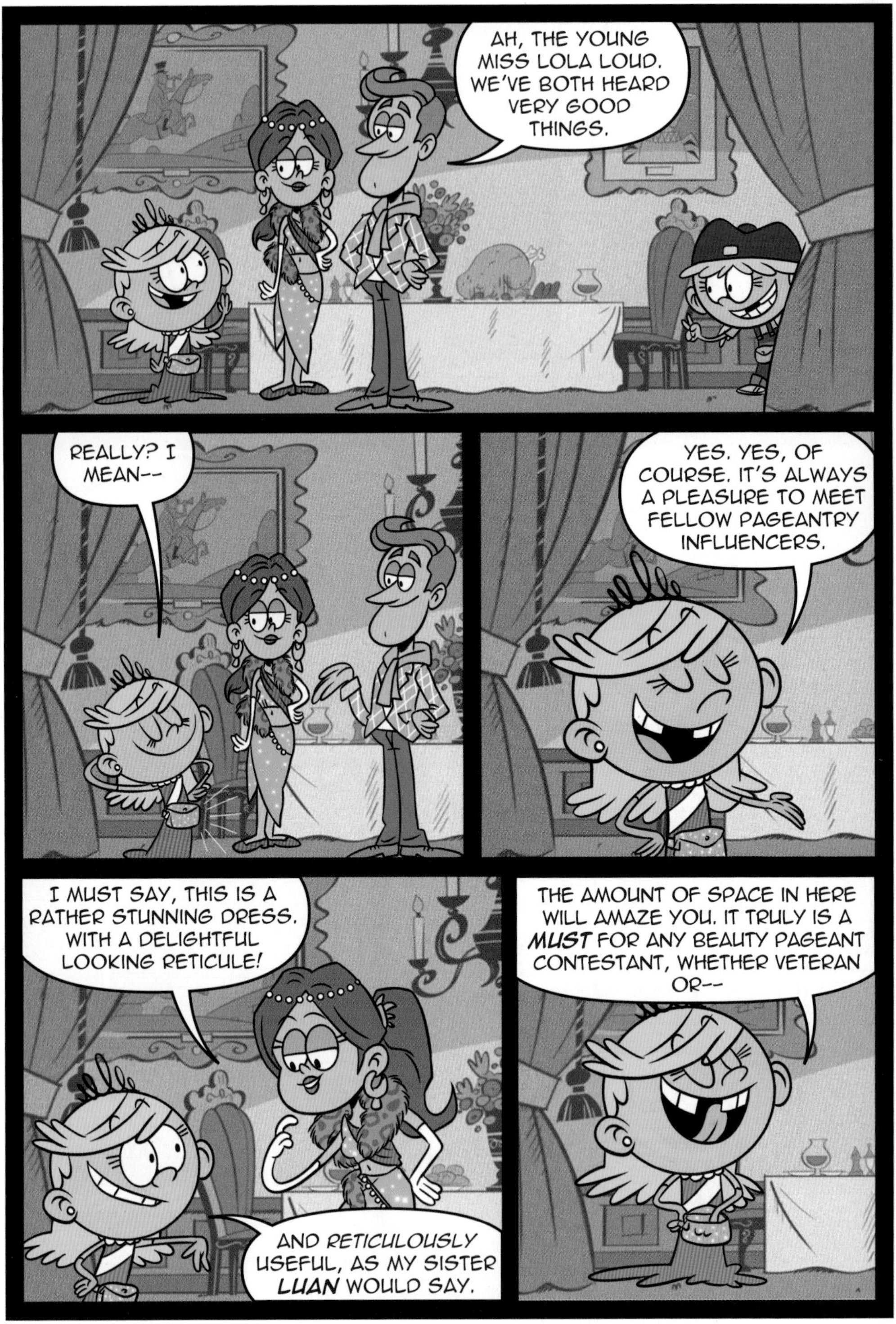
AH, THE YOUNG MISS LOLA LOUD. WE'VE BOTH HEARD VERY GOOD THINGS.
REALLY? I MEAN--
YES. YES, OF COURSE. IT'S ALWAYS A PLEASURE TO MEET FELLOW PAGEANTRY INFLUENCERS.
I MUST SAY, THIS IS A RATHER STUNNING DRESS. WITH A DELIGHTFUL LOOKING RETICULE!
AND RETICULOUSLY USEFUL, AS MY SISTER LUAN WOULD SAY.
THE AMOUNT OF SPACE IN HERE WILL AMAZE YOU. IT TRULY IS A MUST FOR ANY BEAUTY PAGEANT CONTESTANT, WHETHER VETERAN OR--

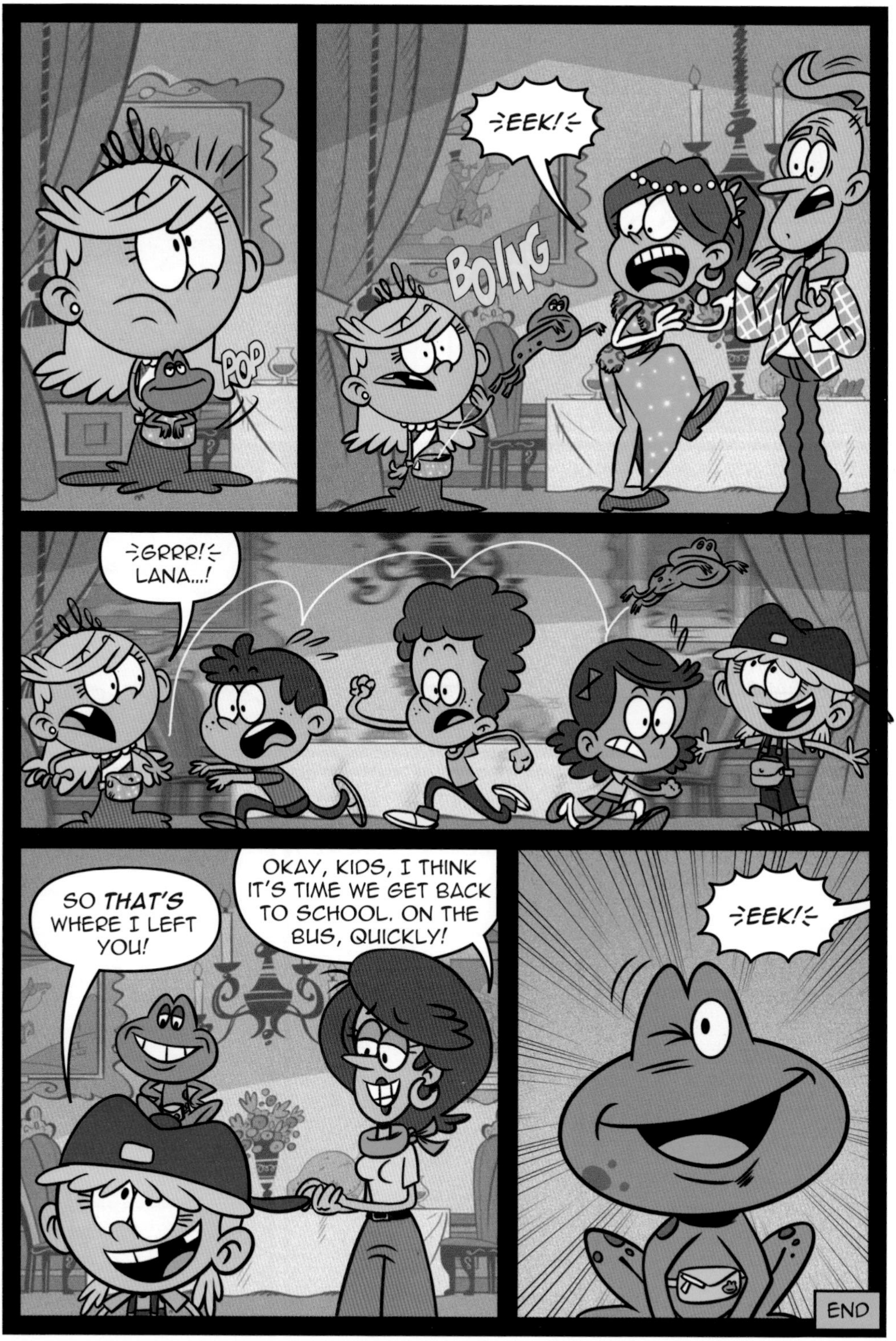
POP
EEK!
BOING
GRRR! LANA...!
SO THAT'S WHERE I LEFT YOU!
OKAY, KIDS, I THINK IT'S TIME WE GET BACK TO SCHOOL. ON THE BUS, QUICKLY!
EEK!
END

"THE HOT GOSS"

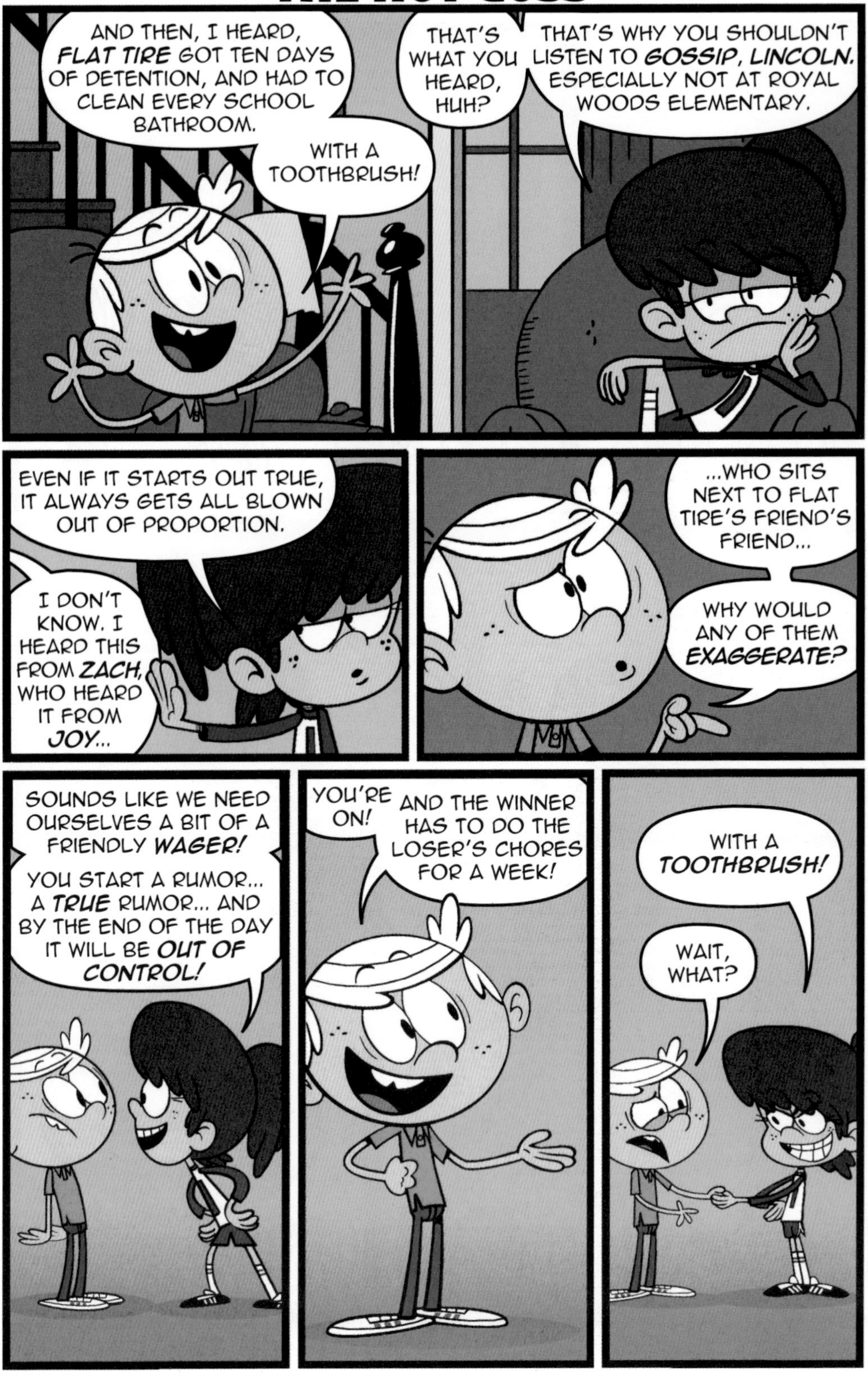
AND THEN, I HEARD, FLAT TIRE GOT TEN DAYS OF DETENTION, AND HAD TO CLEAN EVERY SCHOOL BATHROOM.
WITH A TOOTHBRUSH!
THAT'S WHAT YOU HEARD, HUH?
THAT'S WHY YOU SHOULDN'T LISTEN TO GOSSIP, LINCOLN. ESPECIALLY NOT AT ROYAL WOODS ELEMENTARY.
EVEN IF IT STARTS OUT TRUE, IT ALWAYS GETS ALL BLOWN OUT OF PROPORTION.
I DON'T KNOW. I HEARD THIS FROM ZACH, WHO HEARD IT FROM JOY...
...WHO SITS NEXT TO FLAT TIRE'S FRIEND'S FRIEND...
WHY WOULD ANY OF THEM EXAGGERATE?
SOUNDS LIKE WE NEED OURSELVES A BIT OF A FRIENDLY WAGER!
YOU START A RUMOR... A TRUE RUMOR... AND BY THE END OF THE DAY IT WILL BE OUT OF CONTROL!
YOU'RE ON!
AND THE WINNER HAS TO DO THE LOSER'S CHORES FOR A WEEK!
WITH A TOOTHBRUSH!
WAIT, WHAT?

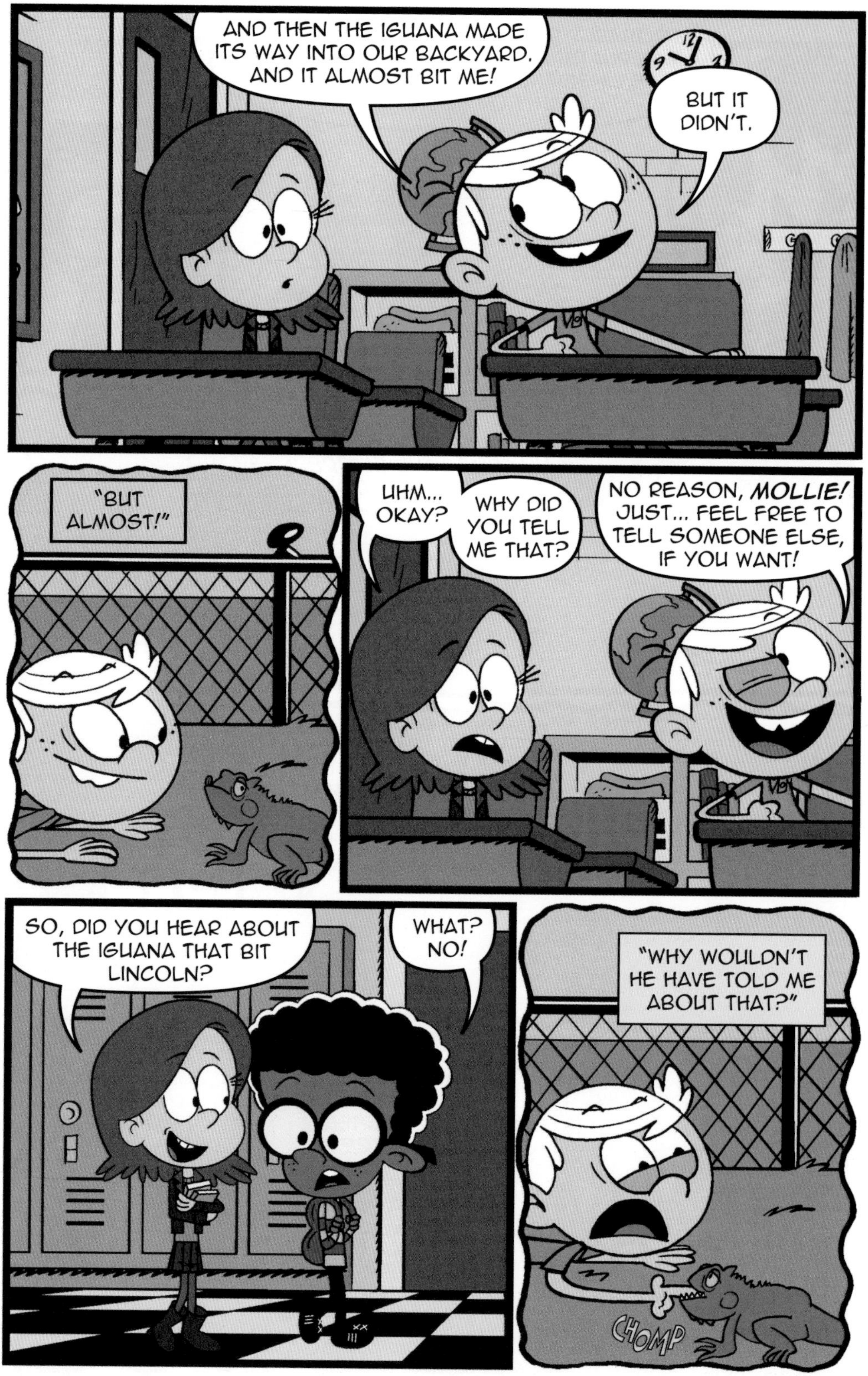
AND THEN THE IGUANA MADE ITS WAY INTO OUR BACKYARD. AND IT ALMOST BIT ME!
BUT IT DIDN'T.
"BUT ALMOST!"
UHM... OKAY?
WHY DID YOU TELL ME THAT?
NO REASON, MOLLIE! JUST... FEEL FREE TO TELL SOMEONE ELSE, IF YOU WANT!
SO, DID YOU HEAR ABOUT THE IGUANA THAT BIT LINCOLN?
WHAT? NO!
"WHY WOULDN'T HE HAVE TOLD ME ABOUT THAT?"
CHOMP

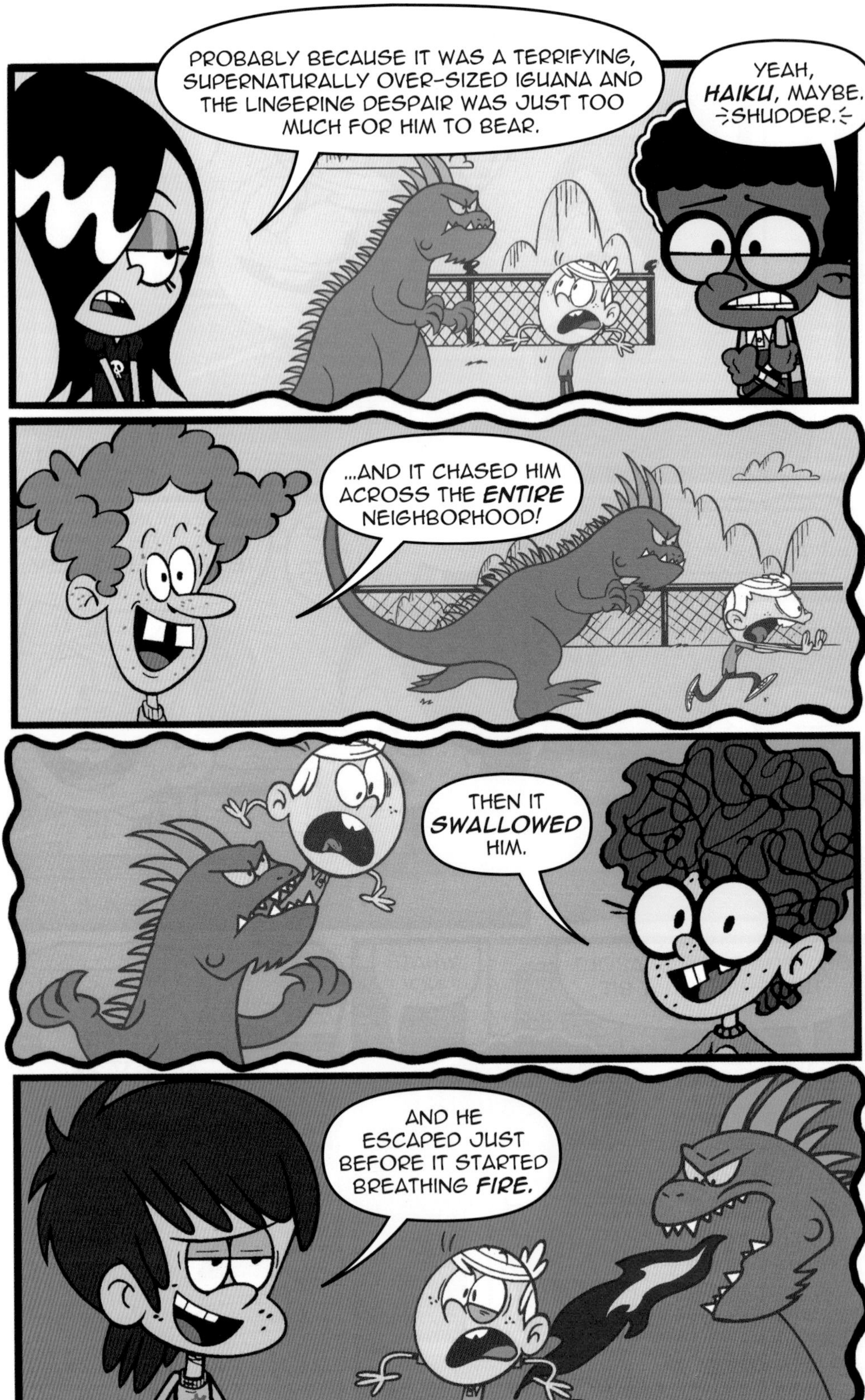
PROBABLY BECAUSE IT WAS A TERRIFYING, SUPERNATURALLY OVER-SIZED IGUANA AND THE LINGERING DESPAIR WAS JUST TOO MUCH FOR HIM TO BEAR.
YEAH, HAIKU, MAYBE. SHUDDER.
...AND IT CHASED HIM ACROSS THE ENTIRE NEIGHBORHOOD!
THEN IT SWALLOWED HIM.
AND HE ESCAPED JUST BEFORE IT STARTED BREATHING FIRE.

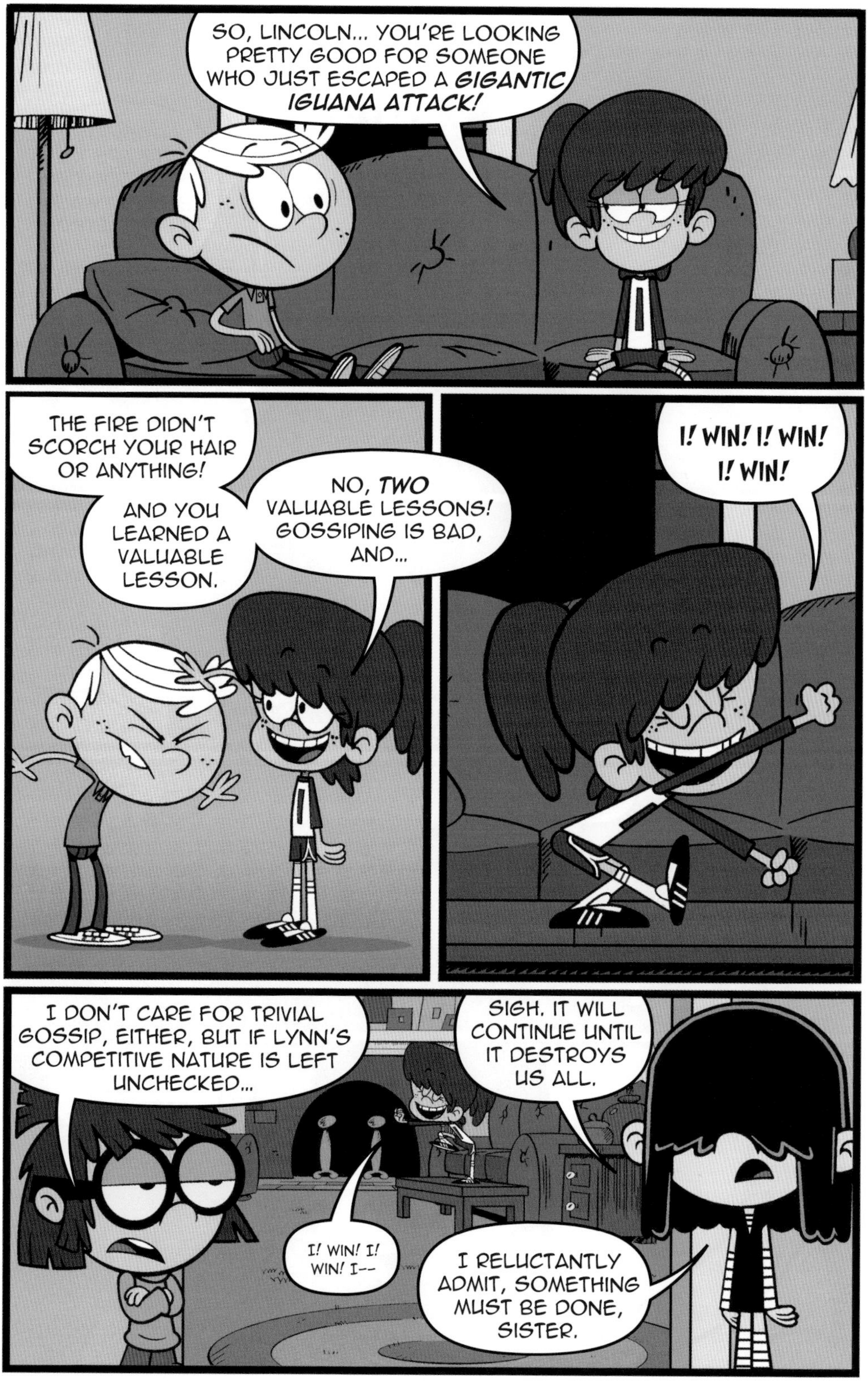
SO, LINCOLN... YOU'RE LOOKING PRETTY GOOD FOR SOMEONE WHO JUST ESCAPED A **GIGANTIC IGUANA ATTACK!**
THE FIRE DIDN'T SCORCH YOUR HAIR OR ANYTHING!
AND YOU LEARNED A VALUABLE LESSON.
NO, **TWO** VALUABLE LESSONS! GOSSIPING IS BAD, AND...
I! WIN! I! WIN! I! WIN!
I DON'T CARE FOR TRIVIAL GOSSIP, EITHER, BUT IF LYNN'S COMPETITIVE NATURE IS LEFT UNCHECKED...
SIGH. IT WILL CONTINUE UNTIL IT DESTROYS US ALL.
I! WIN! I! WIN! I--
I RELUCTANTLY ADMIT, SOMETHING MUST BE DONE, SISTER.

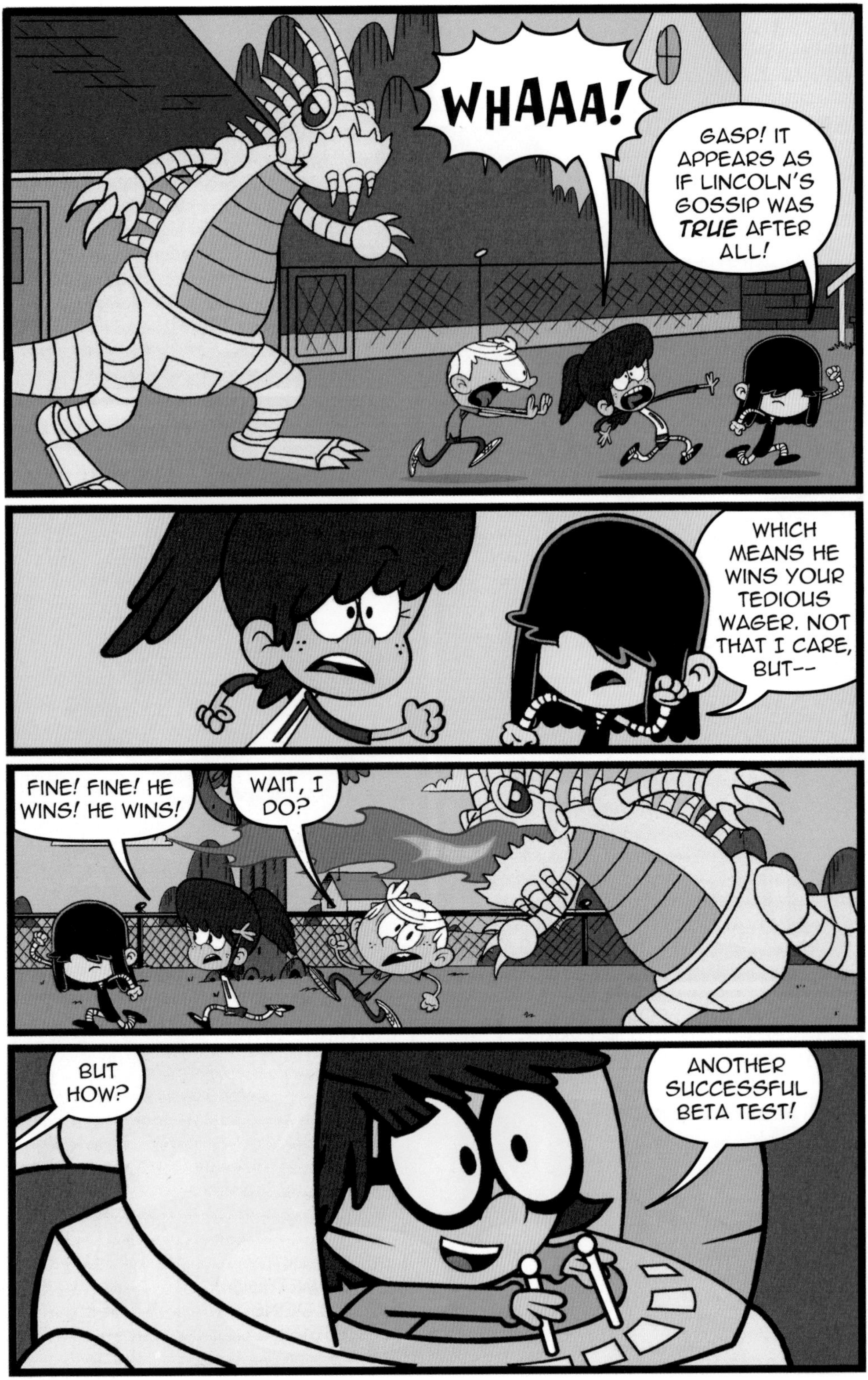
WHAAA!
GASP! IT APPEARS AS IF LINCOLN'S GOSSIP WAS TRUE AFTER ALL!
WHICH MEANS HE WINS YOUR TEDIOUS WAGER. NOT THAT I CARE, BUT--
FINE! FINE! HE WINS! HE WINS!
WAIT, I DO?
BUT HOW?
ANOTHER SUCCESSFUL BETA TEST!

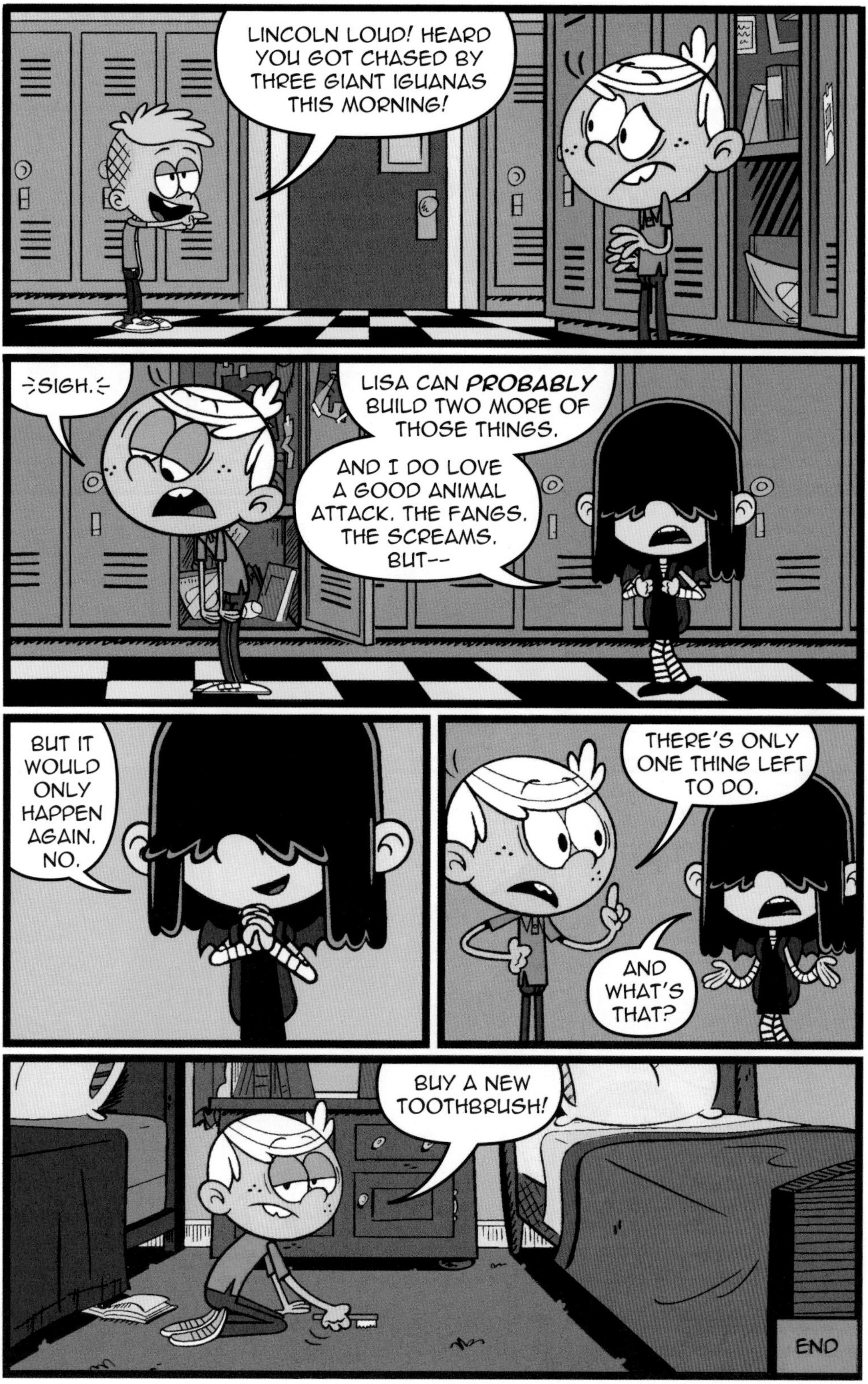
LINCOLN LOUD! HEARD YOU GOT CHASED BY THREE GIANT IGUANAS THIS MORNING!
-SIGH.-
LISA CAN PROBABLY BUILD TWO MORE OF THOSE THINGS.
AND I DO LOVE A GOOD ANIMAL ATTACK. THE FANGS. THE SCREAMS. BUT--
BUT IT WOULD ONLY HAPPEN AGAIN. NO.
THERE'S ONLY ONE THING LEFT TO DO.
AND WHAT'S THAT?
BUY A NEW TOOTHBRUSH!
END

"DON'T CRY FOR ME, AUNTIE FRIDA"

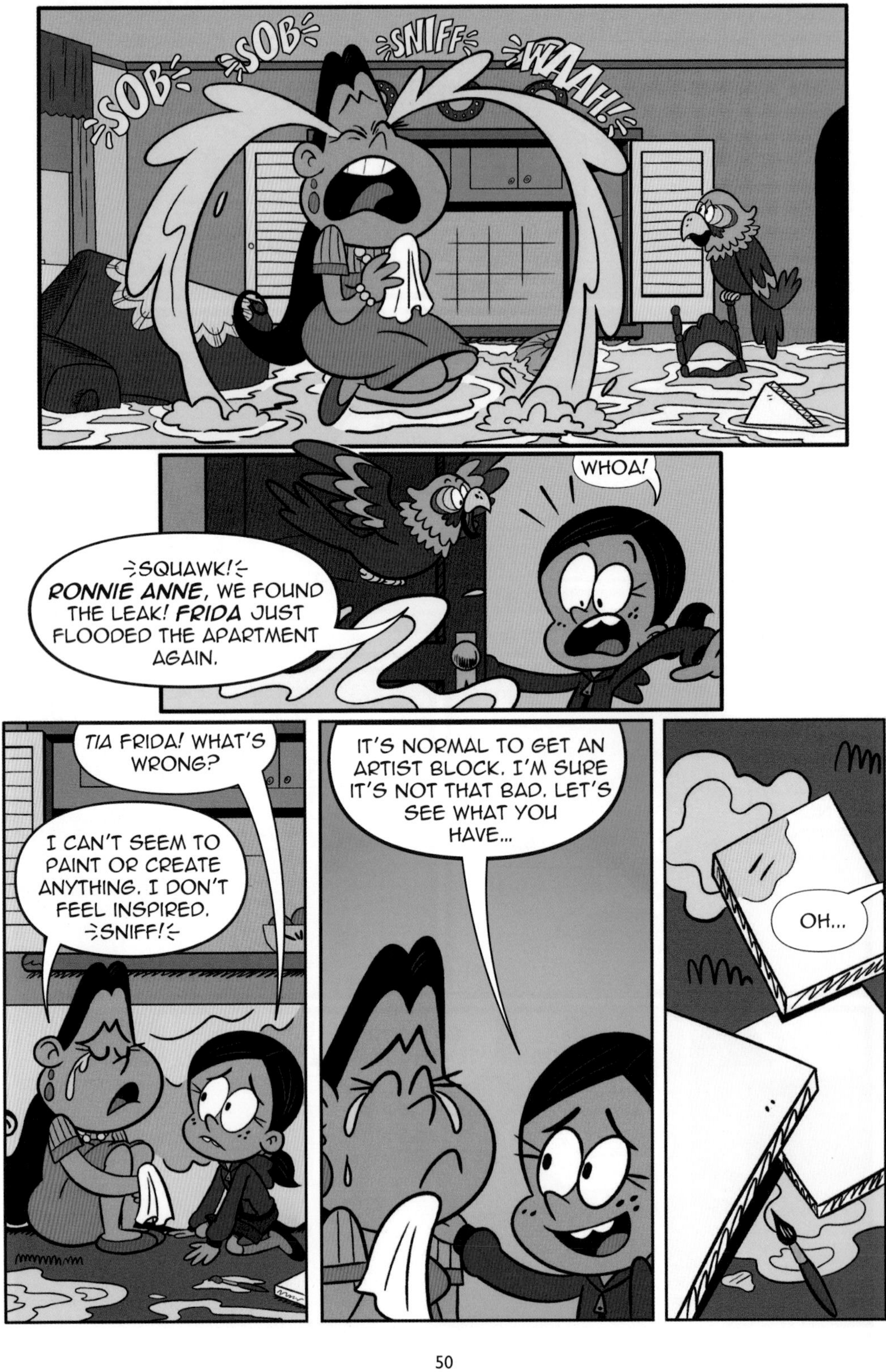
SOB
SOB
SNIFF
WAAAH!
WHOA!
SQUAWK!
RONNIE ANNE, WE FOUND THE LEAK! FRIDA JUST FLOODED THE APARTMENT AGAIN.
TIA FRIDA! WHAT'S WRONG?
I CAN'T SEEM TO PAINT OR CREATE ANYTHING. I DON'T FEEL INSPIRED. SNIFF!
IT'S NORMAL TO GET AN ARTIST BLOCK. I'M SURE IT'S NOT THAT BAD. LET'S SEE WHAT YOU HAVE...
OH...

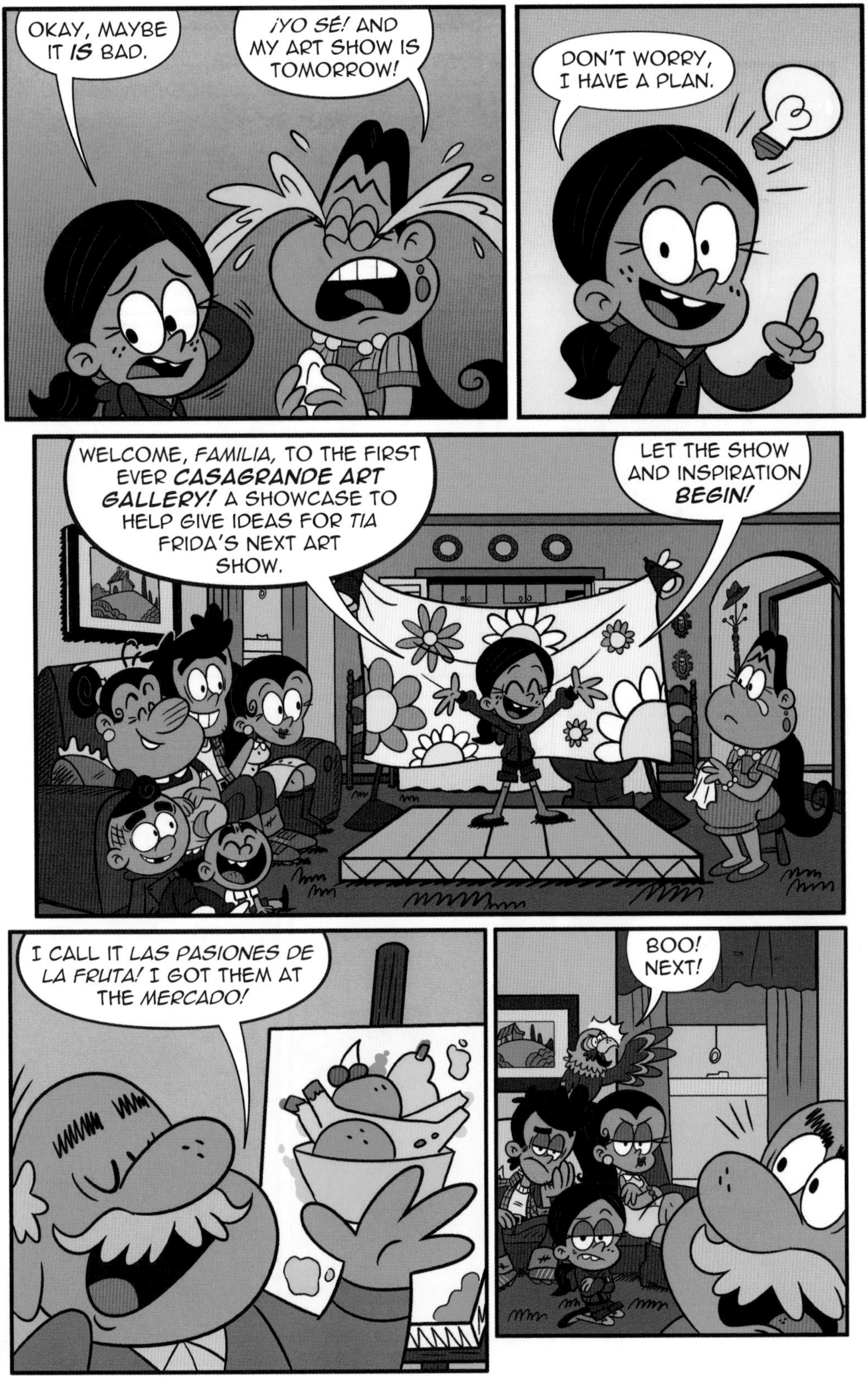
OKAY, MAYBE IT *IS* BAD.
¡YO SÉ! AND MY ART SHOW IS TOMORROW!
DON'T WORRY, I HAVE A PLAN.
WELCOME, *FAMILIA*, TO THE FIRST EVER **CASAGRANDE ART GALLERY!** A SHOWCASE TO HELP GIVE IDEAS FOR *TIA* FRIDA'S NEXT ART SHOW.
LET THE SHOW AND INSPIRATION **BEGIN!**
I CALL IT *LAS PASIONES DE LA FRUTA!* I GOT THEM AT THE *MERCADO!*
BOO! NEXT!

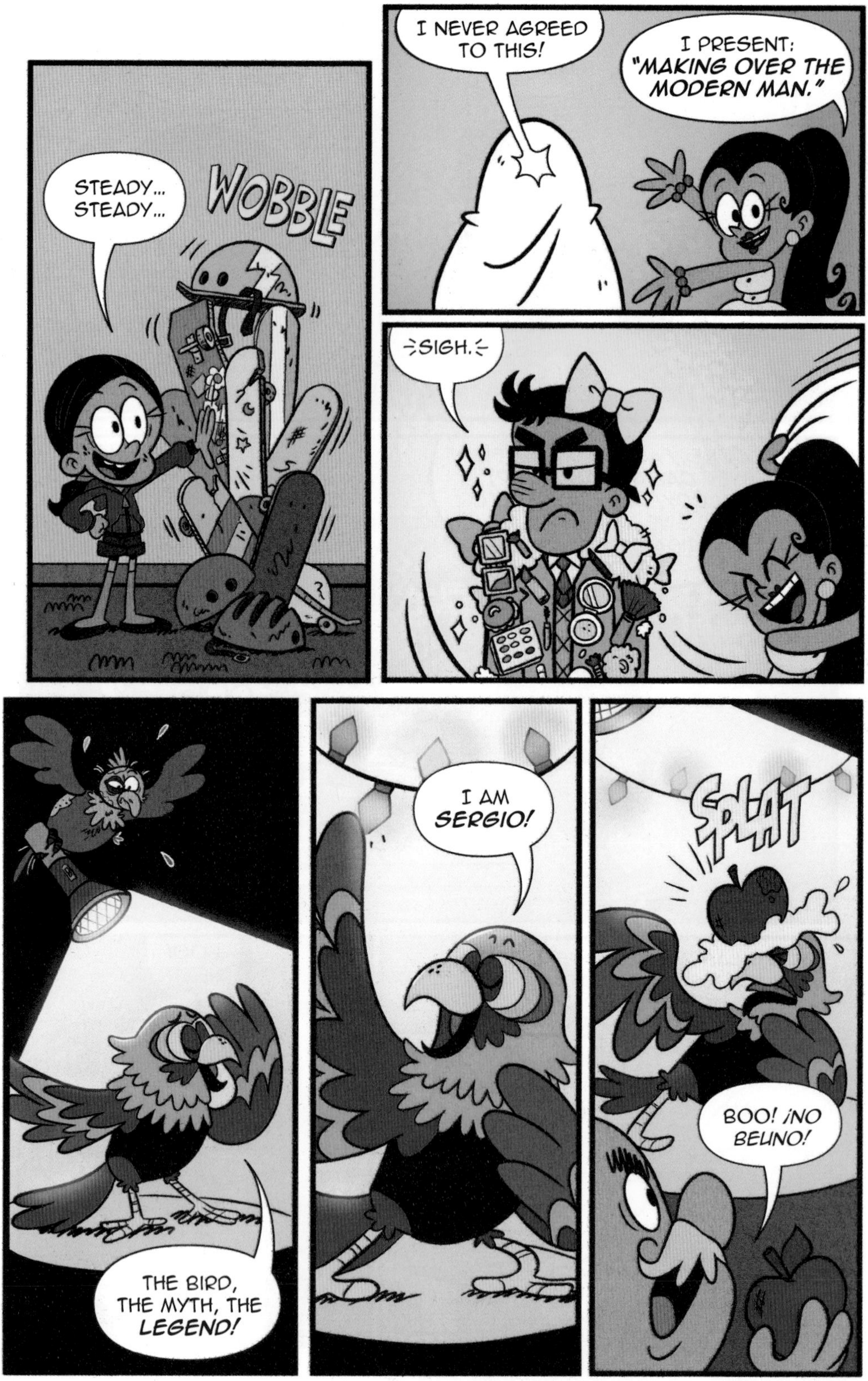
STEADY... STEADY...
WOBBLE
I NEVER AGREED TO THIS!
I PRESENT: "MAKING OVER THE MODERN MAN."
SIGH.
THE BIRD, THE MYTH, THE LEGEND!
I AM SERGIO!
SPLAT
BOO! ¡NO BEUNO!

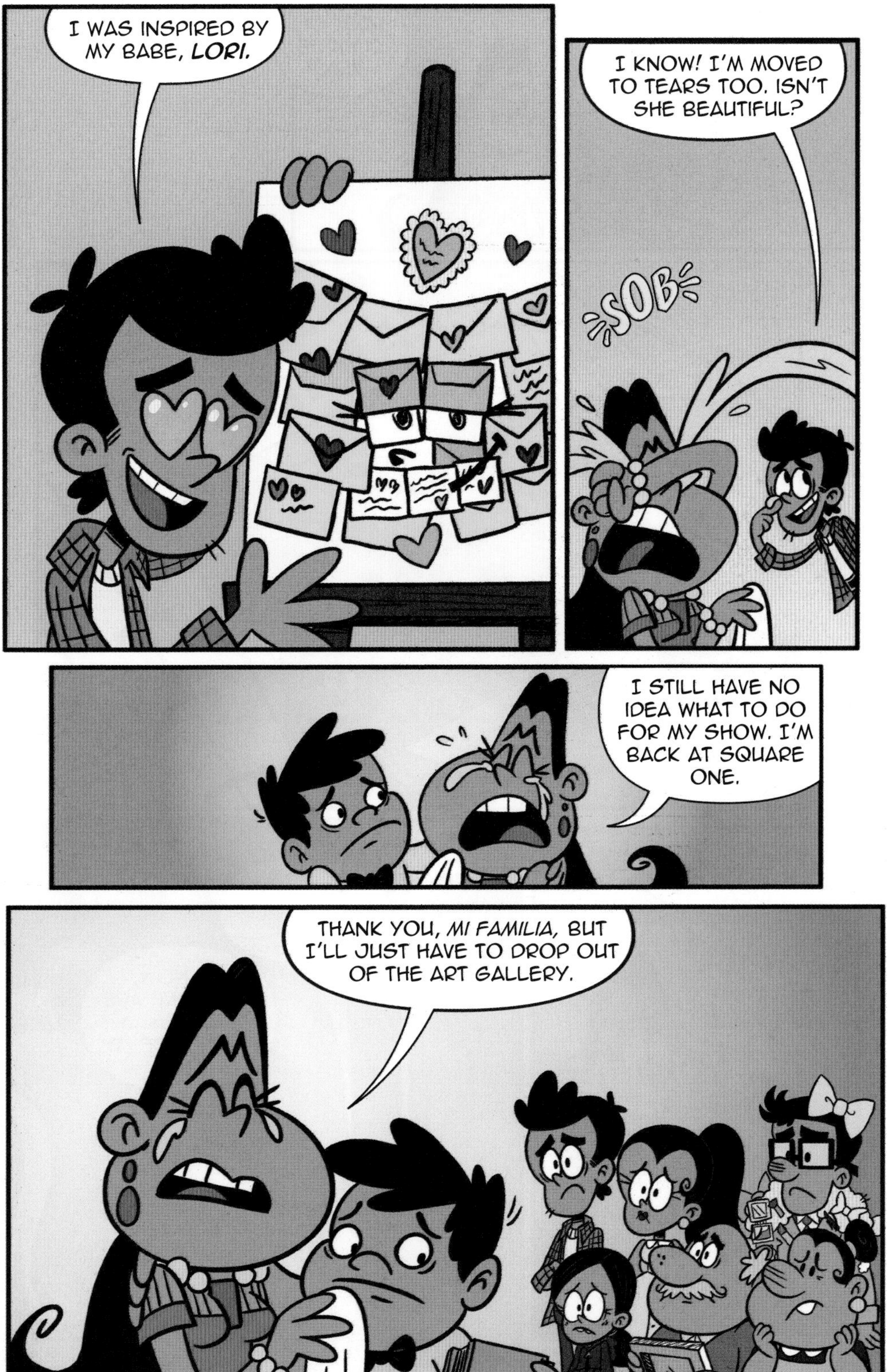
I WAS INSPIRED BY MY BABE, LORI.
I KNOW! I'M MOVED TO TEARS TOO. ISN'T SHE BEAUTIFUL?
SOB
I STILL HAVE NO IDEA WHAT TO DO FOR MY SHOW. I'M BACK AT SQUARE ONE.
THANK YOU, MI FAMILIA, BUT I'LL JUST HAVE TO DROP OUT OF THE ART GALLERY.

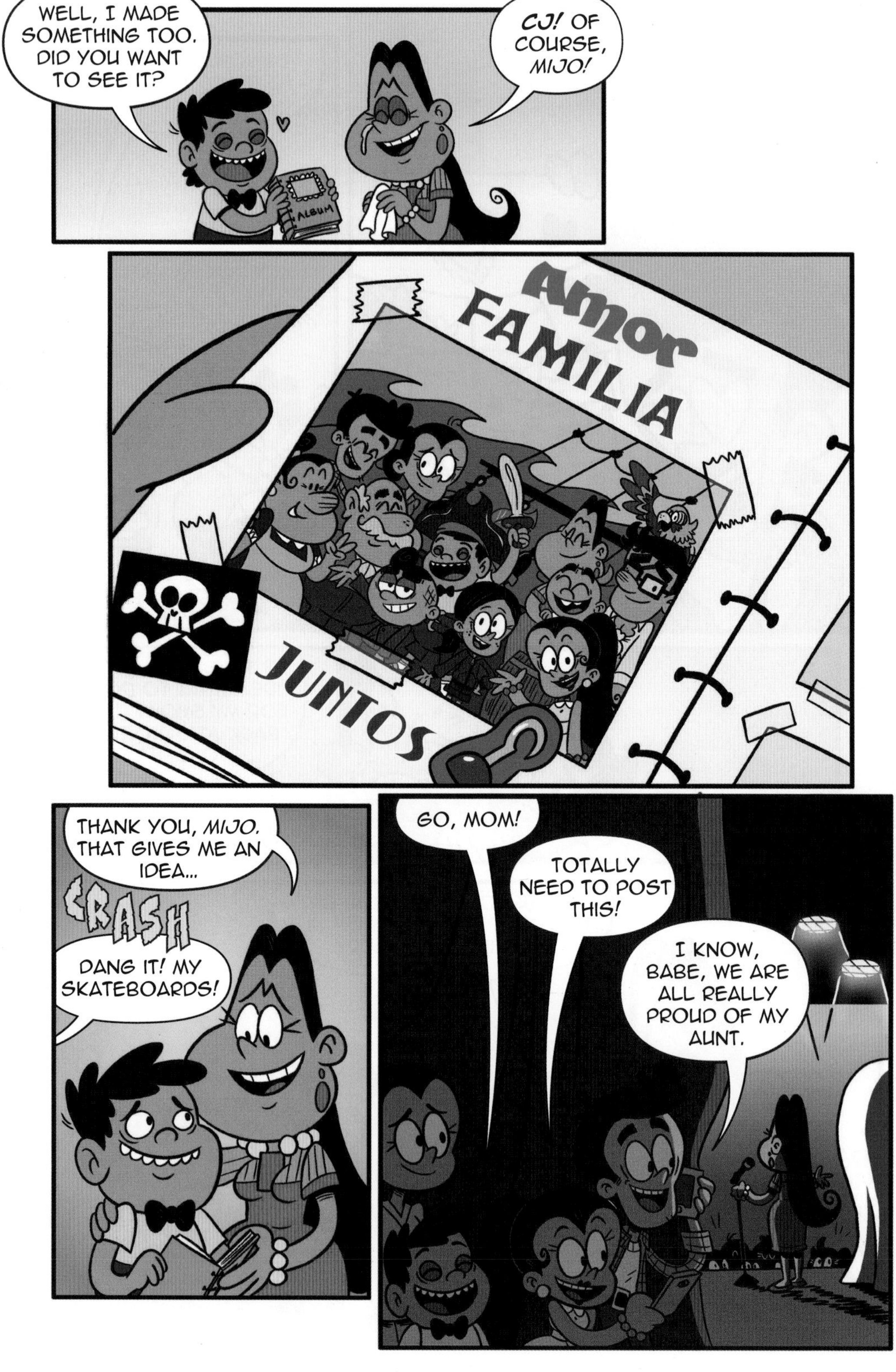
WELL, I MADE SOMETHING TOO. DID YOU WANT TO SEE IT?
CJ! OF COURSE, *MIJO!*
ALBUM
Amor
FAMILIA
JUNTOS
THANK YOU, *MIJO.* THAT GIVES ME AN IDEA...
CRASH
DANG IT! MY SKATEBOARDS!
GO, MOM!
TOTALLY NEED TO POST THIS!
I KNOW, BABE, WE ARE ALL REALLY PROUD OF MY AUNT.

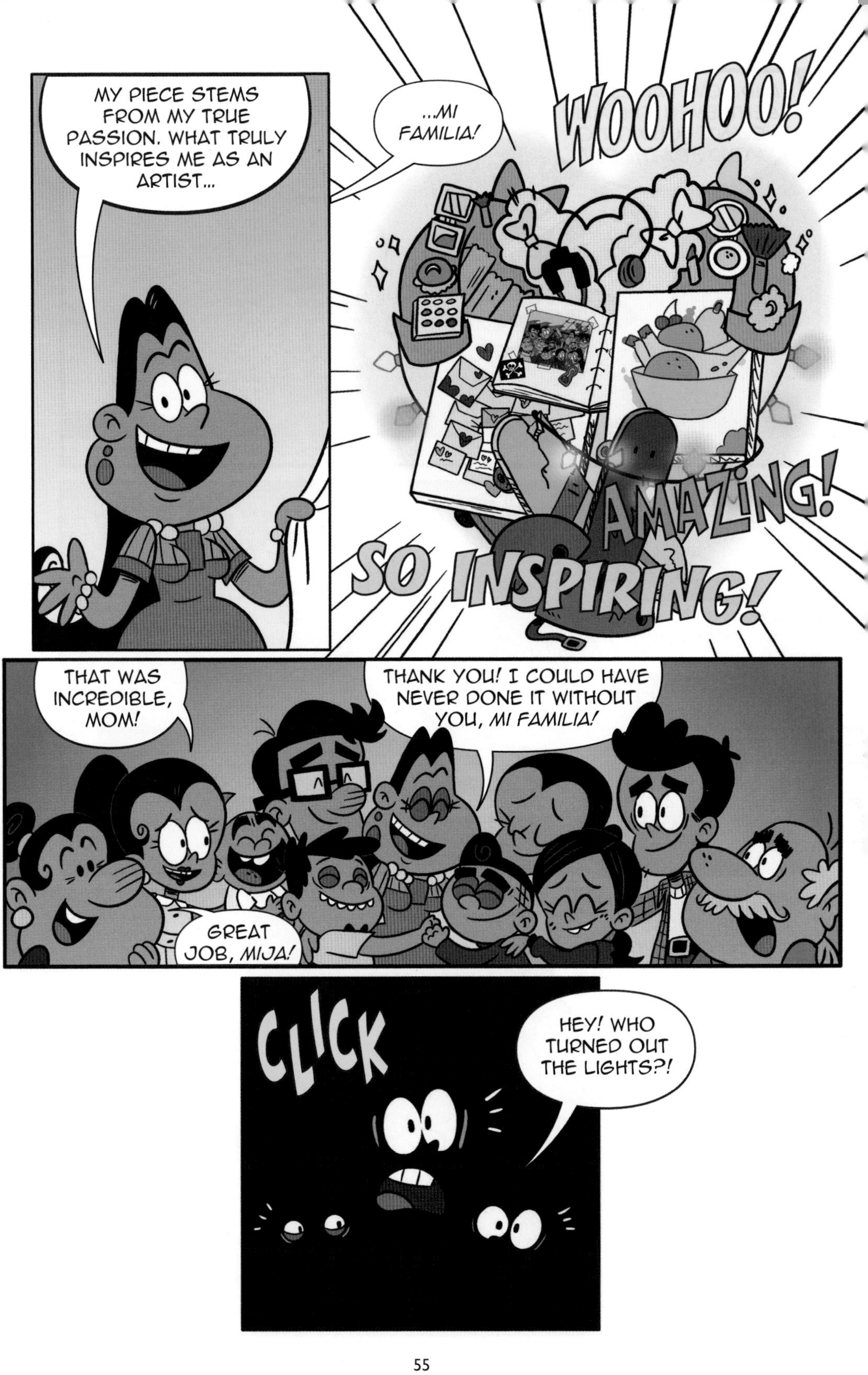
MY PIECE STEMS FROM MY TRUE PASSION. WHAT TRULY INSPIRES ME AS AN ARTIST...
...*MI FAMILIA!*
WOOHOO!
AMAZING!
SO INSPIRING!
THAT WAS INCREDIBLE, MOM!
THANK YOU! I COULD HAVE NEVER DONE IT WITHOUT YOU, *MI FAMILIA!*
GREAT JOB, *MIJA!*
CLICK
HEY! WHO TURNED OUT THE LIGHTS?!

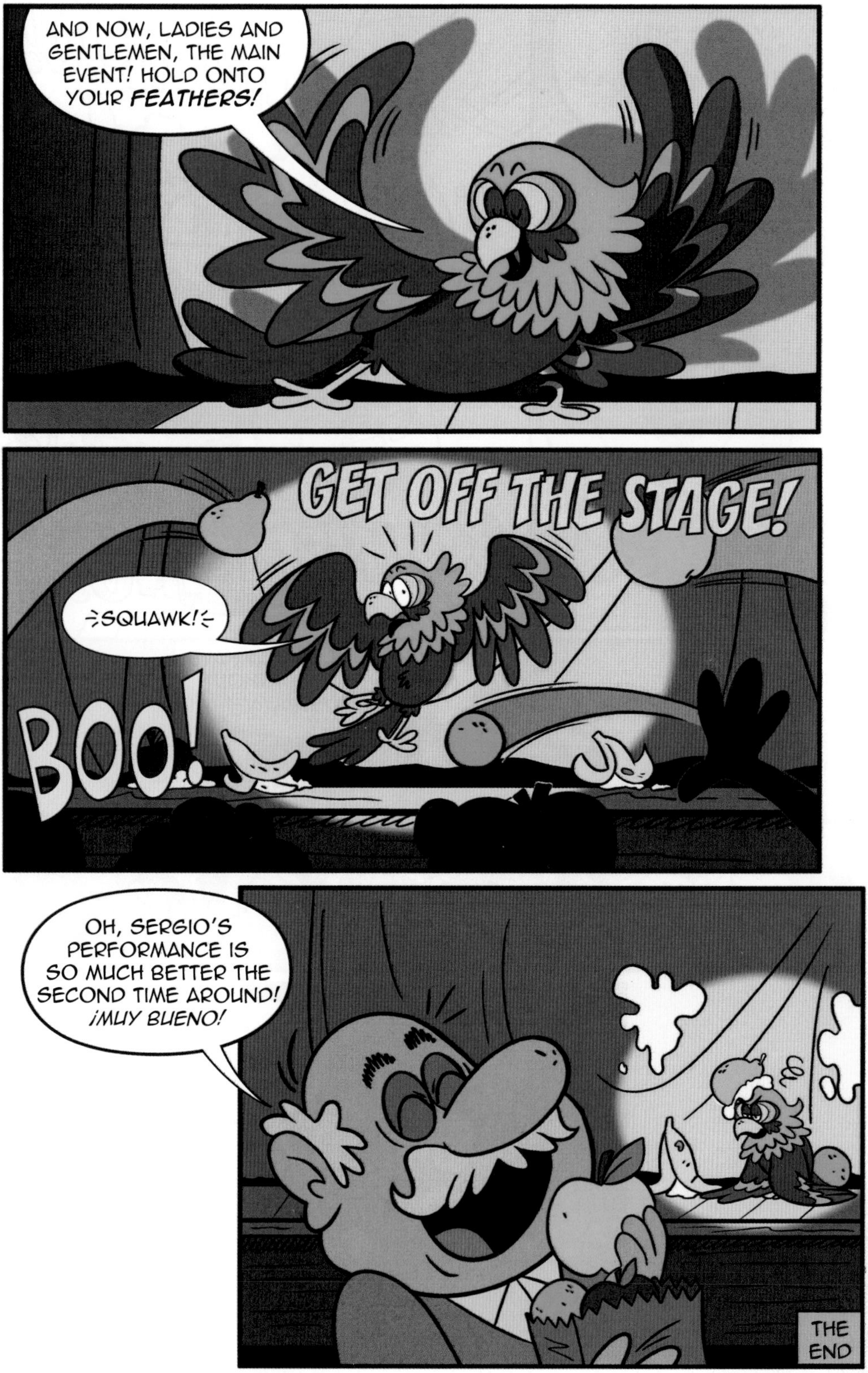
AND NOW, LADIES AND GENTLEMEN, THE MAIN EVENT! HOLD ONTO YOUR **FEATHERS!**
GET OFF THE STAGE!
SQUAWK!
BOO!
OH, SERGIO'S PERFORMANCE IS SO MUCH BETTER THE SECOND TIME AROUND! *¡MUY BUENO!*
THE END

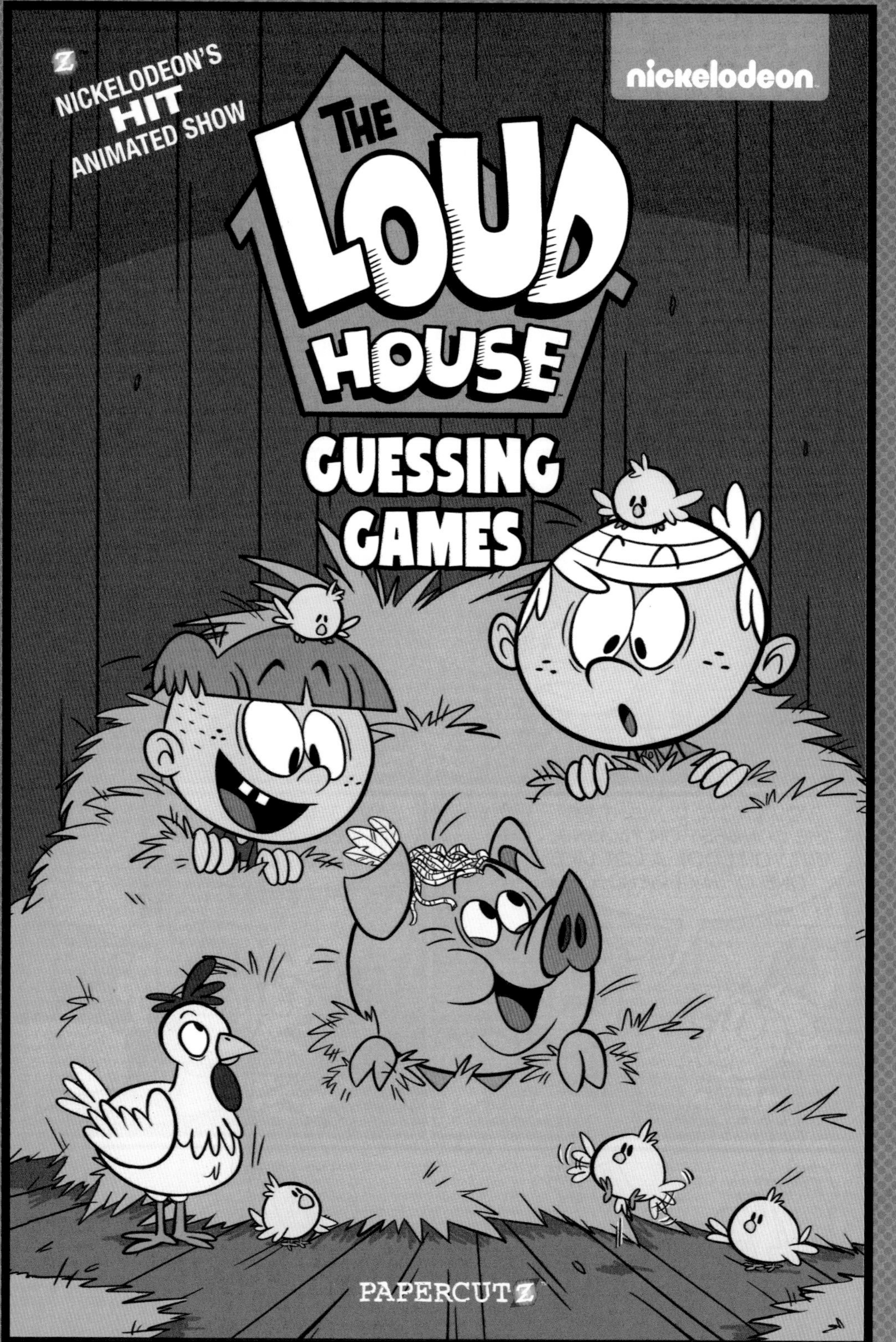
NICKELODEON'S
HIT
ANIMATED SHOW
nickelodeon
THE LOUD HOUSE
GUESSING GAMES
PAPERCUTZ

THE LOUD HOUSE #14 Cover Art by KELSEY WOOLEY

"CRITTER COMFORTS"

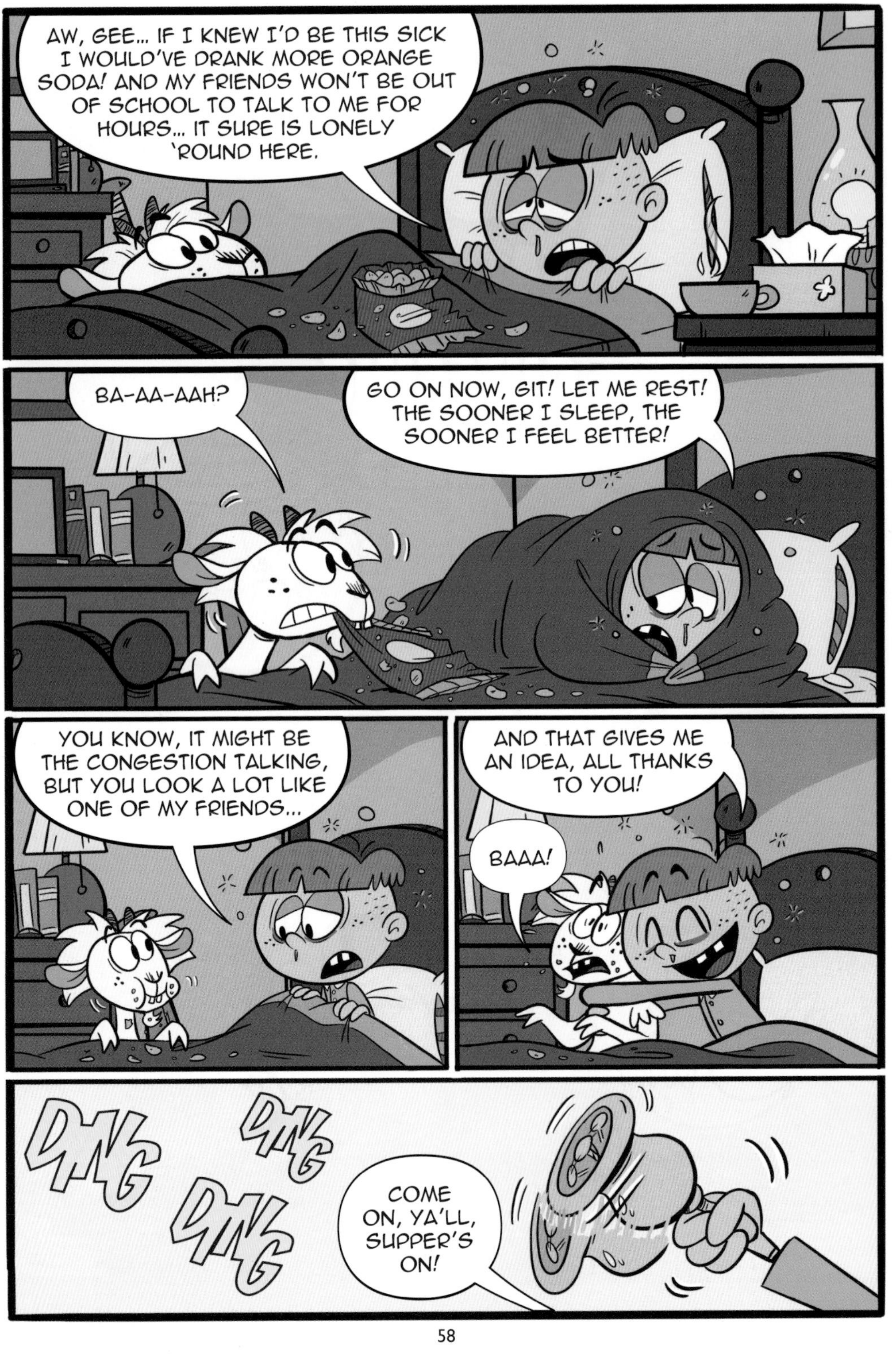
AW, GEE... IF I KNEW I'D BE THIS SICK I WOULD'VE DRANK MORE ORANGE SODA! AND MY FRIENDS WON'T BE OUT OF SCHOOL TO TALK TO ME FOR HOURS... IT SURE IS LONELY 'ROUND HERE.
BA-AA-AAH?
GO ON NOW, GIT! LET ME REST! THE SOONER I SLEEP, THE SOONER I FEEL BETTER!
YOU KNOW, IT MIGHT BE THE CONGESTION TALKING, BUT YOU LOOK A LOT LIKE ONE OF MY FRIENDS...
AND THAT GIVES ME AN IDEA, ALL THANKS TO YOU!
BAAA!
DING
DING
DING
COME ON, YA'LL, SUPPER'S ON!

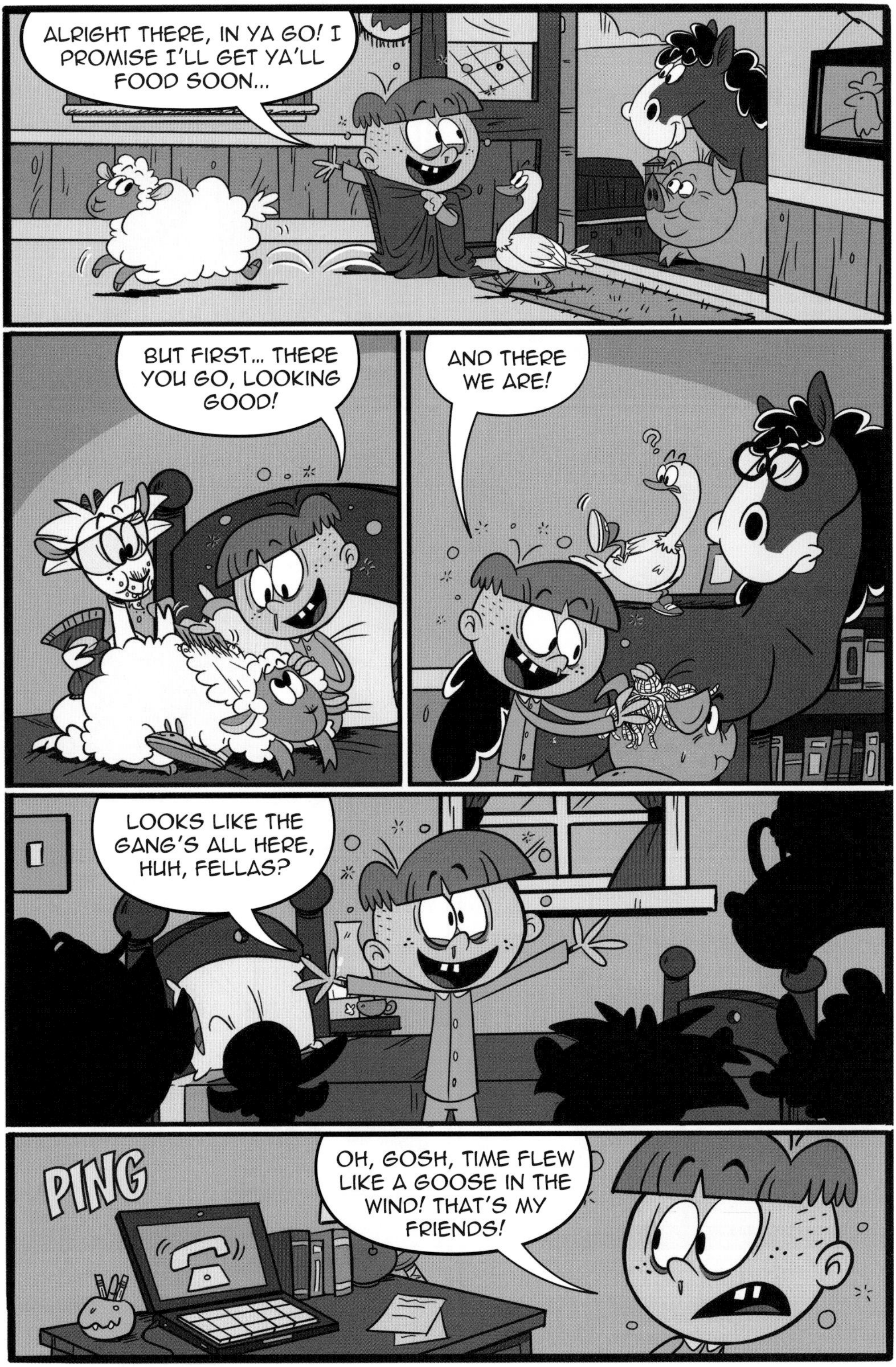
ALRIGHT THERE, IN YA GO! I PROMISE I'LL GET YA'LL FOOD SOON...
BUT FIRST... THERE YOU GO, LOOKING GOOD!
AND THERE WE ARE!
LOOKS LIKE THE GANG'S ALL HERE, HUH, FELLAS?
PING
OH, GOSH, TIME FLEW LIKE A GOOSE IN THE WIND! THAT'S MY FRIENDS!

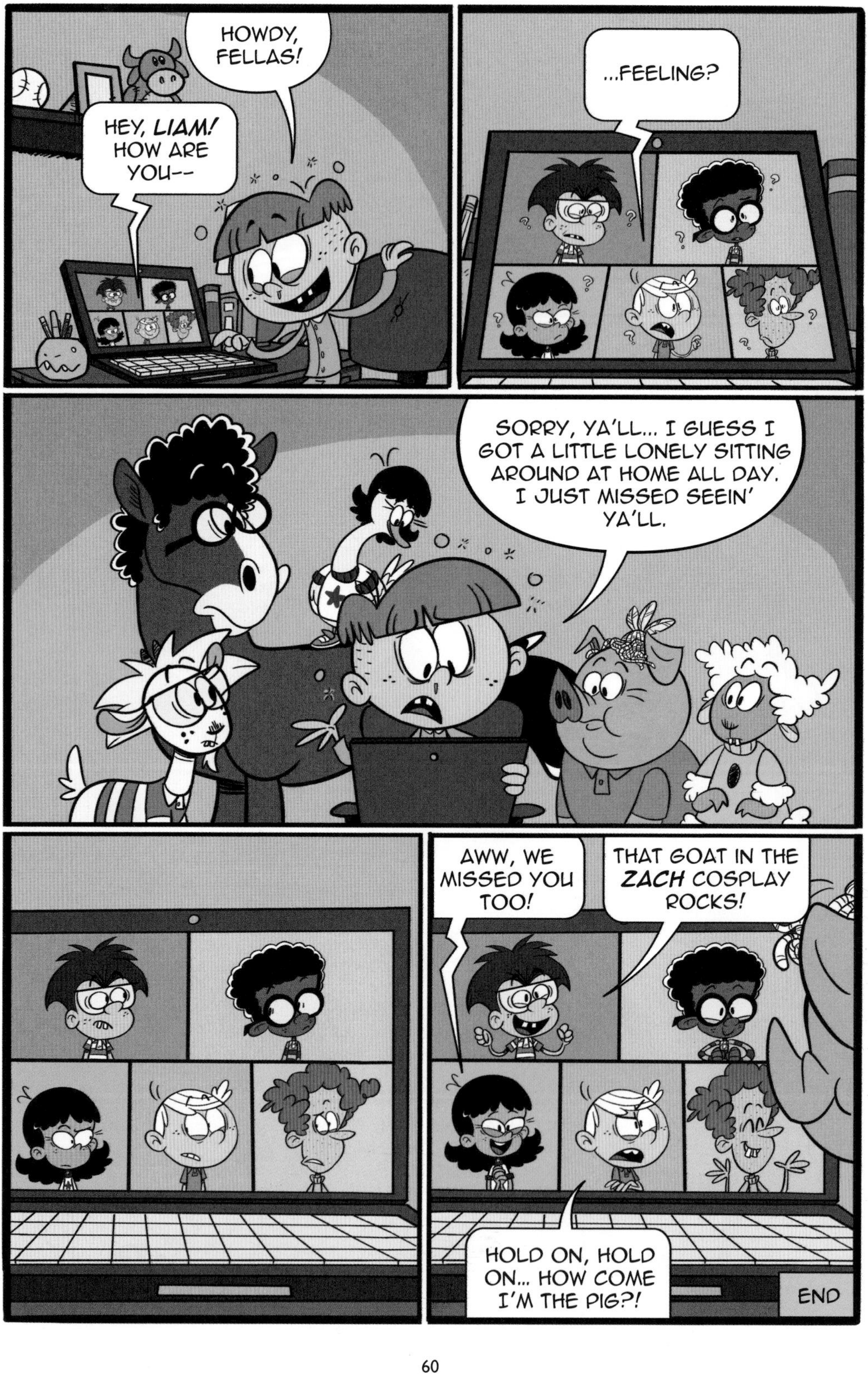
HOWDY, FELLAS!
HEY, LIAM! HOW ARE YOU--
...FEELING?
SORRY, YA'LL... I GUESS I GOT A LITTLE LONELY SITTING AROUND AT HOME ALL DAY. I JUST MISSED SEEIN' YA'LL.
AWW, WE MISSED YOU TOO!
THAT GOAT IN THE ZACH COSPLAY ROCKS!
HOLD ON, HOLD ON... HOW COME I'M THE PIG?!
END

"GUESS WHO?"

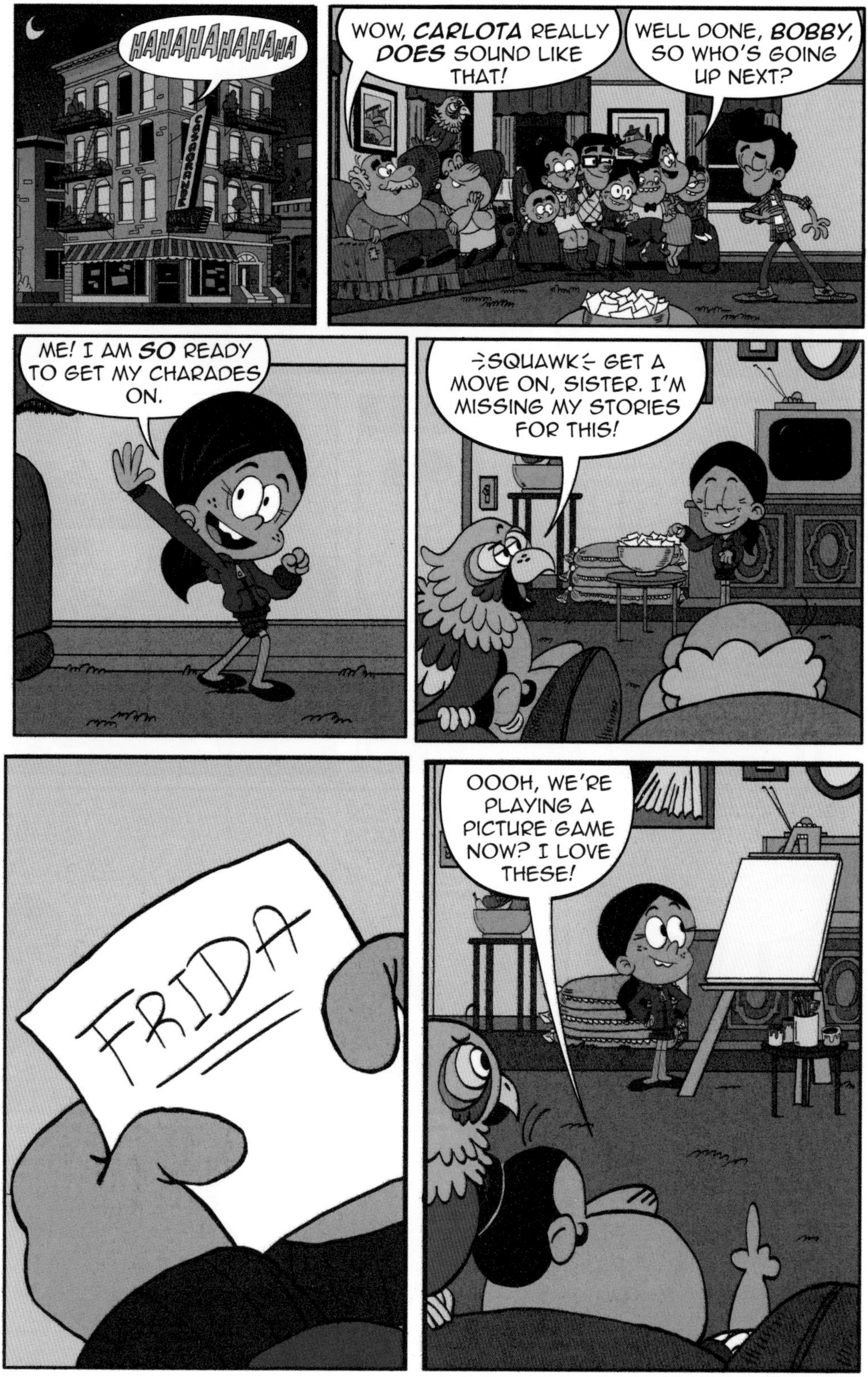
HAHAHAHAHAHAHA
WOW, CARLOTA REALLY DOES SOUND LIKE THAT!
WELL DONE, BOBBY, SO WHO'S GOING UP NEXT?
ME! I AM SO READY TO GET MY CHARADES ON.
⇒SQUAWK⇐ GET A MOVE ON, SISTER. I'M MISSING MY STORIES FOR THIS!
FRIDA
OOOH, WE'RE PLAYING A PICTURE GAME NOW? I LOVE THESE!

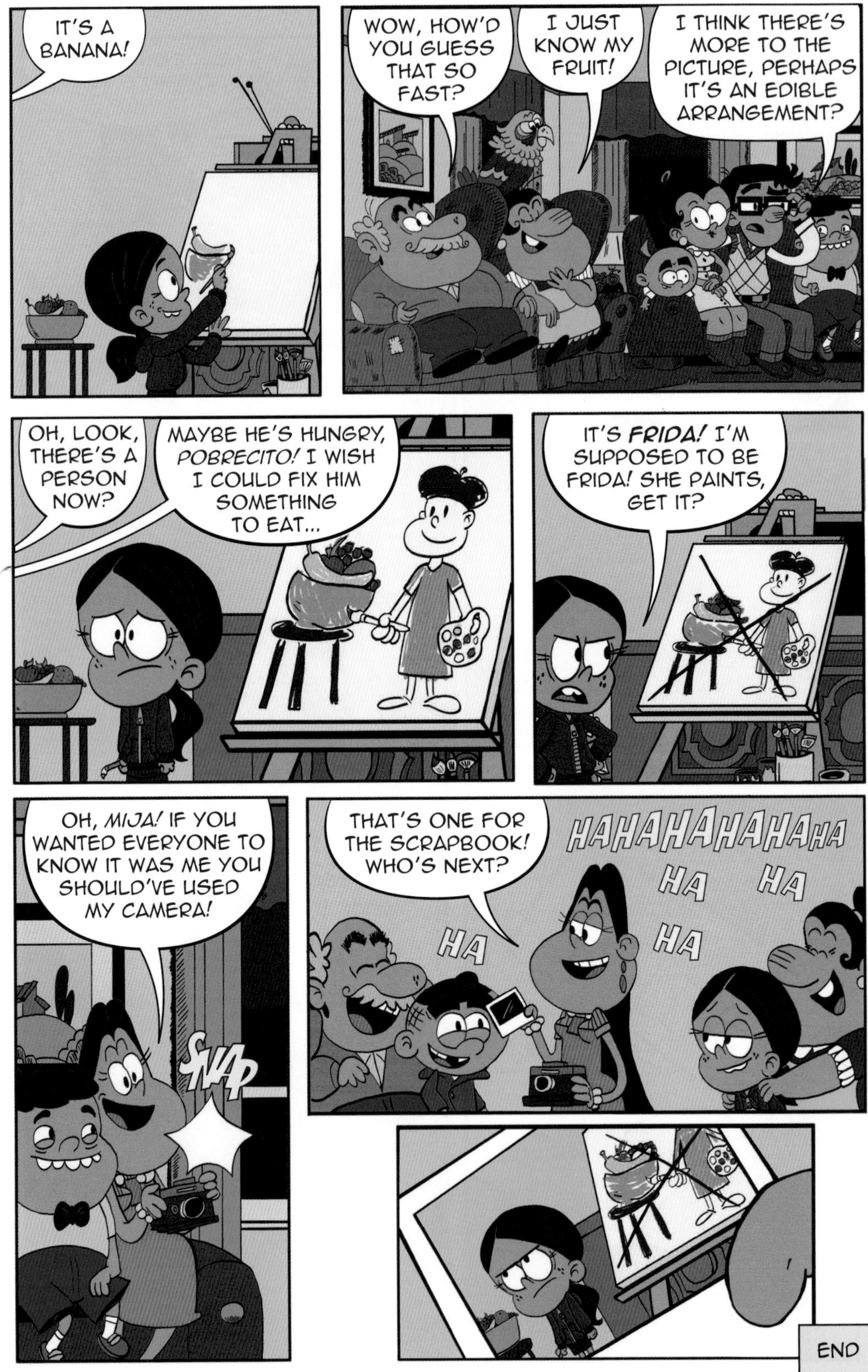
IT'S A BANANA!
WOW, HOW'D YOU GUESS THAT SO FAST?
I JUST KNOW MY FRUIT!
I THINK THERE'S MORE TO THE PICTURE, PERHAPS IT'S AN EDIBLE ARRANGEMENT?
OH, LOOK, THERE'S A PERSON NOW?
MAYBE HE'S HUNGRY, POBRECITO! I WISH I COULD FIX HIM SOMETHING TO EAT...
IT'S FRIDA! I'M SUPPOSED TO BE FRIDA! SHE PAINTS, GET IT?
OH, MIJA! IF YOU WANTED EVERYONE TO KNOW IT WAS ME YOU SHOULD'VE USED MY CAMERA!
SNAP
THAT'S ONE FOR THE SCRAPBOOK! WHO'S NEXT?
HAHAHAHAHAHAHA
HA
HA
HA
HA
END

"TRENDING"

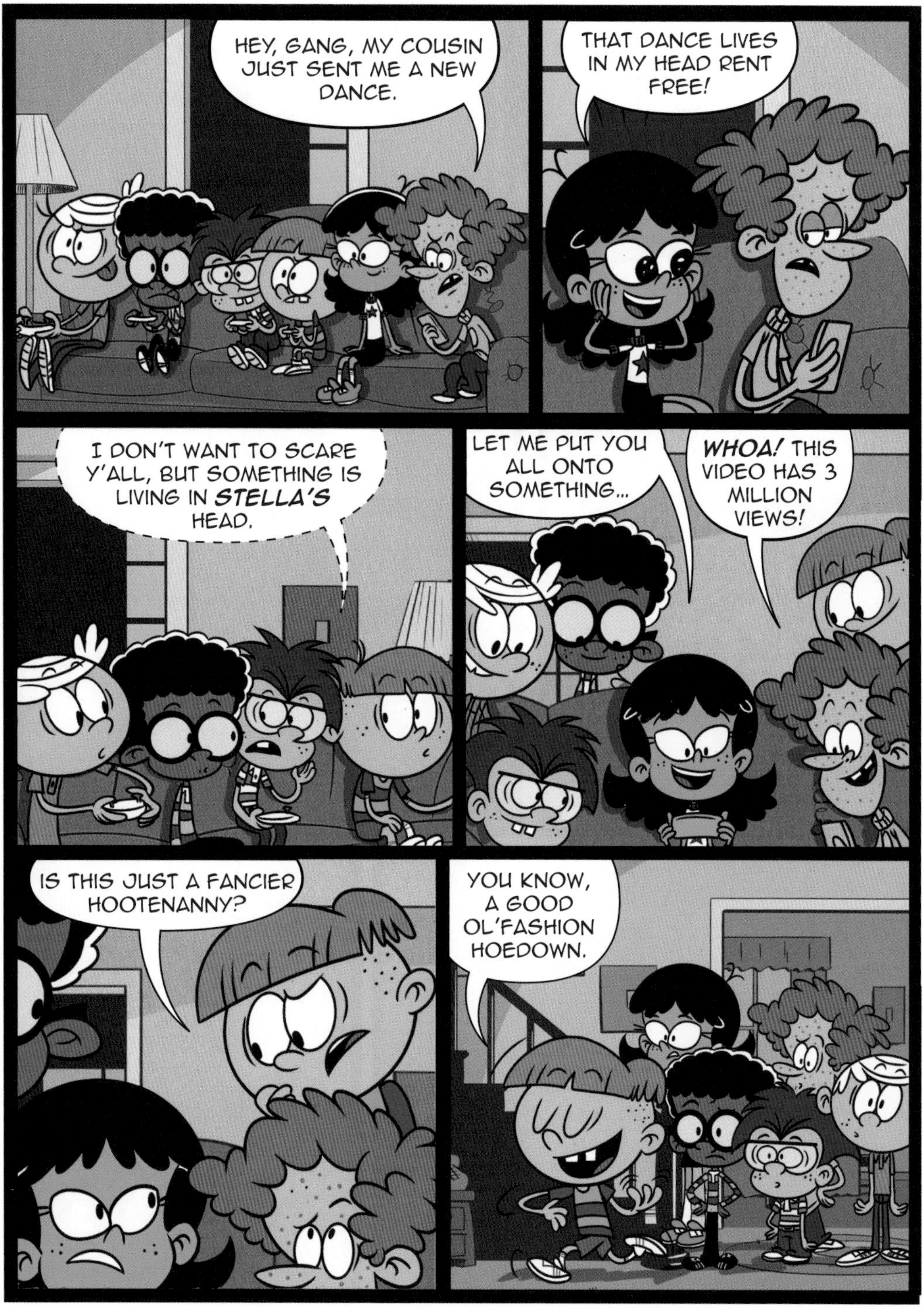
HEY, GANG, MY COUSIN JUST SENT ME A NEW DANCE.
THAT DANCE LIVES IN MY HEAD RENT FREE!
I DON'T WANT TO SCARE Y'ALL, BUT SOMETHING IS LIVING IN STELLA'S HEAD.
LET ME PUT YOU ALL ONTO SOMETHING...
WHOA! THIS VIDEO HAS 3 MILLION VIEWS!
IS THIS JUST A FANCIER HOOTENANNY?
YOU KNOW, A GOOD OL'FASHION HOEDOWN.

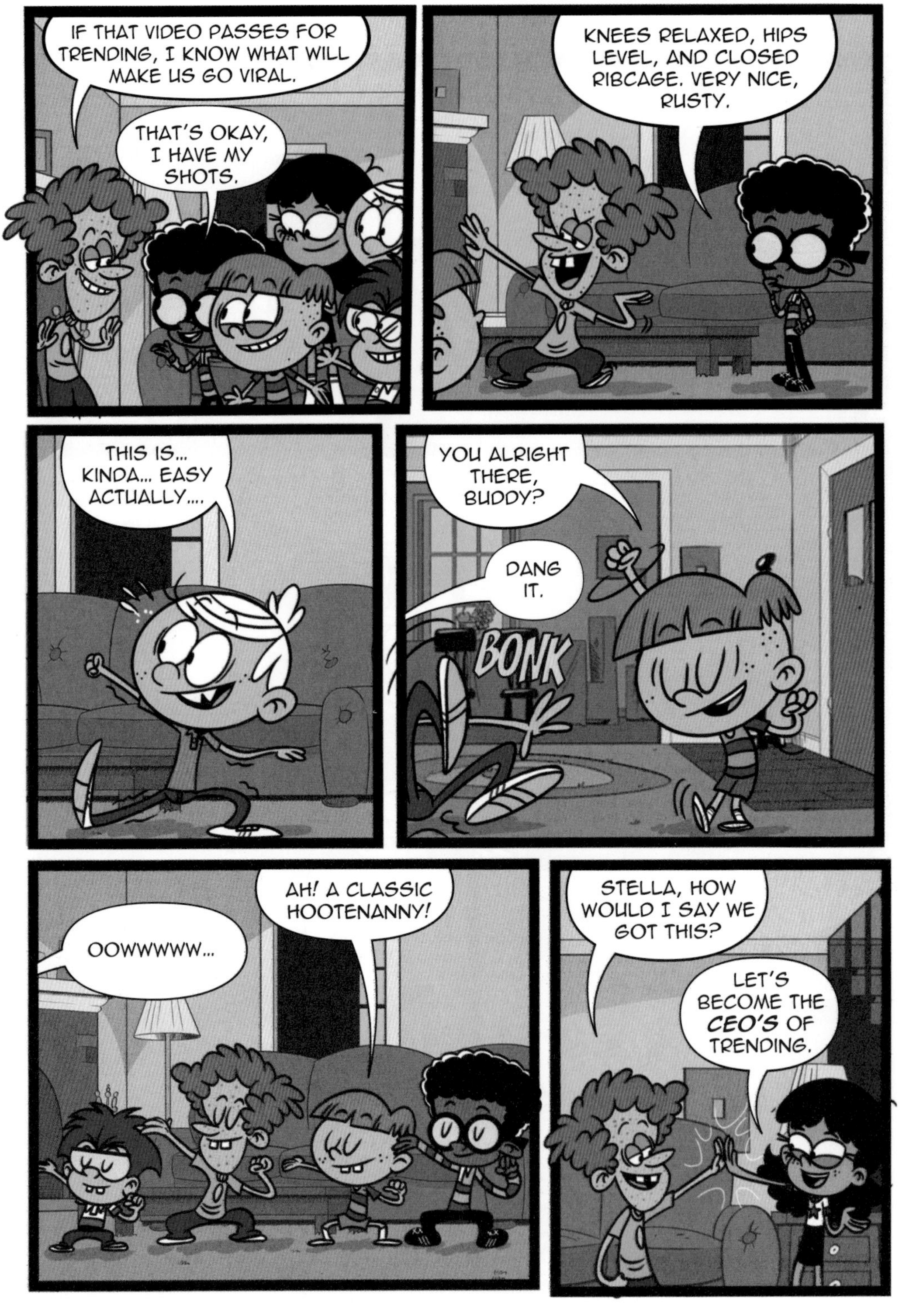
IF THAT VIDEO PASSES FOR TRENDING, I KNOW WHAT WILL MAKE US GO VIRAL.
THAT'S OKAY, I HAVE MY SHOTS.
KNEES RELAXED, HIPS LEVEL, AND CLOSED RIBCAGE. VERY NICE, RUSTY.
THIS IS... KINDA... EASY ACTUALLY....
YOU ALRIGHT THERE, BUDDY?
DANG IT.
BONK
OOWWWWW...
AH! A CLASSIC HOOTENANNY!
STELLA, HOW WOULD I SAY WE GOT THIS?
LET'S BECOME THE ***CEO'S*** OF TRENDING.

WOO-WEE! JUST LIKE LEARNING LINE DANCING.

ALRIGHT, GANG, FROM THE TOP!

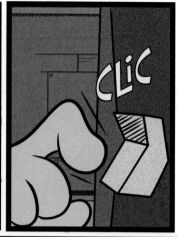

CLiC

DONK

WHOMP

HEY!

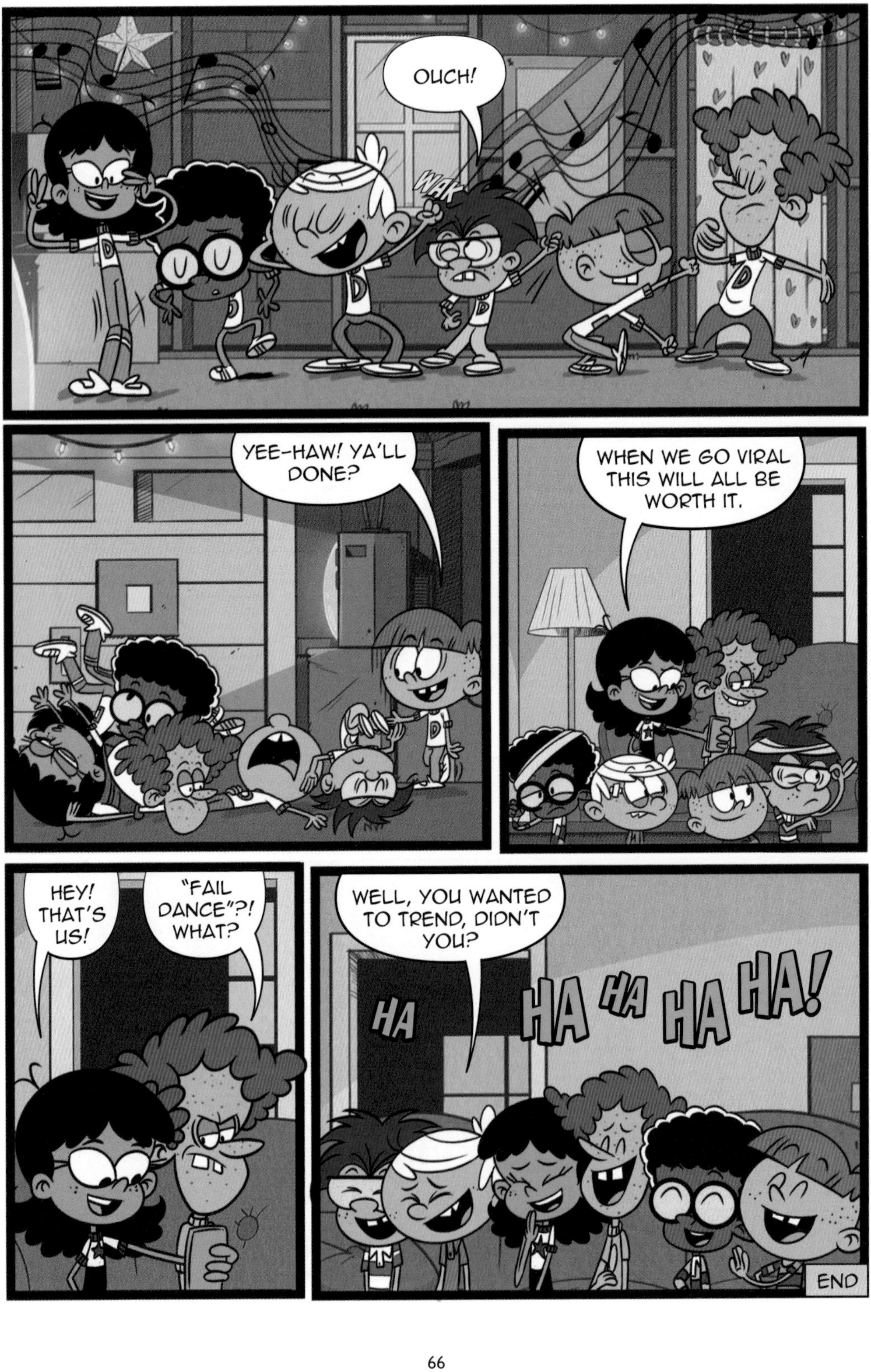
OUCH!
WAK
YEE-HAW! YA'LL DONE?
WHEN WE GO VIRAL THIS WILL ALL BE WORTH IT.
HEY! THAT'S US!
"FAIL DANCE"?! WHAT?
WELL, YOU WANTED TO TREND, DIDN'T YOU?
HA
HA HA HA HA!
END

"PROGRAM POSTPONED"

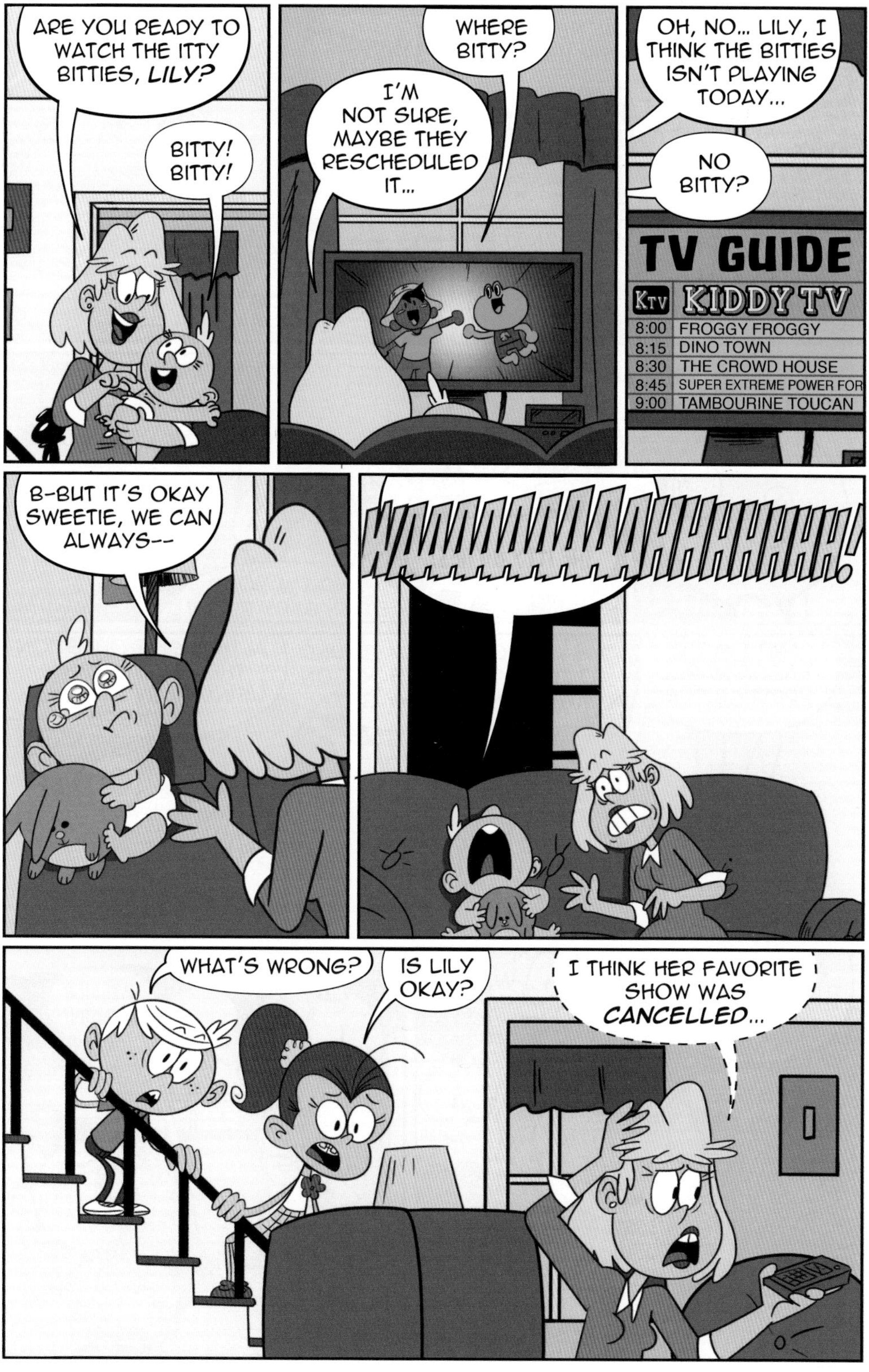

ARE YOU READY TO WATCH THE ITTY BITTIES, *LILY?*
BITTY! BITTY!
WHERE BITTY?
I'M NOT SURE, MAYBE THEY RESCHEDULED IT...
OH, NO... LILY, I THINK THE BITTIES ISN'T PLAYING TODAY...
NO BITTY?
TV GUIDE
KTV KIDDY TV
8:00 FROGGY FROGGY
8:15 DINO TOWN
8:30 THE CROWD HOUSE
8:45 SUPER EXTREME POWER FOR
9:00 TAMBOURINE TOUCAN
B-BUT IT'S OKAY SWEETIE, WE CAN ALWAYS--
WAAAAAAAAAHHHHHHH!
WHAT'S WRONG?
IS LILY OKAY?
I THINK HER FAVORITE SHOW WAS *CANCELLED*...

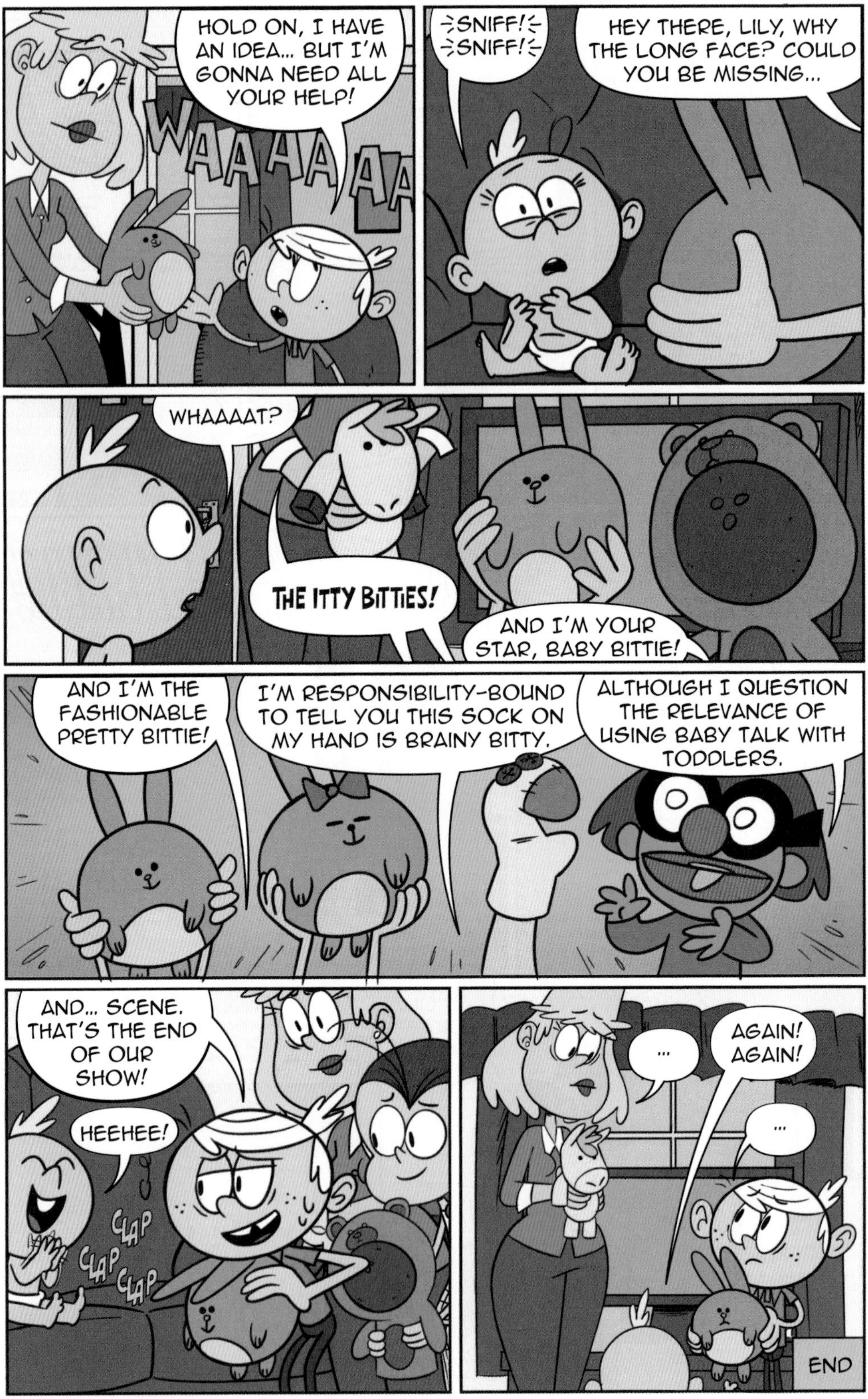
HOLD ON, I HAVE AN IDEA... BUT I'M GONNA NEED ALL YOUR HELP!
WAAAAAAA
SNIFF! SNIFF!
HEY THERE, LILY, WHY THE LONG FACE? COULD YOU BE MISSING...
WHAAAAT?
THE ITTY BITTIES!
AND I'M YOUR STAR, BABY BITTIE!
AND I'M THE FASHIONABLE PRETTY BITTIE!
I'M RESPONSIBILITY-BOUND TO TELL YOU THIS SOCK ON MY HAND IS BRAINY BITTY.
ALTHOUGH I QUESTION THE RELEVANCE OF USING BABY TALK WITH TODDLERS.
AND... SCENE. THAT'S THE END OF OUR SHOW!
HEEHEE!
CLAP CLAP CLAP
...
AGAIN! AGAIN!
...
END

"THE GOLDEN BONE"

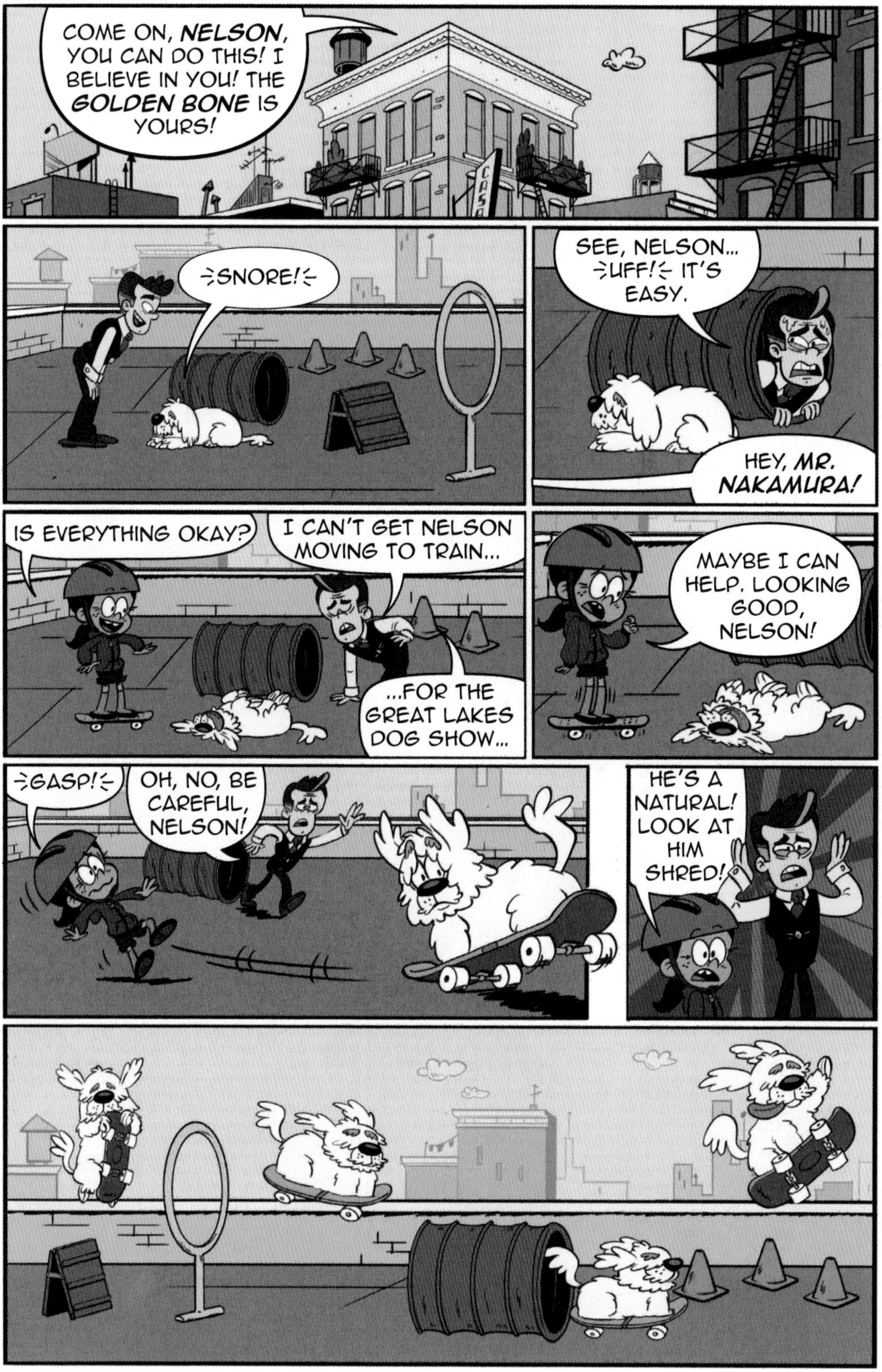

COME ON, NELSON, YOU CAN DO THIS! I BELIEVE IN YOU! THE GOLDEN BONE IS YOURS!
SNORE!
SEE, NELSON... UFF! IT'S EASY.
HEY, MR. NAKAMURA!
IS EVERYTHING OKAY?
I CAN'T GET NELSON MOVING TO TRAIN...
...FOR THE GREAT LAKES DOG SHOW...
MAYBE I CAN HELP. LOOKING GOOD, NELSON!
GASP!
OH, NO, BE CAREFUL, NELSON!
HE'S A NATURAL! LOOK AT HIM SHRED!

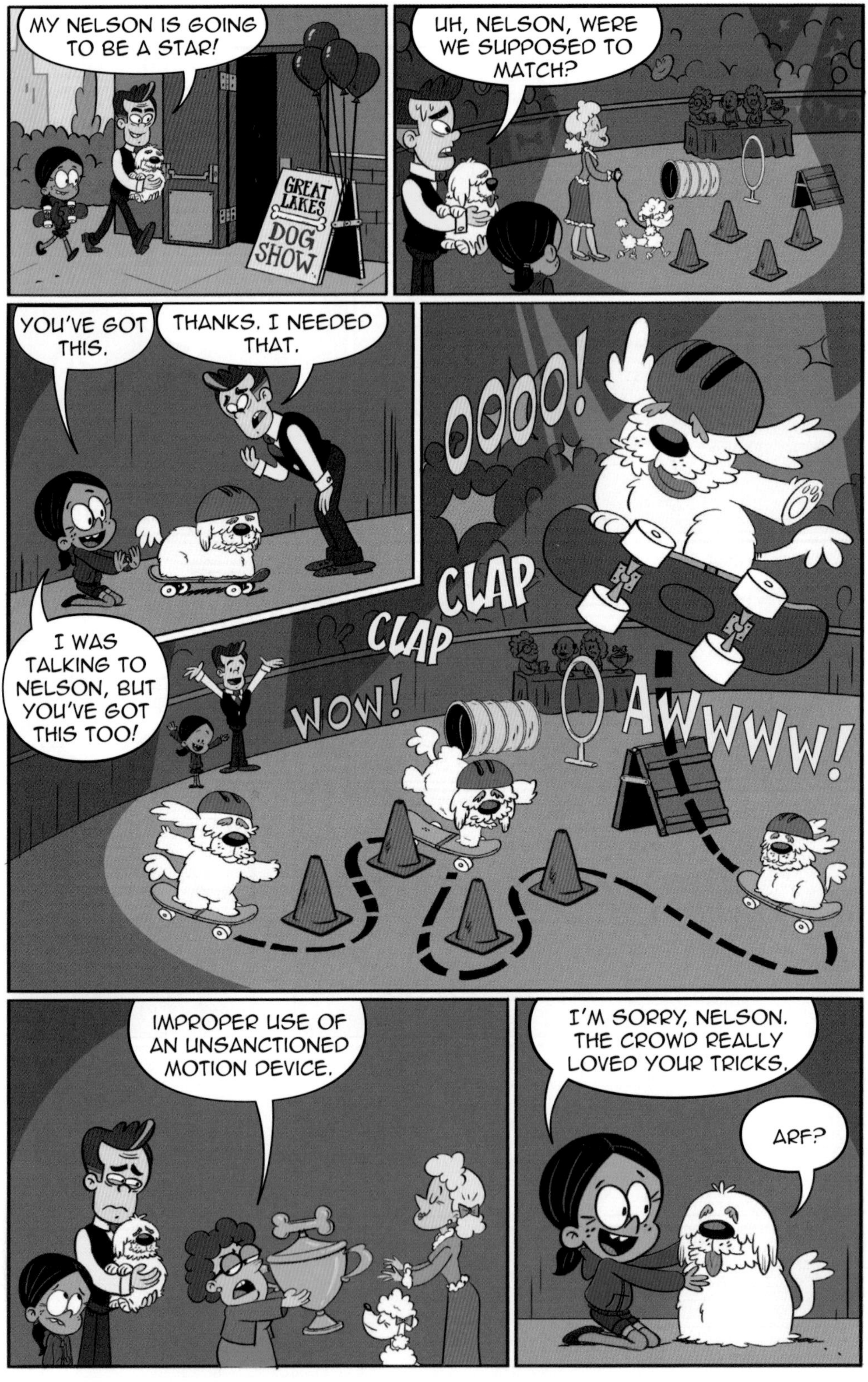
MY NELSON IS GOING TO BE A STAR!
GREAT LAKES DOG SHOW
UH, NELSON, WERE WE SUPPOSED TO MATCH?
YOU'VE GOT THIS.
THANKS. I NEEDED THAT.
I WAS TALKING TO NELSON, BUT YOU'VE GOT THIS TOO!
OOOO!
CLAP
CLAP
WOW!
AWWWWW!
IMPROPER USE OF AN UNSANCTIONED MOTION DEVICE.
I'M SORRY, NELSON. THE CROWD REALLY LOVED YOUR TRICKS.
ARF?

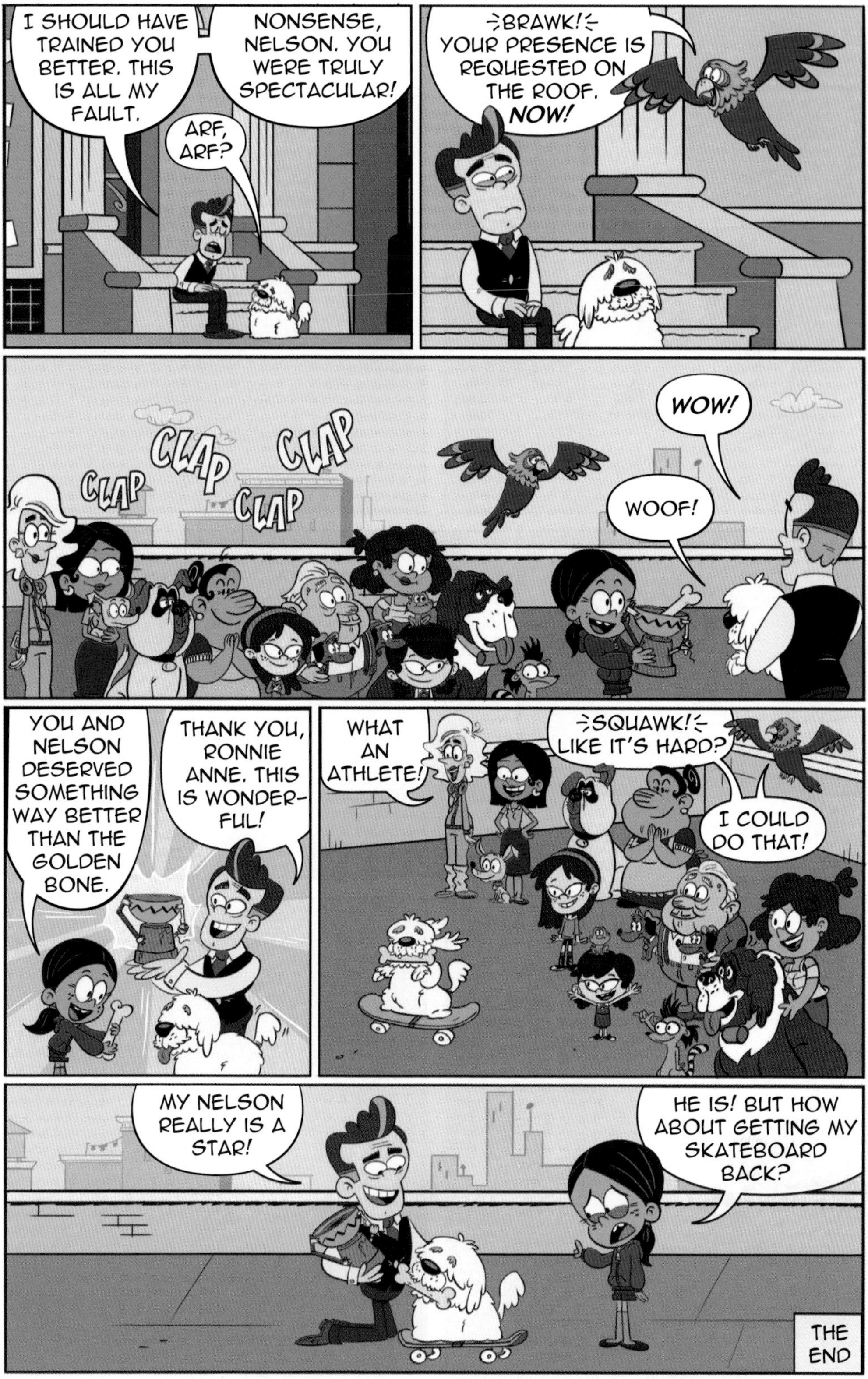
I SHOULD HAVE TRAINED YOU BETTER. THIS IS ALL MY FAULT.
NONSENSE, NELSON. YOU WERE TRULY SPECTACULAR!
ARF, ARF?
BRAWK! YOUR PRESENCE IS REQUESTED ON THE ROOF. NOW!
CLAP
CLAP
CLAP
CLAP
WOW!
WOOF!
YOU AND NELSON DESERVED SOMETHING WAY BETTER THAN THE GOLDEN BONE.
THANK YOU, RONNIE ANNE. THIS IS WONDERFUL!
WHAT AN ATHLETE!
SQUAWK! LIKE IT'S HARD?
I COULD DO THAT!
MY NELSON REALLY IS A STAR!
HE IS! BUT HOW ABOUT GETTING MY SKATEBOARD BACK?
THE END

"SO SUBLIMINAL"

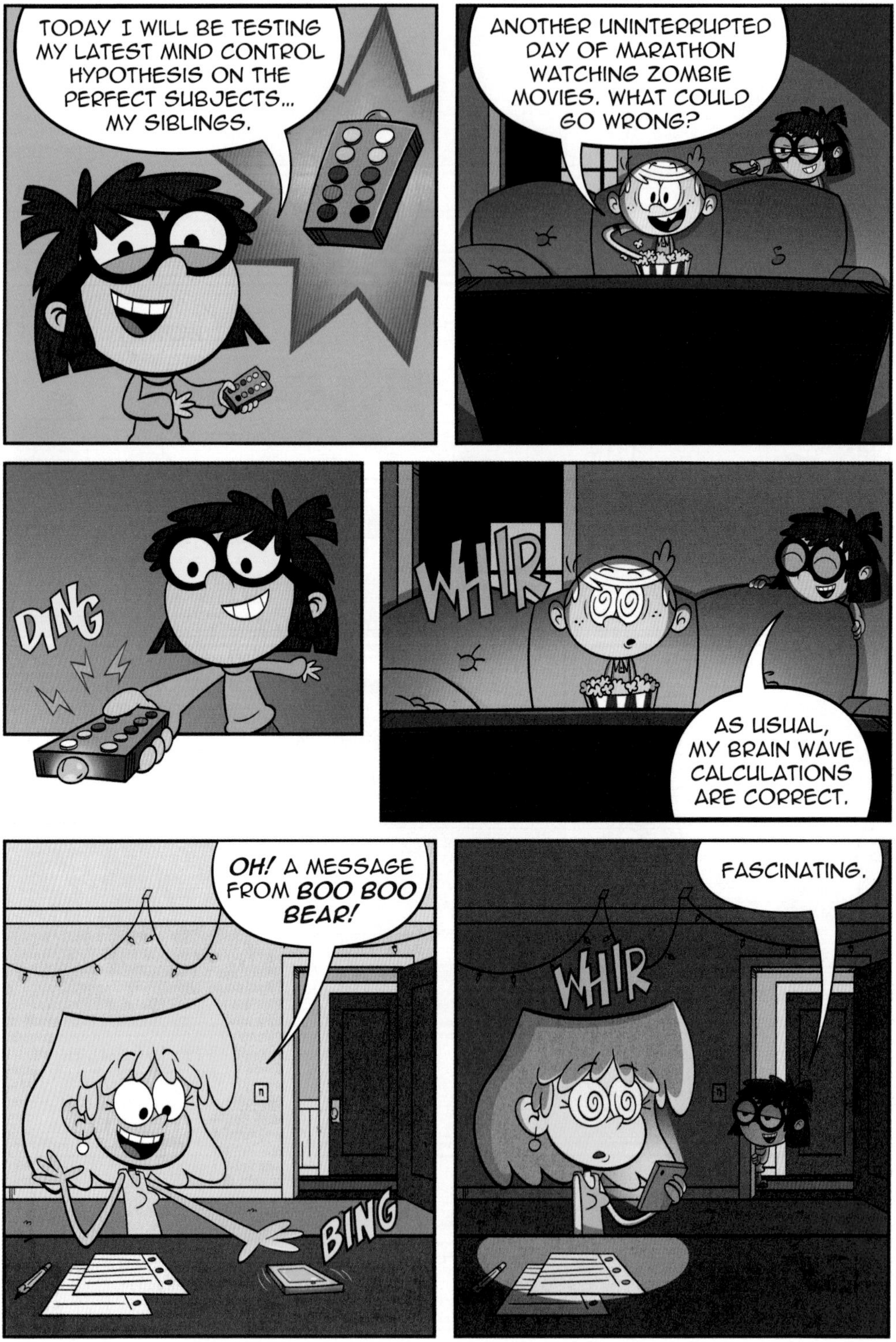
TODAY I WILL BE TESTING MY LATEST MIND CONTROL HYPOTHESIS ON THE PERFECT SUBJECTS... MY SIBLINGS.
ANOTHER UNINTERRUPTED DAY OF MARATHON WATCHING ZOMBIE MOVIES. WHAT COULD GO WRONG?
DING
WHIR
AS USUAL, MY BRAIN WAVE CALCULATIONS ARE CORRECT.
OH! A MESSAGE FROM BOO BOO BEAR!
BING
WHIR
FASCINATING.

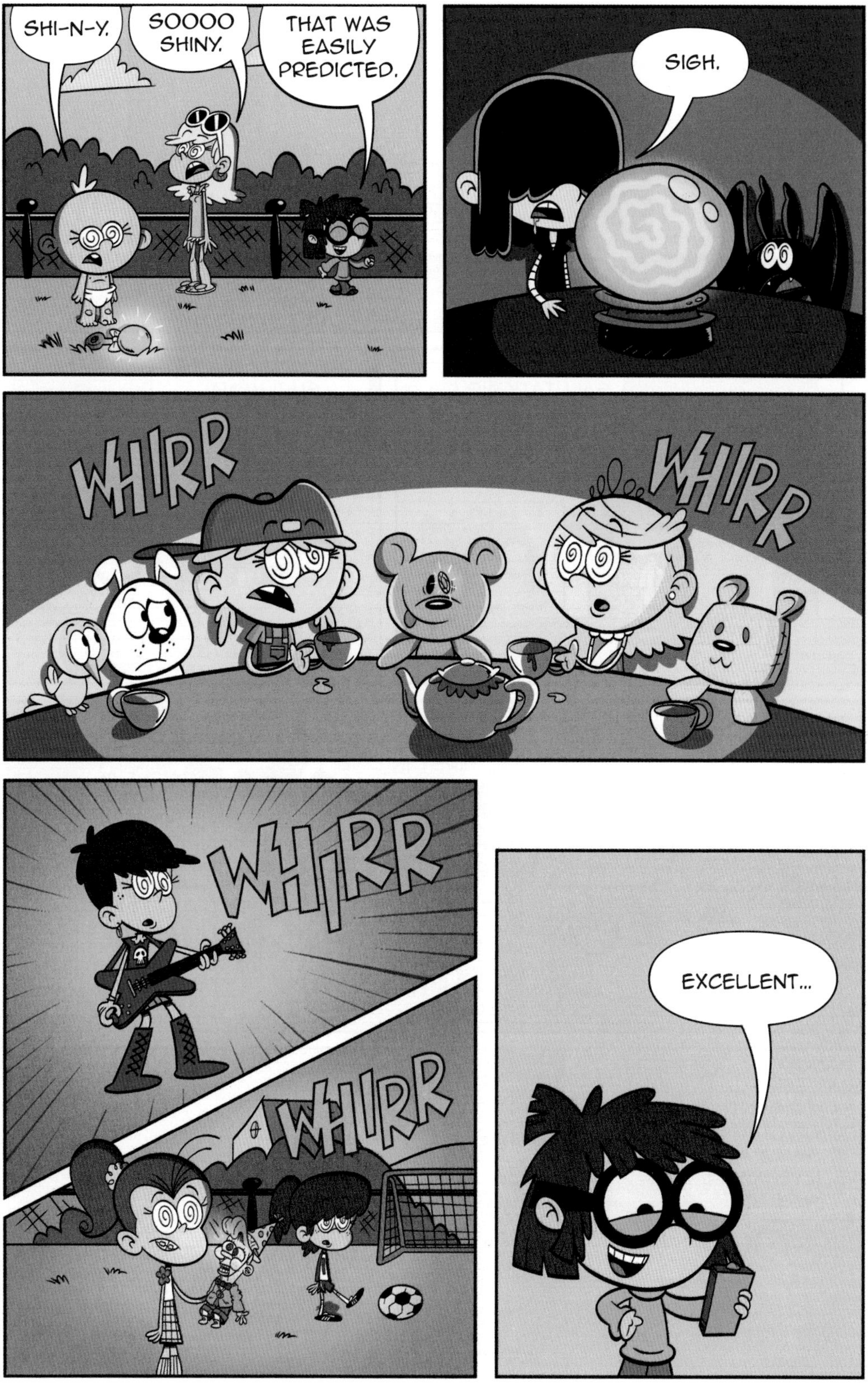
SHI-N-Y.
SOOOO SHINY.
THAT WAS EASILY PREDICTED.
SIGH.
WHIRR
WHIRR
WHIRR
WHIRR
EXCELLENT...

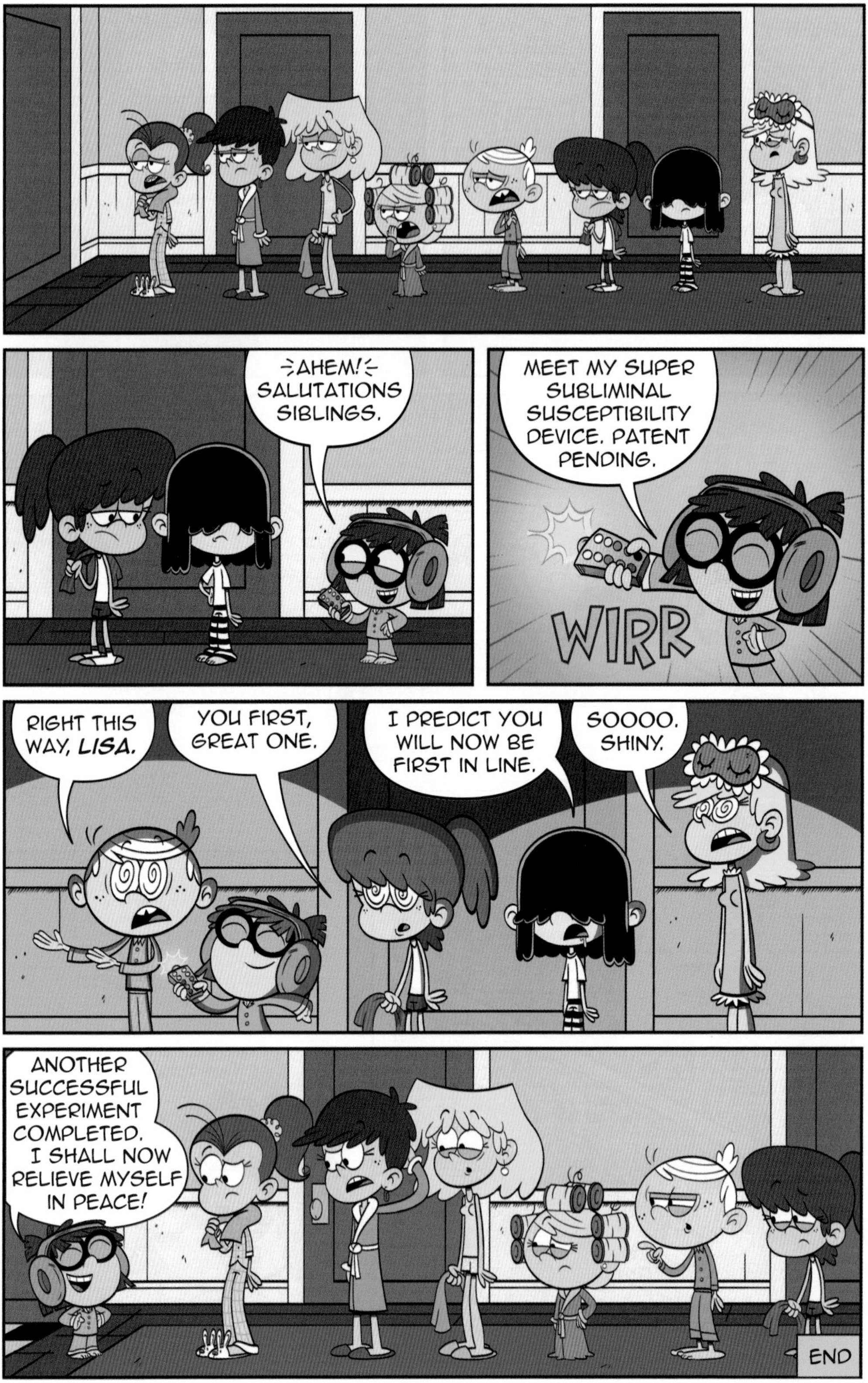

AHEM! SALUTATIONS SIBLINGS.
MEET MY SUPER SUBLIMINAL SUSCEPTIBILITY DEVICE. PATENT PENDING.
WIRR
RIGHT THIS WAY, LISA.
YOU FIRST, GREAT ONE.
I PREDICT YOU WILL NOW BE FIRST IN LINE.
SOOOO. SHINY.
ANOTHER SUCCESSFUL EXPERIMENT COMPLETED. I SHALL NOW RELIEVE MYSELF IN PEACE!
END

"TICKET FOR TWO"

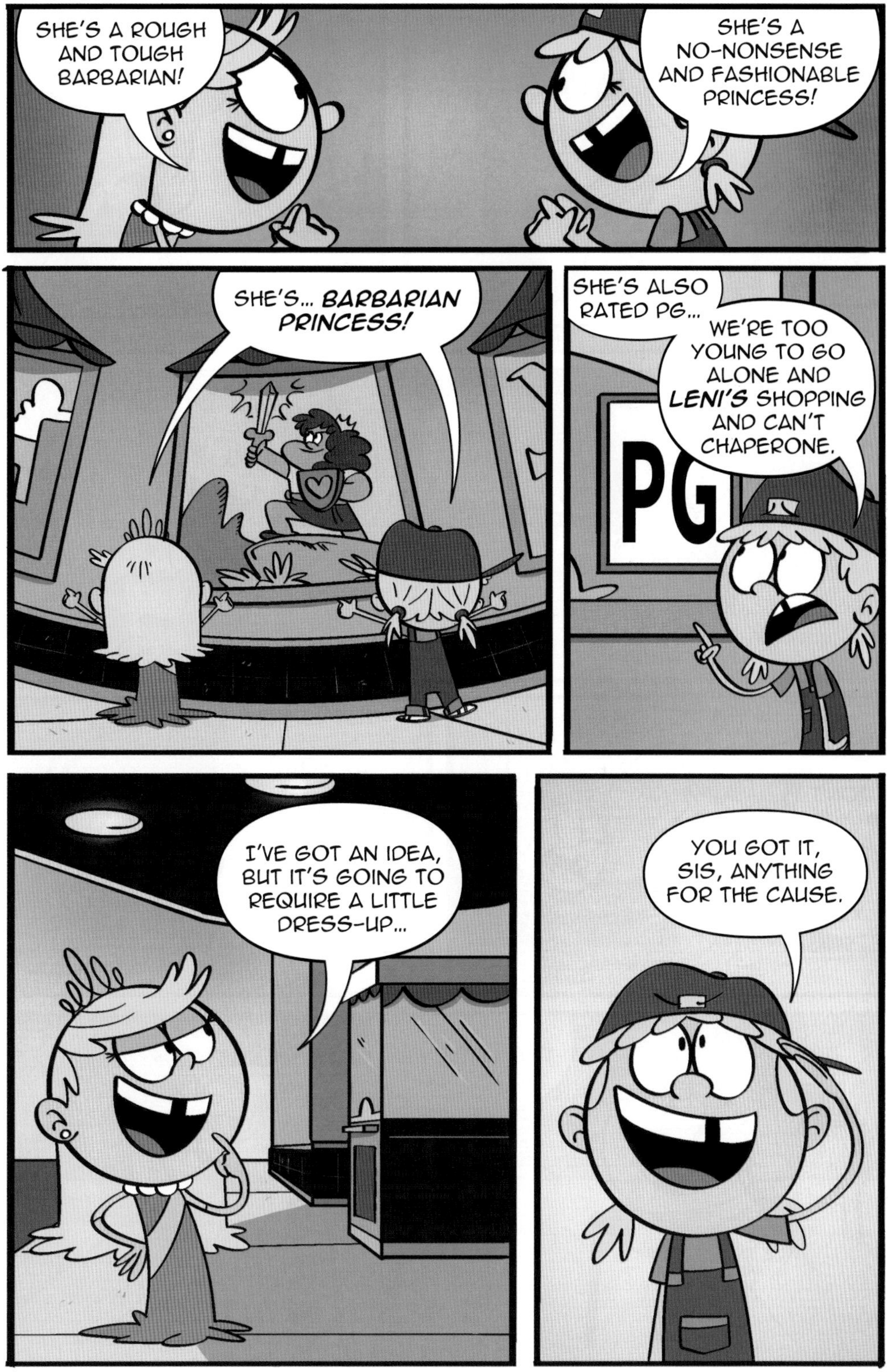
SHE'S A ROUGH AND TOUGH BARBARIAN!
SHE'S A NO-NONSENSE AND FASHIONABLE PRINCESS!
SHE'S... BARBARIAN PRINCESS!
SHE'S ALSO RATED PG...
WE'RE TOO YOUNG TO GO ALONE AND LENI'S SHOPPING AND CAN'T CHAPERONE.
PG
I'VE GOT AN IDEA, BUT IT'S GOING TO REQUIRE A LITTLE DRESS-UP...
YOU GOT IT, SIS, ANYTHING FOR THE CAUSE.

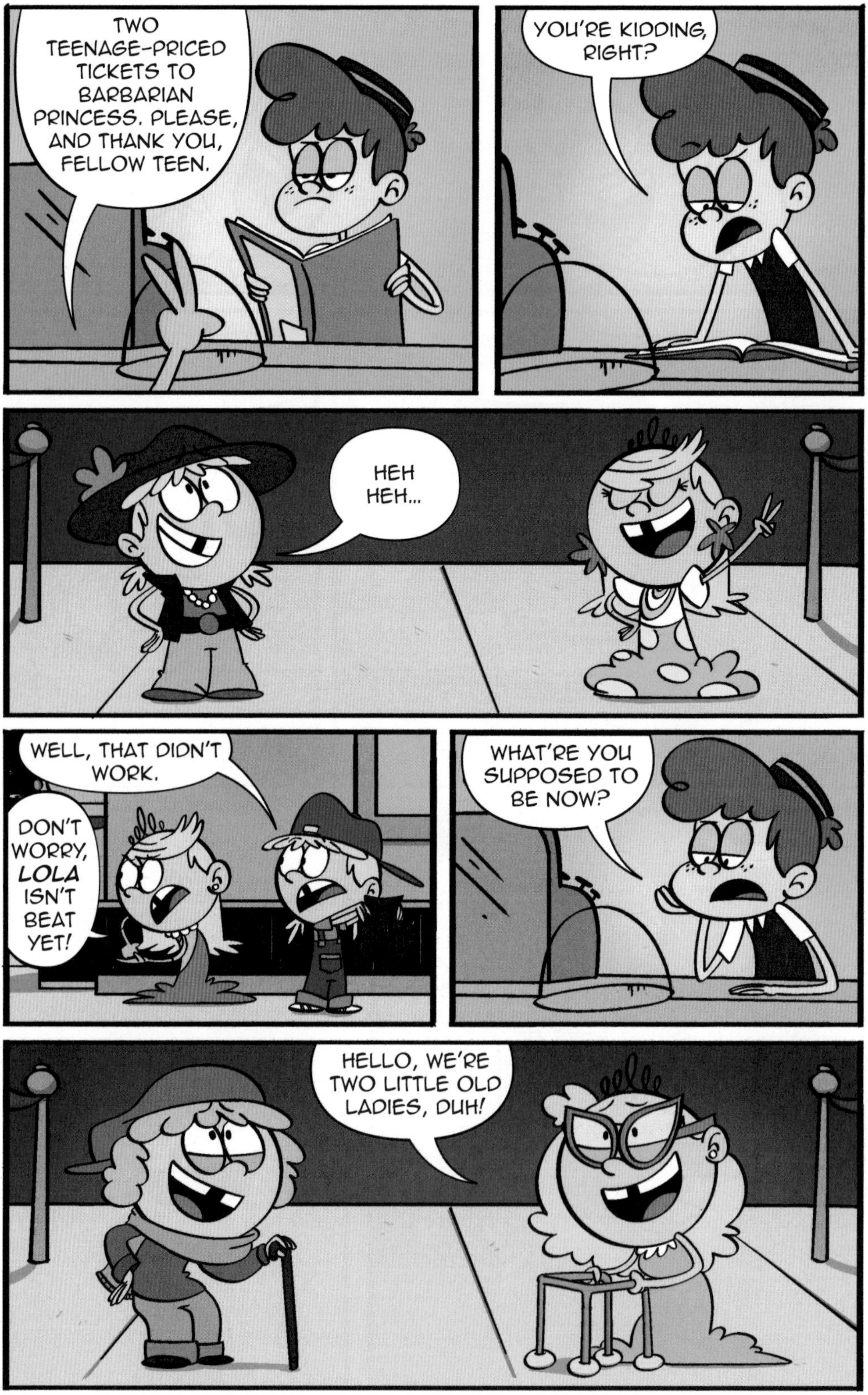
TWO TEENAGE-PRICED TICKETS TO BARBARIAN PRINCESS. PLEASE, AND THANK YOU, FELLOW TEEN.
YOU'RE KIDDING, RIGHT?
HEH HEH...
WELL, THAT DIDN'T WORK.
DON'T WORRY, **LOLA** ISN'T BEAT YET!
WHAT'RE YOU SUPPOSED TO BE NOW?
HELLO, WE'RE TWO LITTLE OLD LADIES, DUH!

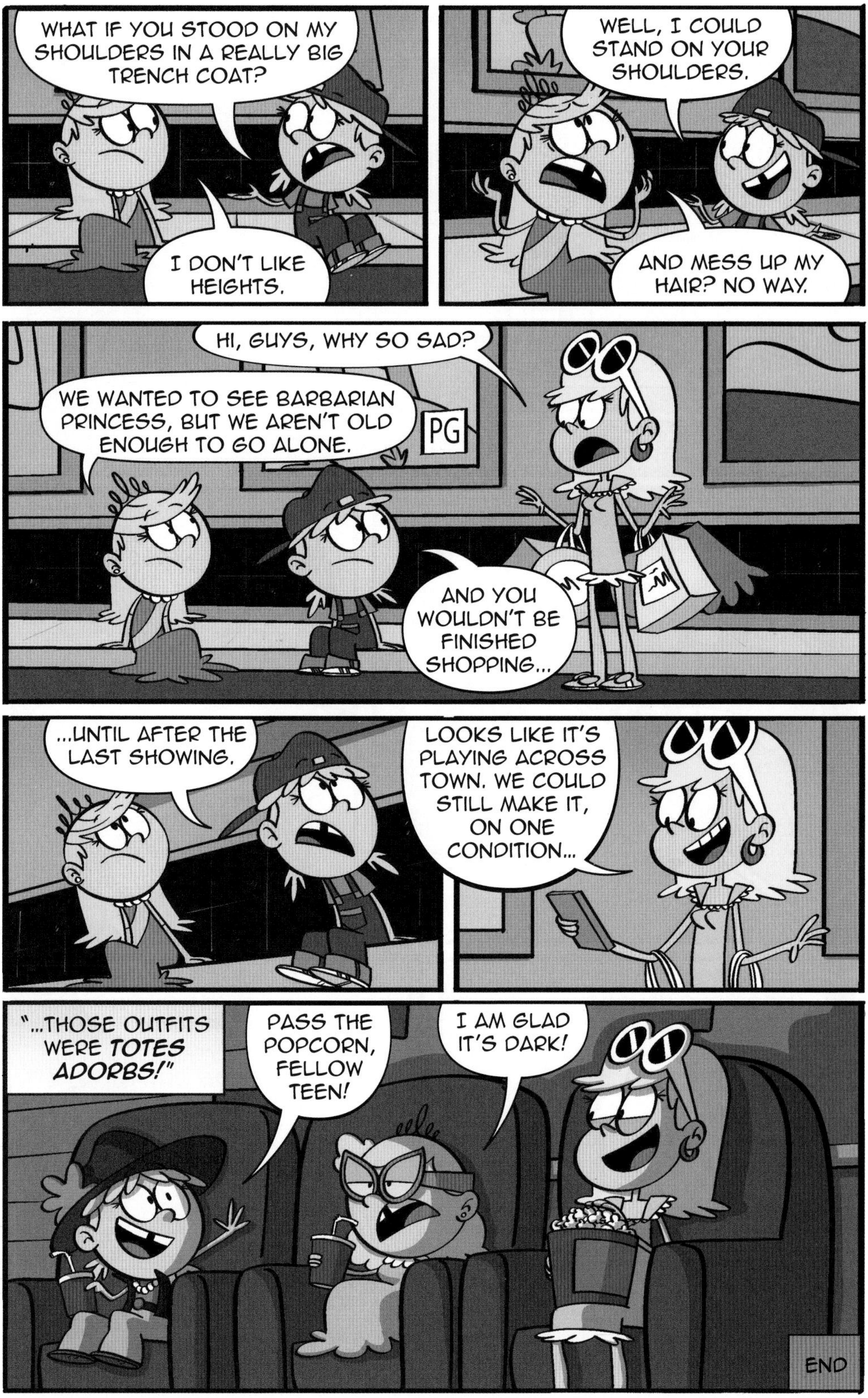
WHAT IF YOU STOOD ON MY SHOULDERS IN A REALLY BIG TRENCH COAT?
I DON'T LIKE HEIGHTS.
WELL, I COULD STAND ON YOUR SHOULDERS.
AND MESS UP MY HAIR? NO WAY.
HI, GUYS, WHY SO SAD?
WE WANTED TO SEE BARBARIAN PRINCESS, BUT WE AREN'T OLD ENOUGH TO GO ALONE.
PG
AND YOU WOULDN'T BE FINISHED SHOPPING...
...UNTIL AFTER THE LAST SHOWING.
LOOKS LIKE IT'S PLAYING ACROSS TOWN. WE COULD STILL MAKE IT, ON ONE CONDITION...
"...THOSE OUTFITS WERE *TOTES ADORBS!*"
PASS THE POPCORN, FELLOW TEEN!
I AM GLAD IT'S DARK!
END

"BOBBY'S WORLD"

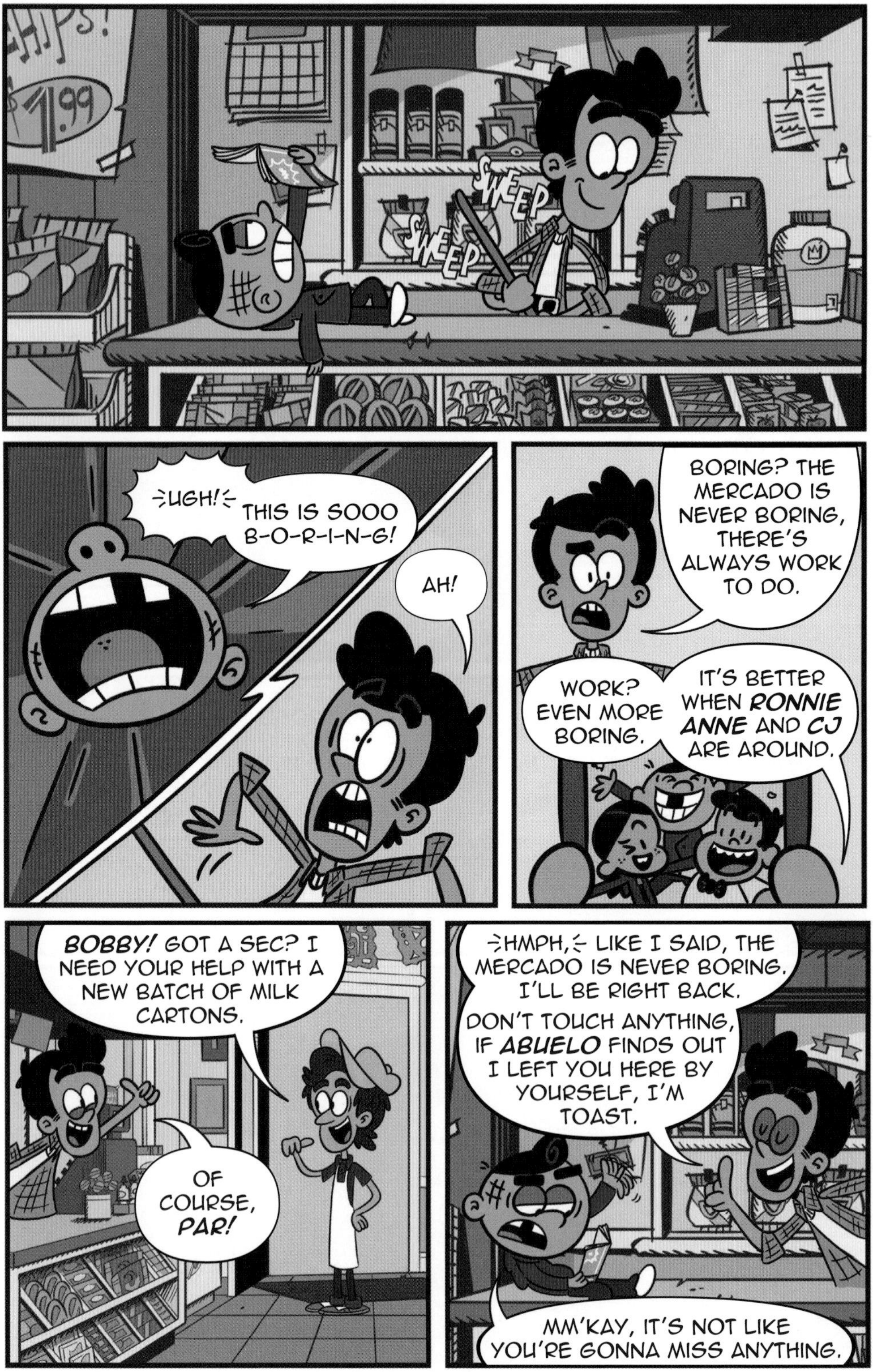

SWEEP
SWEEP
UGH!
THIS IS SOOO B-O-R-I-N-G!
AH!
BORING? THE MERCADO IS NEVER BORING, THERE'S ALWAYS WORK TO DO.
WORK? EVEN MORE BORING.
IT'S BETTER WHEN RONNIE ANNE AND CJ ARE AROUND.
BOBBY! GOT A SEC? I NEED YOUR HELP WITH A NEW BATCH OF MILK CARTONS.
OF COURSE, PAR!
HMPH, LIKE I SAID, THE MERCADO IS NEVER BORING. I'LL BE RIGHT BACK.
DON'T TOUCH ANYTHING, IF ABUELO FINDS OUT I LEFT YOU HERE BY YOURSELF, I'M TOAST.
MM'KAY, IT'S NOT LIKE YOU'RE GONNA MISS ANYTHING.

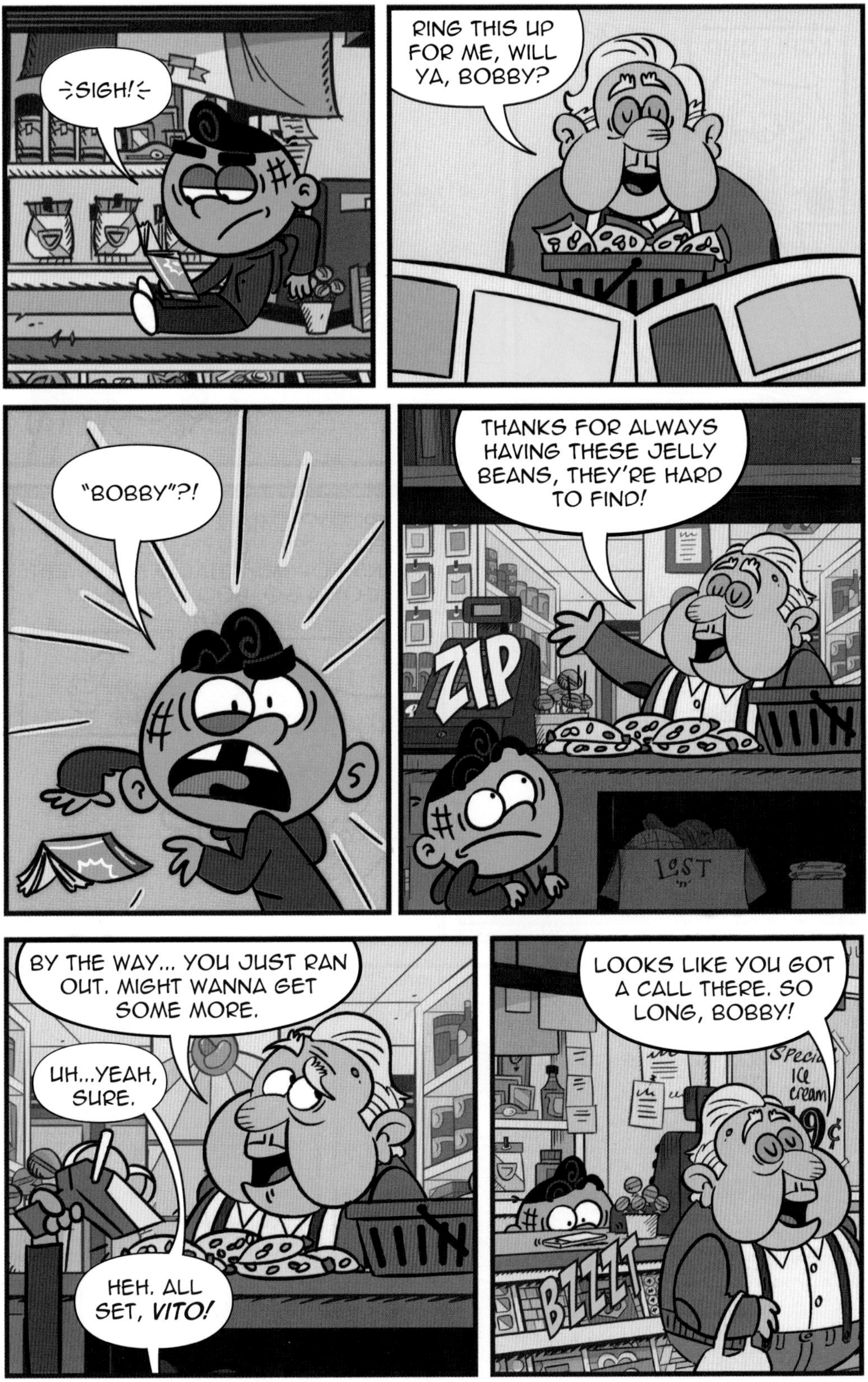

SIGH!
RING THIS UP FOR ME, WILL YA, BOBBY?
"BOBBY"?!
THANKS FOR ALWAYS HAVING THESE JELLY BEANS, THEY'RE HARD TO FIND!
ZIP
LOST
BY THE WAY... YOU JUST RAN OUT. MIGHT WANNA GET SOME MORE.
UH...YEAH, SURE.
HEH. ALL SET, VITO!
LOOKS LIKE YOU GOT A CALL THERE. SO LONG, BOBBY!
Special Ice cream
BZZZT

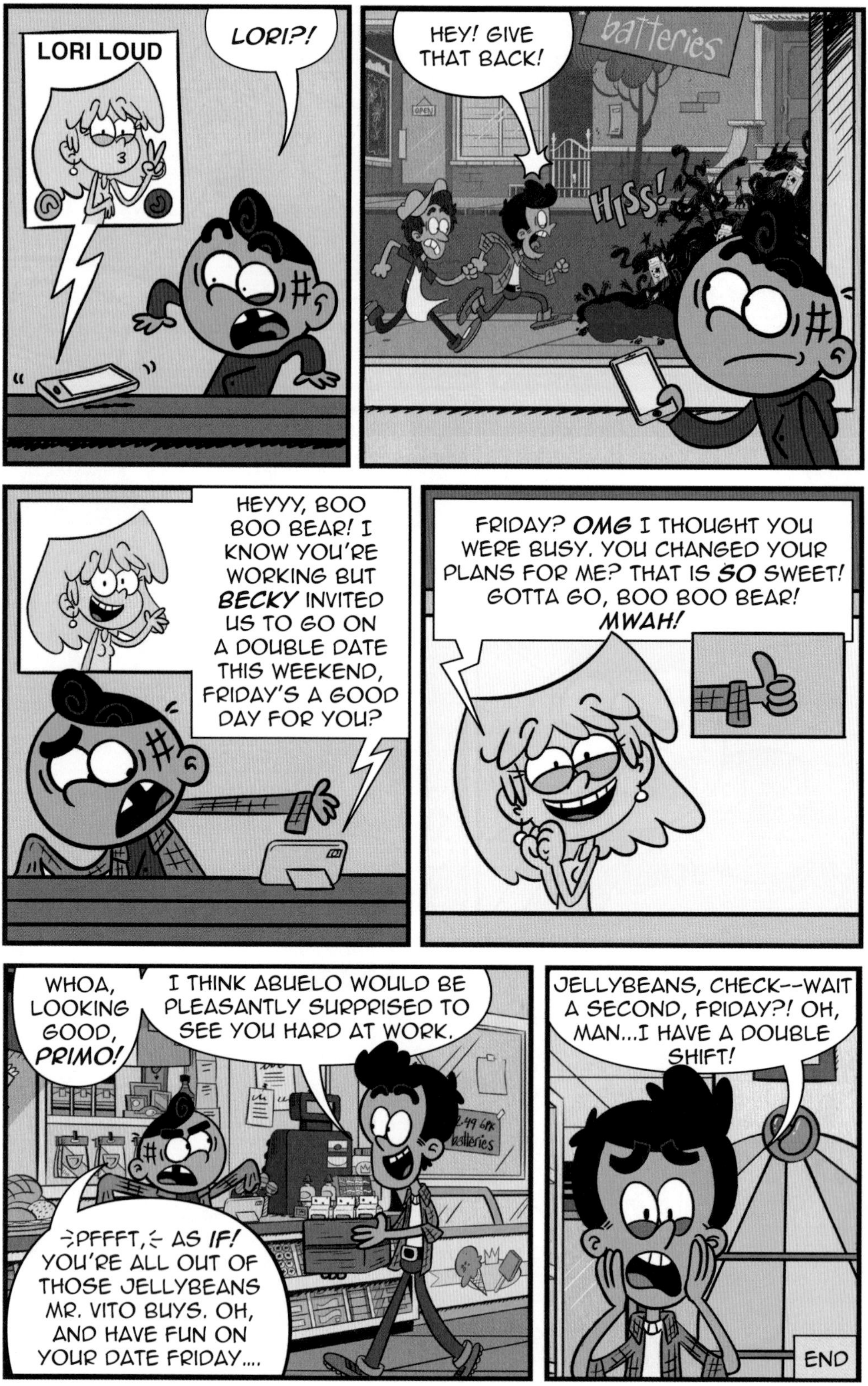
LORI LOUD
LORI?!
HEY! GIVE THAT BACK!
batteries
OPEN
HISS!
HEYYY, BOO BOO BEAR! I KNOW YOU'RE WORKING BUT BECKY INVITED US TO GO ON A DOUBLE DATE THIS WEEKEND, FRIDAY'S A GOOD DAY FOR YOU?
FRIDAY? OMG I THOUGHT YOU WERE BUSY. YOU CHANGED YOUR PLANS FOR ME? THAT IS SO SWEET! GOTTA GO, BOO BOO BEAR! MWAH!
WHOA, LOOKING GOOD, PRIMO!
I THINK ABUELO WOULD BE PLEASANTLY SURPRISED TO SEE YOU HARD AT WORK.
2.49 6PK batteries
PFFFT, AS IF! YOU'RE ALL OUT OF THOSE JELLYBEANS MR. VITO BUYS. OH, AND HAVE FUN ON YOUR DATE FRIDAY....
JELLYBEANS, CHECK--WAIT A SECOND, FRIDAY?! OH, MAN...I HAVE A DOUBLE SHIFT!
END

"ON THE HUSH HUSH"

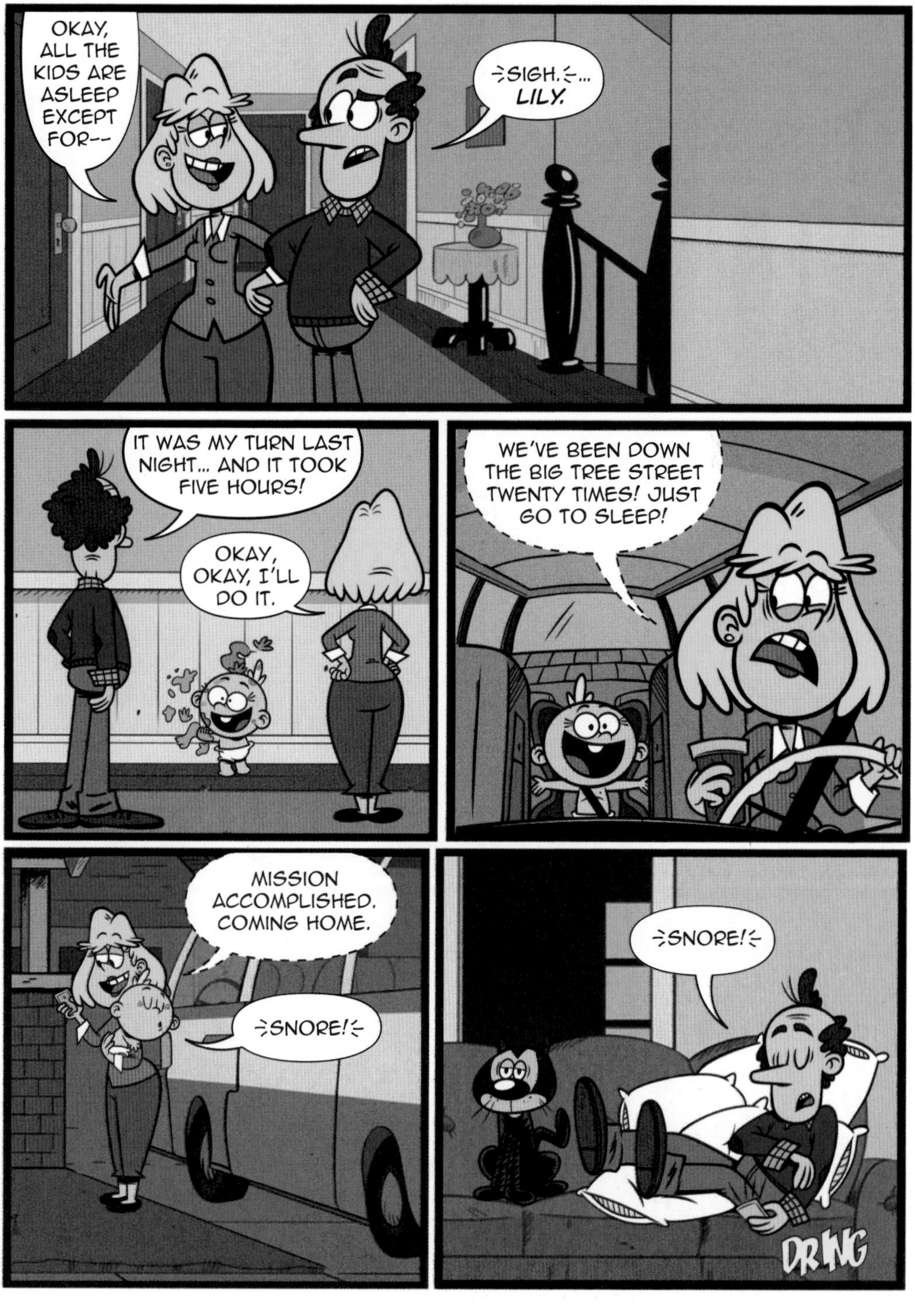
OKAY, ALL THE KIDS ARE ASLEEP EXCEPT FOR--
SIGH. ... LILY.
IT WAS MY TURN LAST NIGHT... AND IT TOOK FIVE HOURS!
OKAY, OKAY, I'LL DO IT.
WE'VE BEEN DOWN THE BIG TREE STREET TWENTY TIMES! JUST GO TO SLEEP!
MISSION ACCOMPLISHED. COMING HOME.
SNORE!
SNORE!
DRING

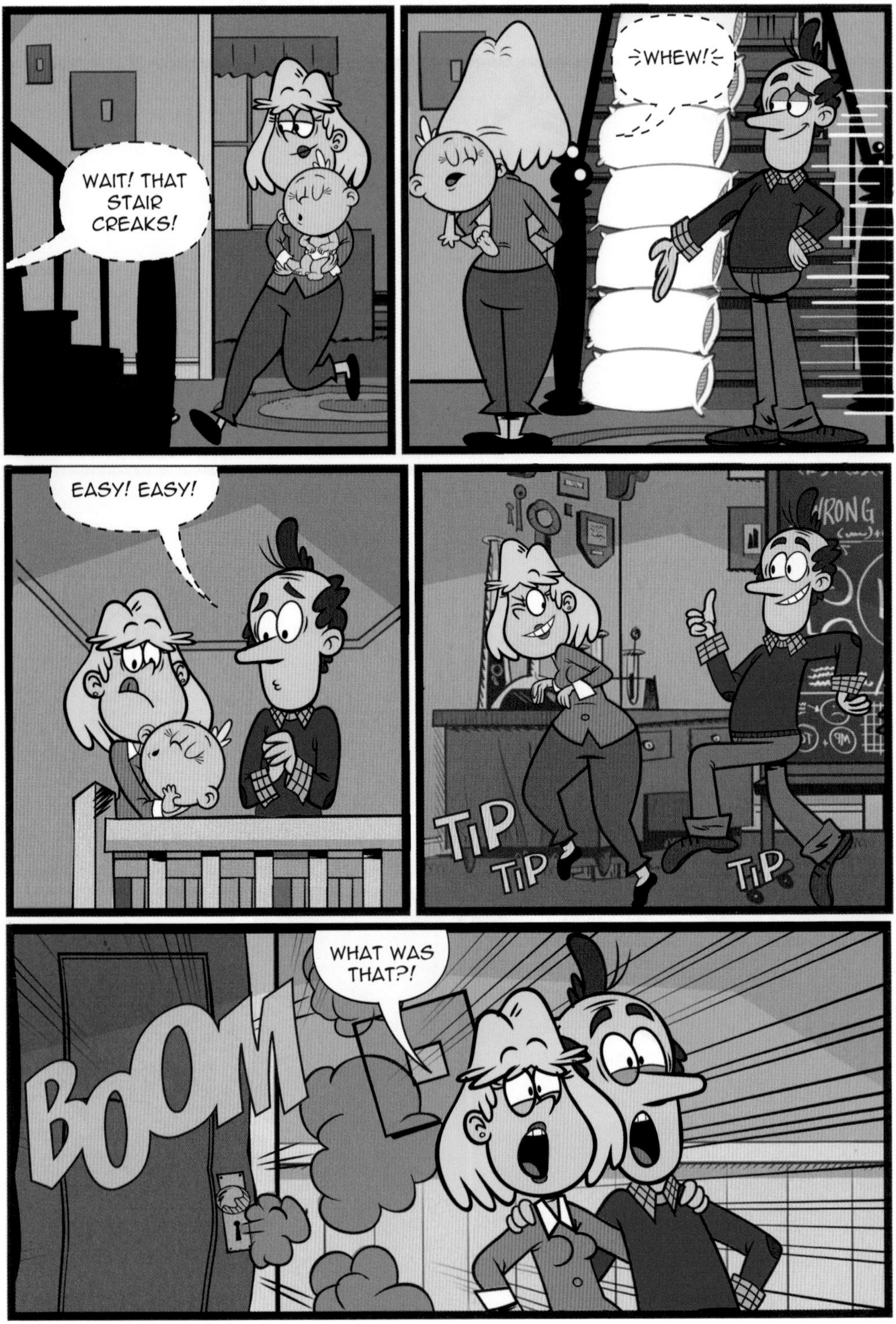
WAIT! THAT STAIR CREAKS!
WHEW!
EASY! EASY!
TIP
TIP
TIP
BOOM
WHAT WAS THAT?!

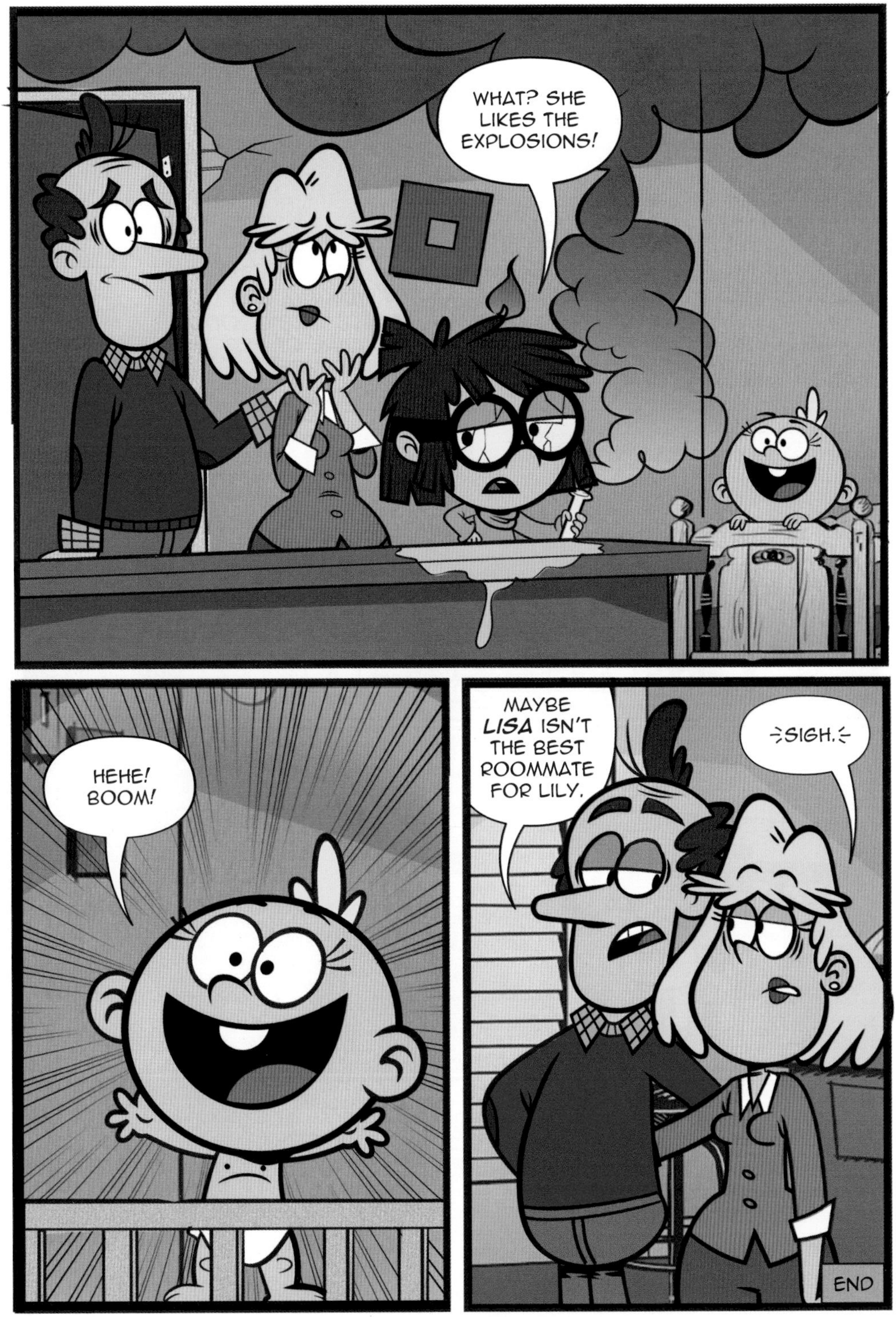
WHAT? SHE LIKES THE EXPLOSIONS!
HEHE! BOOM!
MAYBE *LISA* ISN'T THE BEST ROOMMATE FOR LILY.
SIGH.
END

"COUNTRY MOUSE, SUBURBAN HAMSTER"

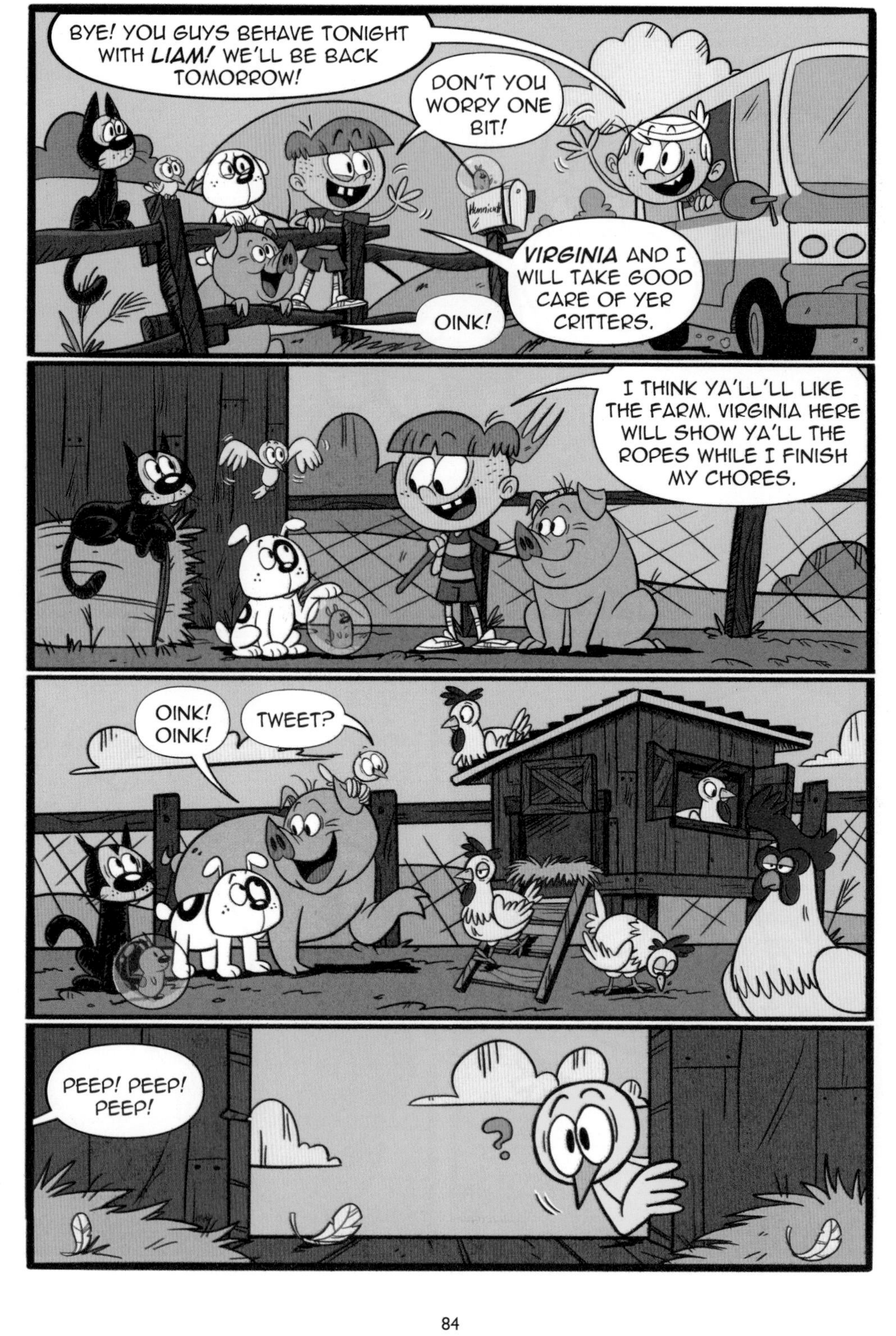
BYE! YOU GUYS BEHAVE TONIGHT WITH LIAM! WE'LL BE BACK TOMORROW!
DON'T YOU WORRY ONE BIT!
VIRGINIA AND I WILL TAKE GOOD CARE OF YER CRITTERS.
OINK!
Hunnicutt
I THINK YA'LL'LL LIKE THE FARM. VIRGINIA HERE WILL SHOW YA'LL THE ROPES WHILE I FINISH MY CHORES.
OINK! OINK!
TWEET?
PEEP! PEEP! PEEP!

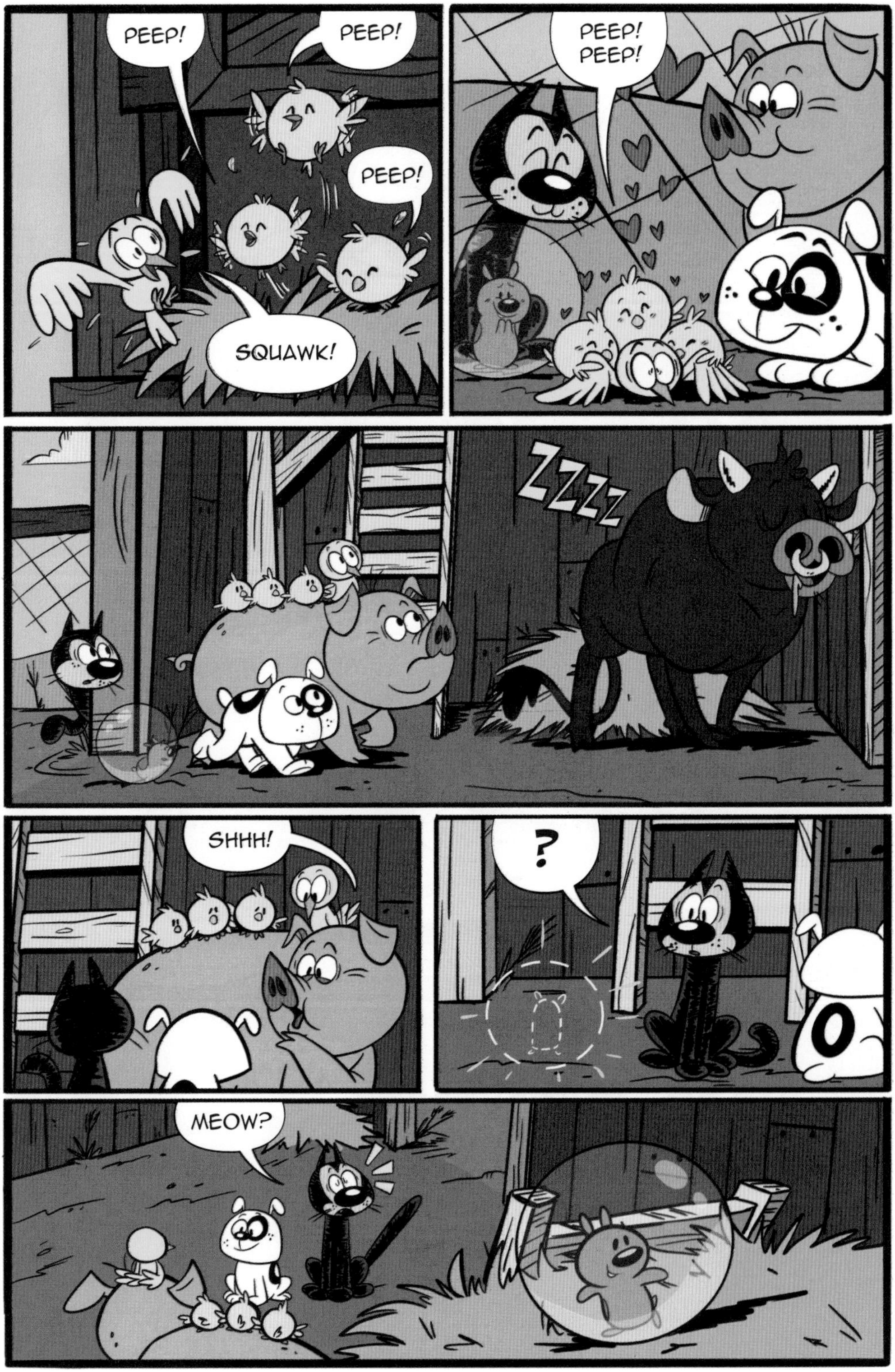
PEEP!
PEEP!
PEEP!
SQUAWK!
PEEP! PEEP!
ZZZZ
SHHH!
?
MEOW?

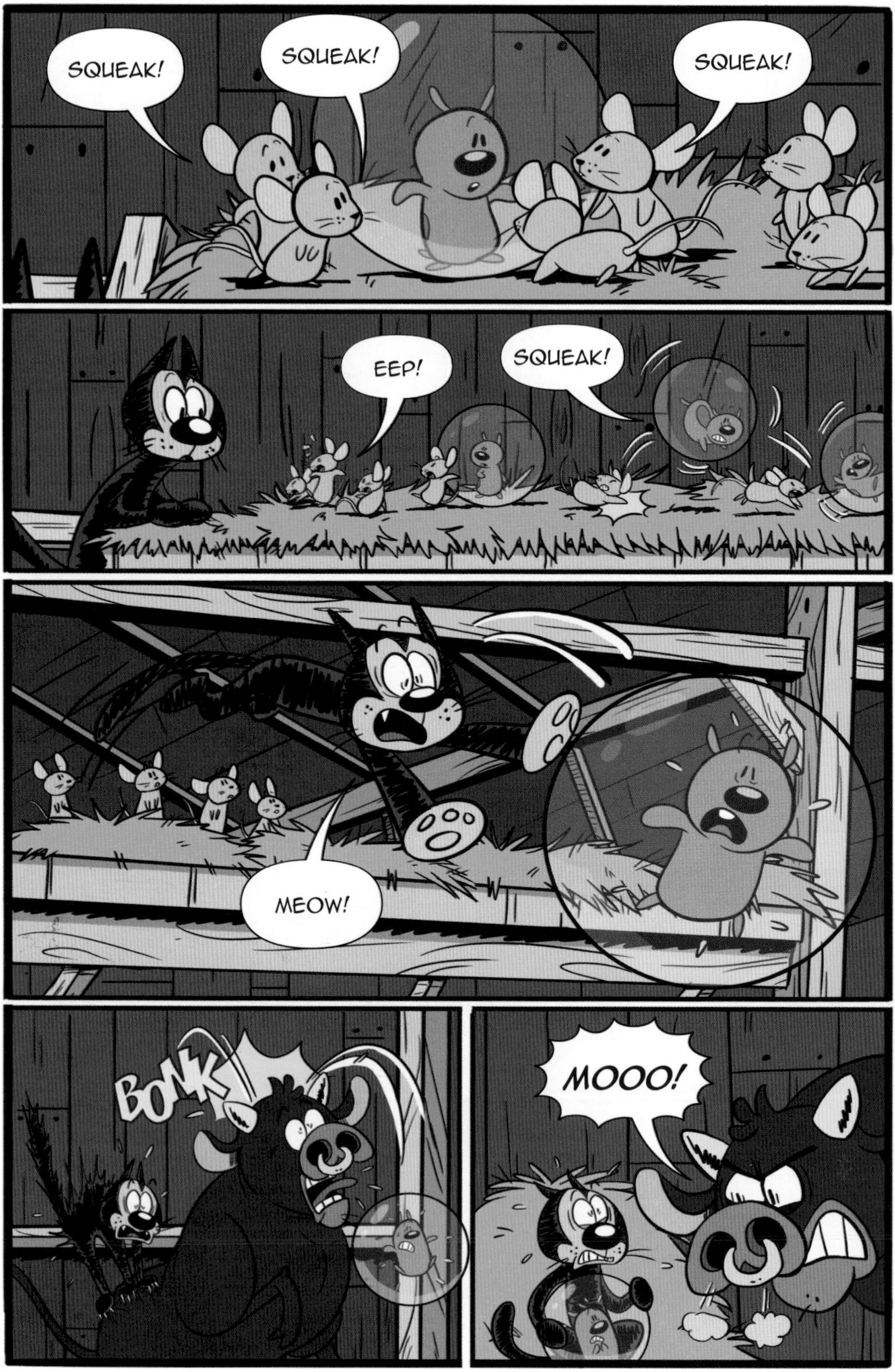
SQUEAK!
SQUEAK!
SQUEAK!
EEP!
SQUEAK!
MEOW!
BONK
MOOO!

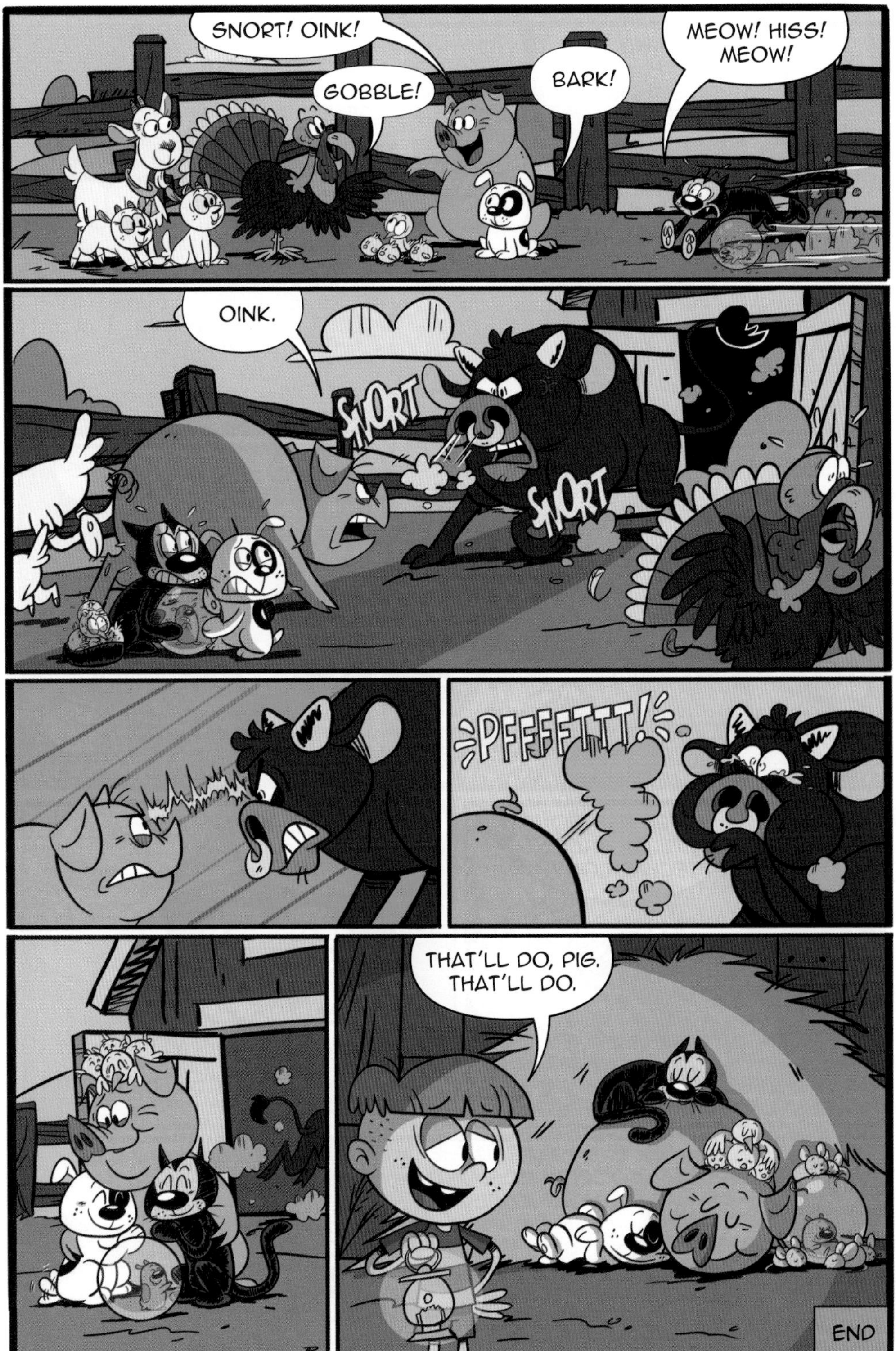
SNORT! OINK!
GOBBLE!
BARK!
MEOW! HISS! MEOW!
OINK.
SNORT
SNORT
PFFFFTTTT!
THAT'LL DO, PIG. THAT'LL DO.
END

"WALKMAN THE LINE"

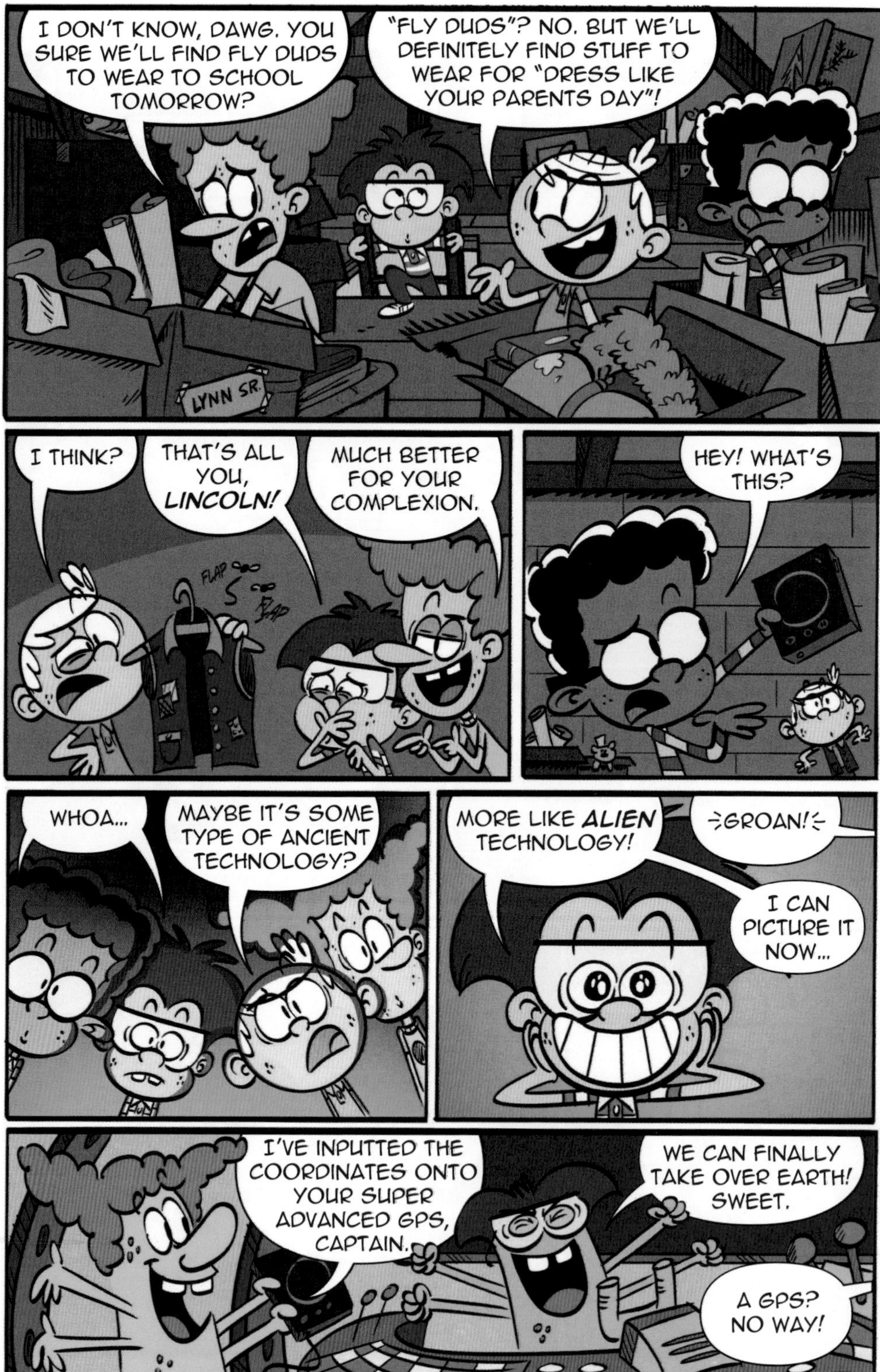
I DON'T KNOW, DAWG. YOU SURE WE'LL FIND FLY DUDS TO WEAR TO SCHOOL TOMORROW?
"FLY DUDS"? NO. BUT WE'LL DEFINITELY FIND STUFF TO WEAR FOR "DRESS LIKE YOUR PARENTS DAY"!
LYNN SR.
I THINK?
THAT'S ALL YOU, LINCOLN!
MUCH BETTER FOR YOUR COMPLEXION.
FLAP
FLAP
HEY! WHAT'S THIS?
WHOA...
MAYBE IT'S SOME TYPE OF ANCIENT TECHNOLOGY?
MORE LIKE ALIEN TECHNOLOGY!
GROAN!
I CAN PICTURE IT NOW...
I'VE INPUTTED THE COORDINATES ONTO YOUR SUPER ADVANCED GPS, CAPTAIN.
WE CAN FINALLY TAKE OVER EARTH! SWEET.
A GPS? NO WAY!

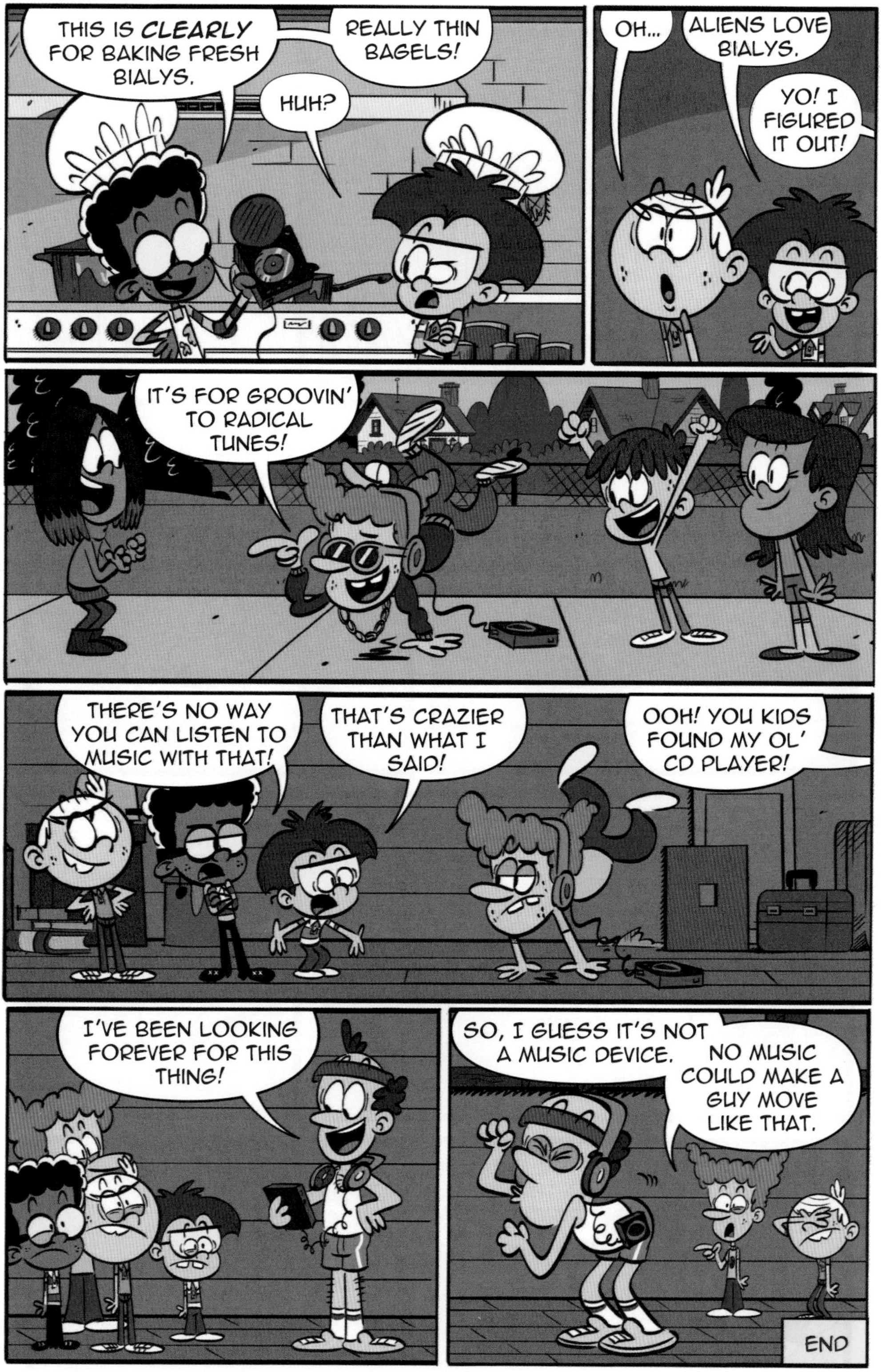
THIS IS CLEARLY FOR BAKING FRESH BIALYS.
REALLY THIN BAGELS!
HUH?
OH...
ALIENS LOVE BIALYS.
YO! I FIGURED IT OUT!
IT'S FOR GROOVIN' TO RADICAL TUNES!
THERE'S NO WAY YOU CAN LISTEN TO MUSIC WITH THAT!
THAT'S CRAZIER THAN WHAT I SAID!
OOH! YOU KIDS FOUND MY OL' CD PLAYER!
I'VE BEEN LOOKING FOREVER FOR THIS THING!
SO, I GUESS IT'S NOT A MUSIC DEVICE.
NO MUSIC COULD MAKE A GUY MOVE LIKE THAT.
END

"SINGING OUT LOUD"

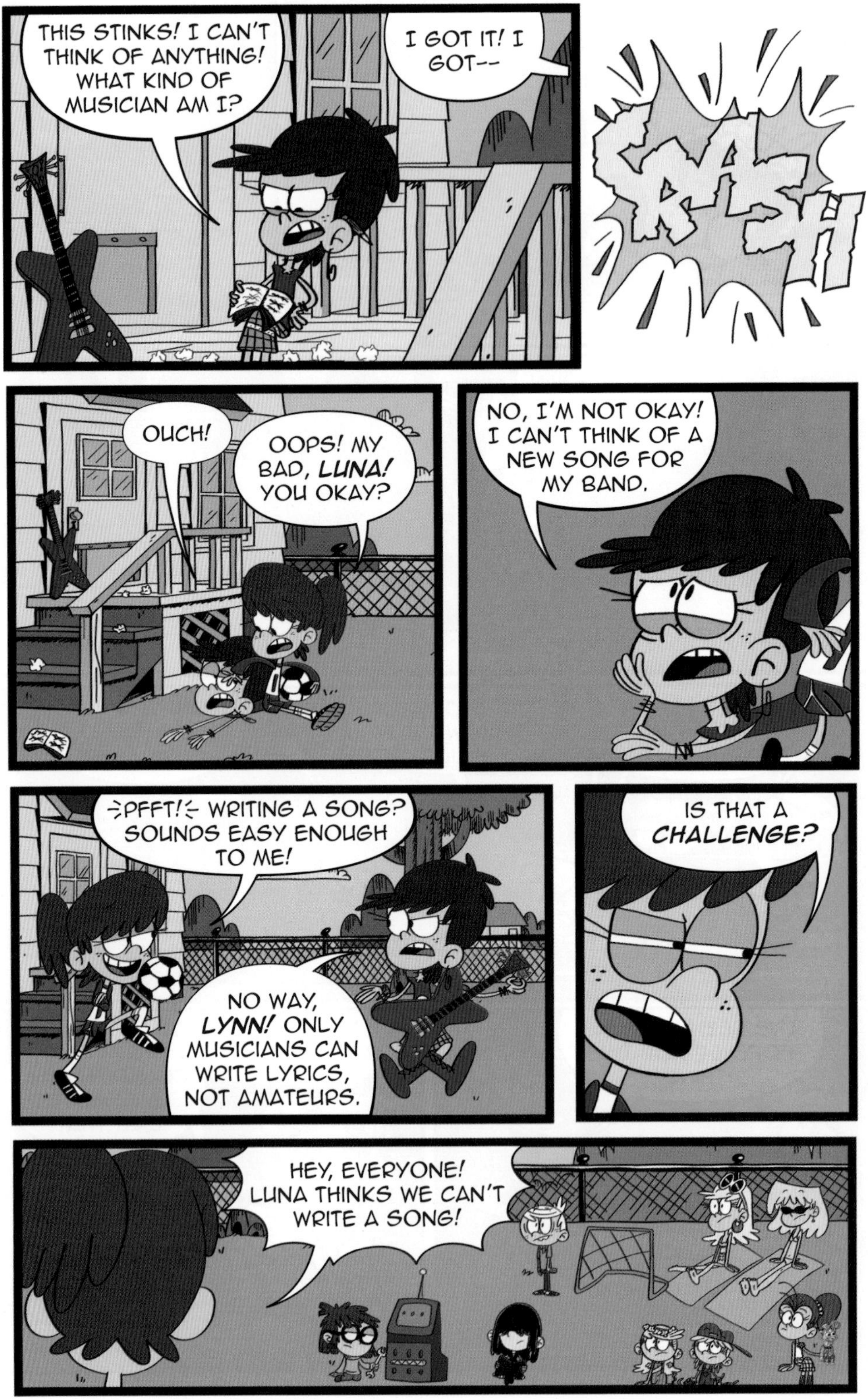

THIS STINKS! I CAN'T THINK OF ANYTHING! WHAT KIND OF MUSICIAN AM I?
I GOT IT! I GOT--
CRASH
OUCH!
OOPS! MY BAD, LUNA! YOU OKAY?
NO, I'M NOT OKAY! I CAN'T THINK OF A NEW SONG FOR MY BAND.
PFFT! WRITING A SONG? SOUNDS EASY ENOUGH TO ME!
NO WAY, LYNN! ONLY MUSICIANS CAN WRITE LYRICS, NOT AMATEURS.
IS THAT A CHALLENGE?
HEY, EVERYONE! LUNA THINKS WE CAN'T WRITE A SONG!

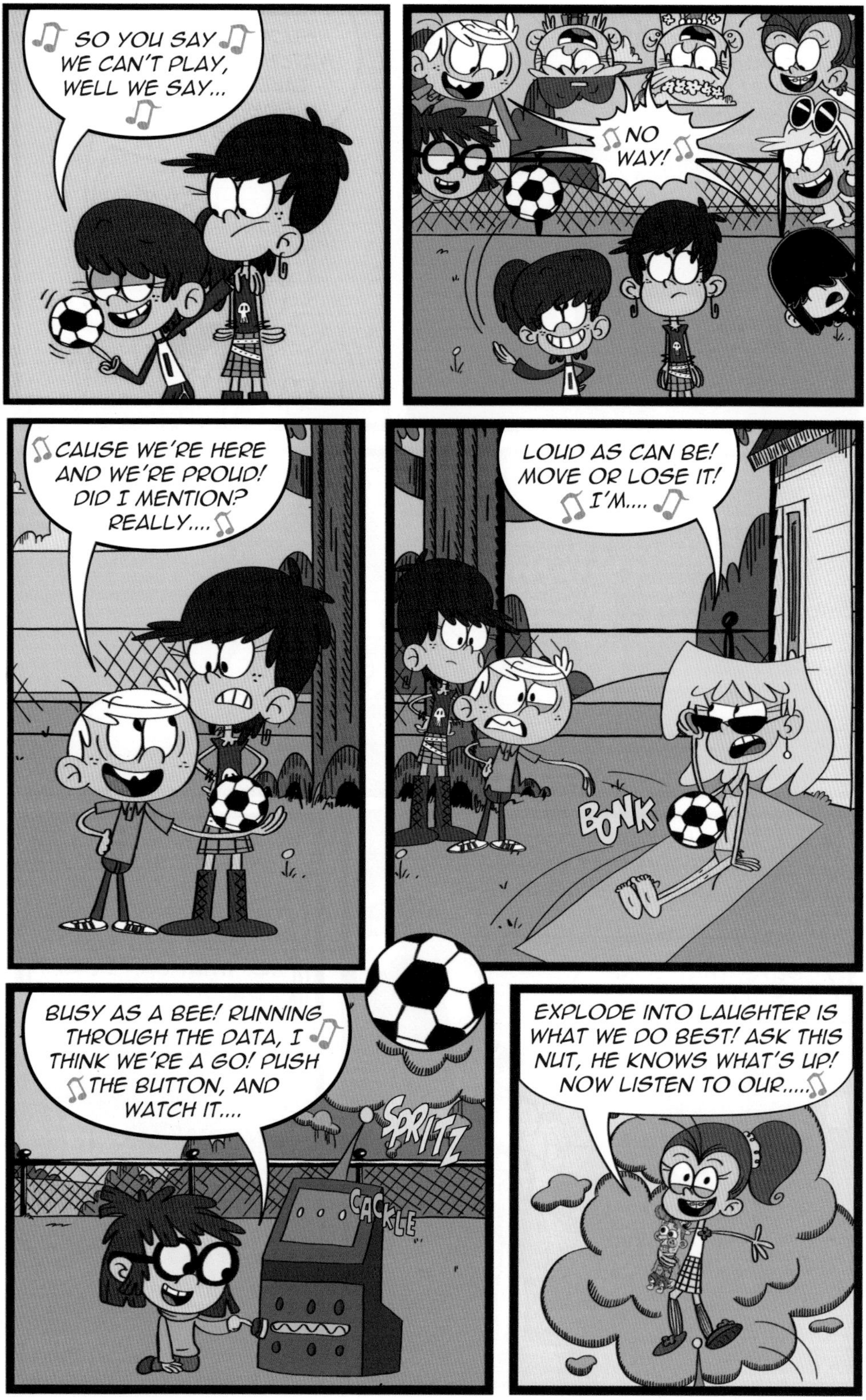
SO YOU SAY WE CAN'T PLAY, WELL WE SAY...
NO WAY!
CAUSE WE'RE HERE AND WE'RE PROUD! DID I MENTION? REALLY....
LOUD AS CAN BE! MOVE OR LOSE IT! I'M....
BONK
BUSY AS A BEE! RUNNING THROUGH THE DATA, I THINK WE'RE A GO! PUSH THE BUTTON, AND WATCH IT....
SPRITZ
CACKLE
EXPLODE INTO LAUGHTER IS WHAT WE DO BEST! ASK THIS NUT, HE KNOWS WHAT'S UP! NOW LISTEN TO OUR.....

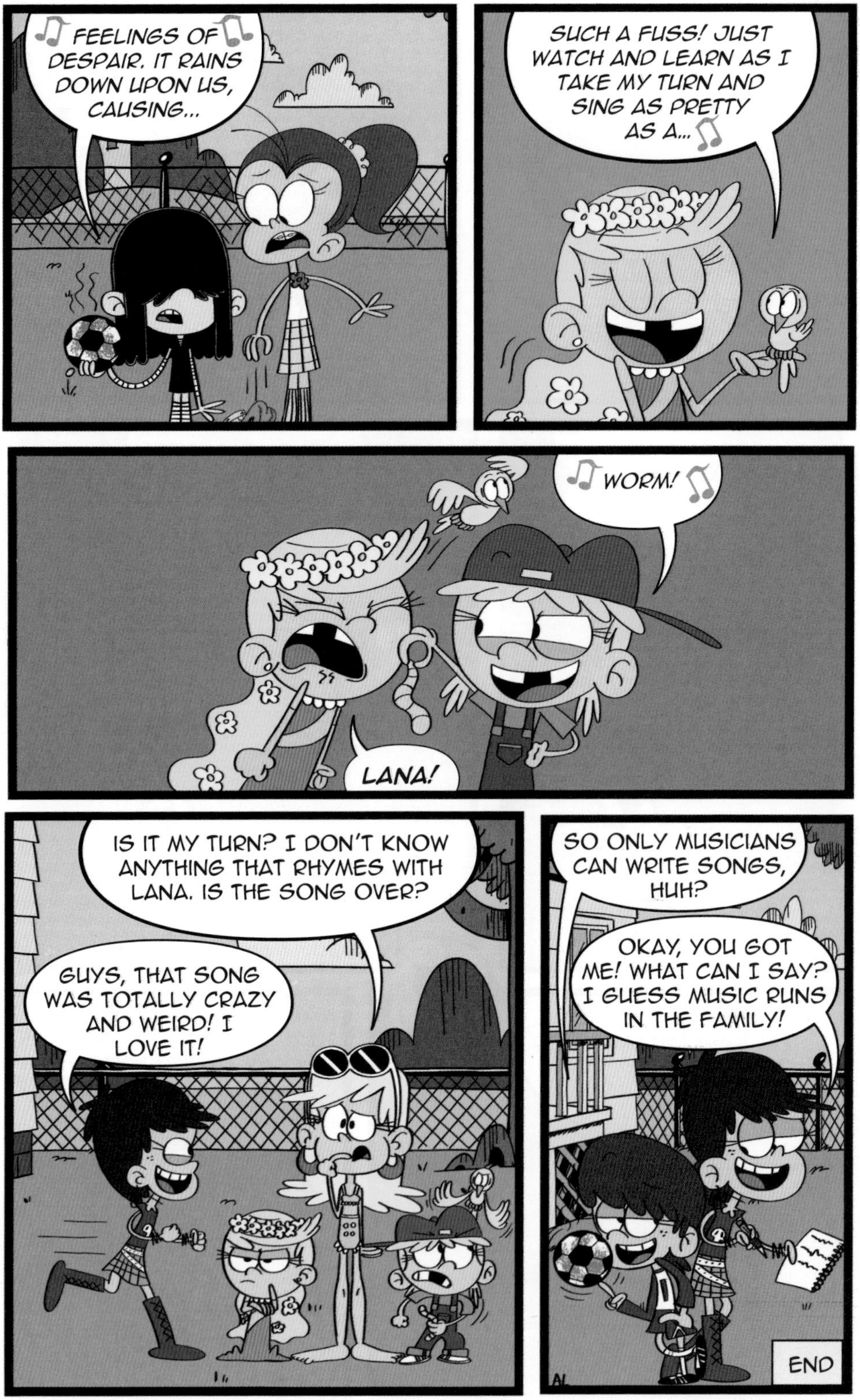
FEELINGS OF DESPAIR. IT RAINS DOWN UPON US, CAUSING...
SUCH A FUSS! JUST WATCH AND LEARN AS I TAKE MY TURN AND SING AS PRETTY AS A...
WORM!
LANA!
IS IT MY TURN? I DON'T KNOW ANYTHING THAT RHYMES WITH LANA. IS THE SONG OVER?
GUYS, THAT SONG WAS TOTALLY CRAZY AND WEIRD! I LOVE IT!
SO ONLY MUSICIANS CAN WRITE SONGS, HUH?
OKAY, YOU GOT ME! WHAT CAN I SAY? I GUESS MUSIC RUNS IN THE FAMILY!
END

"10 SECONDS TO PERFECT"

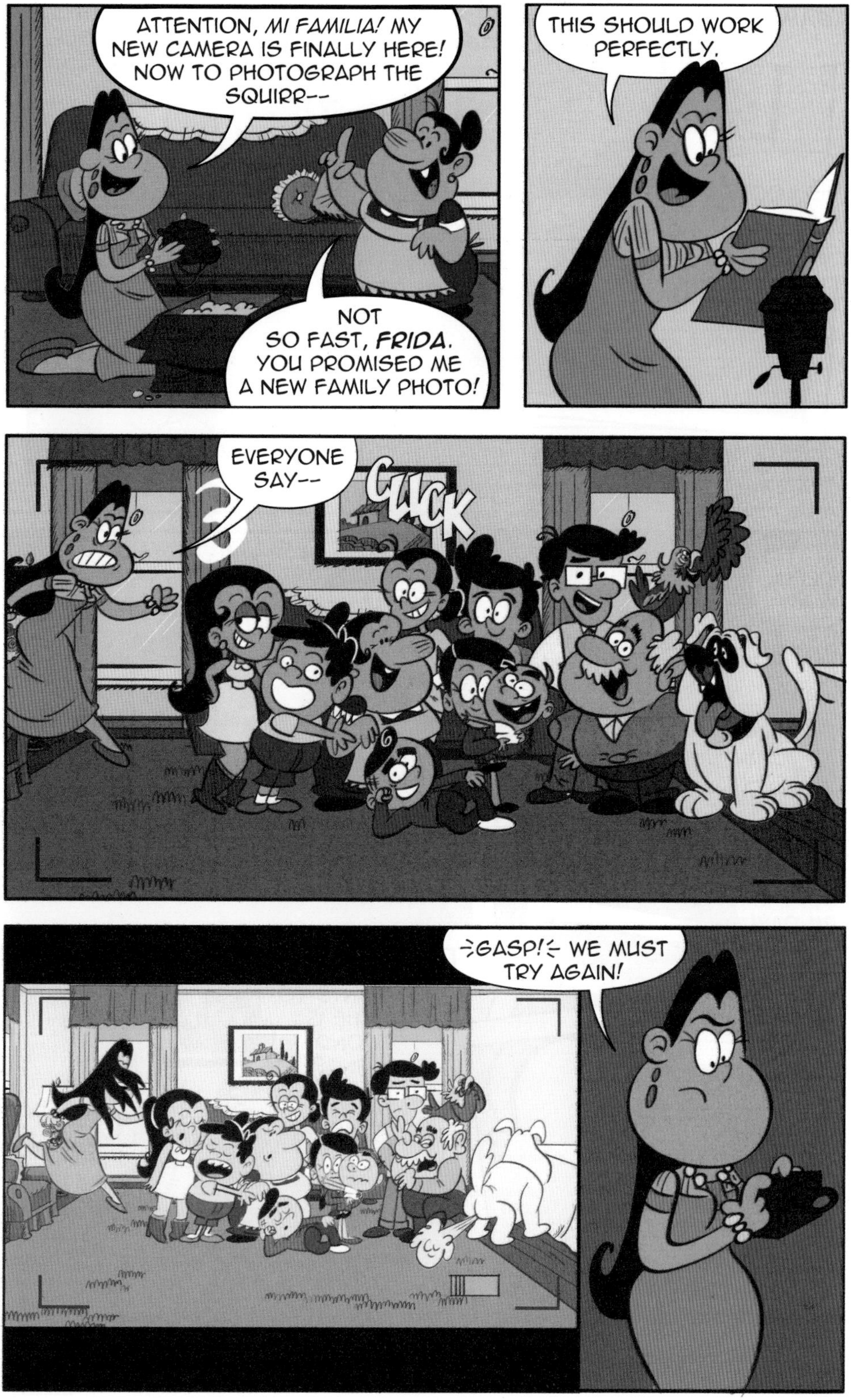
ATTENTION, MI FAMILIA! MY NEW CAMERA IS FINALLY HERE! NOW TO PHOTOGRAPH THE SQUIRR--
NOT SO FAST, FRIDA. YOU PROMISED ME A NEW FAMILY PHOTO!
THIS SHOULD WORK PERFECTLY.
EVERYONE SAY--
CLICK
GASP! WE MUST TRY AGAIN!

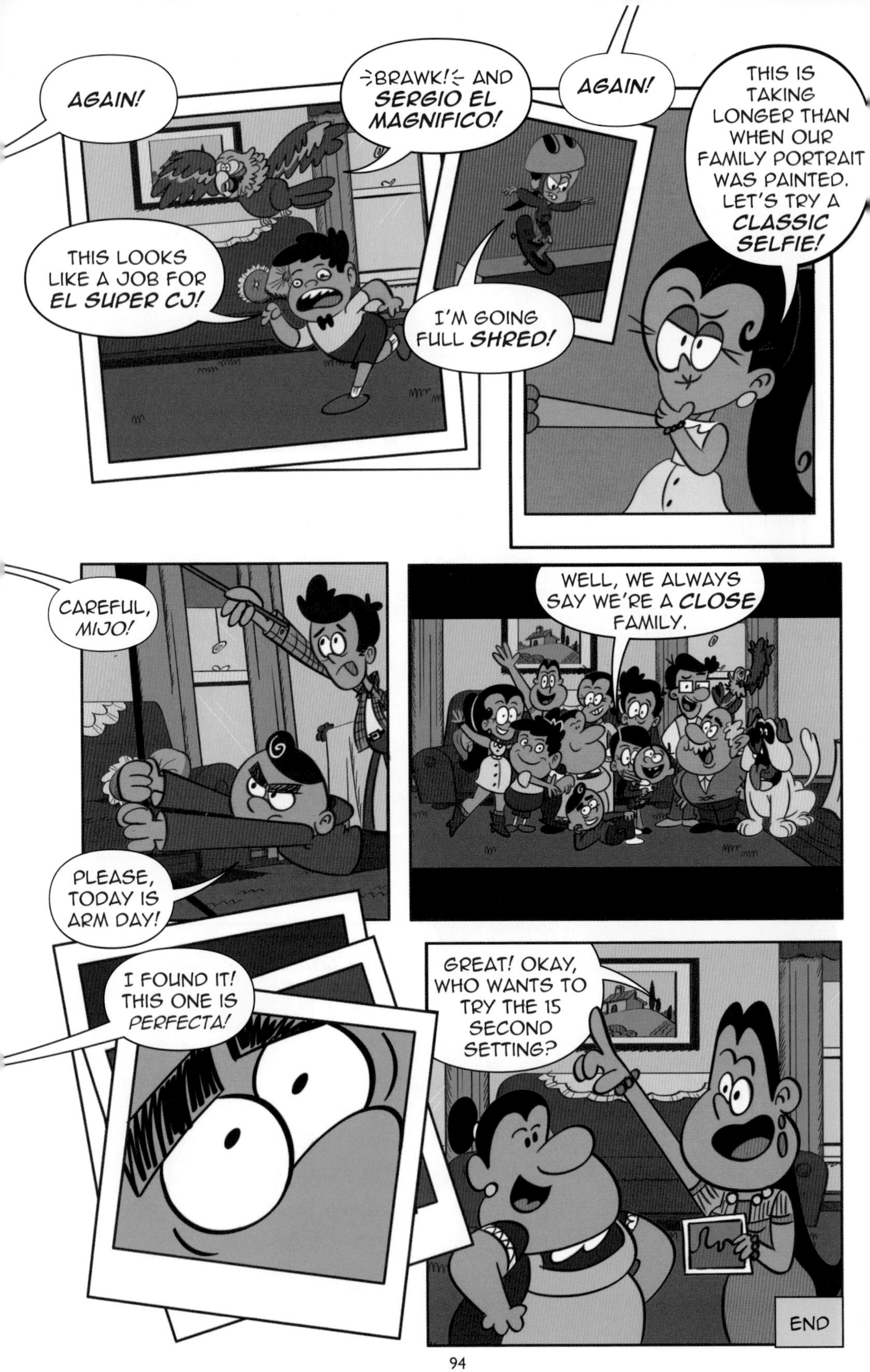
AGAIN!
-BRAWK!- AND SERGIO EL MAGNIFICO!
THIS LOOKS LIKE A JOB FOR EL SUPER CJ!
AGAIN!
I'M GOING FULL SHRED!
THIS IS TAKING LONGER THAN WHEN OUR FAMILY PORTRAIT WAS PAINTED. LET'S TRY A CLASSIC SELFIE!
CAREFUL, MIJO!
PLEASE, TODAY IS ARM DAY!
WELL, WE ALWAYS SAY WE'RE A CLOSE FAMILY.
I FOUND IT! THIS ONE IS PERFECTA!
GREAT! OKAY, WHO WANTS TO TRY THE 15 SECOND SETTING?
END

"TWINTUITION"

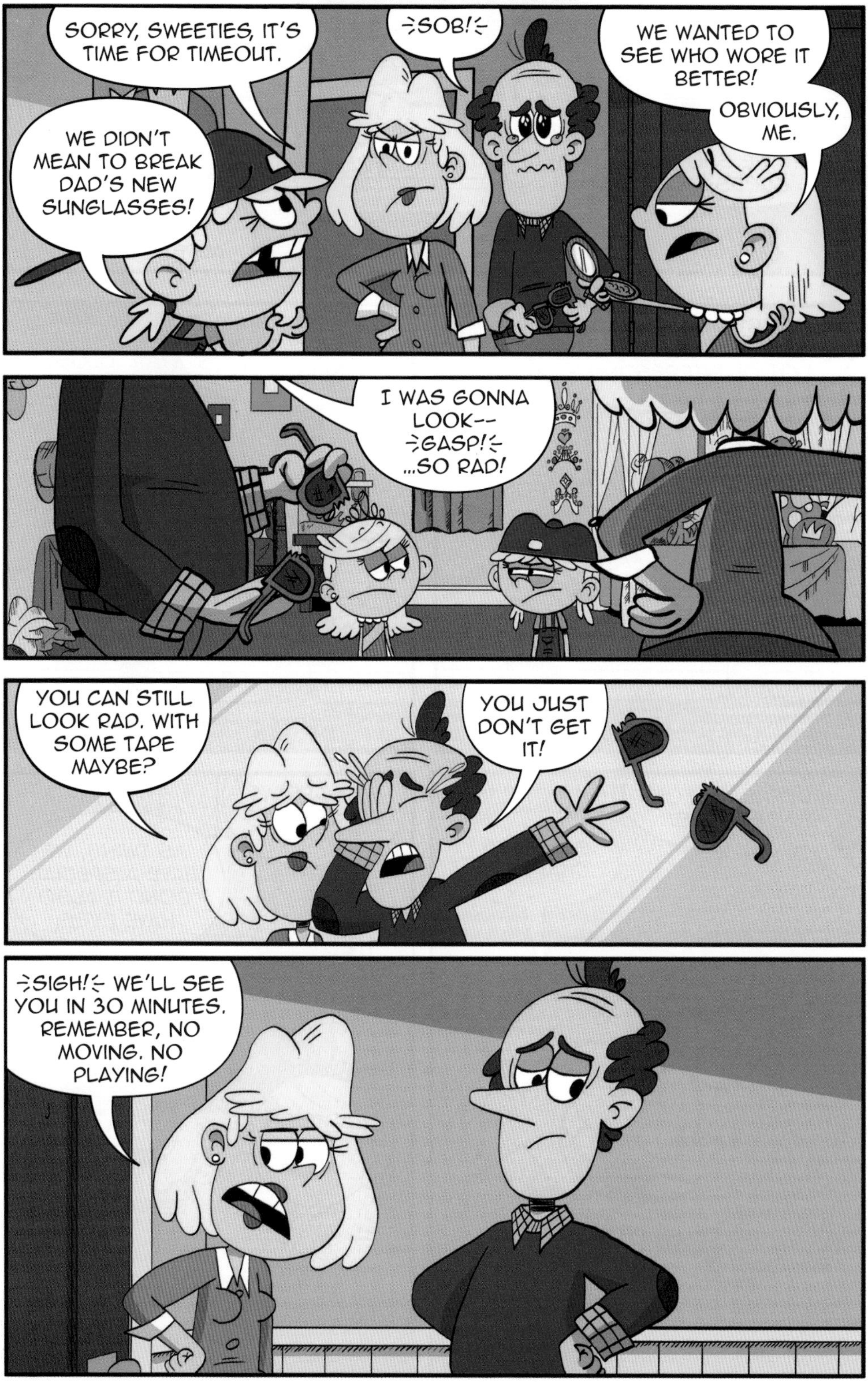

SORRY, SWEETIES, IT'S TIME FOR TIMEOUT.
WE DIDN'T MEAN TO BREAK DAD'S NEW SUNGLASSES!
⫘SOB!⫘
WE WANTED TO SEE WHO WORE IT BETTER!
OBVIOUSLY, ME.
I WAS GONNA LOOK-- ⫘GASP!⫘ ...SO RAD!
YOU CAN STILL LOOK RAD. WITH SOME TAPE MAYBE?
YOU JUST DON'T GET IT!
⫘SIGH!⫘ WE'LL SEE YOU IN 30 MINUTES. REMEMBER, NO MOVING. NO PLAYING!

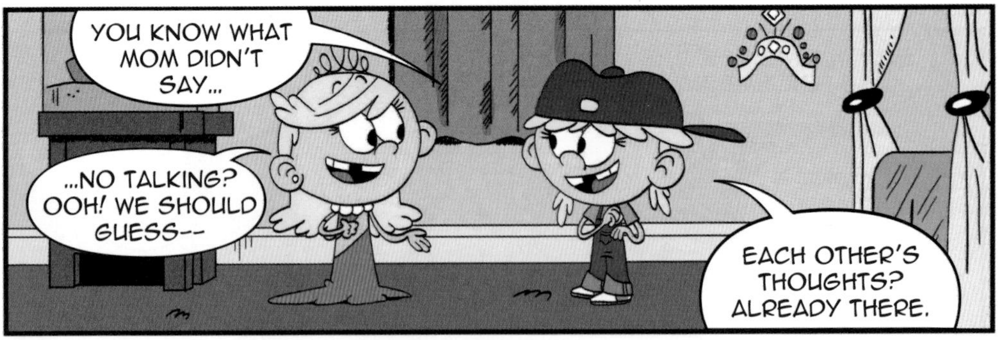
YOU KNOW WHAT MOM DIDN'T SAY...
...NO TALKING? OOH! WE SHOULD GUESS--
EACH OTHER'S THOUGHTS? ALREADY THERE.

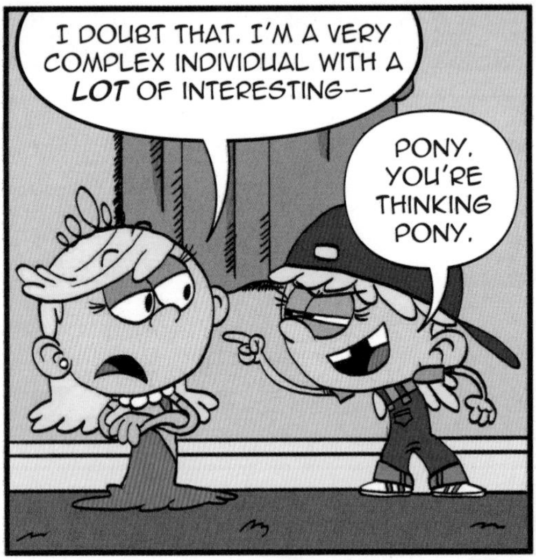
I DOUBT THAT. I'M A VERY COMPLEX INDIVIDUAL WITH A *LOT* OF INTERESTING--
PONY. YOU'RE THINKING PONY.

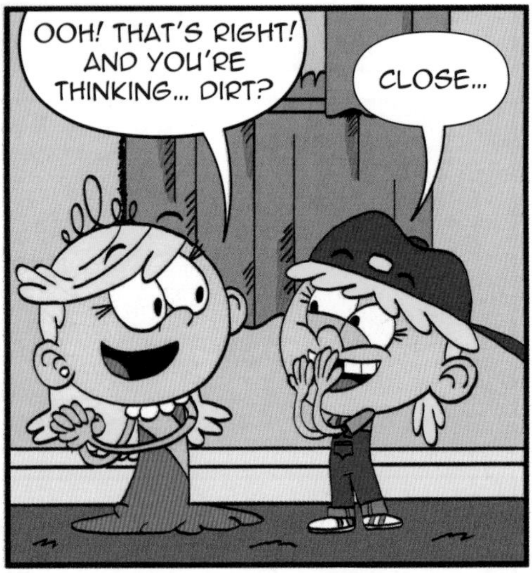
OOH! THAT'S RIGHT! AND YOU'RE THINKING... DIRT?
CLOSE...

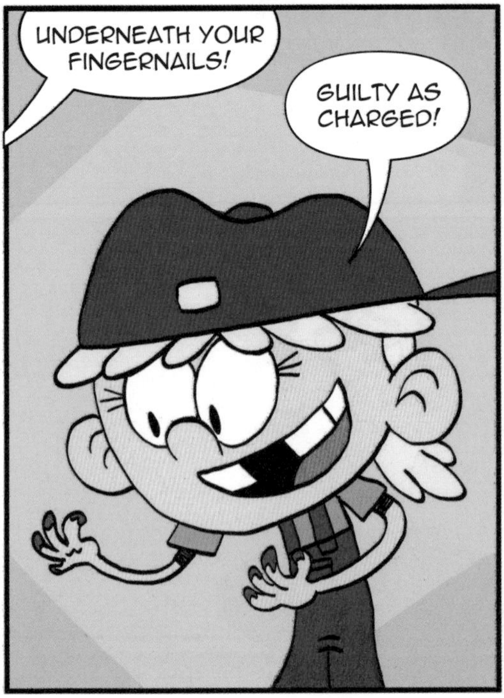
UNDERNEATH YOUR FINGERNAILS!
GUILTY AS CHARGED!

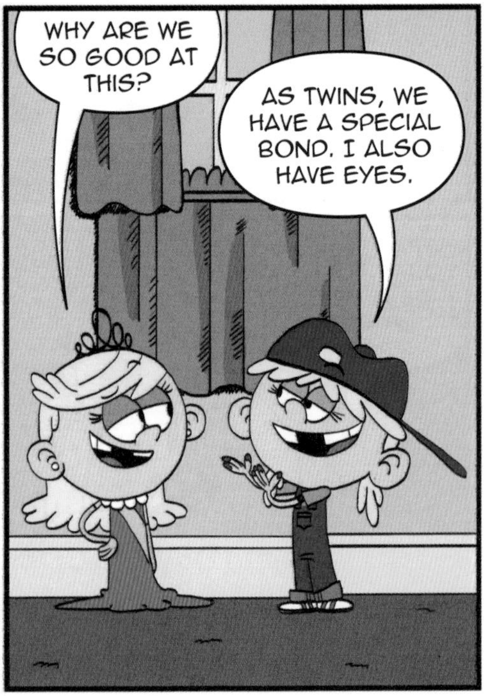
WHY ARE WE SO GOOD AT THIS?
AS TWINS, WE HAVE A SPECIAL BOND. I ALSO HAVE EYES.

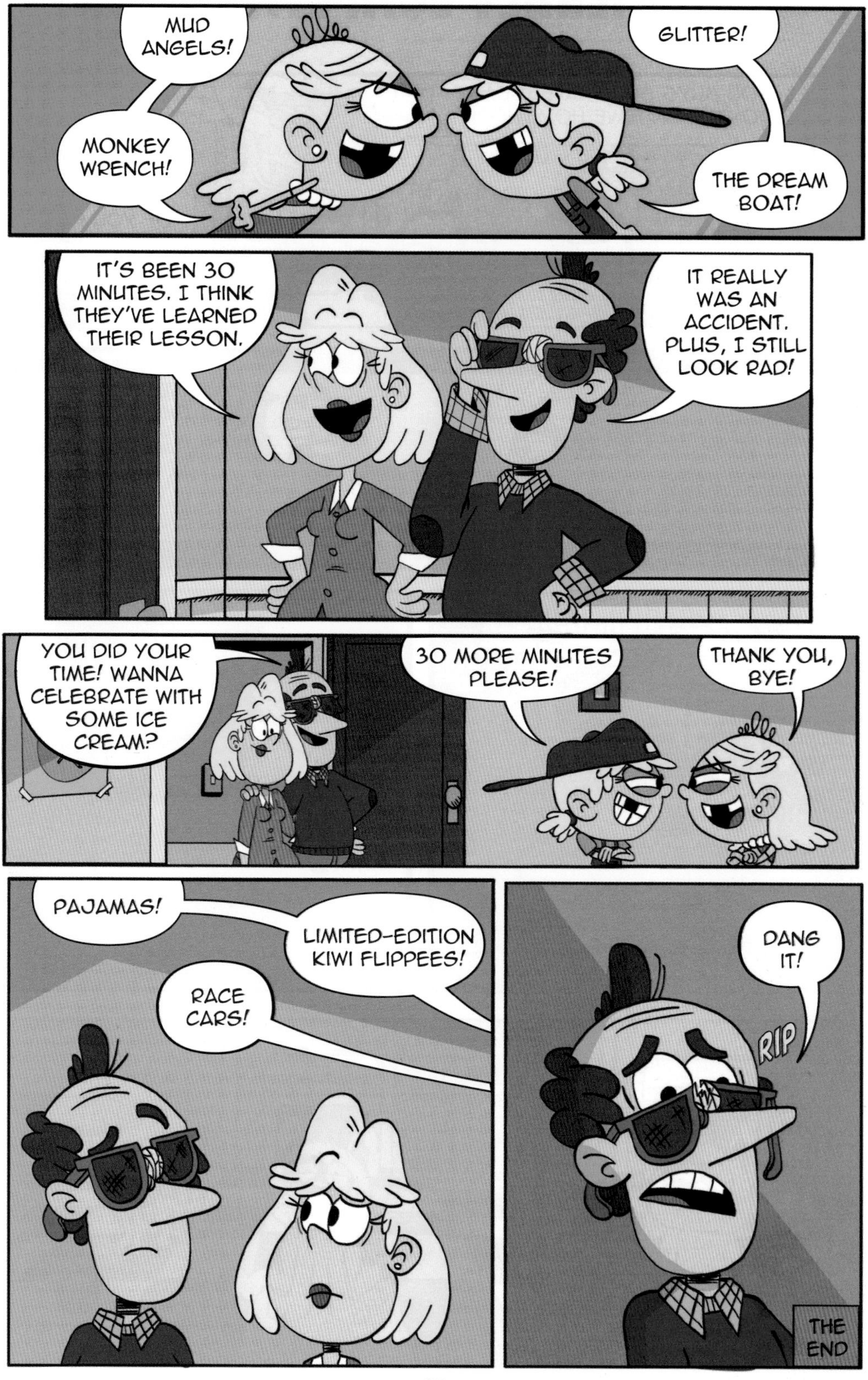
MUD ANGELS!
GLITTER!
MONKEY WRENCH!
THE DREAM BOAT!
IT'S BEEN 30 MINUTES. I THINK THEY'VE LEARNED THEIR LESSON.
IT REALLY WAS AN ACCIDENT. PLUS, I STILL LOOK RAD!
YOU DID YOUR TIME! WANNA CELEBRATE WITH SOME ICE CREAM?
30 MORE MINUTES PLEASE!
THANK YOU, BYE!
PAJAMAS!
LIMITED-EDITION KIWI FLIPPEES!
RACE CARS!
DANG IT!
RIP
THE END

"FURIENDLY COMPETITION"

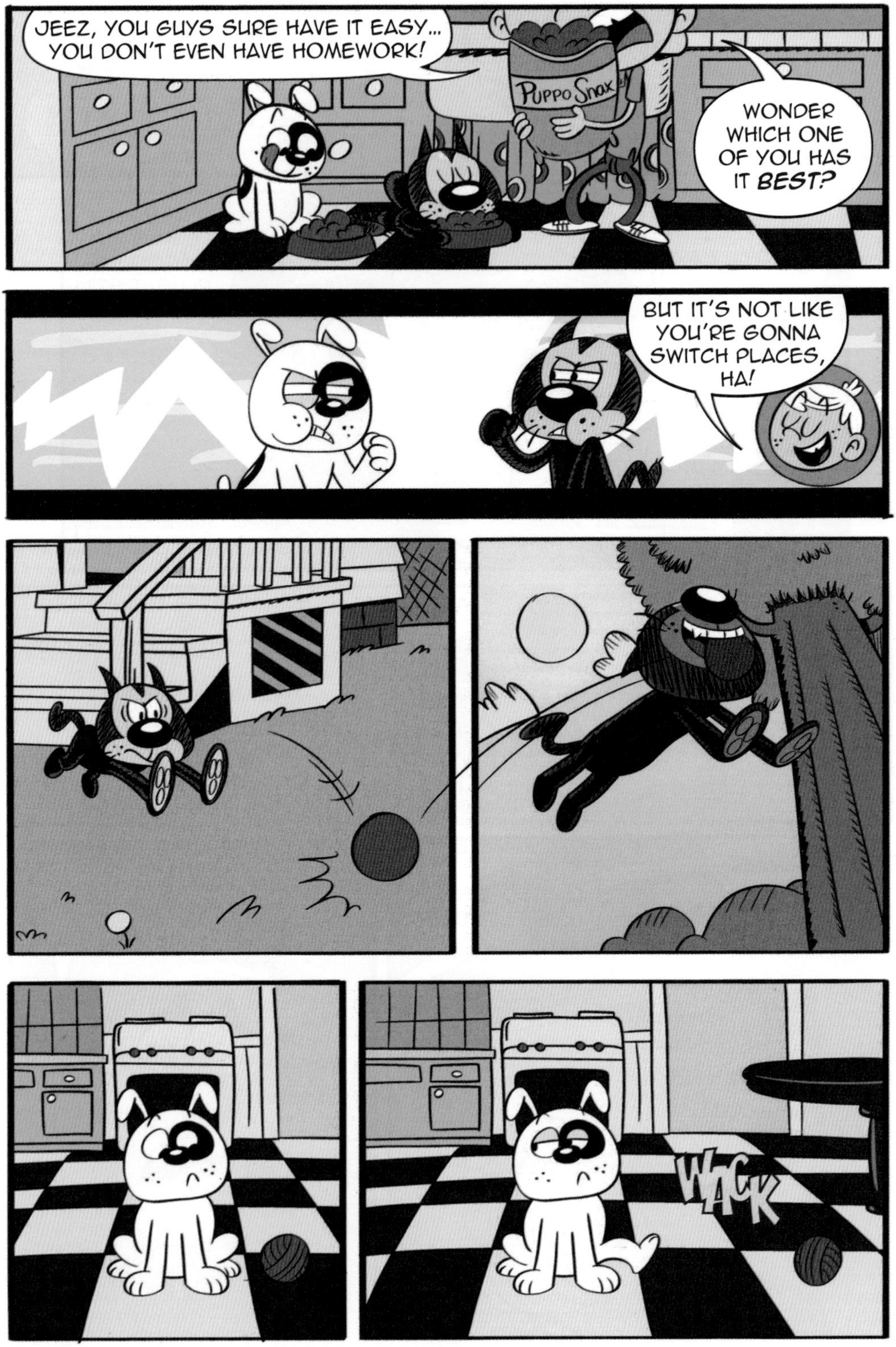

JEEZ, YOU GUYS SURE HAVE IT EASY... YOU DON'T EVEN HAVE HOMEWORK!
Puppo Snax
WONDER WHICH ONE OF YOU HAS IT *BEST?*
BUT IT'S NOT LIKE YOU'RE GONNA SWITCH PLACES, HA!
WACK

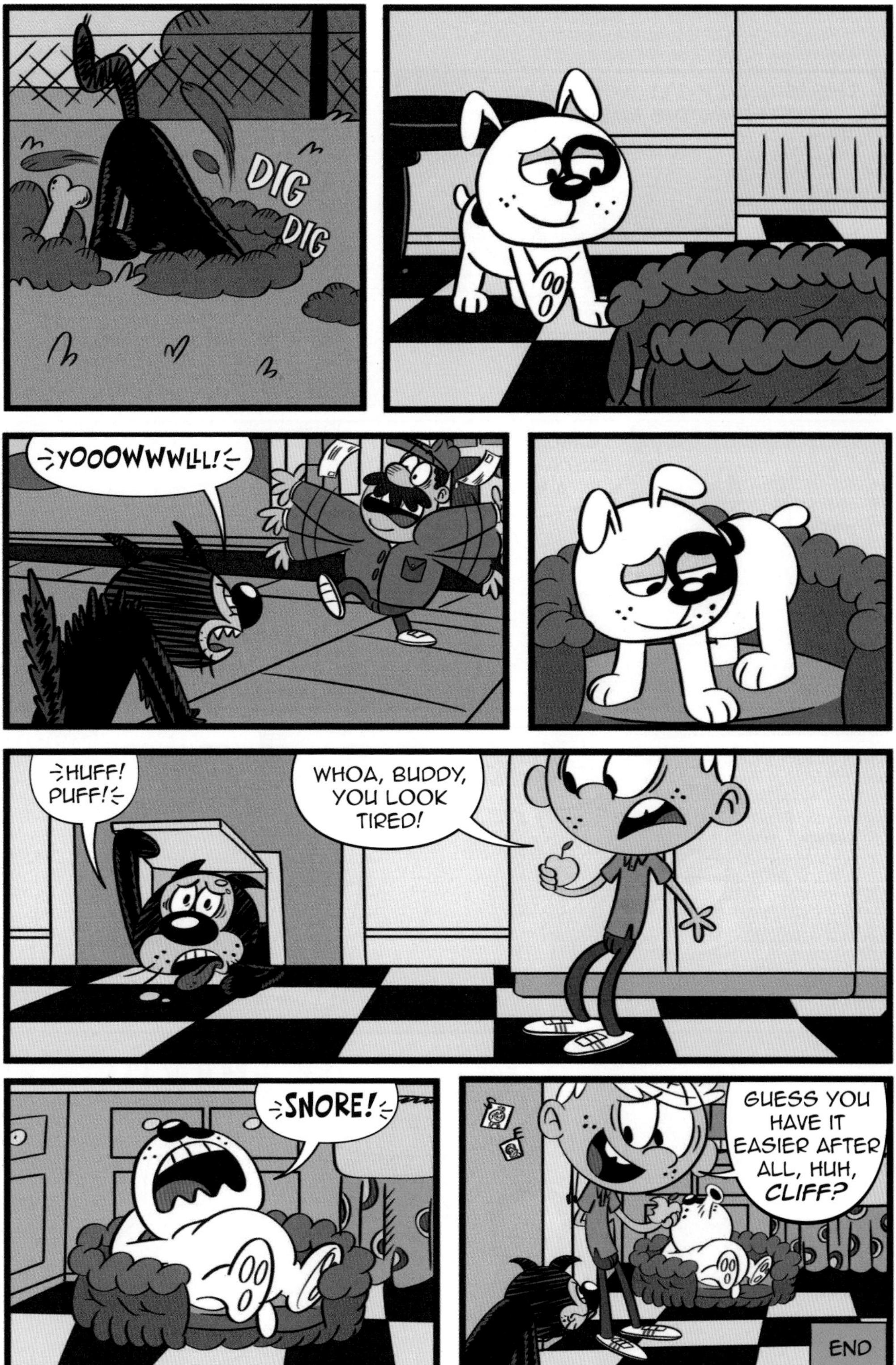
DIG
DIG
YOOOWWWLLL!
HUFF! PUFF!
WHOA, BUDDY, YOU LOOK TIRED!
SNORE!
GUESS YOU HAVE IT EASIER AFTER ALL, HUH, CLIFF?
END

"BUGGIN' OUT"

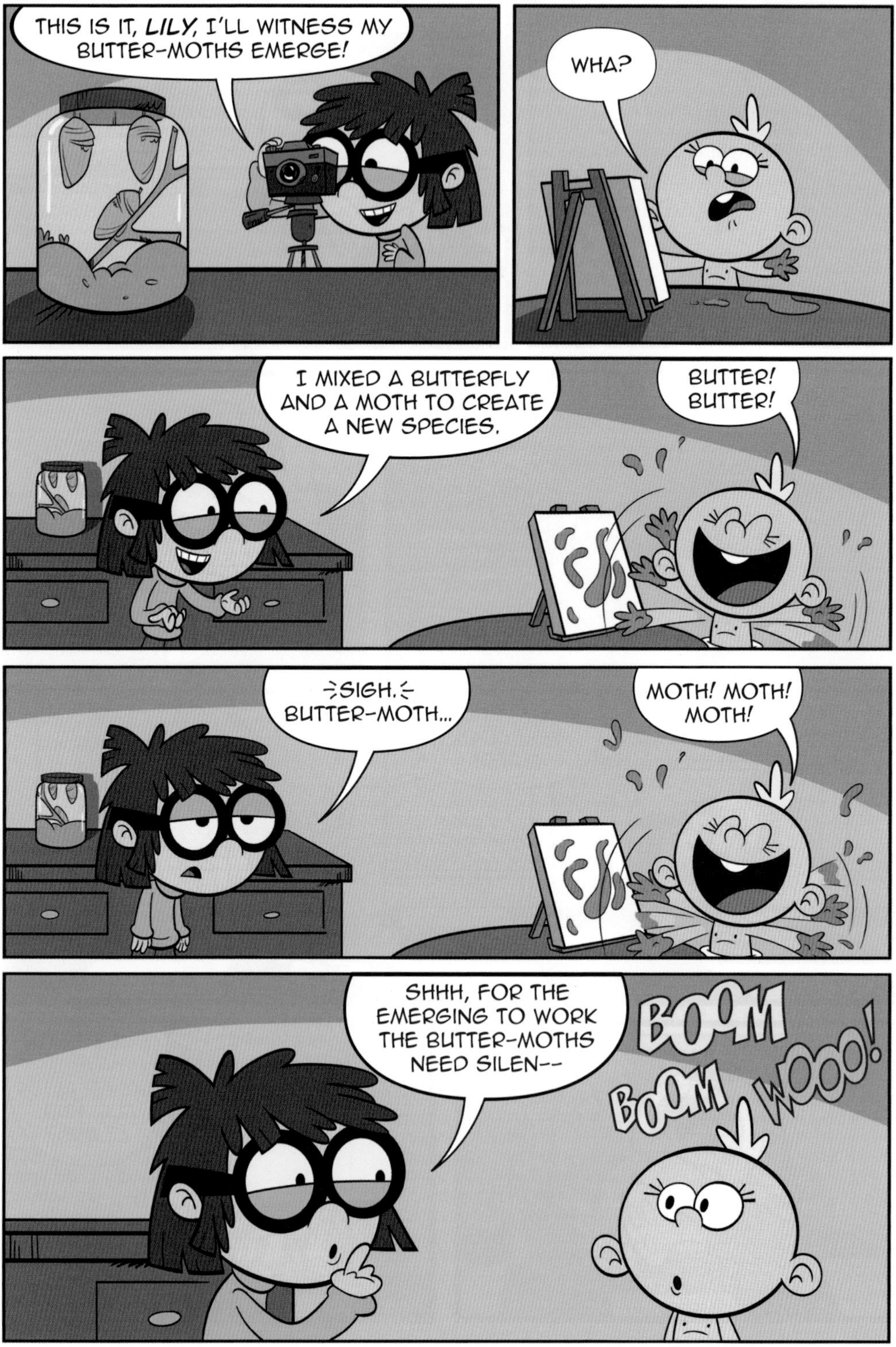
THIS IS IT, *LILY,* I'LL WITNESS MY BUTTER-MOTHS EMERGE!
WHA?
I MIXED A BUTTERFLY AND A MOTH TO CREATE A NEW SPECIES.
BUTTER! BUTTER!
SIGH. BUTTER-MOTH...
MOTH! MOTH! MOTH!
SHHH, FOR THE EMERGING TO WORK THE BUTTER-MOTHS NEED SILEN--
BOOM
BOOM
WOOO!

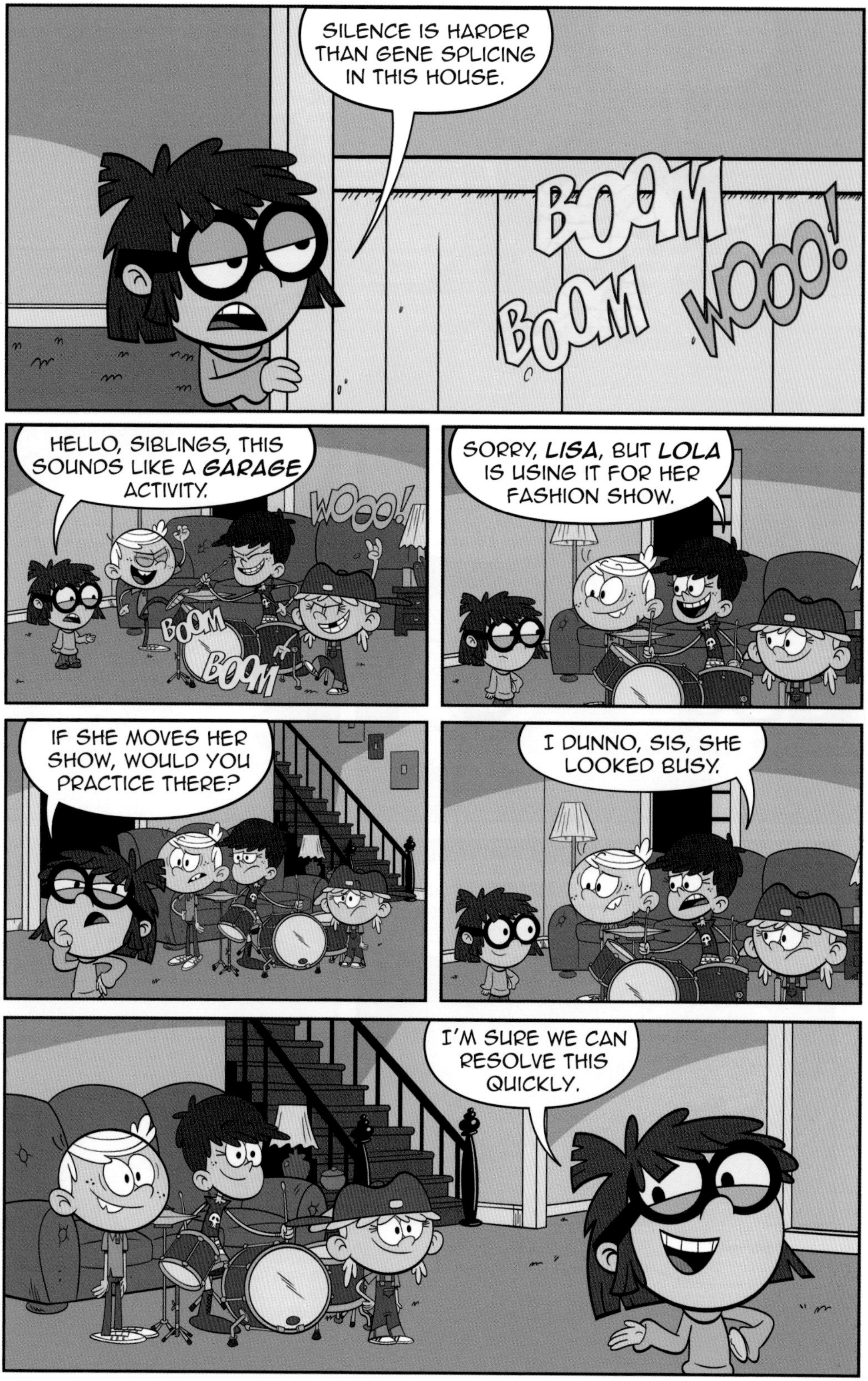
SILENCE IS HARDER THAN GENE SPLICING IN THIS HOUSE.
BOOM
BOOM
WOOO!
HELLO, SIBLINGS, THIS SOUNDS LIKE A **GARAGE** ACTIVITY.
WOOO!
BOOM
BOOM
SORRY, **LISA**, BUT **LOLA** IS USING IT FOR HER FASHION SHOW.
IF SHE MOVES HER SHOW, WOULD YOU PRACTICE THERE?
I DUNNO, SIS, SHE LOOKED BUSY.
I'M SURE WE CAN RESOLVE THIS QUICKLY.

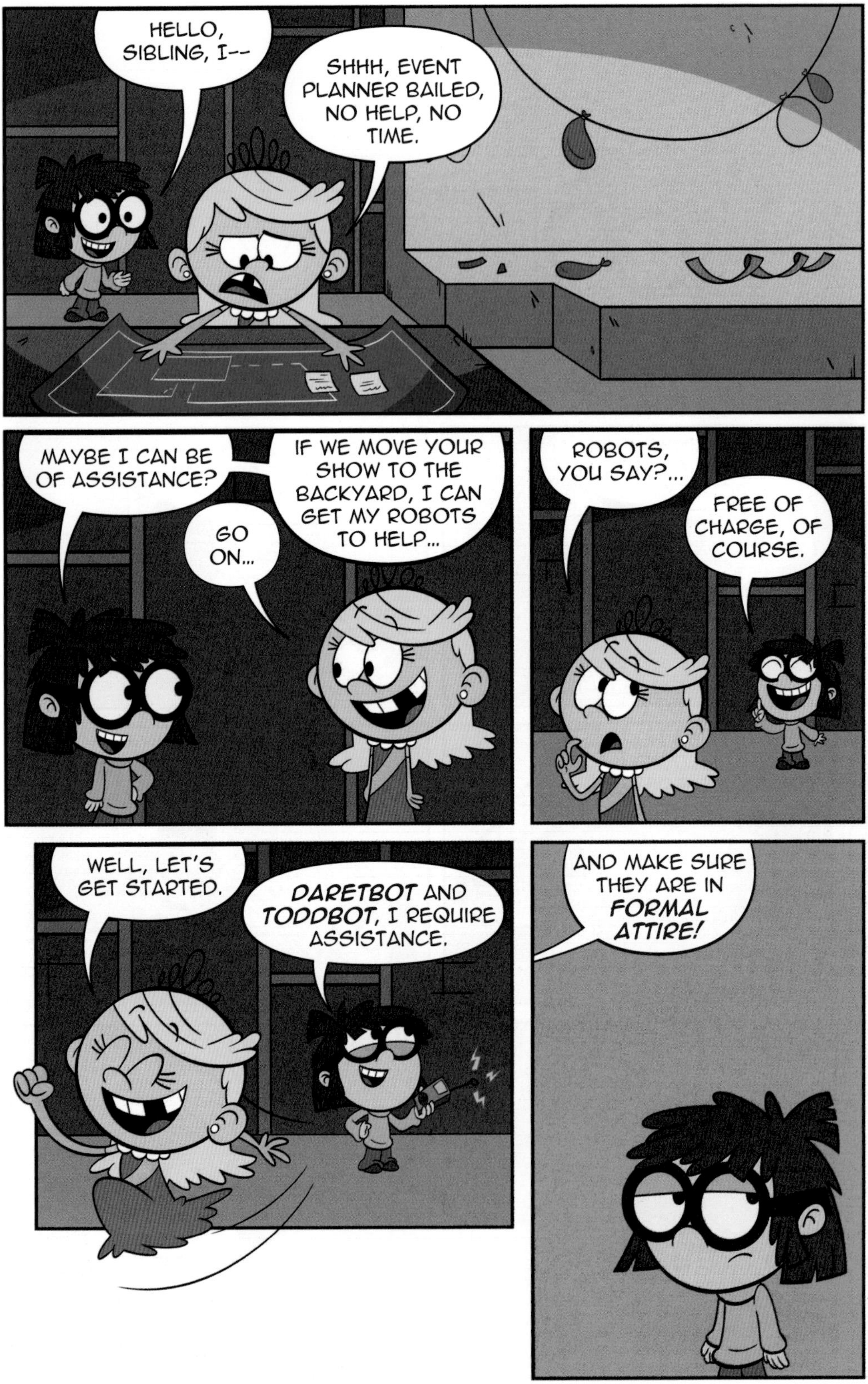
HELLO, SIBLING, I--
SHHH, EVENT PLANNER BAILED, NO HELP, NO TIME.
MAYBE I CAN BE OF ASSISTANCE?
IF WE MOVE YOUR SHOW TO THE BACKYARD, I CAN GET MY ROBOTS TO HELP...
GO ON...
ROBOTS, YOU SAY?...
FREE OF CHARGE, OF COURSE.
WELL, LET'S GET STARTED.
DARETBOT AND TODDBOT, I REQUIRE ASSISTANCE.
AND MAKE SURE THEY ARE IN FORMAL ATTIRE!

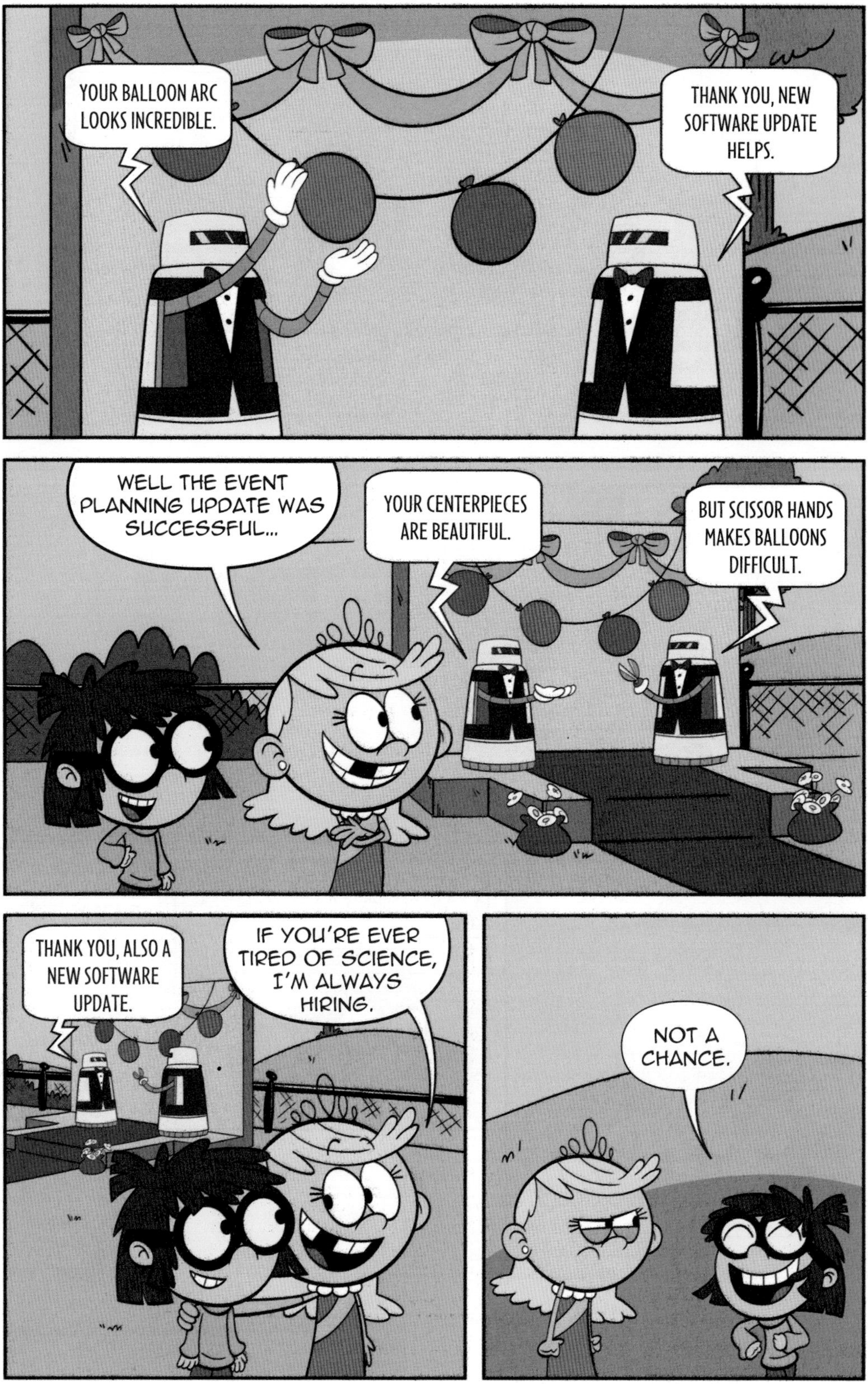
YOUR BALLOON ARC LOOKS INCREDIBLE.
THANK YOU, NEW SOFTWARE UPDATE HELPS.
WELL THE EVENT PLANNING UPDATE WAS SUCCESSFUL...
YOUR CENTERPIECES ARE BEAUTIFUL.
BUT SCISSOR HANDS MAKES BALLOONS DIFFICULT.
THANK YOU, ALSO A NEW SOFTWARE UPDATE.
IF YOU'RE EVER TIRED OF SCIENCE, I'M ALWAYS HIRING.
NOT A CHANCE.

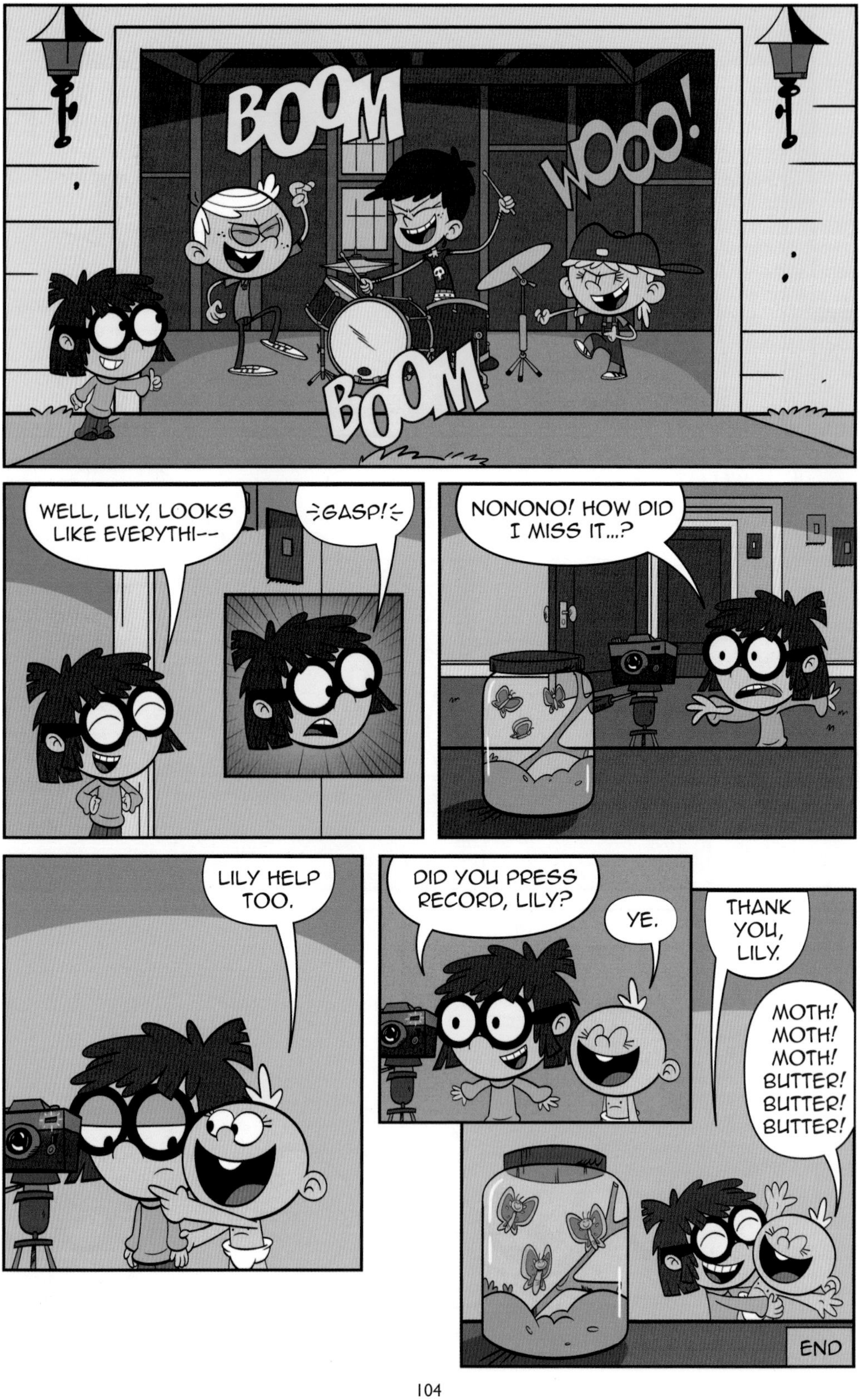
BOOM
WOOO!
BOOM
WELL, LILY, LOOKS LIKE EVERYTHI--
GASP!
NONONO! HOW DID I MISS IT...?
LILY HELP TOO.
DID YOU PRESS RECORD, LILY?
YE.
THANK YOU, LILY.
MOTH! MOTH! MOTH! BUTTER! BUTTER! BUTTER!
END

"SALE FAIL"

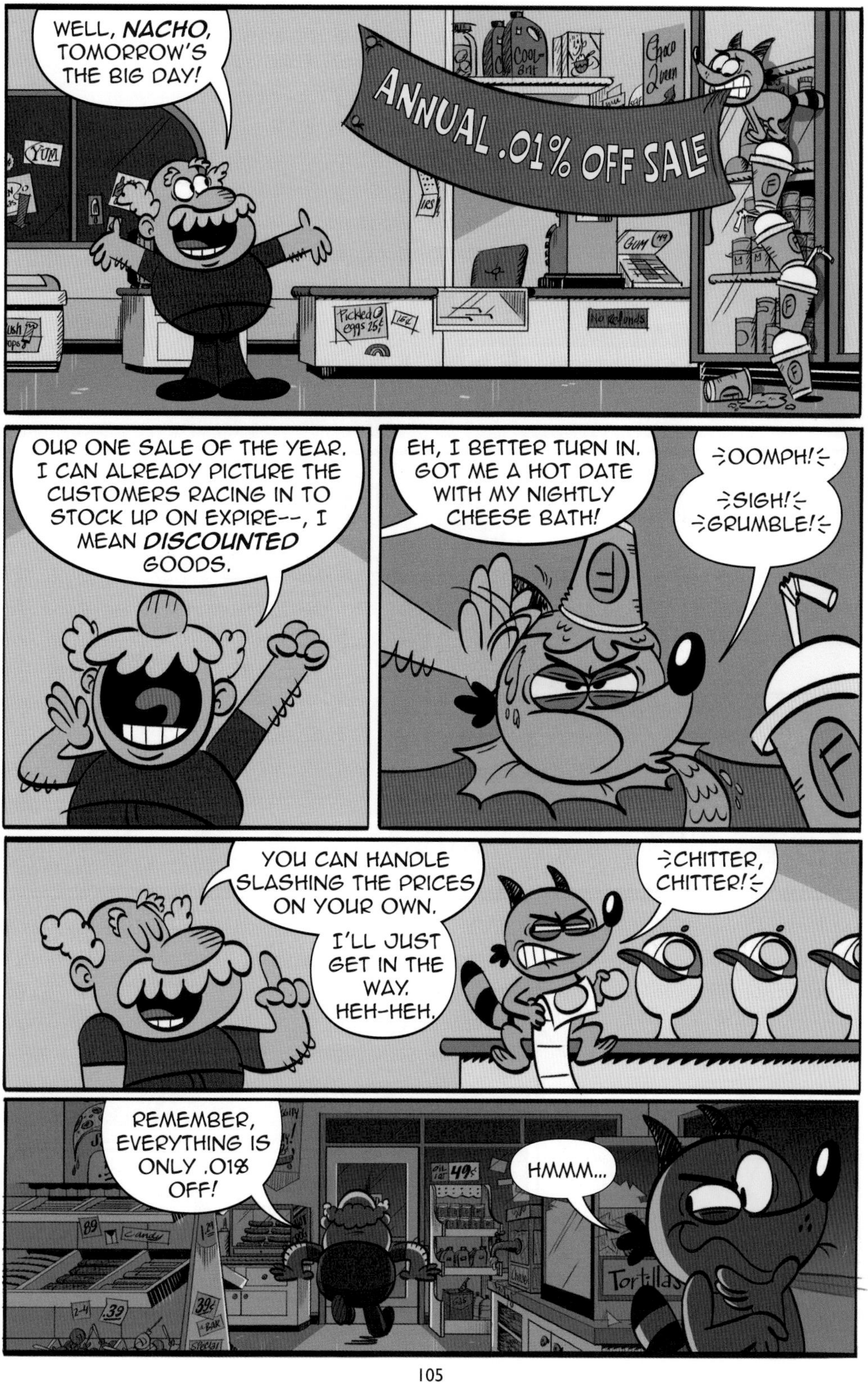

WELL, NACHO, TOMORROW'S THE BIG DAY!
ANNUAL .01% OFF SALE
OUR ONE SALE OF THE YEAR. I CAN ALREADY PICTURE THE CUSTOMERS RACING IN TO STOCK UP ON EXPIRE--, I MEAN DISCOUNTED GOODS.
EH, I BETTER TURN IN. GOT ME A HOT DATE WITH MY NIGHTLY CHEESE BATH!
OOMPH!
SIGH!
GRUMBLE!
YOU CAN HANDLE SLASHING THE PRICES ON YOUR OWN.
I'LL JUST GET IN THE WAY. HEH-HEH.
CHITTER, CHITTER!
REMEMBER, EVERYTHING IS ONLY .01% OFF!
HMMM...
Tortillas

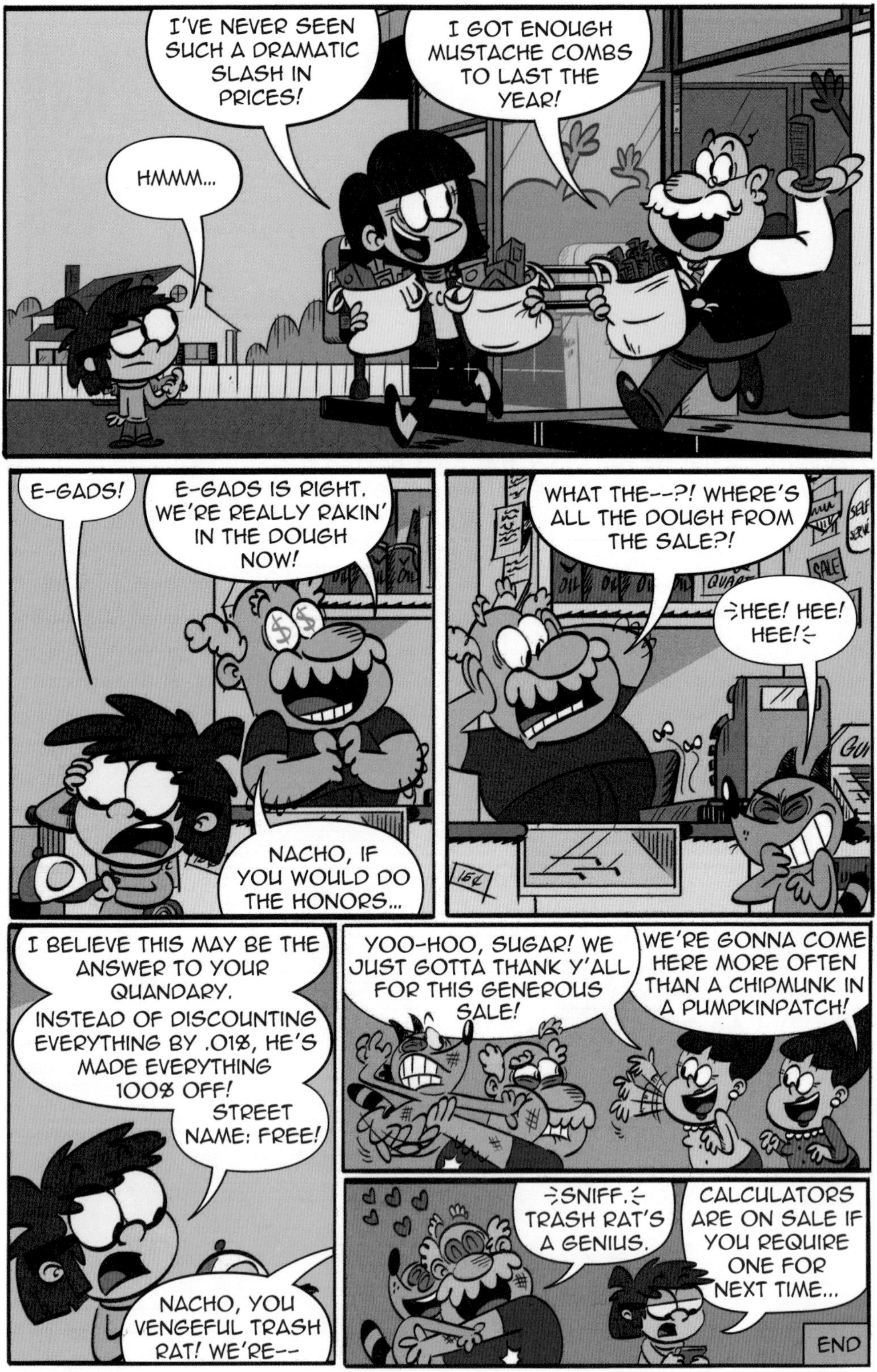
I'VE NEVER SEEN SUCH A DRAMATIC SLASH IN PRICES!
I GOT ENOUGH MUSTACHE COMBS TO LAST THE YEAR!
HMMM...
E-GADS!
E-GADS IS RIGHT. WE'RE REALLY RAKIN' IN THE DOUGH NOW!
NACHO, IF YOU WOULD DO THE HONORS...
WHAT THE--?! WHERE'S ALL THE DOUGH FROM THE SALE?!
HEE! HEE! HEE!
I BELIEVE THIS MAY BE THE ANSWER TO YOUR QUANDARY.
INSTEAD OF DISCOUNTING EVERYTHING BY .01%, HE'S MADE EVERYTHING 100% OFF!
STREET NAME: FREE!
NACHO, YOU VENGEFUL TRASH RAT! WE'RE--
YOO-HOO, SUGAR! WE JUST GOTTA THANK Y'ALL FOR THIS GENEROUS SALE!
WE'RE GONNA COME HERE MORE OFTEN THAN A CHIPMUNK IN A PUMPKINPATCH!
SNIFF. TRASH RAT'S A GENIUS.
CALCULATORS ARE ON SALE IF YOU REQUIRE ONE FOR NEXT TIME...
END

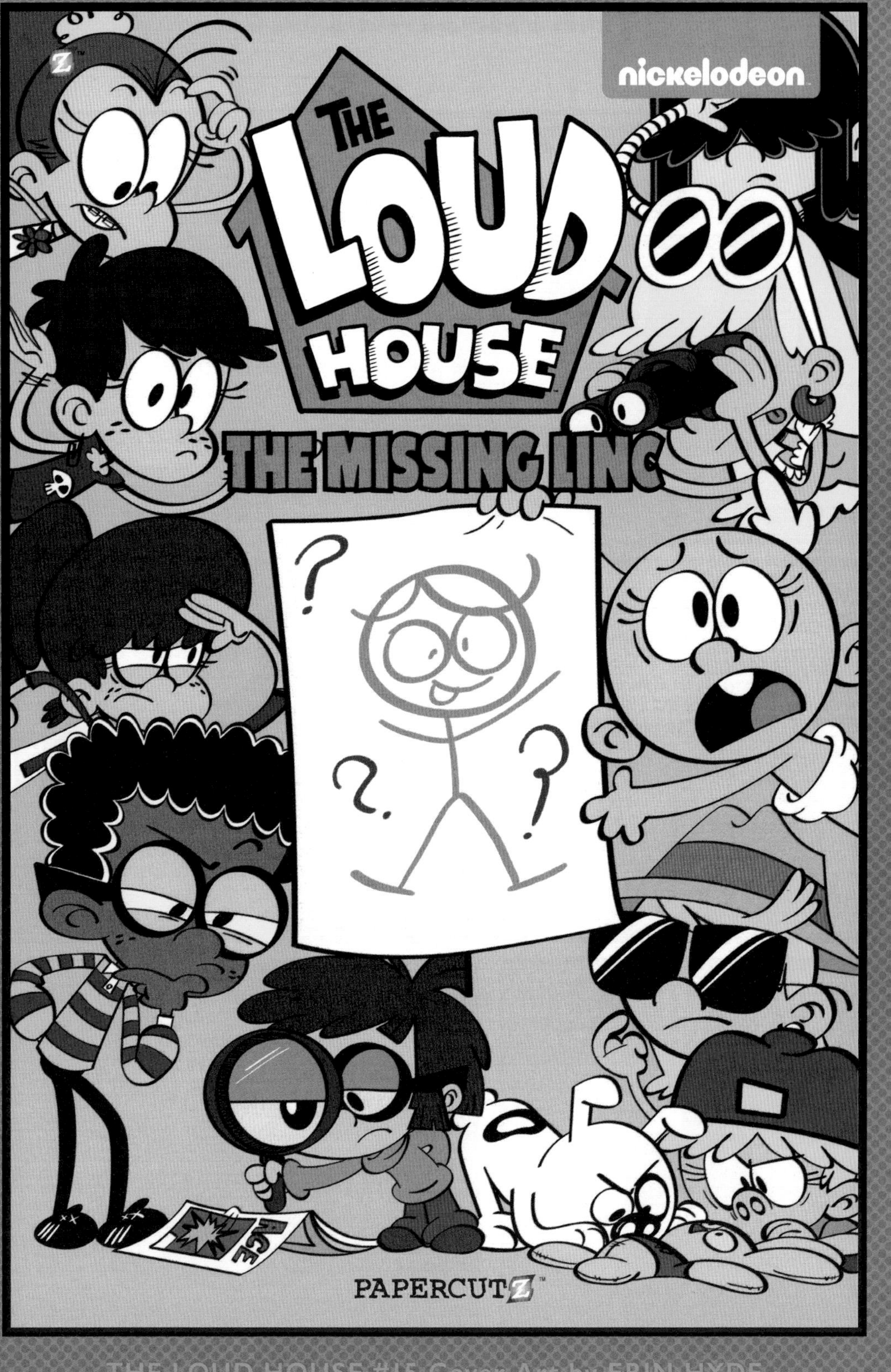
nickelodeon
THE LOUD HOUSE
THE MISSING LINC
PAPERCUTZ

THE LOUD HOUSE #15 Cover Art by ERIN HYDE

"THE MISSING LINC"

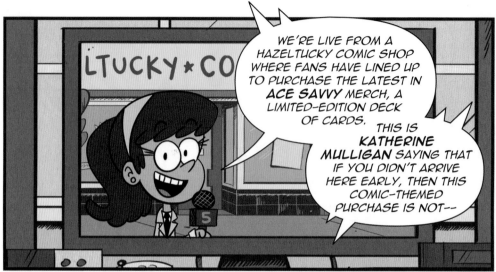

WE'RE LIVE FROM A HAZELTUCKY COMIC SHOP WHERE FANS HAVE LINED UP TO PURCHASE THE LATEST IN **ACE SAVVY** MERCH, A LIMITED-EDITION DECK OF CARDS.

THIS IS **KATHERINE MULLIGAN** SAYING THAT IF YOU DIDN'T ARRIVE HERE EARLY, THEN THIS COMIC-THEMED PURCHASE IS NOT--

--IN THE CARDS.

HEY! SHE HAS A DECK OF CARDS. GET HER!

⇒OOF⇐ MULLIGAN OUT!

YO, STINKIN'! THE NEWS IS COVERING JUNK YOU LIKE!

LINCOLN! GET OVER HERE!

HUH. HE MUST NOT BE HOME.

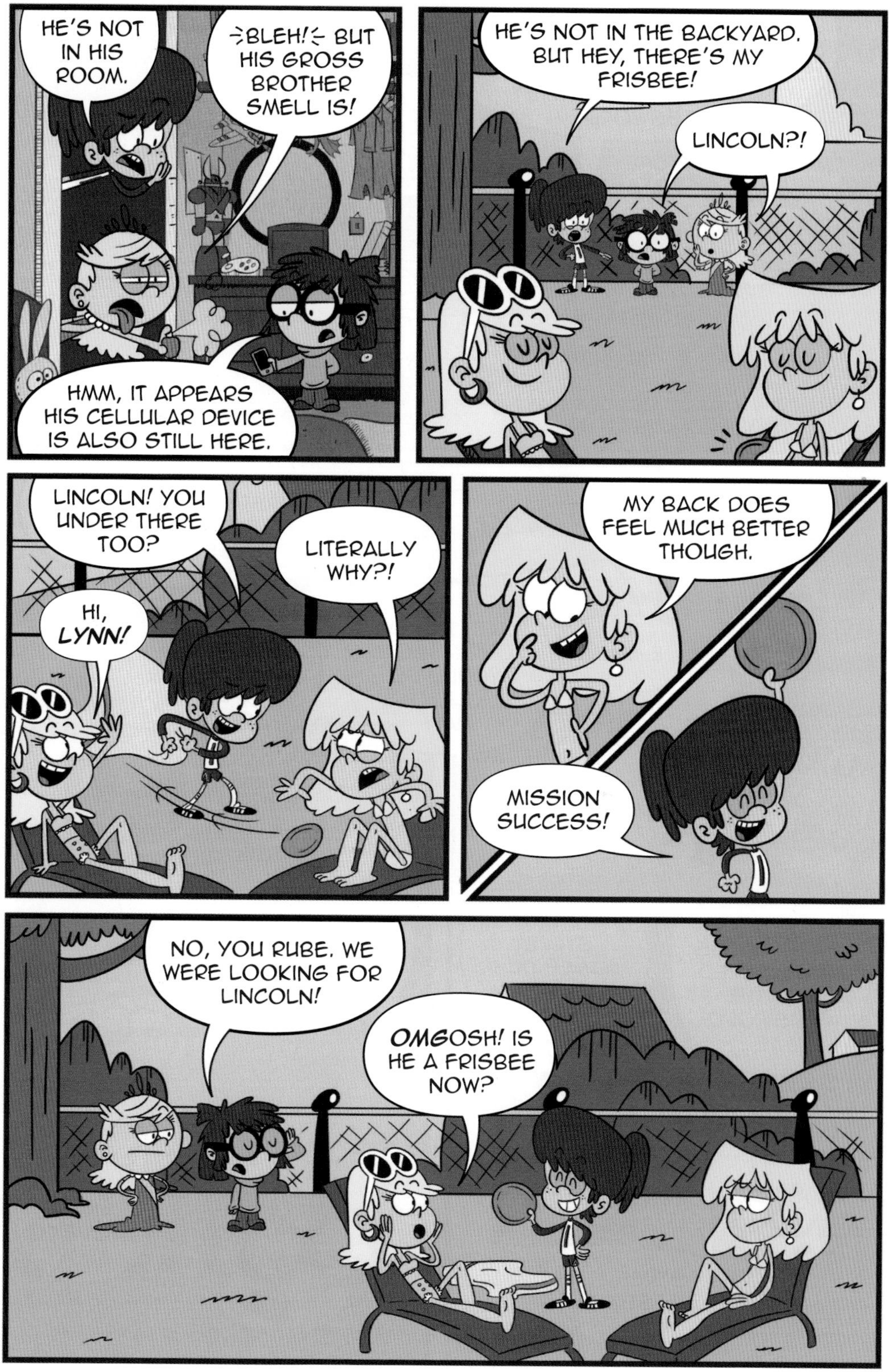
HE'S NOT IN HIS ROOM.
BLEH! BUT HIS GROSS BROTHER SMELL IS!
HMM, IT APPEARS HIS CELLULAR DEVICE IS ALSO STILL HERE.
HE'S NOT IN THE BACKYARD. BUT HEY, THERE'S MY FRISBEE!
LINCOLN?!
LINCOLN! YOU UNDER THERE TOO?
LITERALLY WHY?!
HI, LYNN!
MY BACK DOES FEEL MUCH BETTER THOUGH.
MISSION SUCCESS!
NO, YOU RUBE. WE WERE LOOKING FOR LINCOLN!
OMGOSH! IS HE A FRISBEE NOW?

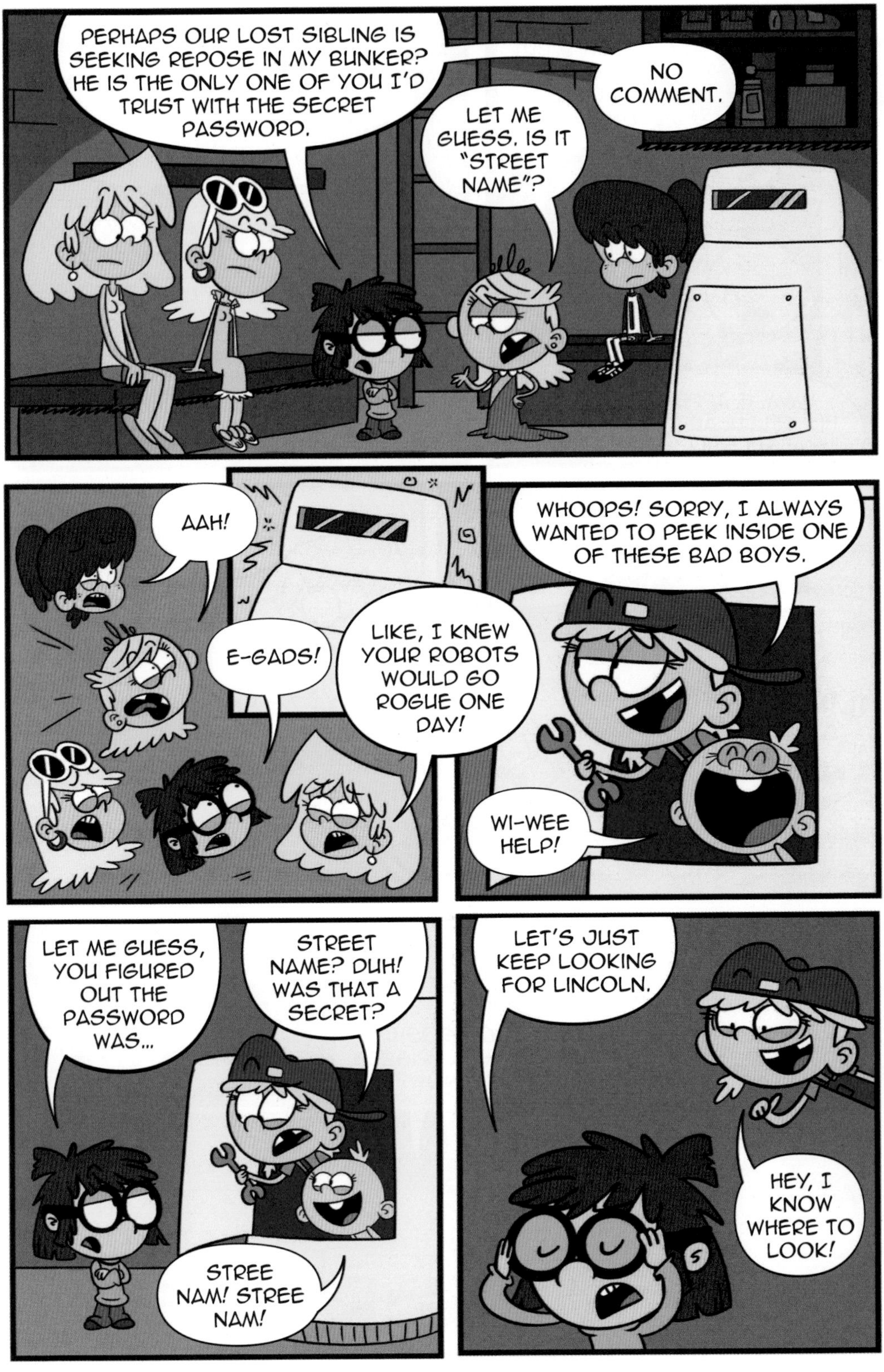
PERHAPS OUR LOST SIBLING IS SEEKING REPOSE IN MY BUNKER? HE IS THE ONLY ONE OF YOU I'D TRUST WITH THE SECRET PASSWORD.
NO COMMENT.
LET ME GUESS. IS IT "STREET NAME"?
AAH!
E-GADS!
LIKE, I KNEW YOUR ROBOTS WOULD GO ROGUE ONE DAY!
WHOOPS! SORRY, I ALWAYS WANTED TO PEEK INSIDE ONE OF THESE BAD BOYS.
WI-WEE HELP!
LET ME GUESS, YOU FIGURED OUT THE PASSWORD WAS...
STREET NAME? DUH! WAS THAT A SECRET?
STREE NAM! STREE NAM!
LET'S JUST KEEP LOOKING FOR LINCOLN.
HEY, I KNOW WHERE TO LOOK!

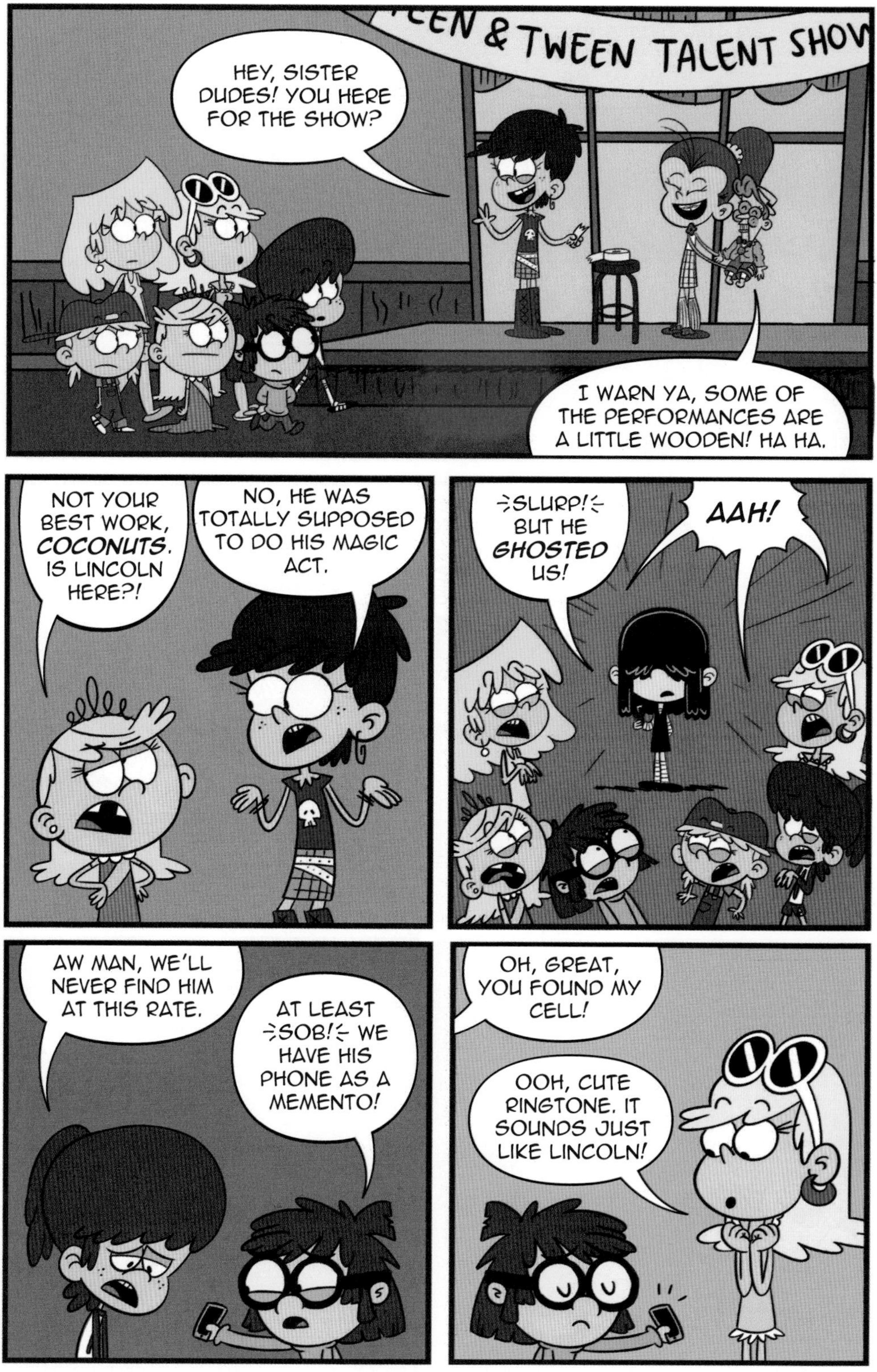
EEN & TWEEN TALENT SHOW
HEY, SISTER DUDES! YOU HERE FOR THE SHOW?
I WARN YA, SOME OF THE PERFORMANCES ARE A LITTLE WOODEN! HA HA.
NOT YOUR BEST WORK, COCONUTS. IS LINCOLN HERE?!
NO, HE WAS TOTALLY SUPPOSED TO DO HIS MAGIC ACT.
SLURP! BUT HE GHOSTED US!
AAH!
AW MAN, WE'LL NEVER FIND HIM AT THIS RATE.
AT LEAST SOB! WE HAVE HIS PHONE AS A MEMENTO!
OH, GREAT, YOU FOUND MY CELL!
OOH, CUTE RINGTONE. IT SOUNDS JUST LIKE LINCOLN!

UM, THAT'S BECAUSE IT IS LINCOLN? I MEAN, ME.

÷GASP!÷

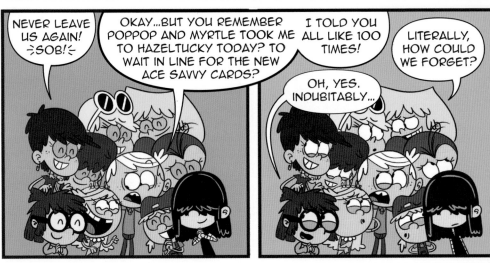

NEVER LEAVE US AGAIN! ÷SOB!÷

OKAY...BUT YOU REMEMBER POPPOP AND MYRTLE TOOK ME TO HAZELTUCKY TODAY? TO WAIT IN LINE FOR THE NEW ACE SAVVY CARDS?

I TOLD YOU ALL LIKE 100 TIMES!

LITERALLY, HOW COULD WE FORGET?

OH, YES. INDUBITABLY...

WELL, WE HAD A SUPER DAY. WE WERE ON TV!

WE SURE WERE! I DO REGRET TACKLING THAT NICE REPORTER LADY THOUGH.

--IN THE CARDS.

HEY! SHE HAS A DECK OF CARDS. GET HER!

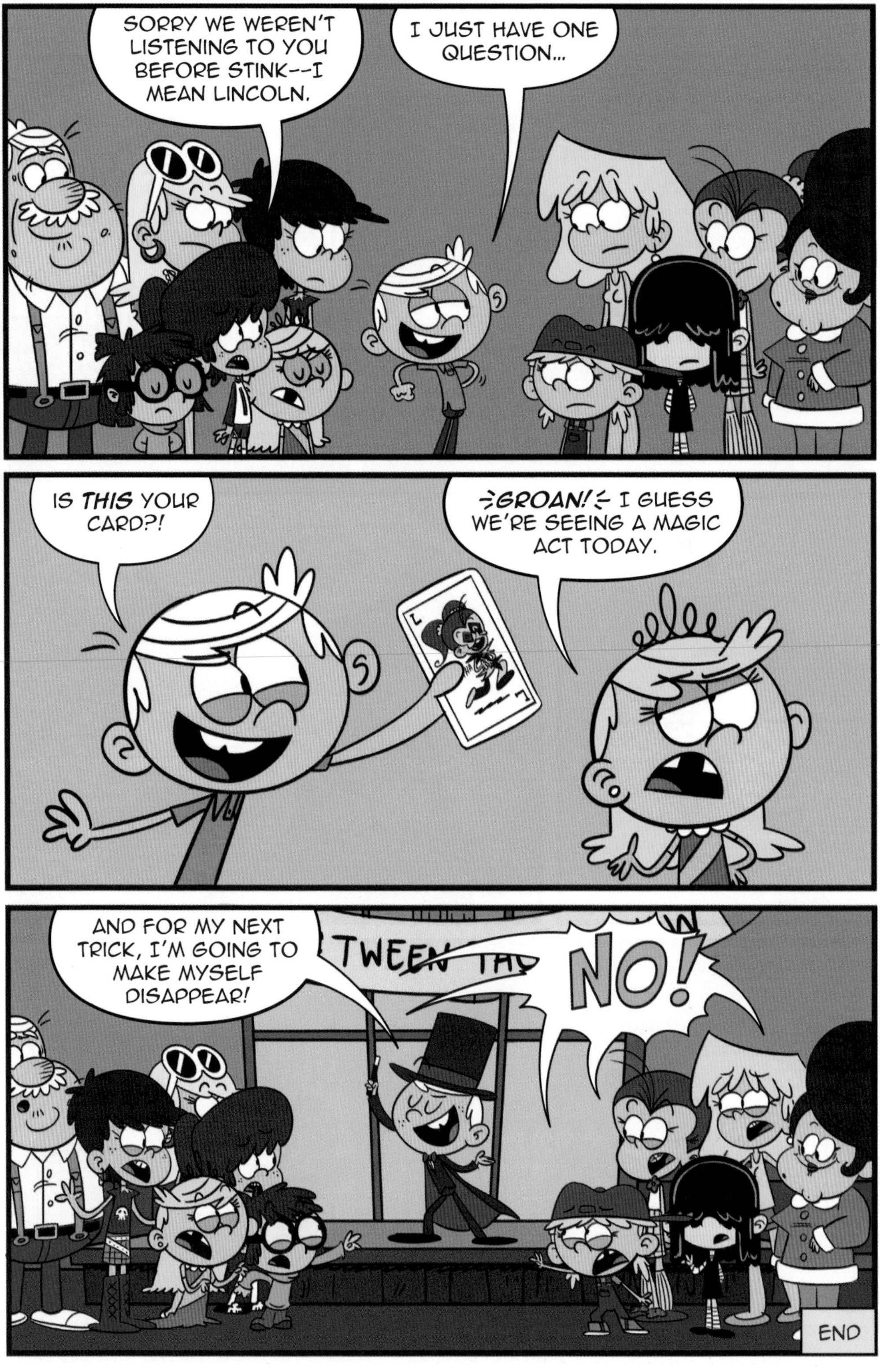
SORRY WE WEREN'T LISTENING TO YOU BEFORE STINK--I MEAN LINCOLN.
I JUST HAVE ONE QUESTION...
IS THIS YOUR CARD?!
GROAN! I GUESS WE'RE SEEING A MAGIC ACT TODAY.
AND FOR MY NEXT TRICK, I'M GOING TO MAKE MYSELF DISAPPEAR!
TWEEN
NO!
END

"I BELIEVE"

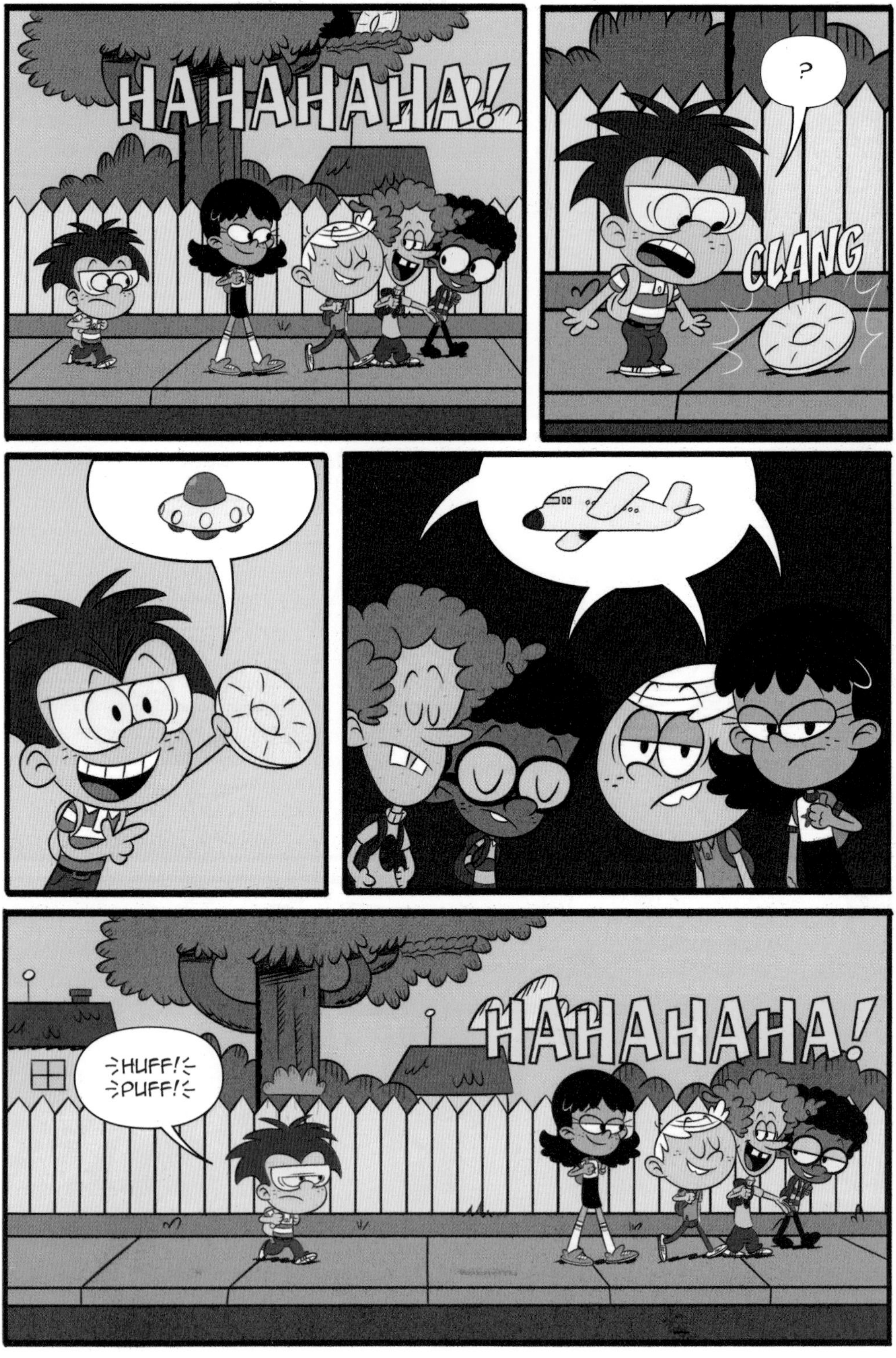
HAHAHAHA!
?
CLANG
HAHAHAHA!
HUFF!
PUFF!

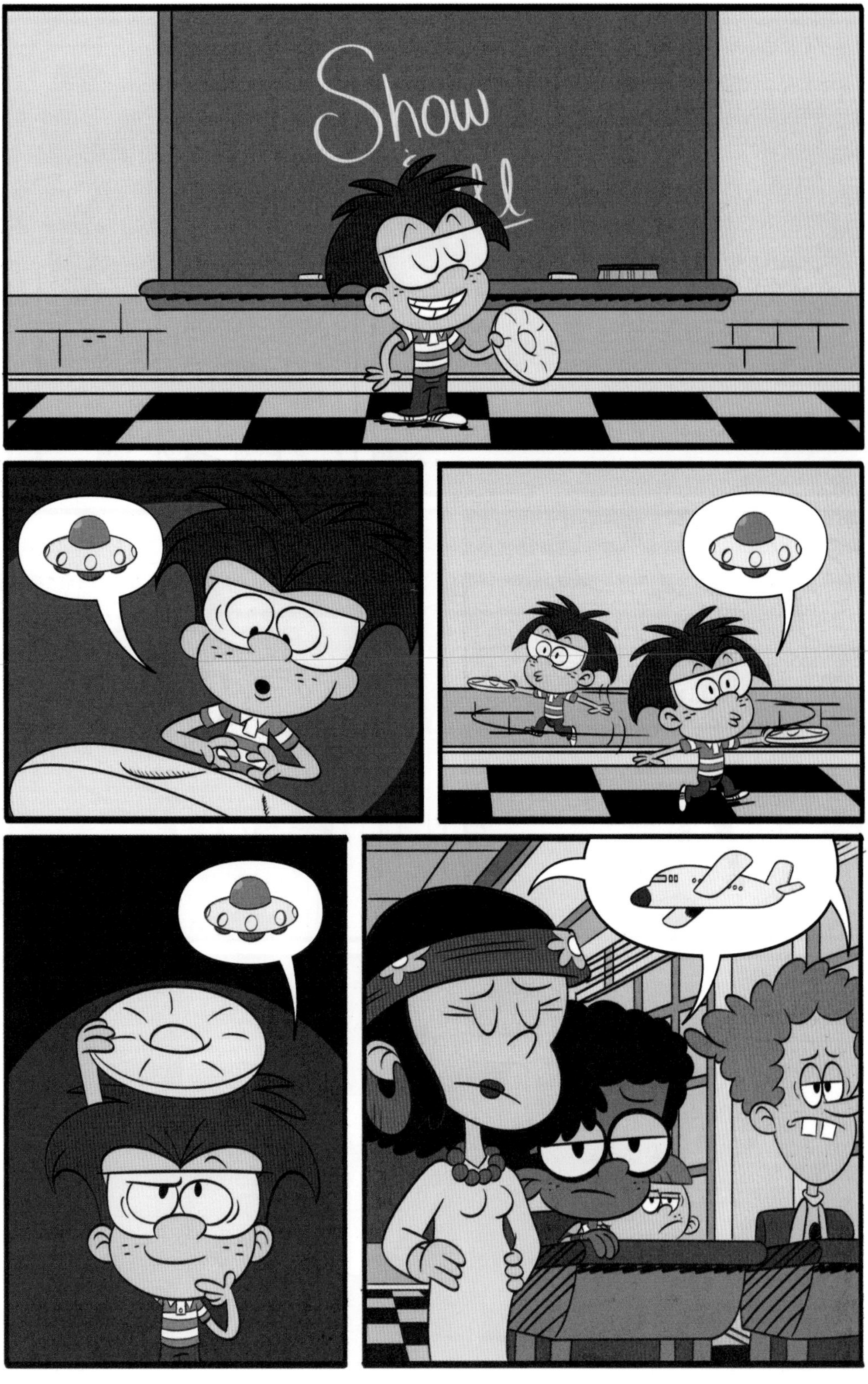
Show

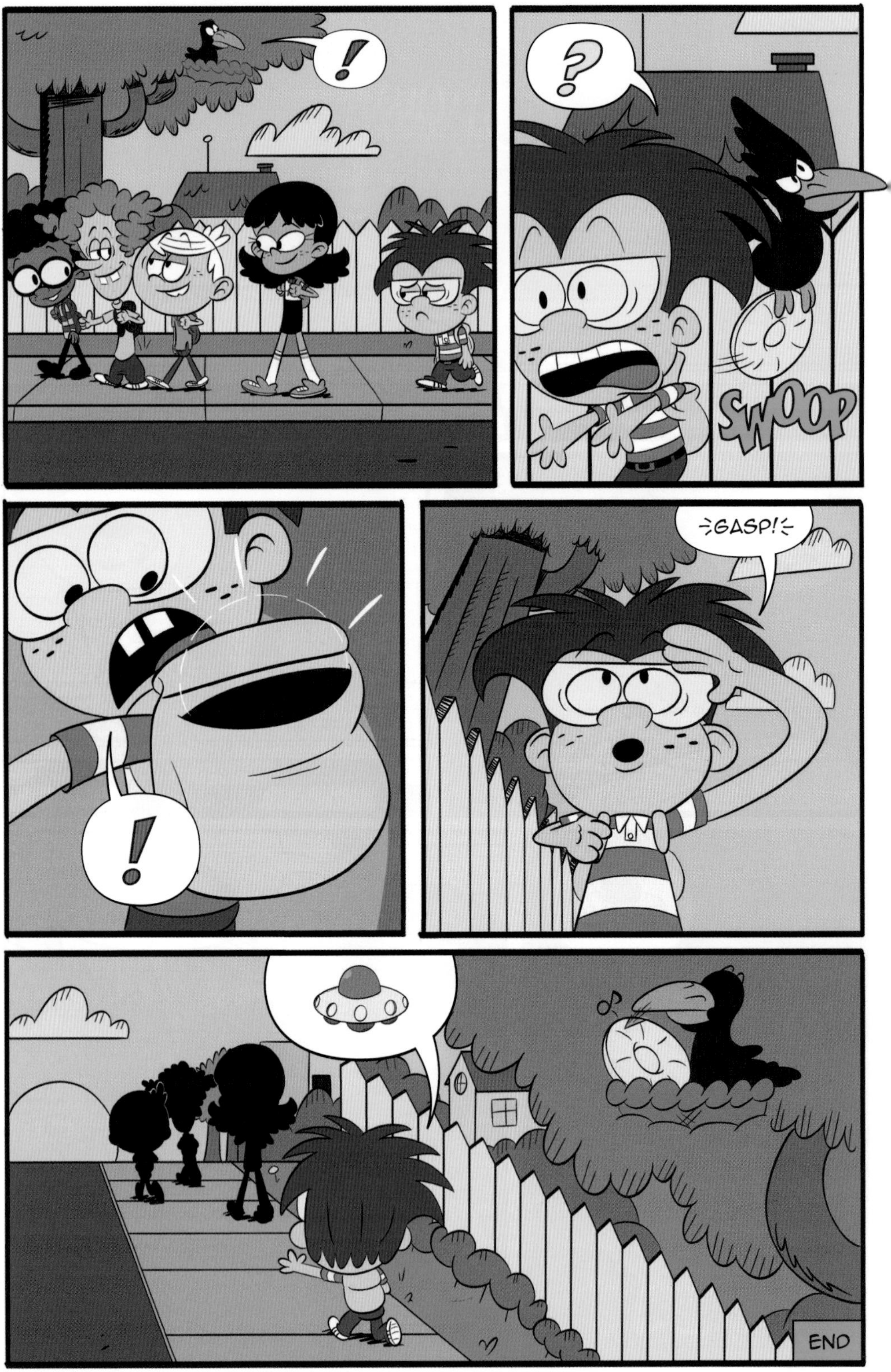
!
?
SWOOP
!
GASP!
END

"AN UNDEAD DEBATE"

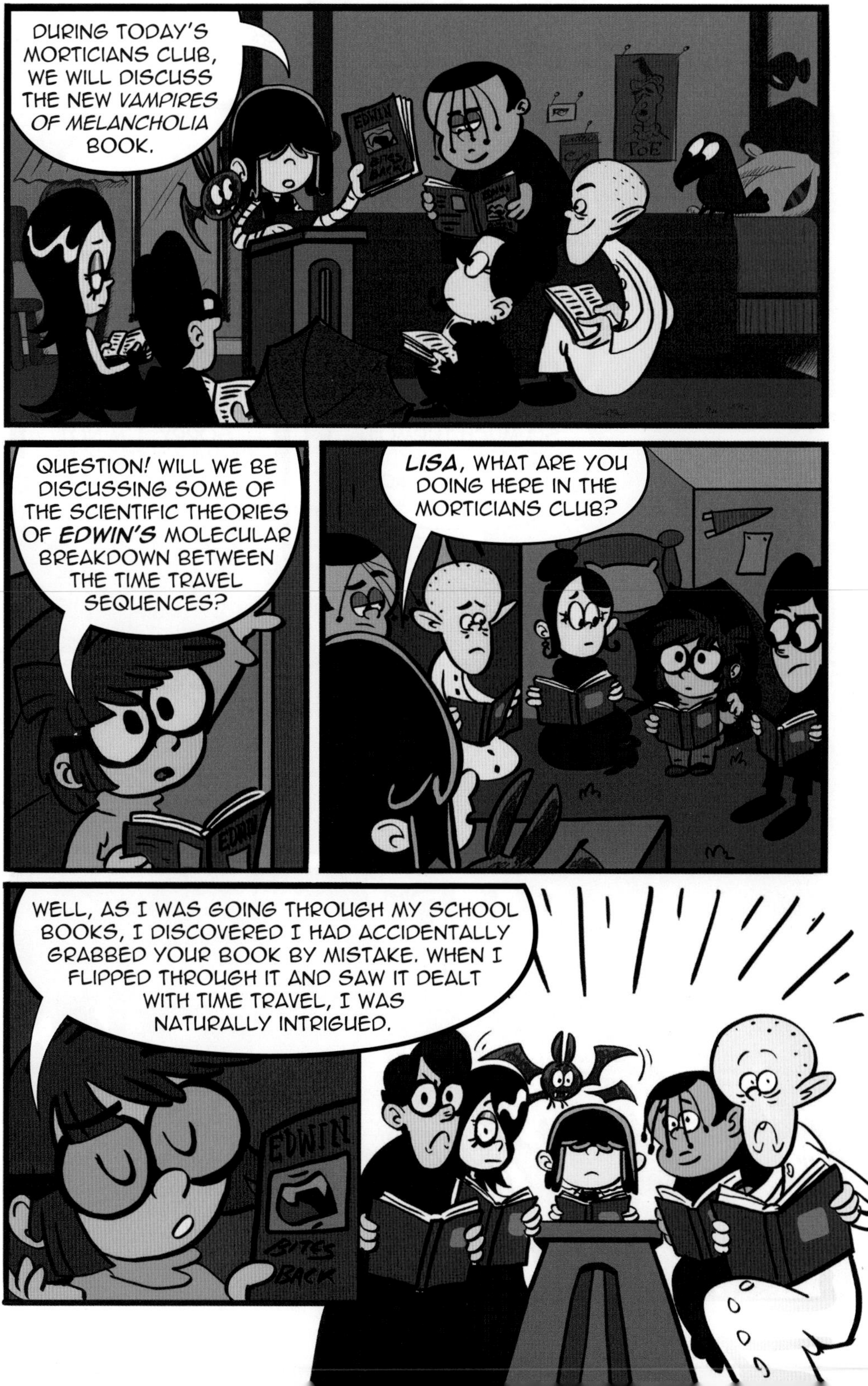
DURING TODAY'S MORTICIANS CLUB, WE WILL DISCUSS THE NEW *VAMPIRES OF MELANCHOLIA* BOOK.
EDWIN
BITES BACK
POE
QUESTION! WILL WE BE DISCUSSING SOME OF THE SCIENTIFIC THEORIES OF ***EDWIN'S*** MOLECULAR BREAKDOWN BETWEEN THE TIME TRAVEL SEQUENCES?
LISA, WHAT ARE YOU DOING HERE IN THE MORTICIANS CLUB?
WELL, AS I WAS GOING THROUGH MY SCHOOL BOOKS, I DISCOVERED I HAD ACCIDENTALLY GRABBED YOUR BOOK BY MISTAKE. WHEN I FLIPPED THROUGH IT AND SAW IT DEALT WITH TIME TRAVEL, I WAS NATURALLY INTRIGUED.
EDWIN
BITES BACK

YES, TIME TRAVEL IS A THEME OF THE BOOK BUT WHAT ABOUT THE CHARACTERS' EXISTENSIAL CRISIS?

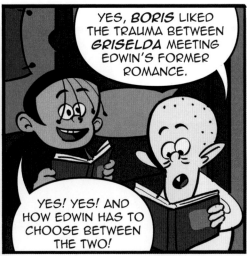

YES, *BORIS* LIKED THE TRAUMA BETWEEN *GRISELDA* MEETING EDWIN'S FORMER ROMANCE.

YES! YES! AND HOW EDWIN HAS TO CHOOSE BETWEEN THE TWO!

SO MUCH TURMOIL AND JEALOUSY! MY HEART...IS DEAD! ⸕WAHWAH!⸕

SORRY, I'M NOT REALLY INTERESTED IN THEIR PETTY ROMANCES.

GASP! SQUAWK

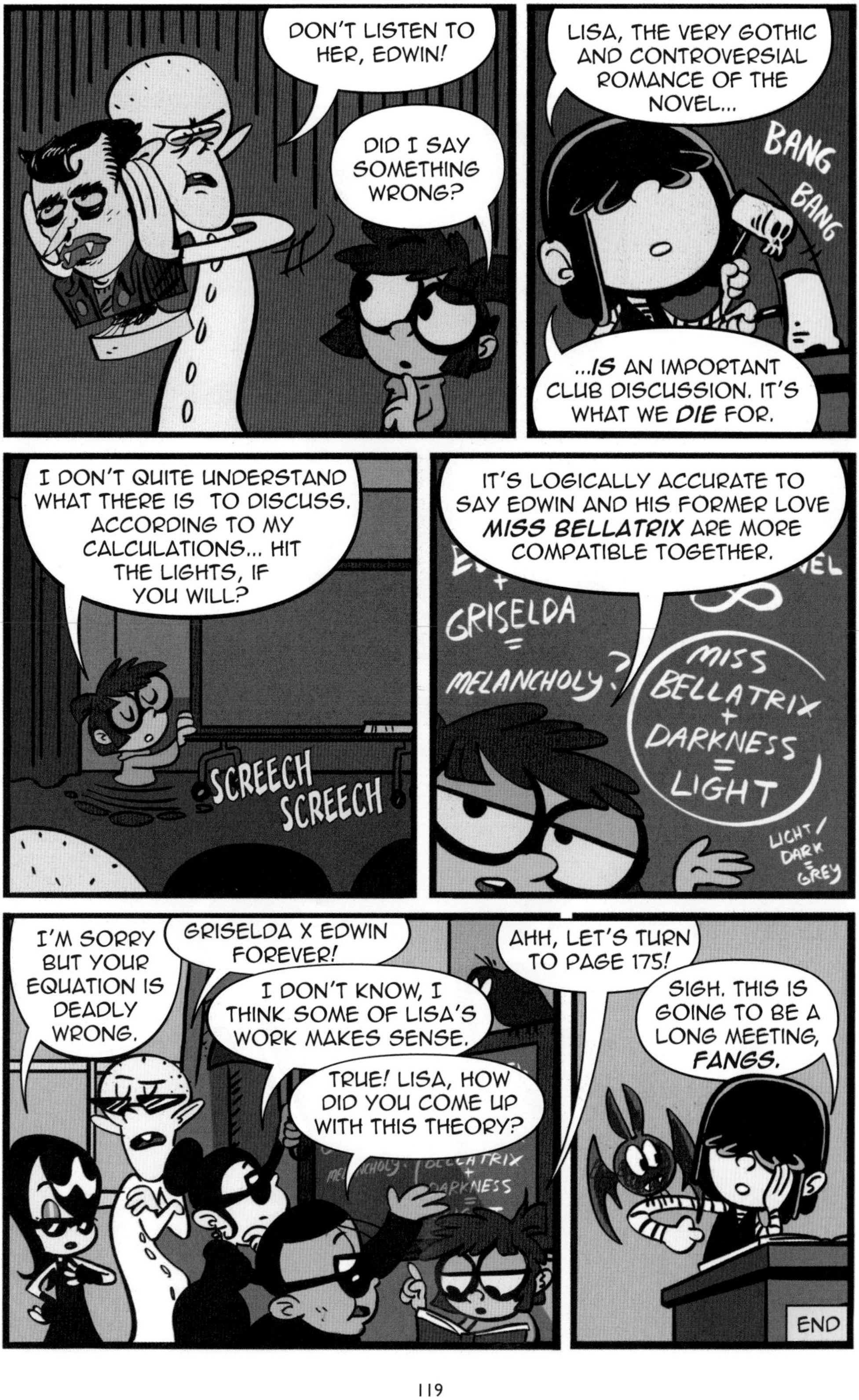
DON'T LISTEN TO HER, EDWIN!
DID I SAY SOMETHING WRONG?
LISA, THE VERY GOTHIC AND CONTROVERSIAL ROMANCE OF THE NOVEL...
BANG
BANG
...IS AN IMPORTANT CLUB DISCUSSION. IT'S WHAT WE DIE FOR.
I DON'T QUITE UNDERSTAND WHAT THERE IS TO DISCUSS. ACCORDING TO MY CALCULATIONS... HIT THE LIGHTS, IF YOU WILL?
SCREECH
SCREECH
IT'S LOGICALLY ACCURATE TO SAY EDWIN AND HIS FORMER LOVE MISS BELLATRIX ARE MORE COMPATIBLE TOGETHER.
GRISELDA
=
MELANCHOLY?
MISS BELLATRIX + DARKNESS = LIGHT
LIGHT / DARK = GREY
I'M SORRY BUT YOUR EQUATION IS DEADLY WRONG.
GRISELDA X EDWIN FOREVER!
I DON'T KNOW, I THINK SOME OF LISA'S WORK MAKES SENSE.
TRUE! LISA, HOW DID YOU COME UP WITH THIS THEORY?
AHH, LET'S TURN TO PAGE 175!
SIGH. THIS IS GOING TO BE A LONG MEETING, FANGS.
END

"MALL TRIP"

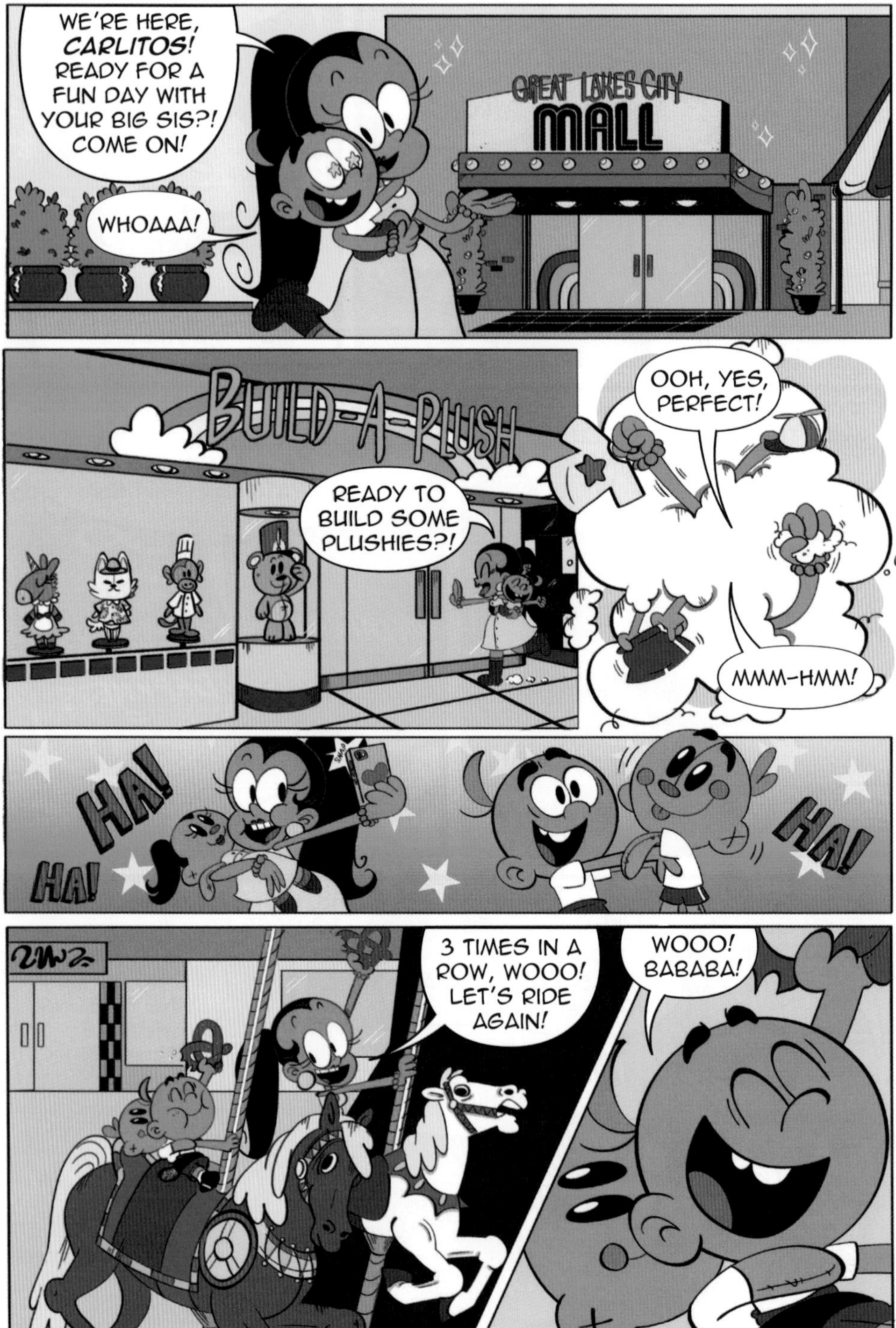
WE'RE HERE, CARLITOS! READY FOR A FUN DAY WITH YOUR BIG SIS?! COME ON!
WHOAAA!
GREAT LAKES CITY MALL
BUILD-A-PLUSH
READY TO BUILD SOME PLUSHIES?!
OOH, YES, PERFECT!
MMM-HMM!
HA!
HA!
HA!
3 TIMES IN A ROW, WOOO! LET'S RIDE AGAIN!
WOOO! BABABA!

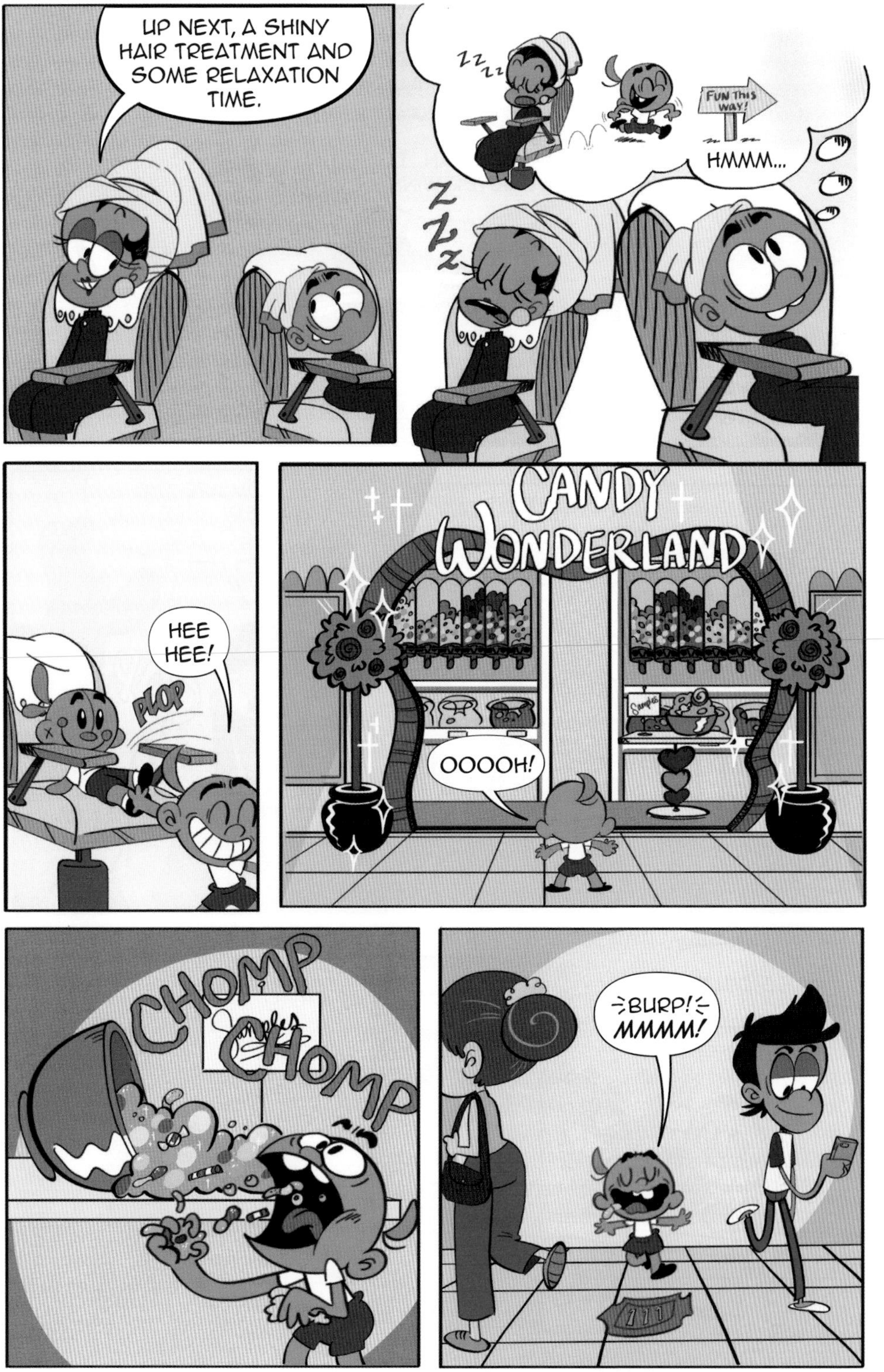
UP NEXT, A SHINY HAIR TREATMENT AND SOME RELAXATION TIME.
Z Z Z Z
FUN THIS WAY!
HMMM...
Z Z Z
HEE HEE!
PLOP
CANDY WONDERLAND
OOOOH!
CHOMP
CHOMP
BURP!
MMMM!

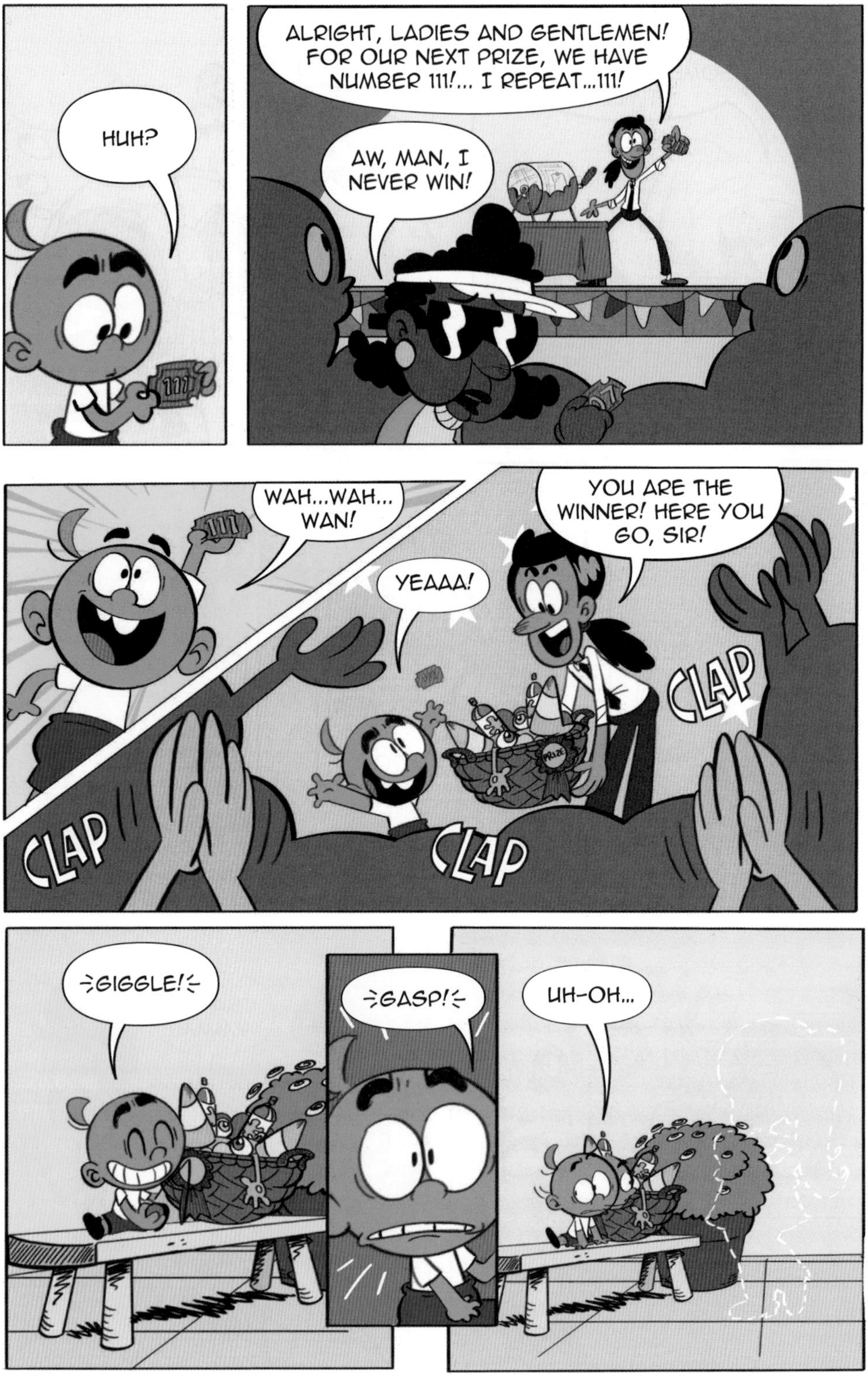
HUH?
ALRIGHT, LADIES AND GENTLEMEN! FOR OUR NEXT PRIZE, WE HAVE NUMBER 111!... I REPEAT...111!
AW, MAN, I NEVER WIN!
111
WAH...WAH... WAN!
YOU ARE THE WINNER! HERE YOU GO, SIR!
YEAAA!
CLAP
CLAP
CLAP
PRIZE
≈GIGGLE!≈
≈GASP!≈
UH-OH...

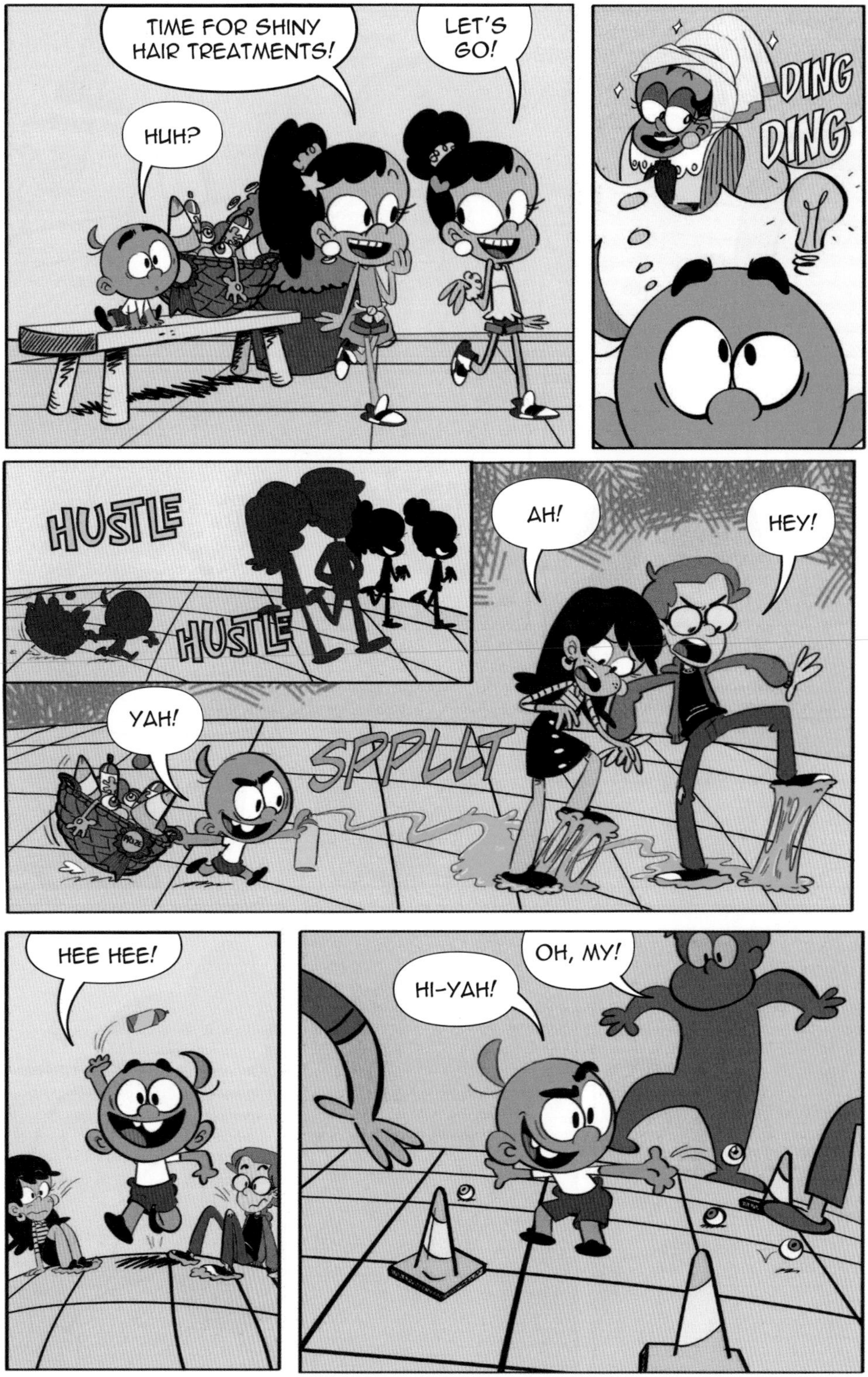

TIME FOR SHINY HAIR TREATMENTS!
LET'S GO!
HUH?
DING
DING
HUSTLE
HUSTLE
AH!
HEY!
YAH!
SPPLLT
HEE HEE!
OH, MY!
HI-YAH!

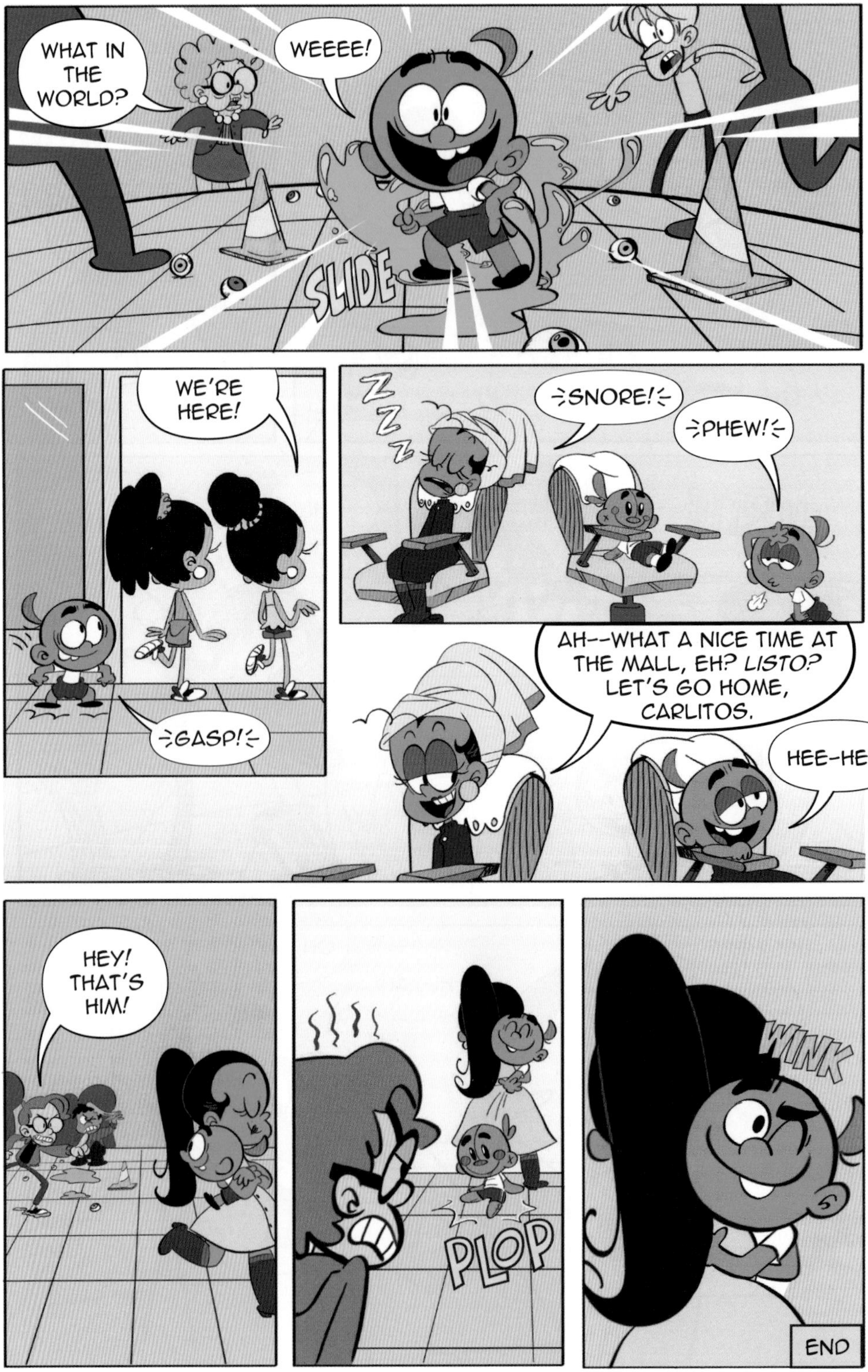
WHAT IN THE WORLD?
WEEEE!
SLIDE
WE'RE HERE!
GASP!
SNORE!
PHEW!
AH--WHAT A NICE TIME AT THE MALL, EH? *LISTO?* LET'S GO HOME, CARLITOS.
HEE-HEE!
HEY! THAT'S HIM!
PLOP
WINK
END

"PLAYING TO THE CROWD"

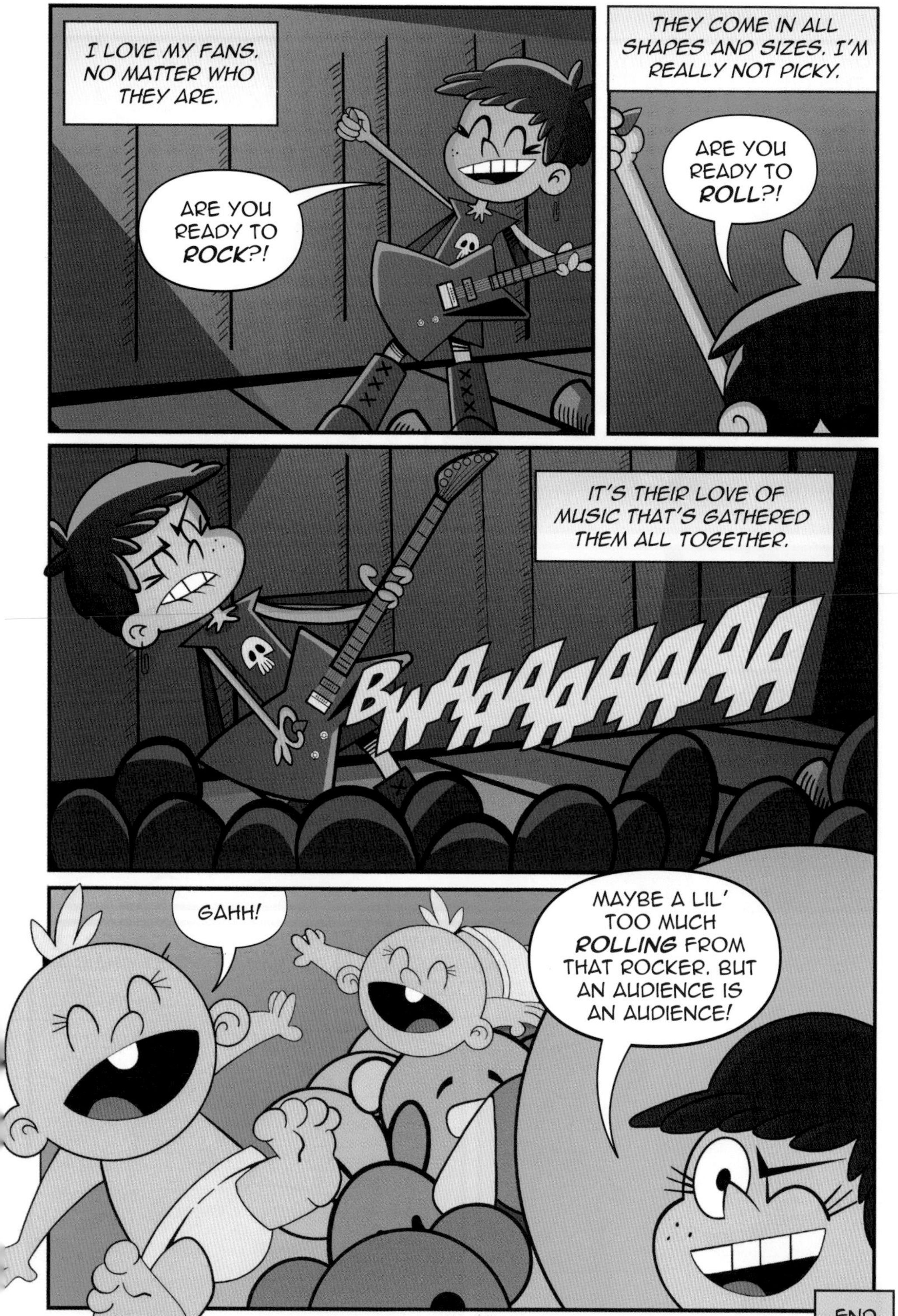
I LOVE MY FANS, NO MATTER WHO THEY ARE.
ARE YOU READY TO ROCK?!
THEY COME IN ALL SHAPES AND SIZES. I'M REALLY NOT PICKY.
ARE YOU READY TO ROLL?!
IT'S THEIR LOVE OF MUSIC THAT'S GATHERED THEM ALL TOGETHER.
BWAAAAAAAAA
GAHH!
MAYBE A LIL' TOO MUCH ROLLING FROM THAT ROCKER, BUT AN AUDIENCE IS AN AUDIENCE!
END

"CONSTRUCTION CONUNDRUM"

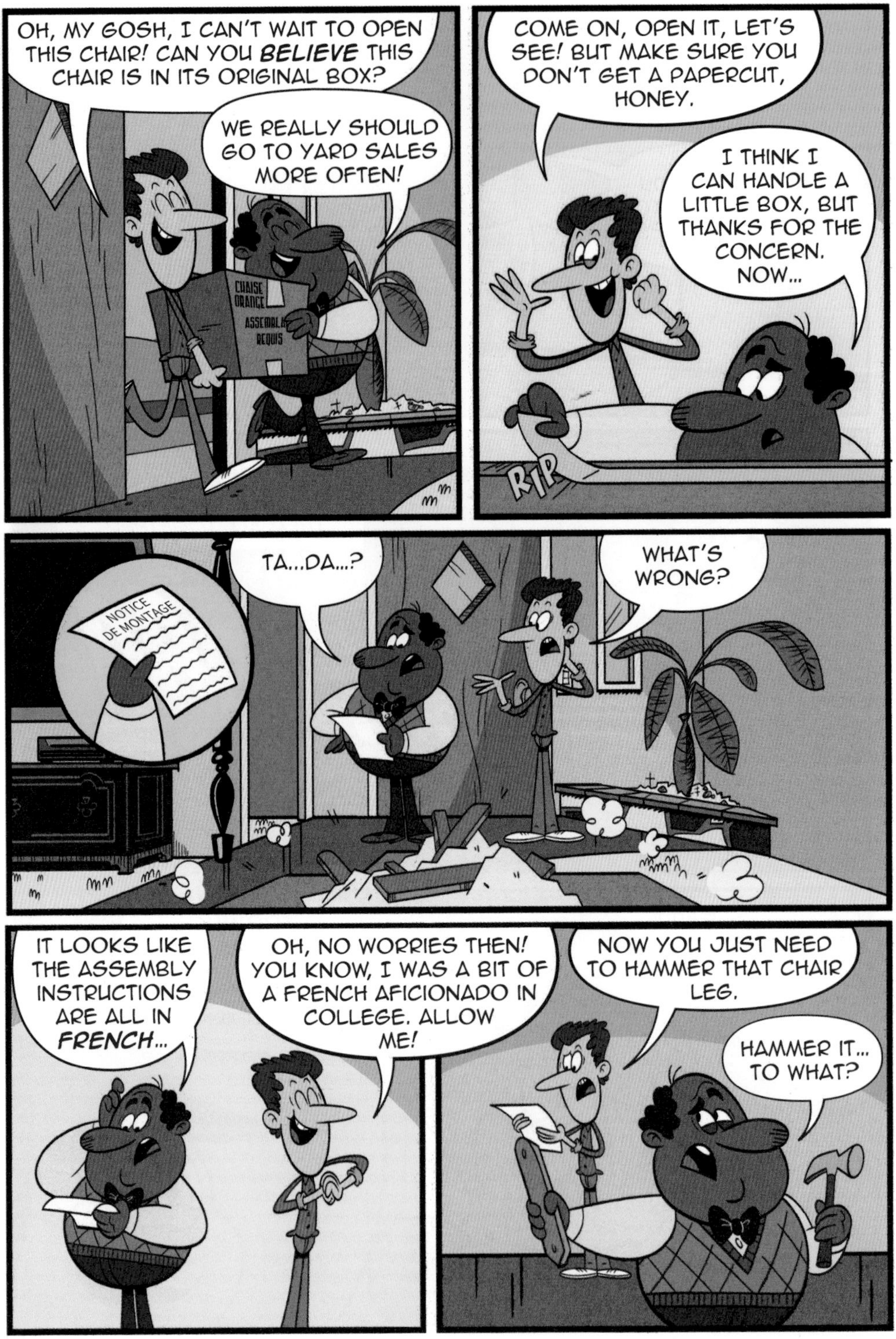
OH, MY GOSH, I CAN'T WAIT TO OPEN THIS CHAIR! CAN YOU *BELIEVE* THIS CHAIR IS IN ITS ORIGINAL BOX?
WE REALLY SHOULD GO TO YARD SALES MORE OFTEN!
CHAISE ORANGE
ASSEMBLAGE REQUIS
COME ON, OPEN IT, LET'S SEE! BUT MAKE SURE YOU DON'T GET A PAPERCUT, HONEY.
I THINK I CAN HANDLE A LITTLE BOX, BUT THANKS FOR THE CONCERN. NOW...
RIP
NOTICE DE MONTAGE
TA...DA...?
WHAT'S WRONG?
IT LOOKS LIKE THE ASSEMBLY INSTRUCTIONS ARE ALL IN *FRENCH*...
OH, NO WORRIES THEN! YOU KNOW, I WAS A BIT OF A FRENCH AFICIONADO IN COLLEGE. ALLOW ME!
NOW YOU JUST NEED TO HAMMER THAT CHAIR LEG.
HAMMER IT... TO WHAT?

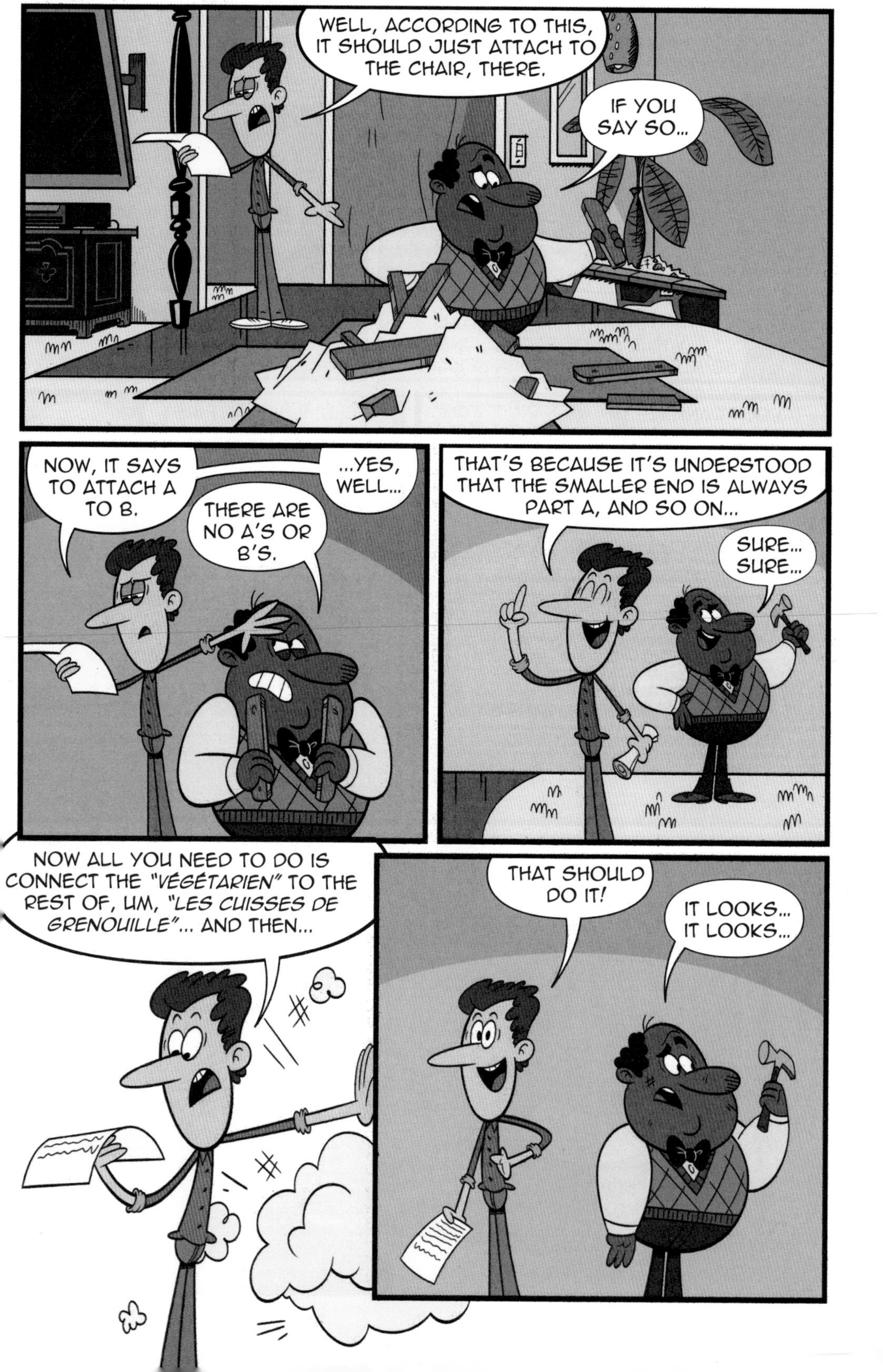
WELL, ACCORDING TO THIS, IT SHOULD JUST ATTACH TO THE CHAIR, THERE.
IF YOU SAY SO...
NOW, IT SAYS TO ATTACH A TO B.
THERE ARE NO A'S OR B'S.
...YES, WELL...
THAT'S BECAUSE IT'S UNDERSTOOD THAT THE SMALLER END IS ALWAYS PART A, AND SO ON...
SURE... SURE...
NOW ALL YOU NEED TO DO IS CONNECT THE "*VÉGÉTARIEN*" TO THE REST OF, UM, "*LES CUISSES DE GRENOUILLE*"... AND THEN...
THAT SHOULD DO IT!
IT LOOKS... IT LOOKS...

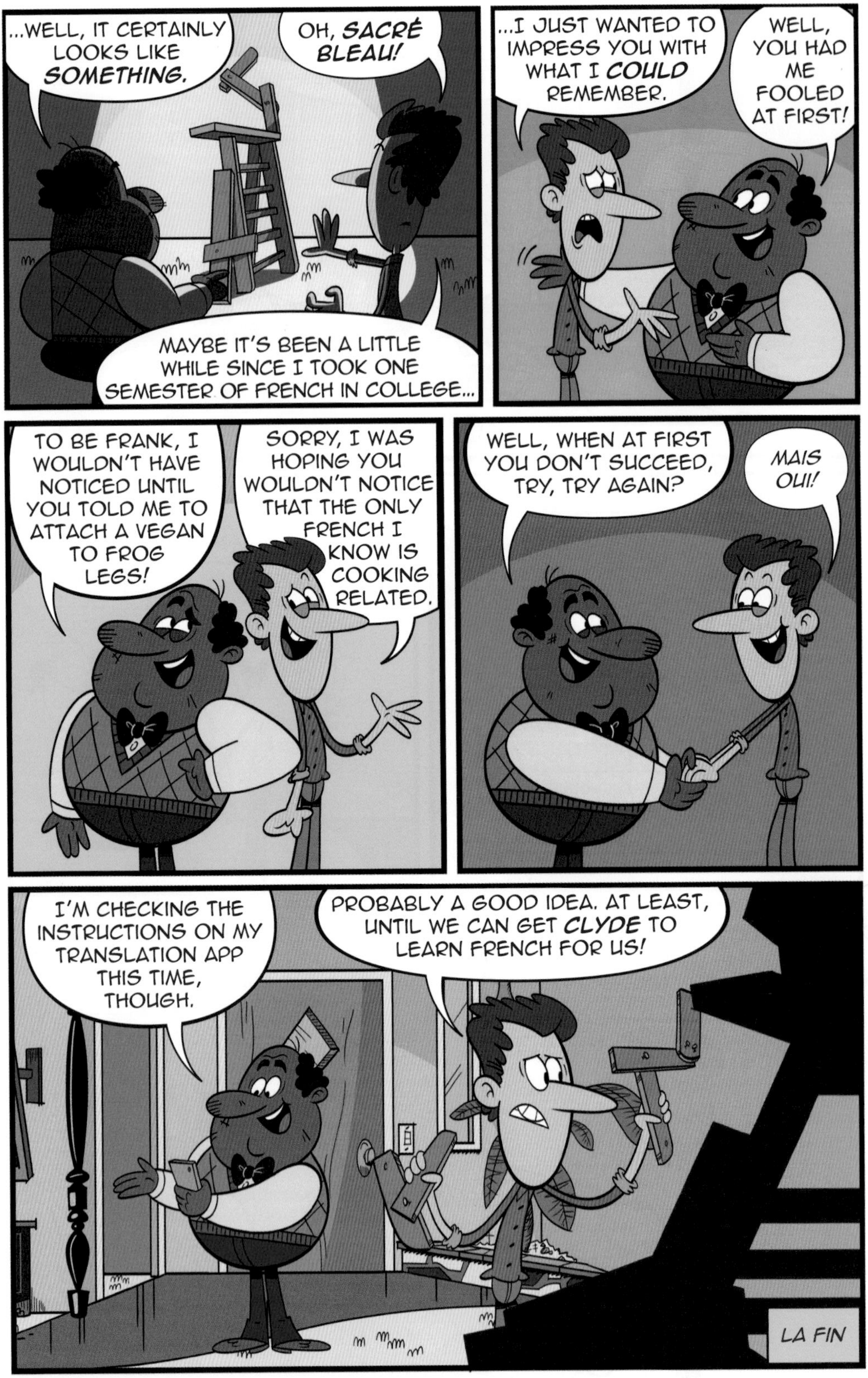
...WELL, IT CERTAINLY LOOKS LIKE SOMETHING.
OH, SACRÉ BLEAU!
MAYBE IT'S BEEN A LITTLE WHILE SINCE I TOOK ONE SEMESTER OF FRENCH IN COLLEGE...
...I JUST WANTED TO IMPRESS YOU WITH WHAT I COULD REMEMBER.
WELL, YOU HAD ME FOOLED AT FIRST!
TO BE FRANK, I WOULDN'T HAVE NOTICED UNTIL YOU TOLD ME TO ATTACH A VEGAN TO FROG LEGS!
SORRY, I WAS HOPING YOU WOULDN'T NOTICE THAT THE ONLY FRENCH I KNOW IS COOKING RELATED.
WELL, WHEN AT FIRST YOU DON'T SUCCEED, TRY, TRY AGAIN?
MAIS OUI!
I'M CHECKING THE INSTRUCTIONS ON MY TRANSLATION APP THIS TIME, THOUGH.
PROBABLY A GOOD IDEA. AT LEAST, UNTIL WE CAN GET CLYDE TO LEARN FRENCH FOR US!
LA FIN

"THE TEAM-UP"

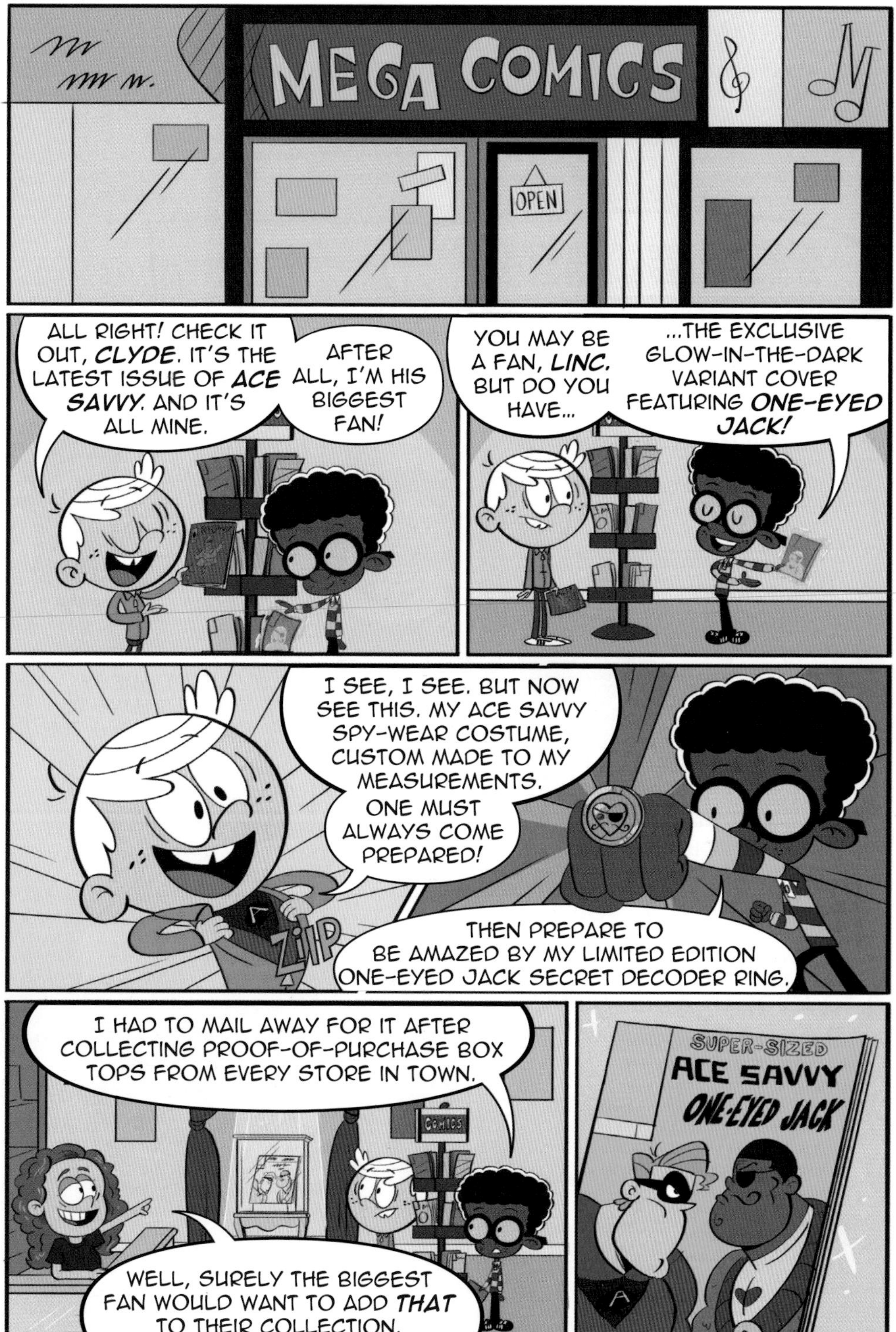
MEGA COMICS
OPEN
ALL RIGHT! CHECK IT OUT, CLYDE. IT'S THE LATEST ISSUE OF ACE SAVVY. AND IT'S ALL MINE.
AFTER ALL, I'M HIS BIGGEST FAN!
YOU MAY BE A FAN, LINC. BUT DO YOU HAVE...
...THE EXCLUSIVE GLOW-IN-THE-DARK VARIANT COVER FEATURING ONE-EYED JACK!
I SEE, I SEE. BUT NOW SEE THIS. MY ACE SAVVY SPY-WEAR COSTUME, CUSTOM MADE TO MY MEASUREMENTS.
ONE MUST ALWAYS COME PREPARED!
ZIIP
THEN PREPARE TO BE AMAZED BY MY LIMITED EDITION ONE-EYED JACK SECRET DECODER RING.
I HAD TO MAIL AWAY FOR IT AFTER COLLECTING PROOF-OF-PURCHASE BOX TOPS FROM EVERY STORE IN TOWN.
COMICS
WELL, SURELY THE BIGGEST FAN WOULD WANT TO ADD THAT TO THEIR COLLECTION.
SUPER-SIZED
ACE SAVVY
ONE-EYED JACK

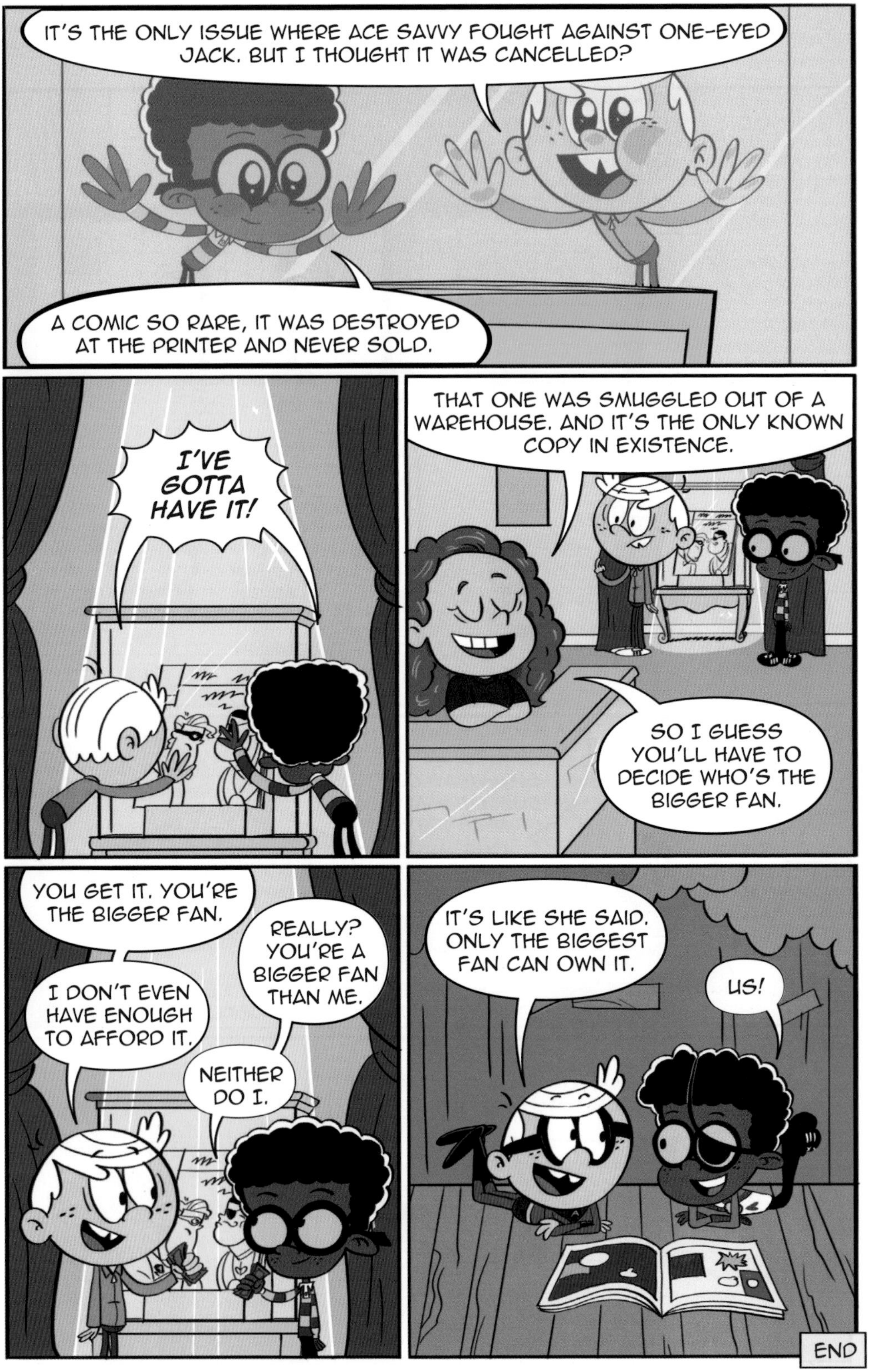
IT'S THE ONLY ISSUE WHERE ACE SAVVY FOUGHT AGAINST ONE-EYED JACK. BUT I THOUGHT IT WAS CANCELLED?
A COMIC SO RARE, IT WAS DESTROYED AT THE PRINTER AND NEVER SOLD.
I'VE GOTTA HAVE IT!
THAT ONE WAS SMUGGLED OUT OF A WAREHOUSE. AND IT'S THE ONLY KNOWN COPY IN EXISTENCE.
SO I GUESS YOU'LL HAVE TO DECIDE WHO'S THE BIGGER FAN.
YOU GET IT. YOU'RE THE BIGGER FAN.
REALLY? YOU'RE A BIGGER FAN THAN ME.
I DON'T EVEN HAVE ENOUGH TO AFFORD IT.
NEITHER DO I.
IT'S LIKE SHE SAID. ONLY THE BIGGEST FAN CAN OWN IT.
US!
END

"SISTER NATURE"

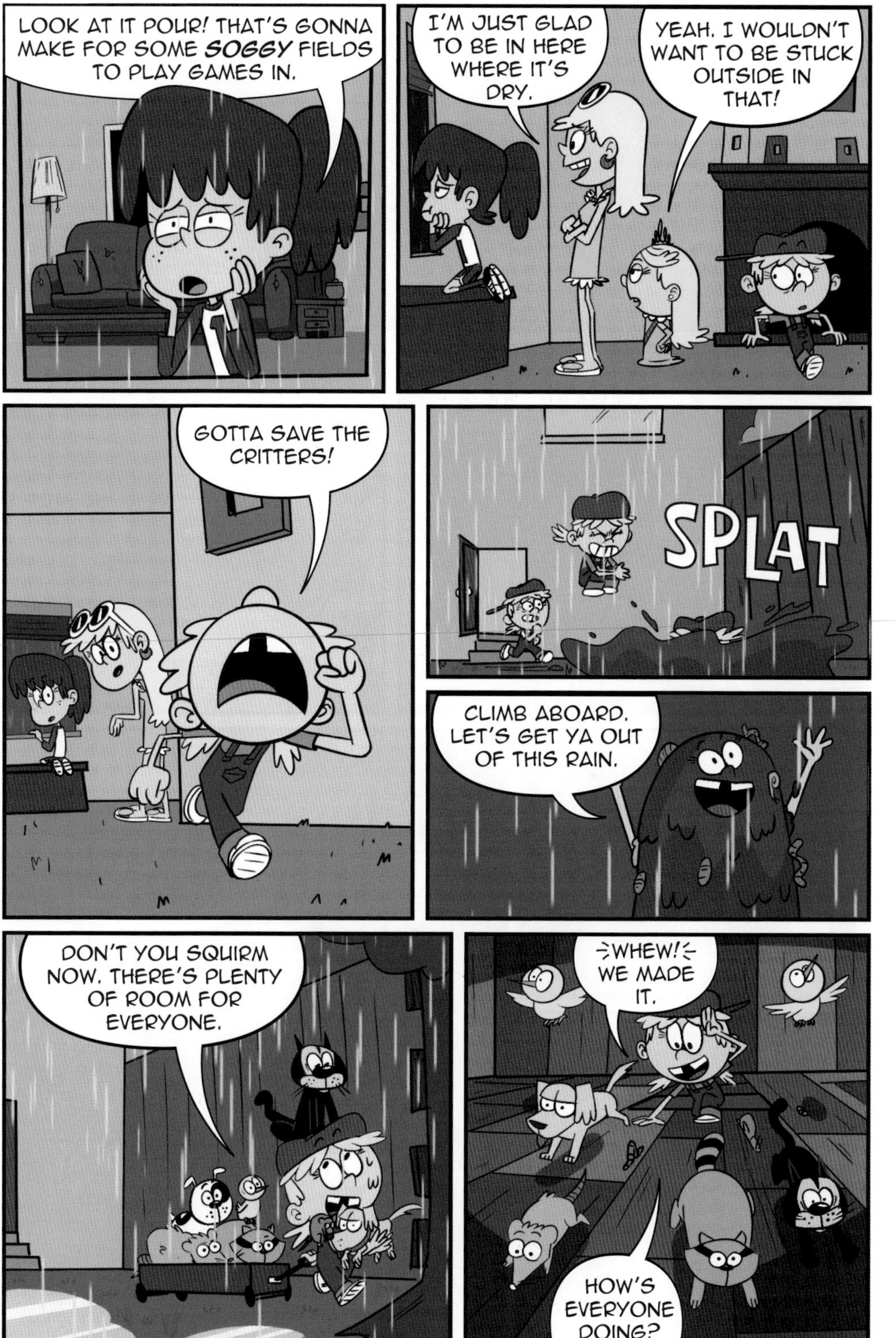
LOOK AT IT POUR! THAT'S GONNA MAKE FOR SOME SOGGY FIELDS TO PLAY GAMES IN.
I'M JUST GLAD TO BE IN HERE WHERE IT'S DRY.
YEAH. I WOULDN'T WANT TO BE STUCK OUTSIDE IN THAT!
GOTTA SAVE THE CRITTERS!
SPLAT
CLIMB ABOARD. LET'S GET YA OUT OF THIS RAIN.
DON'T YOU SQUIRM NOW. THERE'S PLENTY OF ROOM FOR EVERYONE.
WHEW! WE MADE IT.
HOW'S EVERYONE DOING?

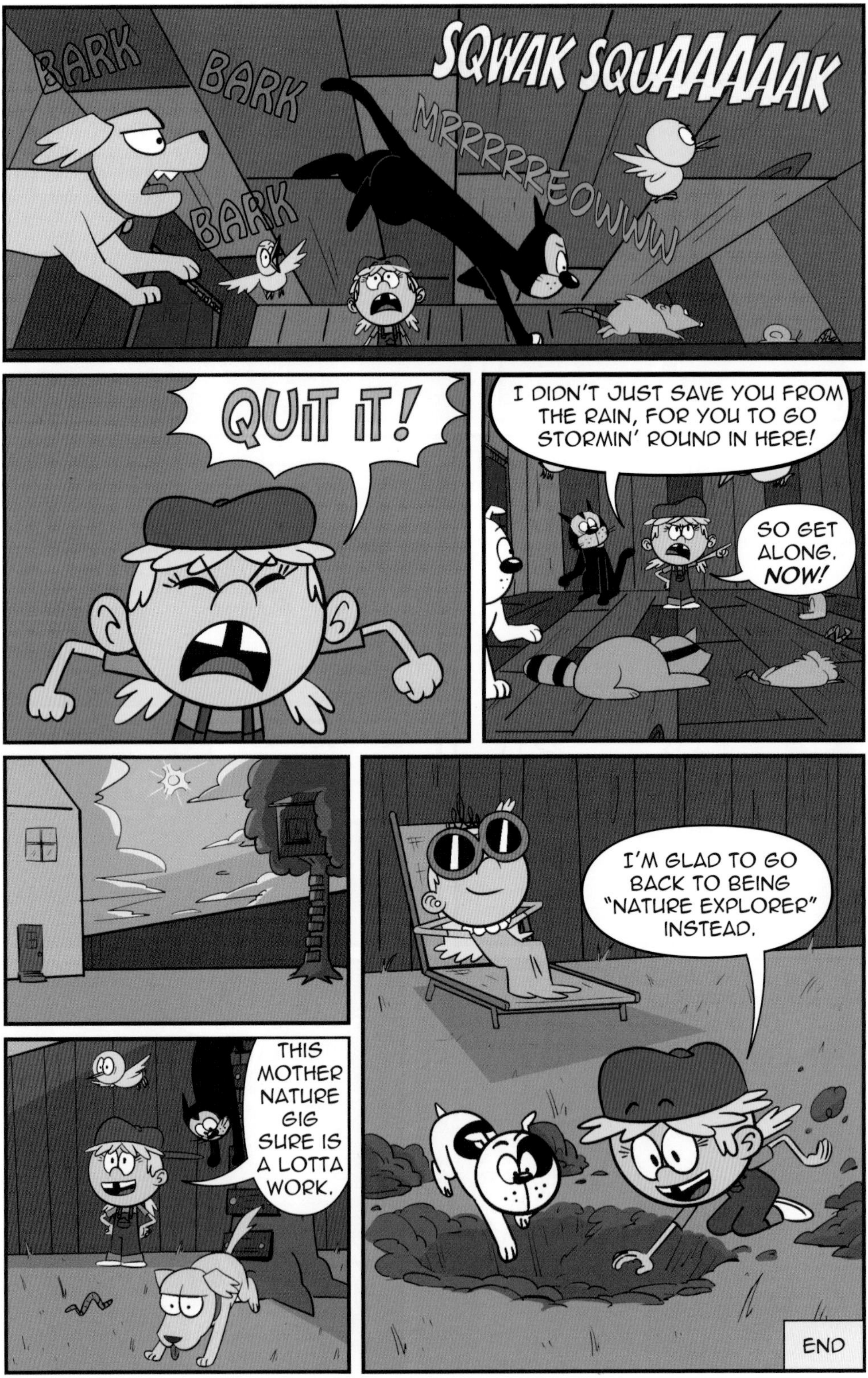
BARK
BARK
BARK
MRRRRREOWWW
SQWAK SQUAAAAAK
QUIT IT!
I DIDN'T JUST SAVE YOU FROM THE RAIN, FOR YOU TO GO STORMIN' ROUND IN HERE!
SO GET ALONG. NOW!
THIS MOTHER NATURE GIG SURE IS A LOTTA WORK.
I'M GLAD TO GO BACK TO BEING "NATURE EXPLORER" INSTEAD.
END

"A DIRTY RESCUE"

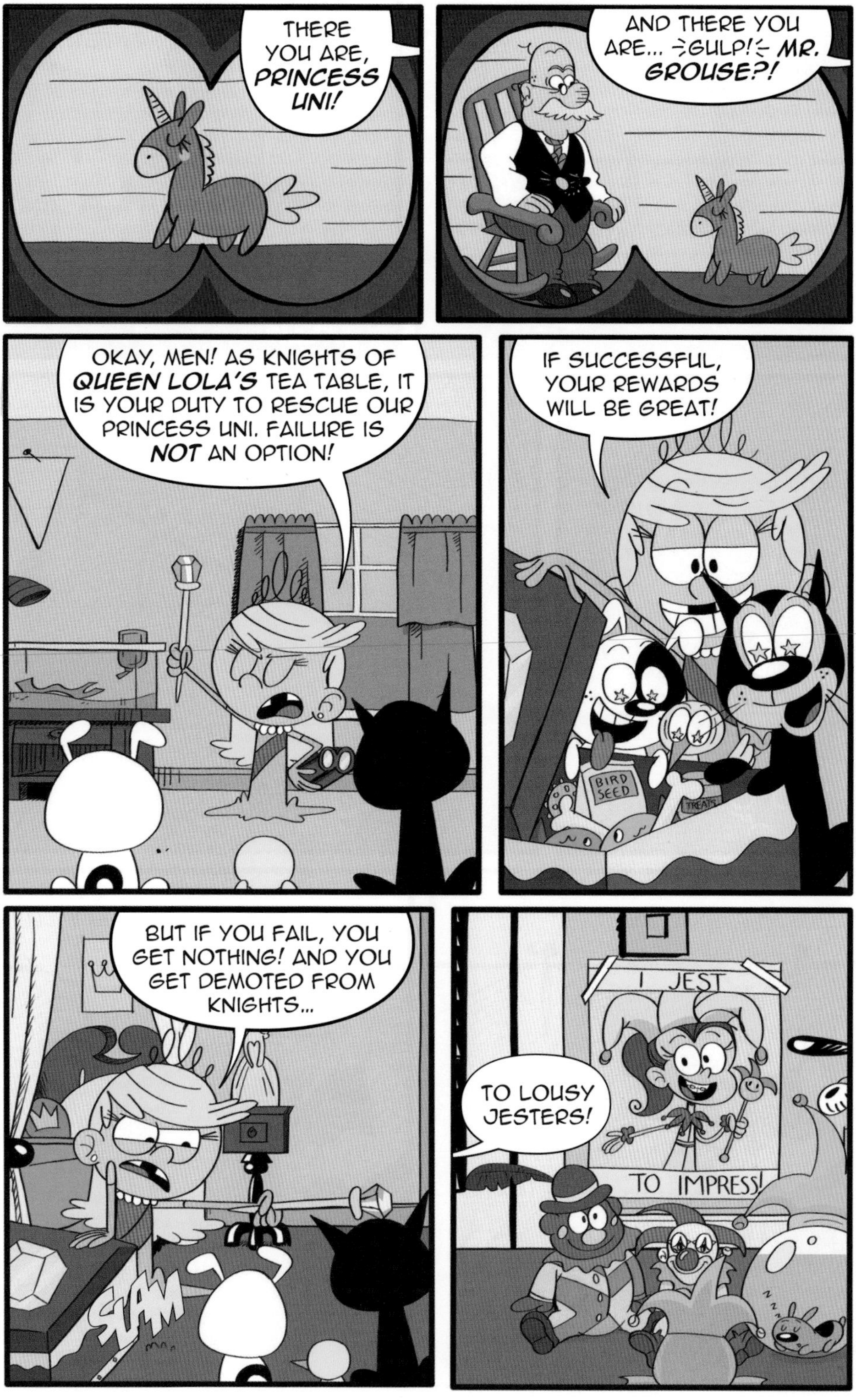

THERE YOU ARE, PRINCESS UNI!
AND THERE YOU ARE... ⇉GULP!⇇ MR. GROUSE?!
OKAY, MEN! AS KNIGHTS OF QUEEN LOLA'S TEA TABLE, IT IS YOUR DUTY TO RESCUE OUR PRINCESS UNI. FAILURE IS NOT AN OPTION!
IF SUCCESSFUL, YOUR REWARDS WILL BE GREAT!
BIRD SEED
TREATS
BUT IF YOU FAIL, YOU GET NOTHING! AND YOU GET DEMOTED FROM KNIGHTS...
SLAM
I JEST TO IMPRESS!
TO LOUSY JESTERS!

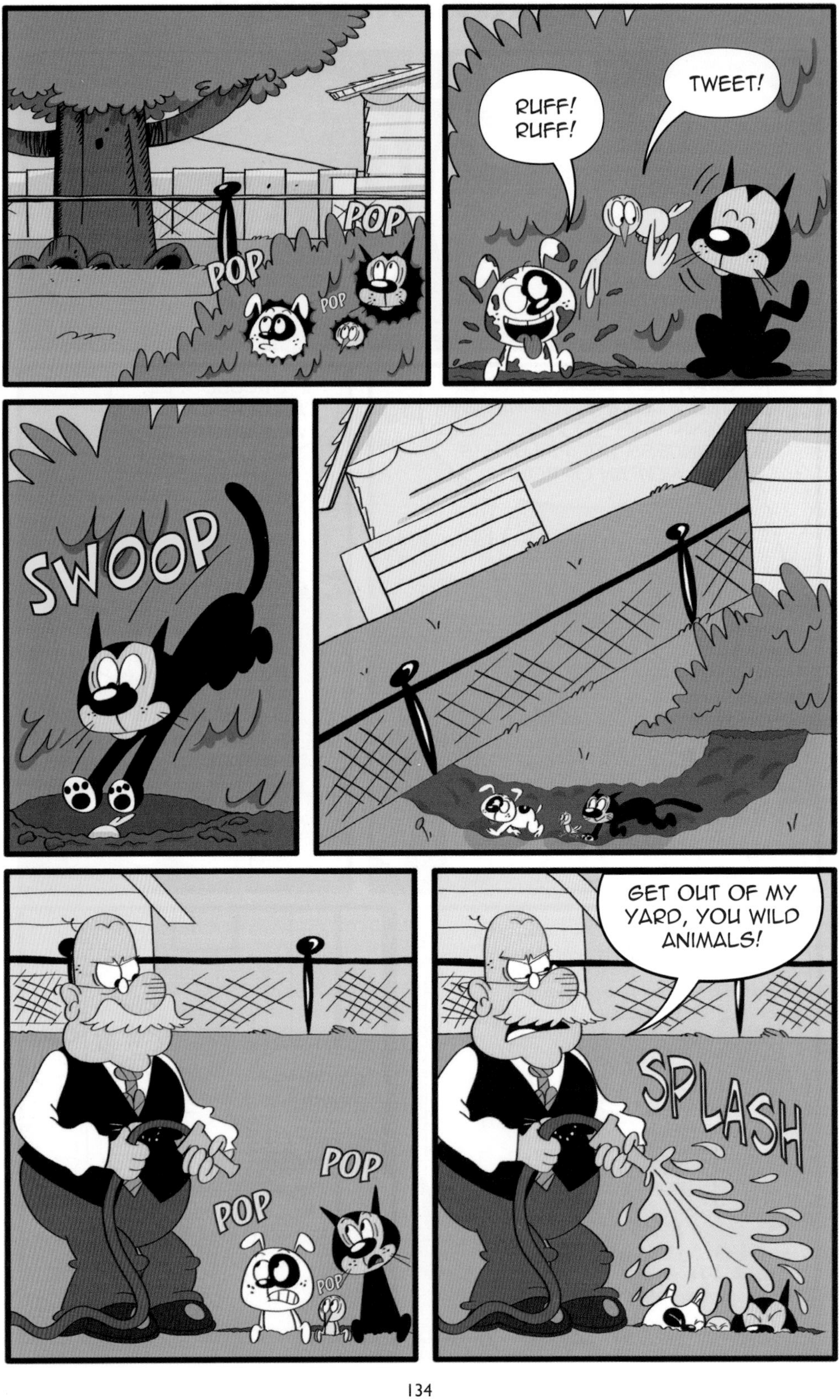
POP
POP
POP
RUFF! RUFF!
TWEET!
SWOOP
POP
POP
POP
GET OUT OF MY YARD, YOU WILD ANIMALS!
SPLASH

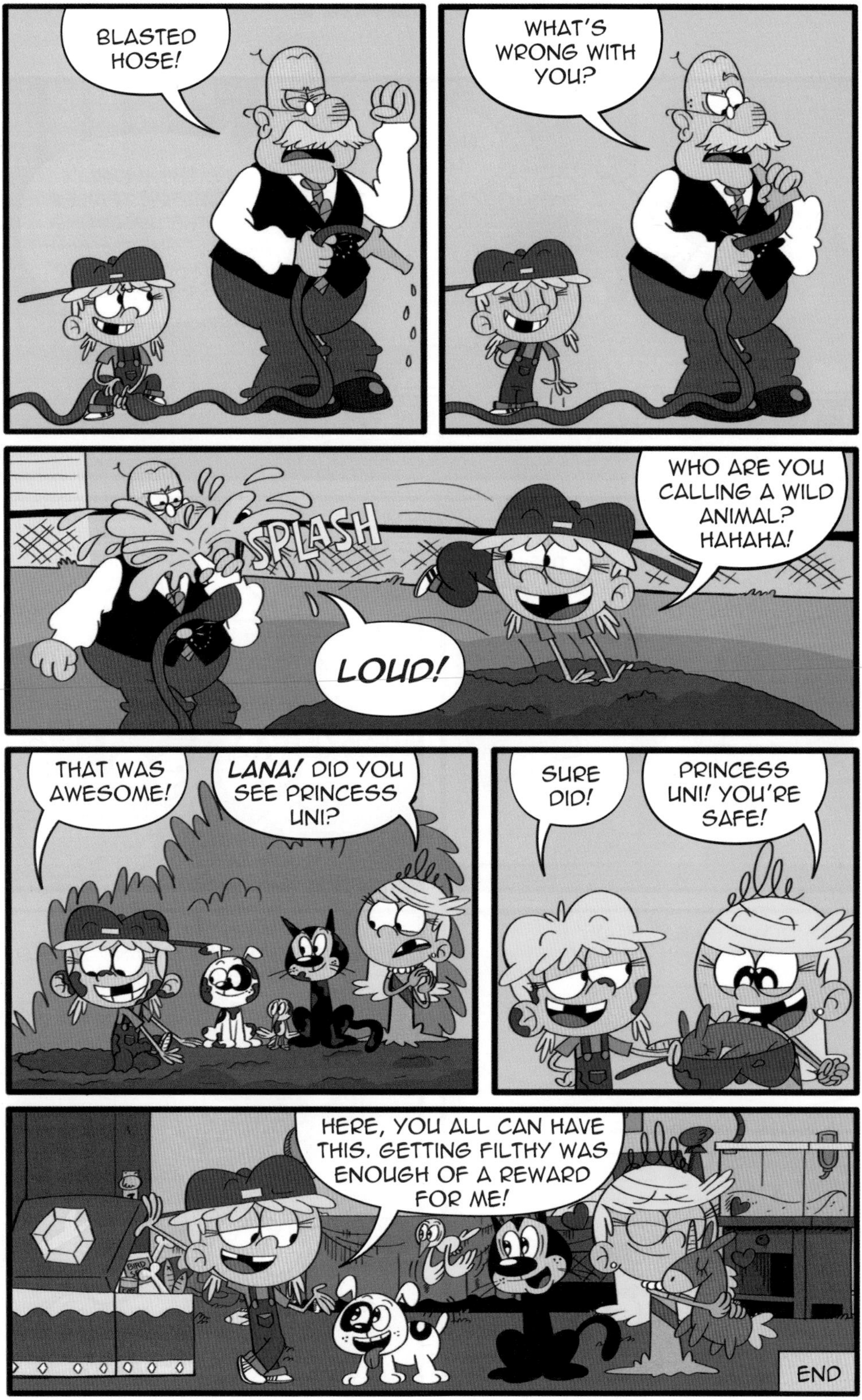
BLASTED HOSE!
WHAT'S WRONG WITH YOU?
SPLASH
LOUD!
WHO ARE YOU CALLING A WILD ANIMAL? HAHAHA!
THAT WAS AWESOME!
LANA! DID YOU SEE PRINCESS UNI?
SURE DID!
PRINCESS UNI! YOU'RE SAFE!
HERE, YOU ALL CAN HAVE THIS. GETTING FILTHY WAS ENOUGH OF A REWARD FOR ME!
END

"FAN FRENZY"

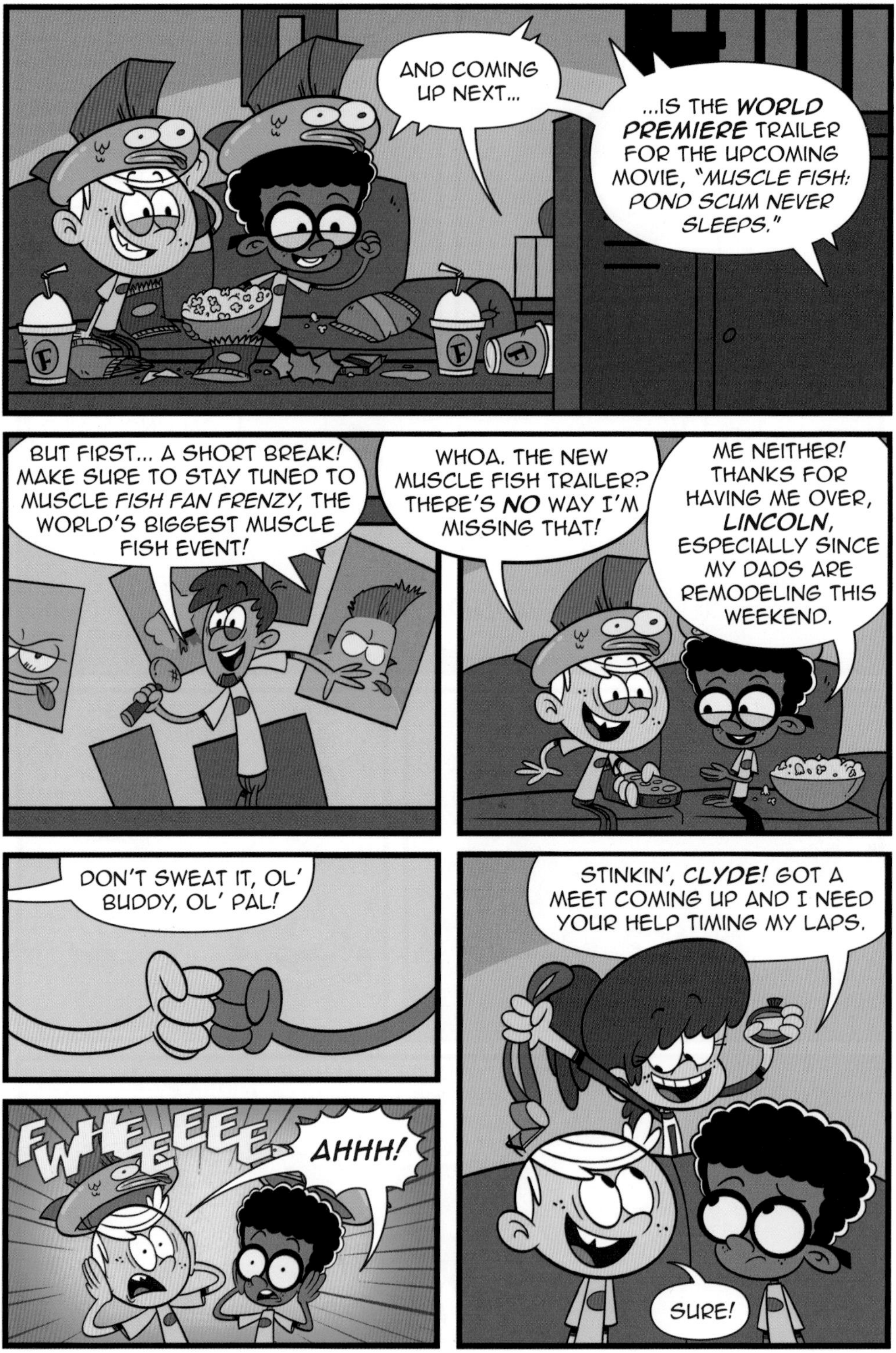
AND COMING UP NEXT...
...IS THE *WORLD PREMIERE* TRAILER FOR THE UPCOMING MOVIE, "*MUSCLE FISH: POND SCUM NEVER SLEEPS.*"
BUT FIRST... A SHORT BREAK! MAKE SURE TO STAY TUNED TO MUSCLE *FISH FAN FRENZY*, THE WORLD'S BIGGEST MUSCLE FISH EVENT!
WHOA. THE NEW MUSCLE FISH TRAILER? THERE'S ***NO*** WAY I'M MISSING THAT!
ME NEITHER! THANKS FOR HAVING ME OVER, ***LINCOLN***, ESPECIALLY SINCE MY DADS ARE REMODELING THIS WEEKEND.
DON'T SWEAT IT, OL' BUDDY, OL' PAL!
FWHEEEEE
AHHH!
STINKIN', ***CLYDE!*** GOT A MEET COMING UP AND I NEED YOUR HELP TIMING MY LAPS.
SURE!

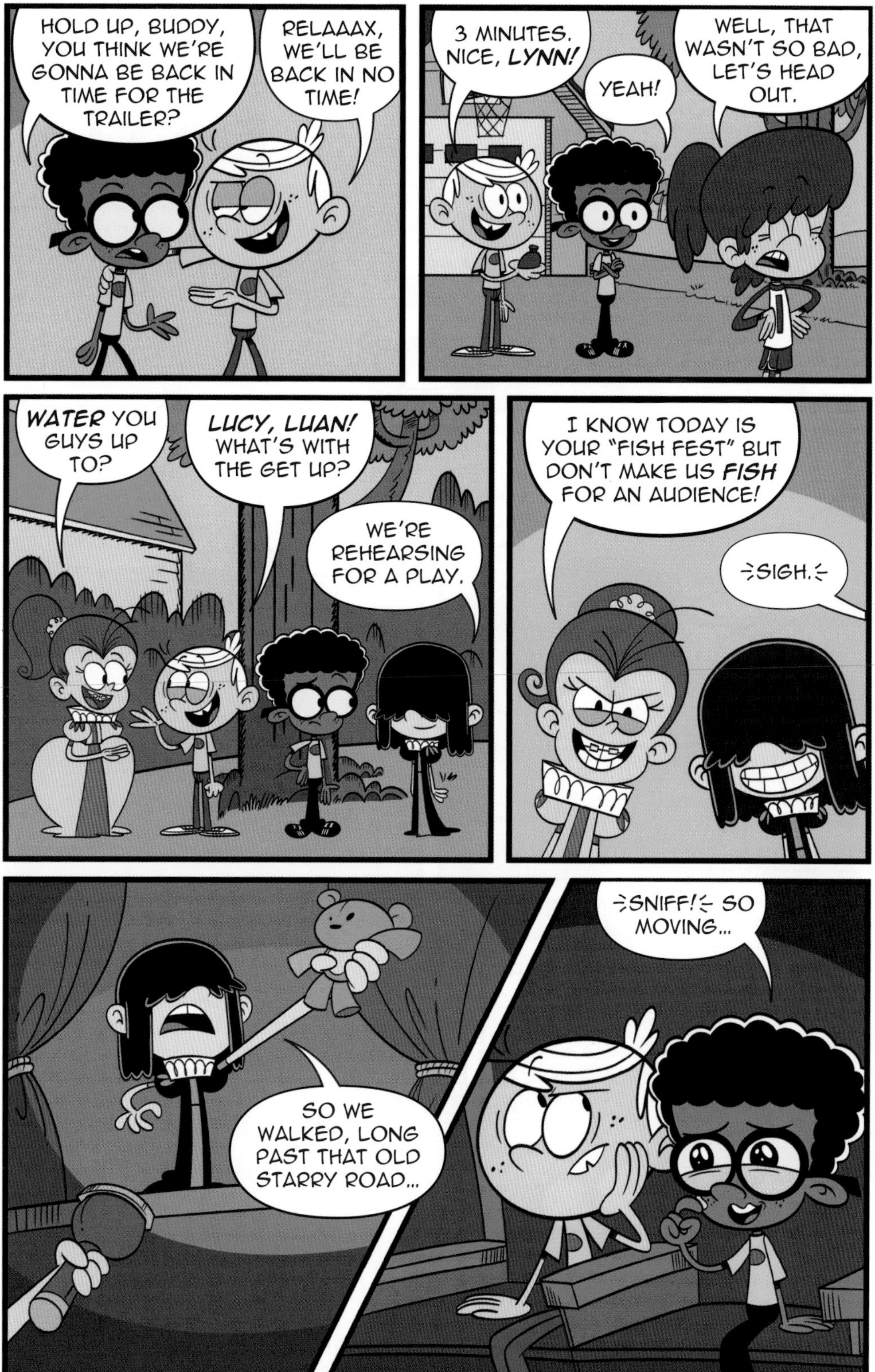
HOLD UP, BUDDY, YOU THINK WE'RE GONNA BE BACK IN TIME FOR THE TRAILER?
RELAAAX, WE'LL BE BACK IN NO TIME!
3 MINUTES. NICE, LYNN!
YEAH!
WELL, THAT WASN'T SO BAD, LET'S HEAD OUT.
WATER YOU GUYS UP TO?
LUCY, LUAN! WHAT'S WITH THE GET UP?
WE'RE REHEARSING FOR A PLAY.
I KNOW TODAY IS YOUR "FISH FEST" BUT DON'T MAKE US FISH FOR AN AUDIENCE!
SIGH.
SO WE WALKED, LONG PAST THAT OLD STARRY ROAD...
SNIFF! SO MOVING...

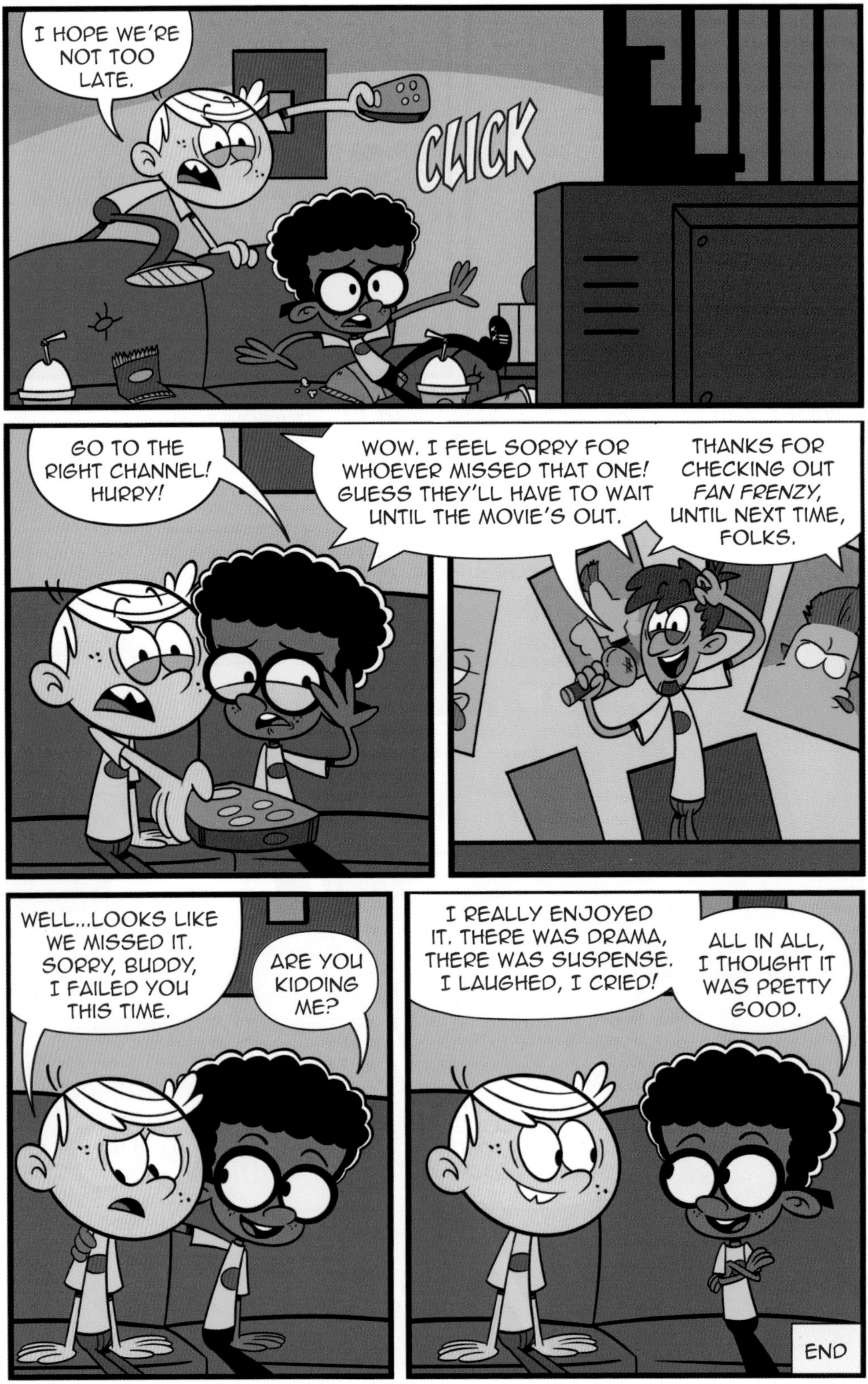
I HOPE WE'RE NOT TOO LATE.
CLICK
GO TO THE RIGHT CHANNEL! HURRY!
WOW. I FEEL SORRY FOR WHOEVER MISSED THAT ONE! GUESS THEY'LL HAVE TO WAIT UNTIL THE MOVIE'S OUT.
THANKS FOR CHECKING OUT *FAN FRENZY*, UNTIL NEXT TIME, FOLKS.
WELL...LOOKS LIKE WE MISSED IT. SORRY, BUDDY, I FAILED YOU THIS TIME.
ARE YOU KIDDING ME?
I REALLY ENJOYED IT. THERE WAS DRAMA, THERE WAS SUSPENSE. I LAUGHED, I CRIED!
ALL IN ALL, I THOUGHT IT WAS PRETTY GOOD.
END

"LISA'S PAPER VIEW"

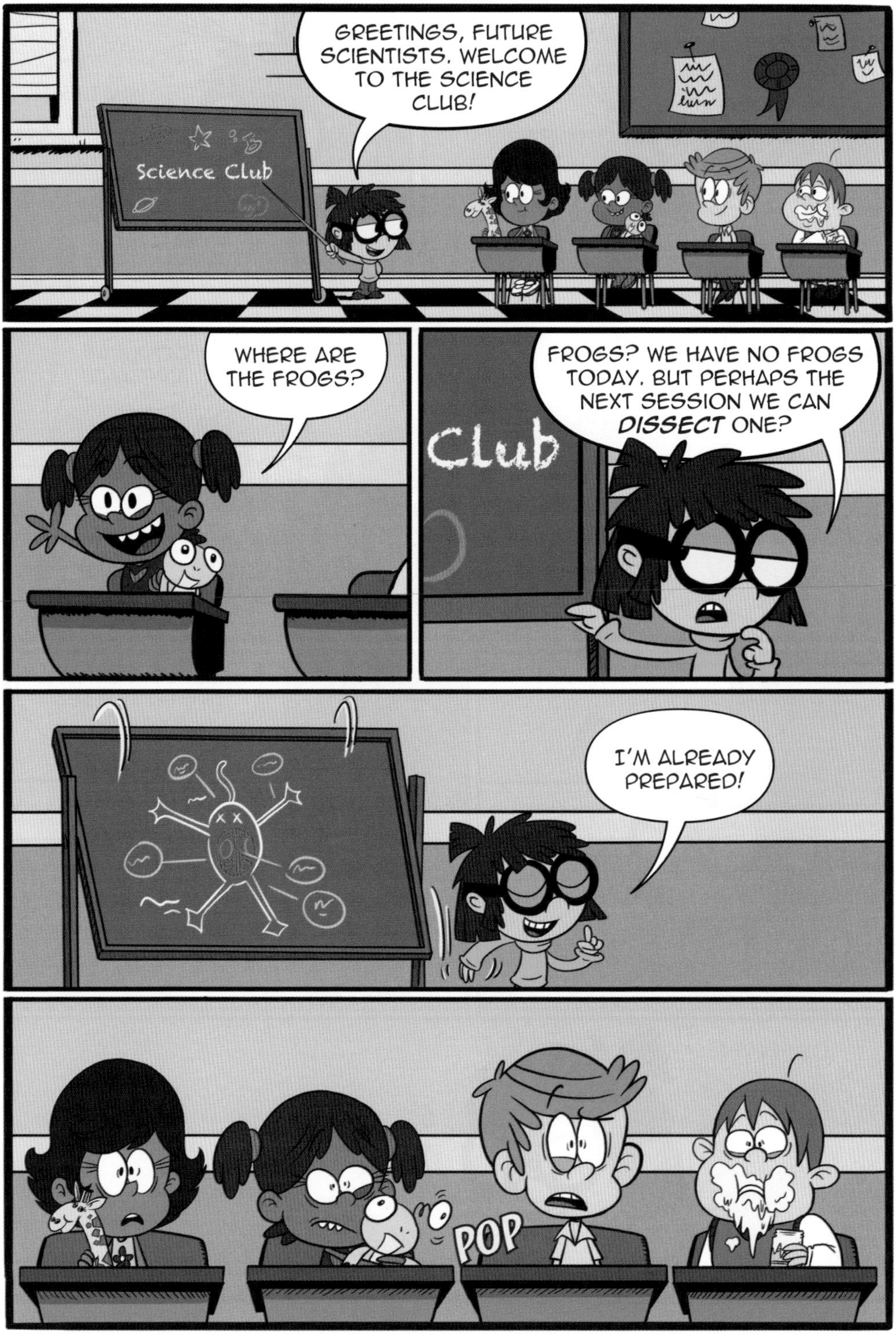

GREETINGS, FUTURE SCIENTISTS. WELCOME TO THE SCIENCE CLUB!
Science Club
WHERE ARE THE FROGS?
Club
FROGS? WE HAVE NO FROGS TODAY. BUT PERHAPS THE NEXT SESSION WE CAN DISSECT ONE?
I'M ALREADY PREPARED!
POP

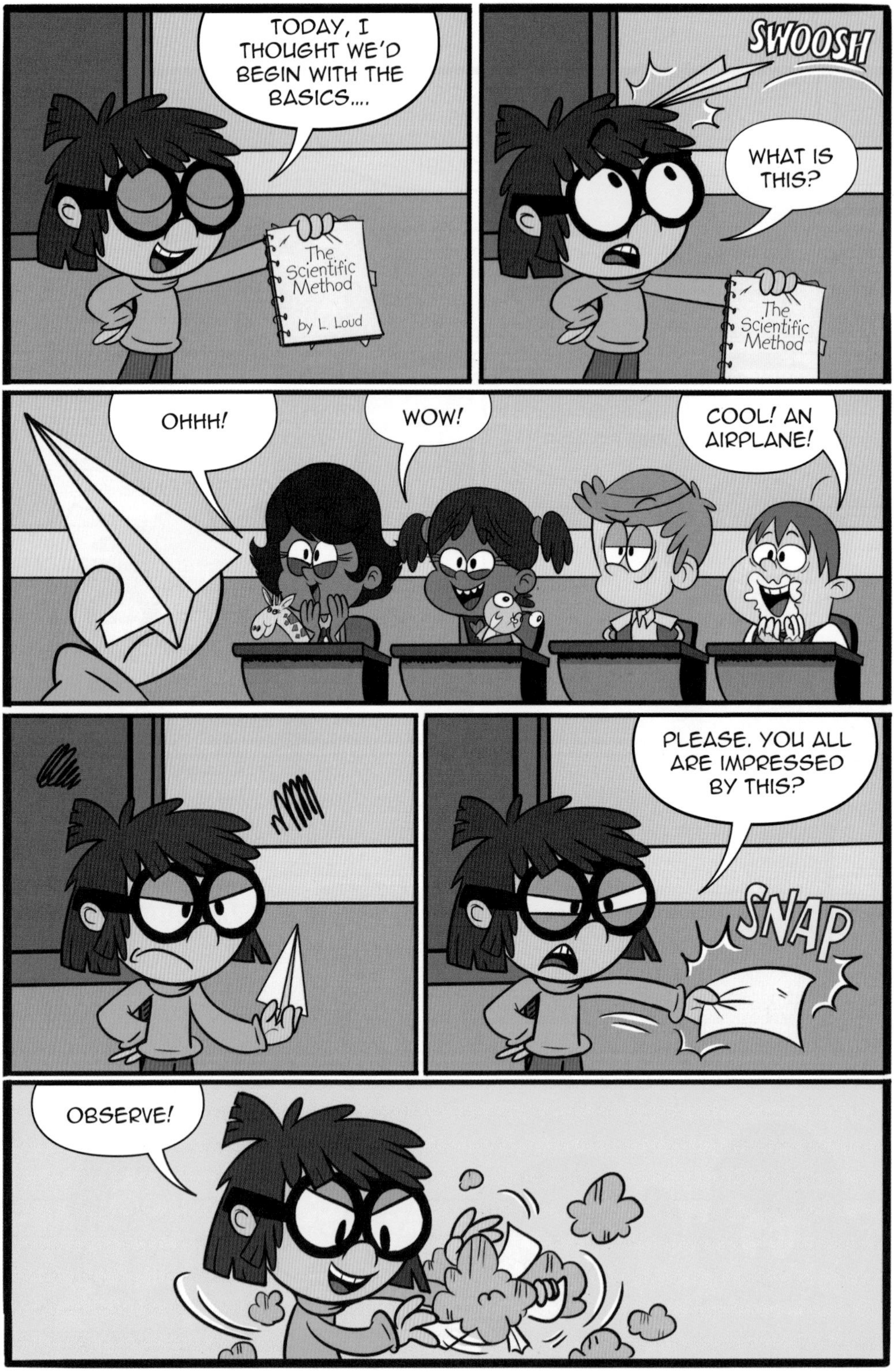
TODAY, I THOUGHT WE'D BEGIN WITH THE BASICS....
The Scientific Method
by L. Loud
SWOOSH
WHAT IS THIS?
The Scientific Method
OHHH!
WOW!
COOL! AN AIRPLANE!
PLEASE. YOU ALL ARE IMPRESSED BY THIS?
SNAP
OBSERVE!

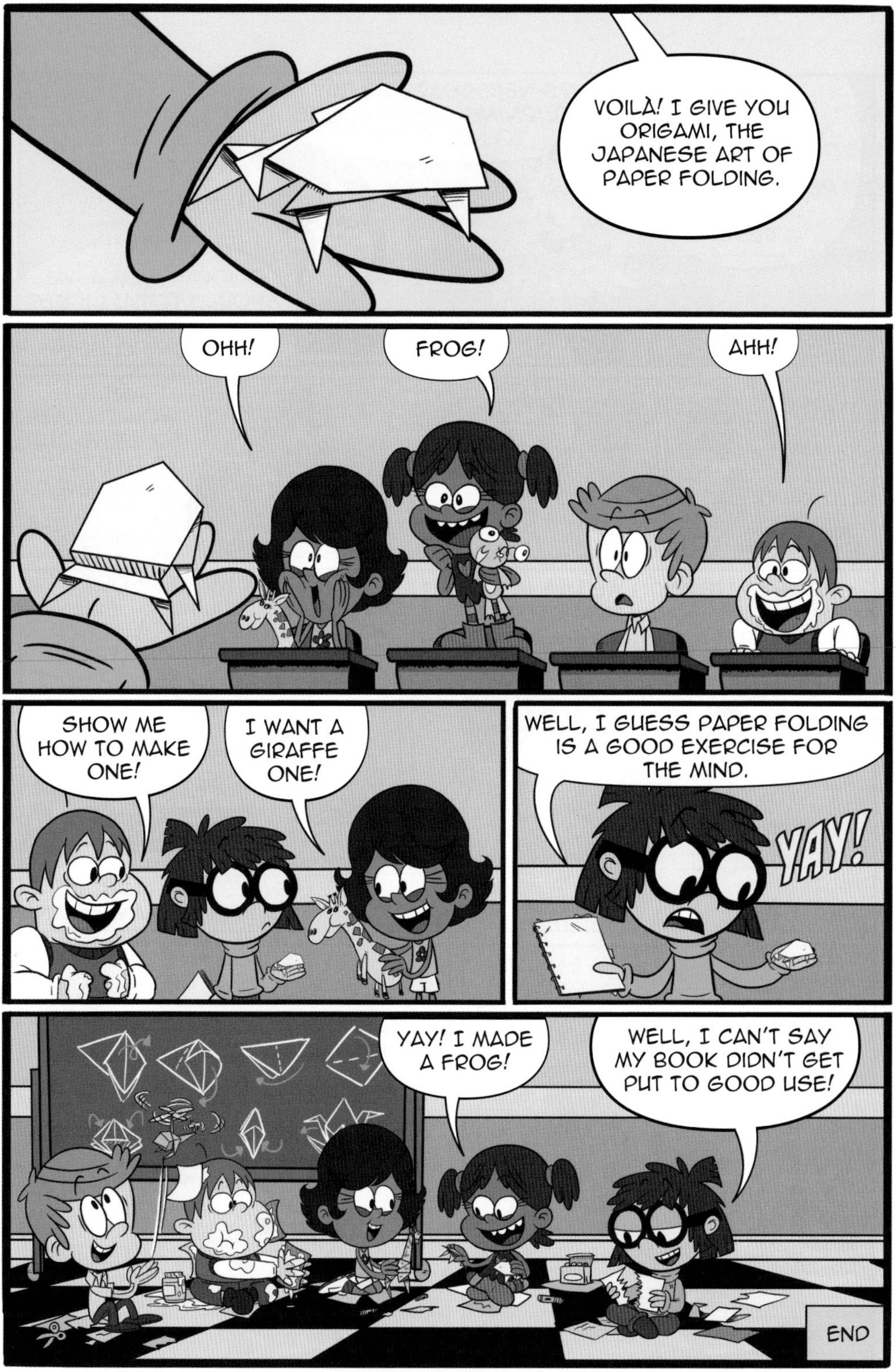

VOILÀ! I GIVE YOU ORIGAMI, THE JAPANESE ART OF PAPER FOLDING.
OHH!
FROG!
AHH!
SHOW ME HOW TO MAKE ONE!
I WANT A GIRAFFE ONE!
WELL, I GUESS PAPER FOLDING IS A GOOD EXERCISE FOR THE MIND.
YAY!
YAY! I MADE A FROG!
WELL, I CAN'T SAY MY BOOK DIDN'T GET PUT TO GOOD USE!
END

"CLOSING MIME"

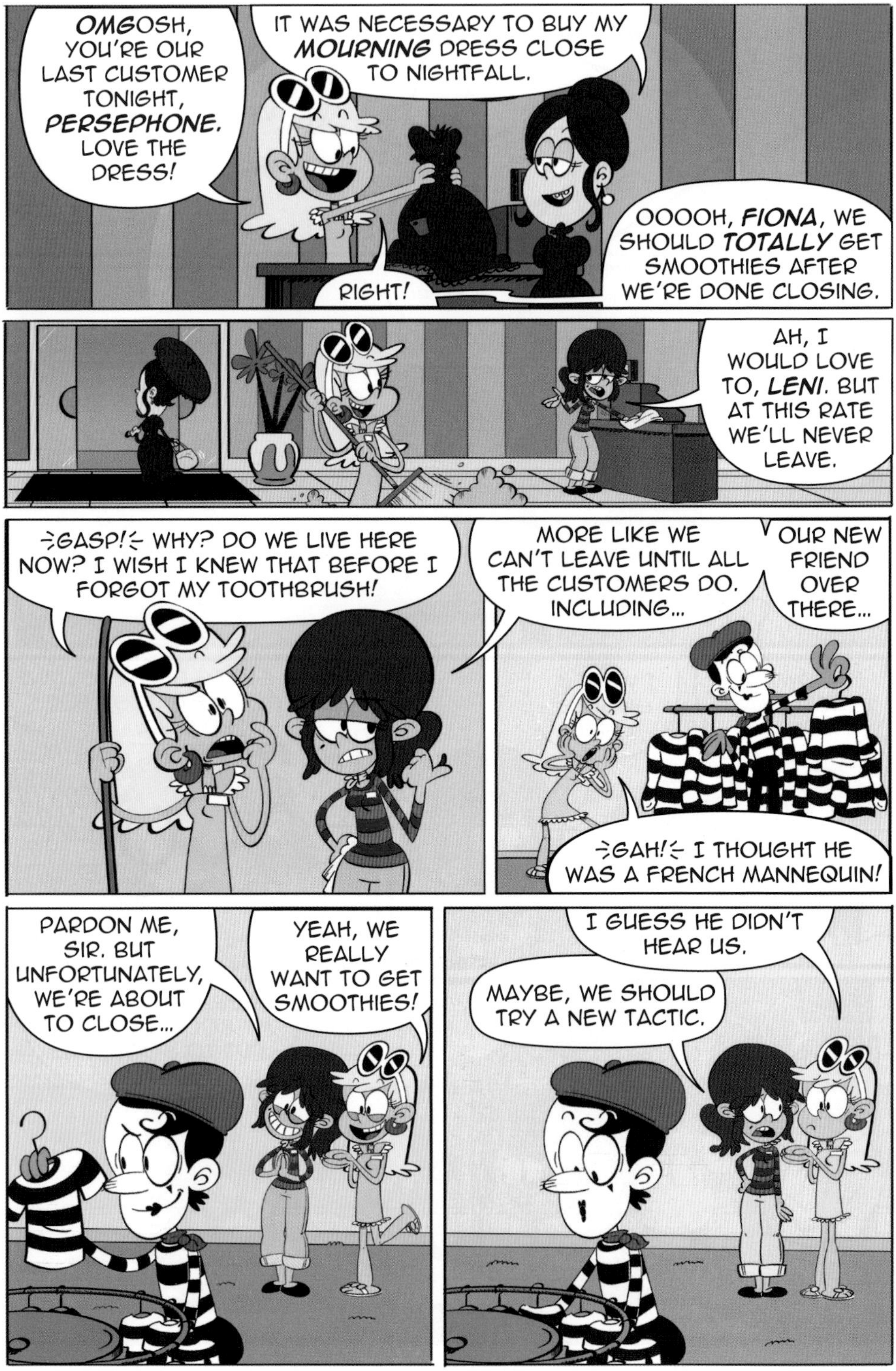

OMGOSH, YOU'RE OUR LAST CUSTOMER TONIGHT, PERSEPHONE. LOVE THE DRESS!
IT WAS NECESSARY TO BUY MY MOURNING DRESS CLOSE TO NIGHTFALL.
RIGHT!
OOOOH, FIONA, WE SHOULD TOTALLY GET SMOOTHIES AFTER WE'RE DONE CLOSING.
AH, I WOULD LOVE TO, LENI. BUT AT THIS RATE WE'LL NEVER LEAVE.
GASP! WHY? DO WE LIVE HERE NOW? I WISH I KNEW THAT BEFORE I FORGOT MY TOOTHBRUSH!
MORE LIKE WE CAN'T LEAVE UNTIL ALL THE CUSTOMERS DO. INCLUDING...
OUR NEW FRIEND OVER THERE...
GAH! I THOUGHT HE WAS A FRENCH MANNEQUIN!
PARDON ME, SIR. BUT UNFORTUNATELY, WE'RE ABOUT TO CLOSE...
YEAH, WE REALLY WANT TO GET SMOOTHIES!
I GUESS HE DIDN'T HEAR US.
MAYBE, WE SHOULD TRY A NEW TACTIC.

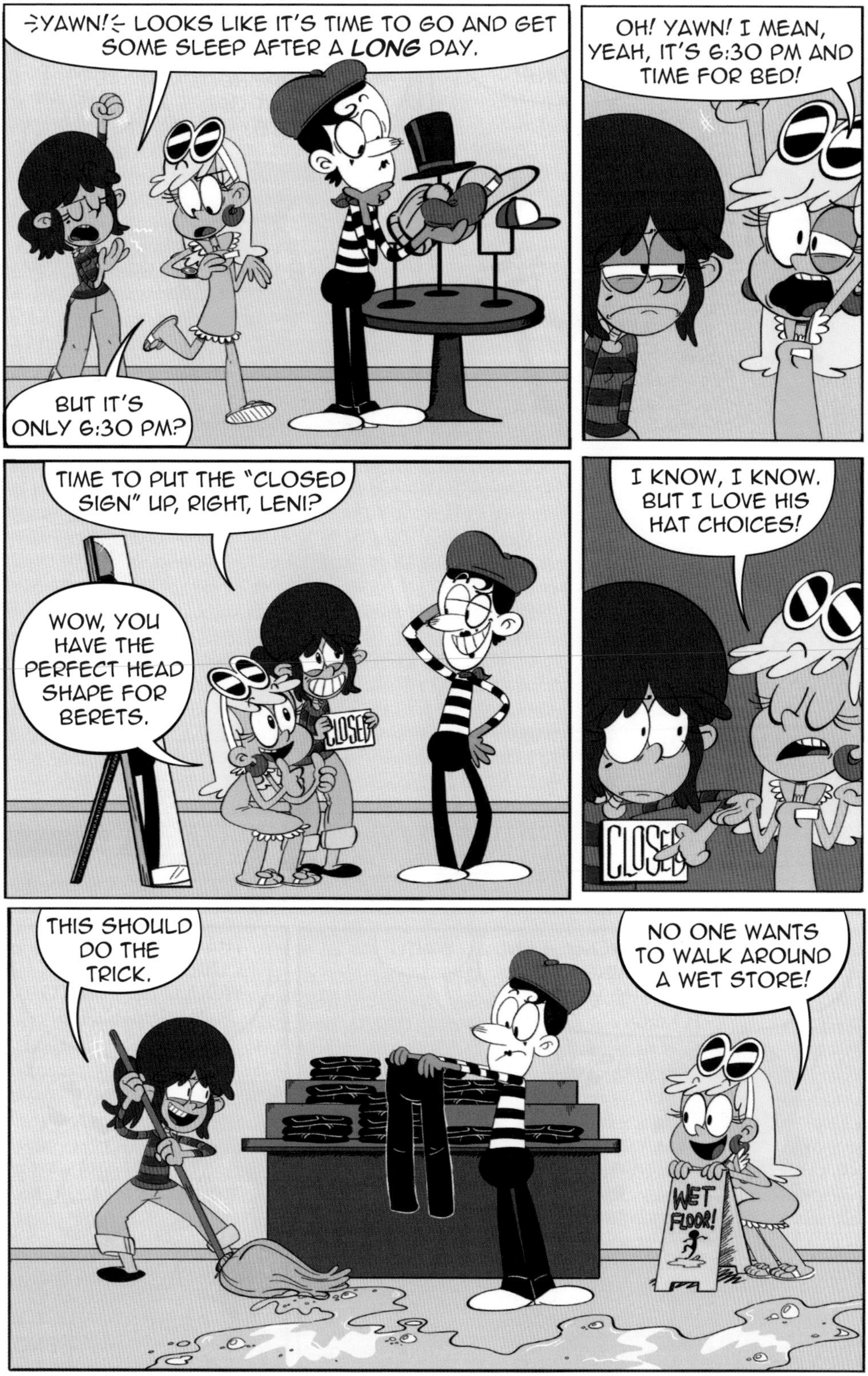
YAWN! LOOKS LIKE IT'S TIME TO GO AND GET SOME SLEEP AFTER A LONG DAY.
BUT IT'S ONLY 6:30 PM?
OH! YAWN! I MEAN, YEAH, IT'S 6:30 PM AND TIME FOR BED!
TIME TO PUT THE "CLOSED SIGN" UP, RIGHT, LENI?
WOW, YOU HAVE THE PERFECT HEAD SHAPE FOR BERETS.
CLOSED
I KNOW, I KNOW. BUT I LOVE HIS HAT CHOICES!
THIS SHOULD DO THE TRICK.
NO ONE WANTS TO WALK AROUND A WET STORE!
WET FLOOR!

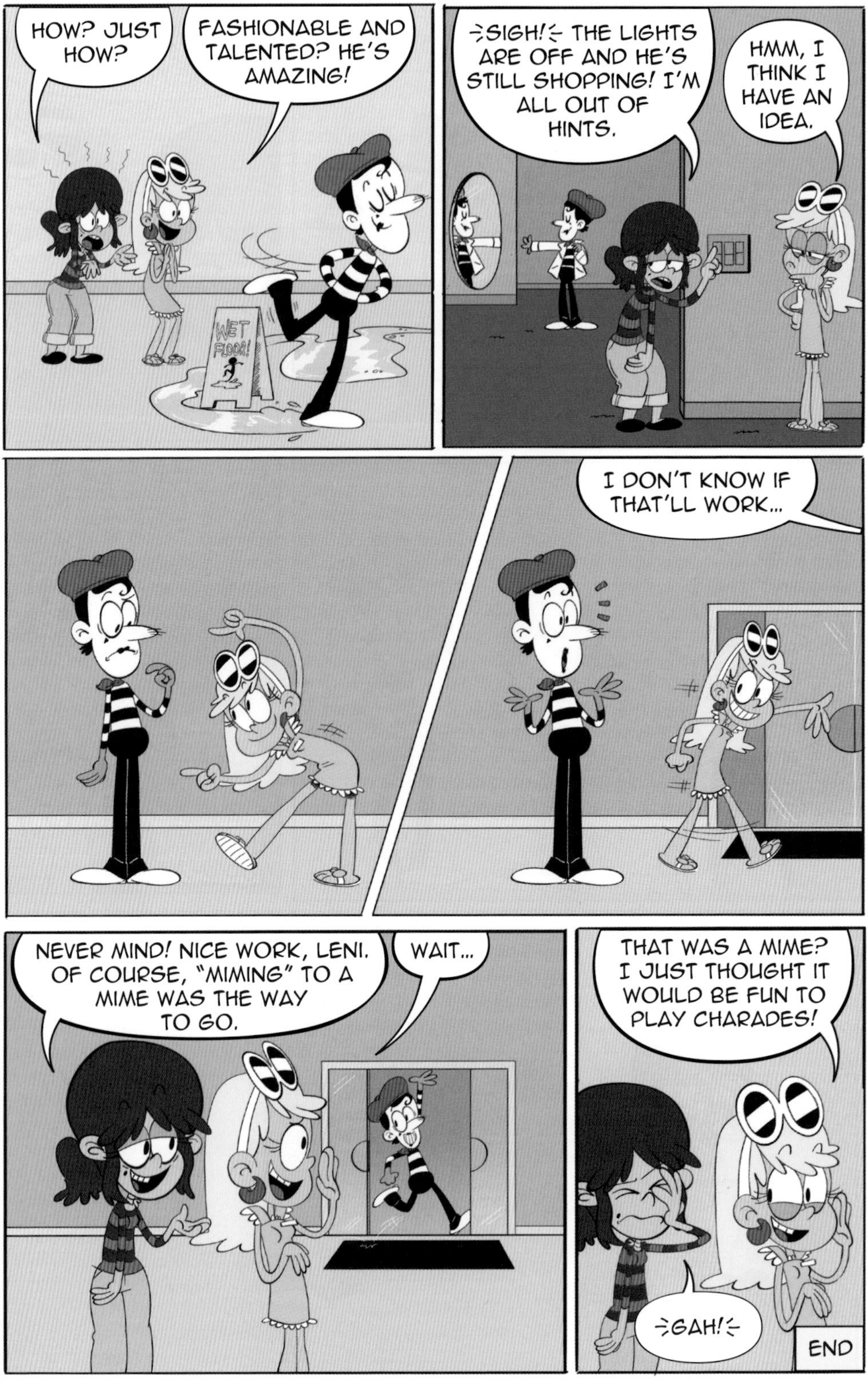
HOW? JUST HOW?
FASHIONABLE AND TALENTED? HE'S AMAZING!
WET FLOOR!
⇒SIGH!⇐ THE LIGHTS ARE OFF AND HE'S STILL SHOPPING! I'M ALL OUT OF HINTS.
HMM, I THINK I HAVE AN IDEA.
I DON'T KNOW IF THAT'LL WORK...
NEVER MIND! NICE WORK, LENI. OF COURSE, "MIMING" TO A MIME WAS THE WAY TO GO.
WAIT...
THAT WAS A MIME? I JUST THOUGHT IT WOULD BE FUN TO PLAY CHARADES!
⇒GAH!⇐
END

"GONE GNOME"

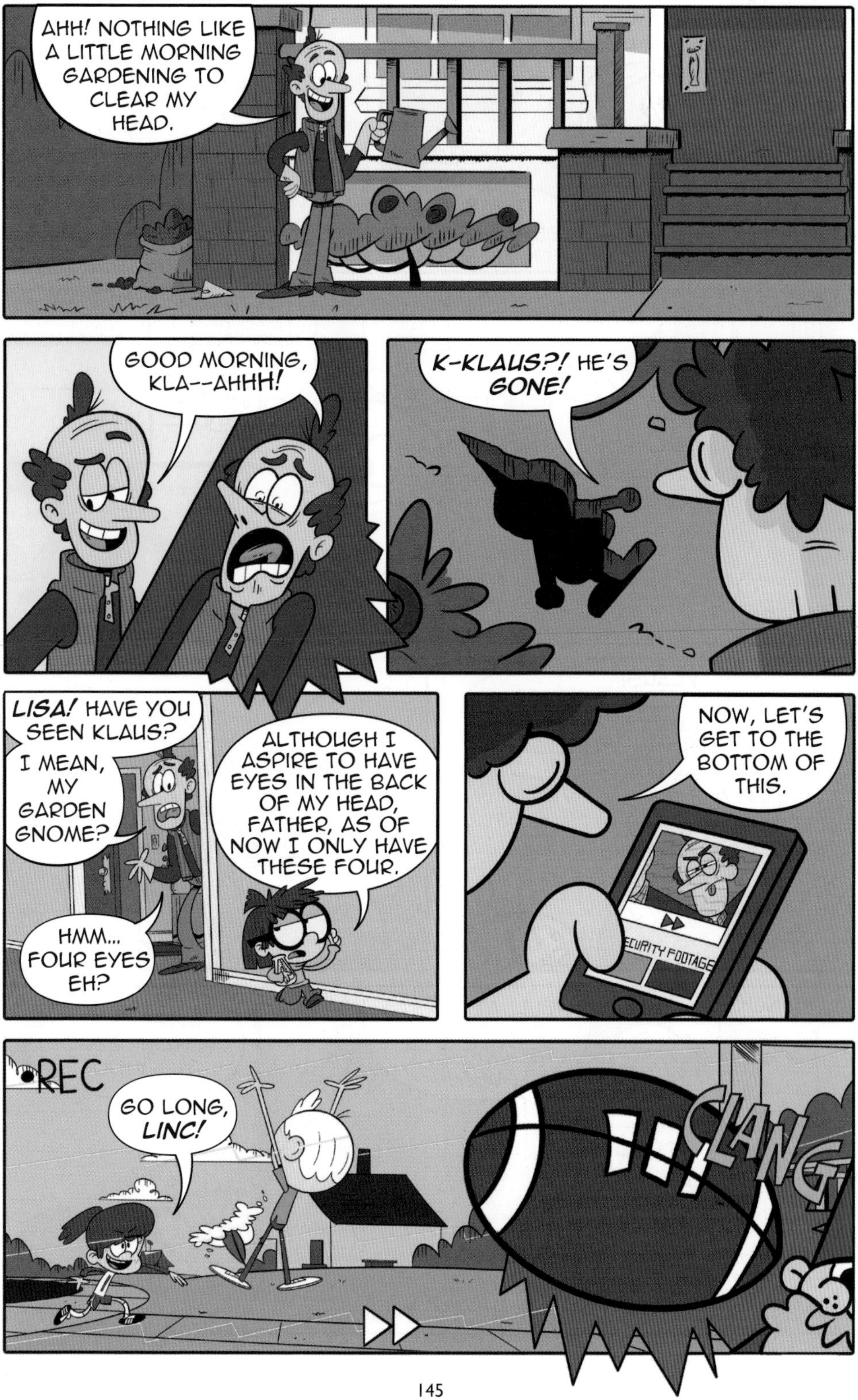
AHH! NOTHING LIKE A LITTLE MORNING GARDENING TO CLEAR MY HEAD.
GOOD MORNING, KLA--AHHH!
K-KLAUS?! HE'S GONE!
LISA! HAVE YOU SEEN KLAUS?
I MEAN, MY GARDEN GNOME?
ALTHOUGH I ASPIRE TO HAVE EYES IN THE BACK OF MY HEAD, FATHER, AS OF NOW I ONLY HAVE THESE FOUR.
HMM... FOUR EYES EH?
NOW, LET'S GET TO THE BOTTOM OF THIS.
SECURITY FOOTAGE
•REC
GO LONG, LINC!
CLANG

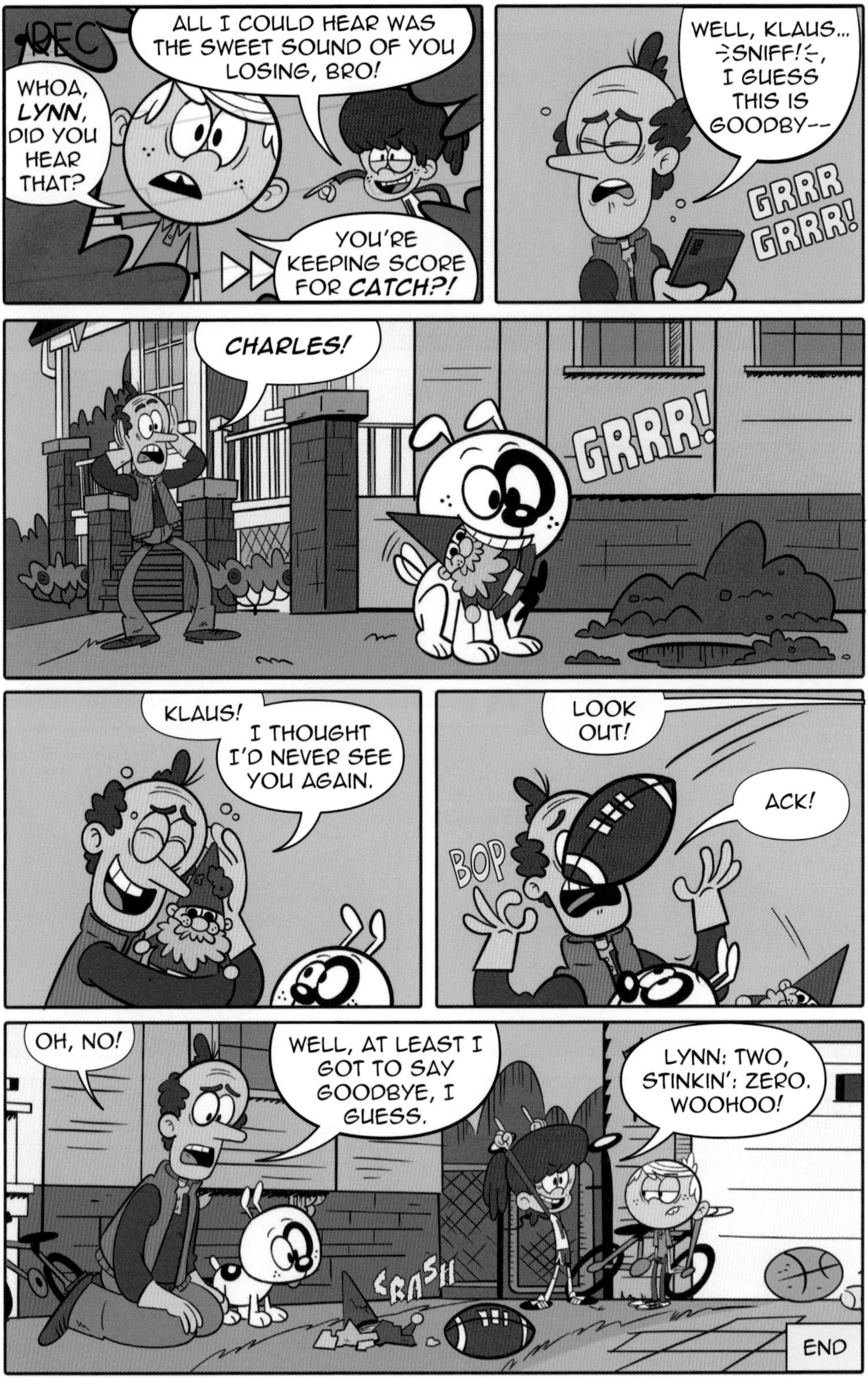
REC
ALL I COULD HEAR WAS THE SWEET SOUND OF YOU LOSING, BRO!
WHOA, LYNN, DID YOU HEAR THAT?
YOU'RE KEEPING SCORE FOR CATCH?!
WELL, KLAUS... SNIFF!, I GUESS THIS IS GOODBY--
GRRR GRRR!
CHARLES!
GRRR!
KLAUS! I THOUGHT I'D NEVER SEE YOU AGAIN.
LOOK OUT!
ACK!
BOP
OH, NO!
WELL, AT LEAST I GOT TO SAY GOODBYE, I GUESS.
LYNN: TWO, STINKIN': ZERO. WOOHOO!
CRASH
END

"FRIENDS FUR-EVER"

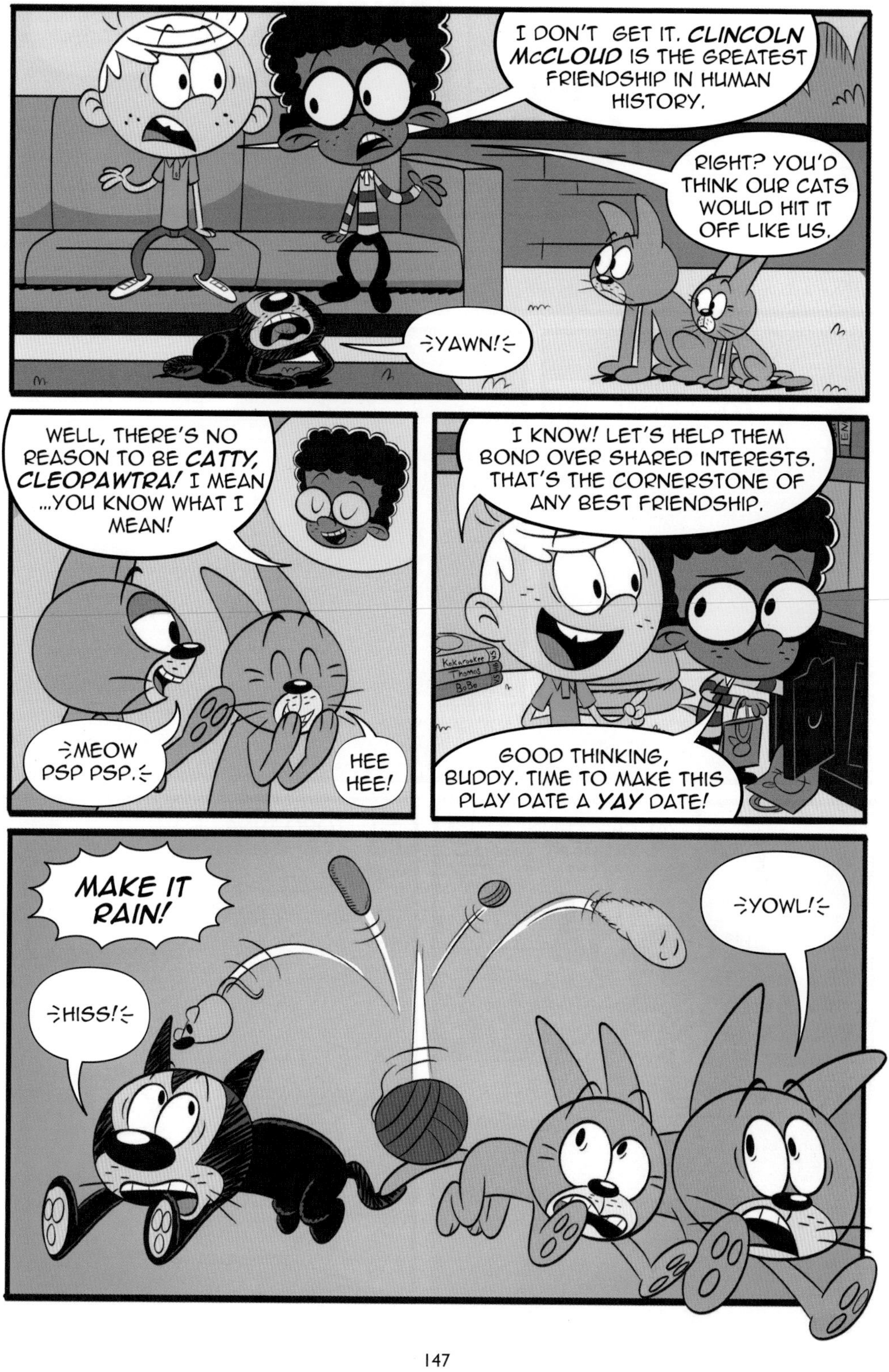
I DON'T GET IT. CLINCOLN McCLOUD IS THE GREATEST FRIENDSHIP IN HUMAN HISTORY.
RIGHT? YOU'D THINK OUR CATS WOULD HIT IT OFF LIKE US.
YAWN!
WELL, THERE'S NO REASON TO BE CATTY, CLEOPAWTRA! I MEAN ...YOU KNOW WHAT I MEAN!
MEOW PSP PSP.
HEE HEE!
I KNOW! LET'S HELP THEM BOND OVER SHARED INTERESTS. THAT'S THE CORNERSTONE OF ANY BEST FRIENDSHIP.
Kokarooker
Thomas
BoBo
GOOD THINKING, BUDDY. TIME TO MAKE THIS PLAY DATE A YAY DATE!
MAKE IT RAIN!
HISS!
YOWL!

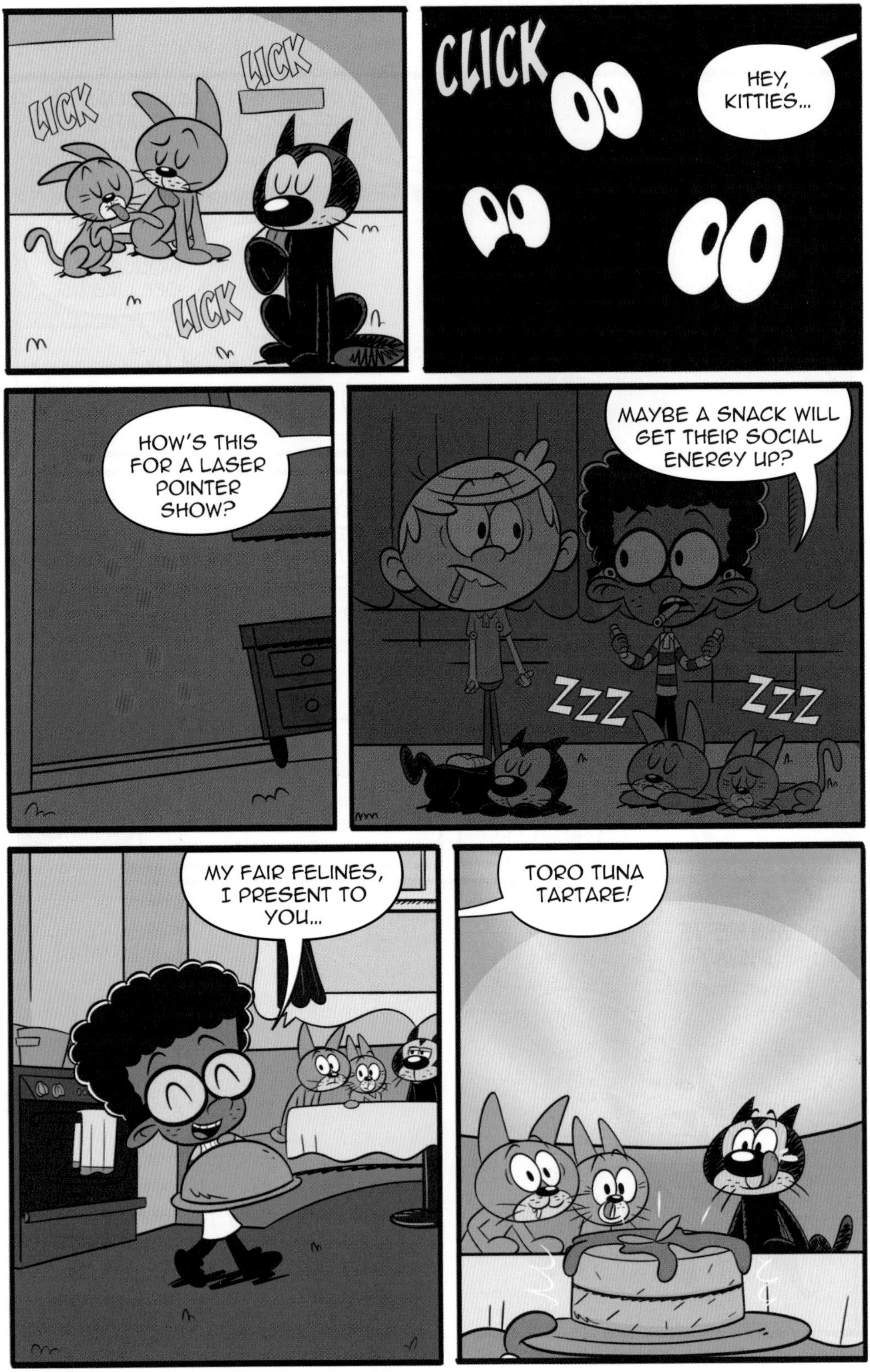
LICK
LICK
LICK
CLICK
HEY, KITTIES...
HOW'S THIS FOR A LASER POINTER SHOW?
MAYBE A SNACK WILL GET THEIR SOCIAL ENERGY UP?
ZZZ
ZZZ
MY FAIR FELINES, I PRESENT TO YOU...
TORO TUNA TARTARE!

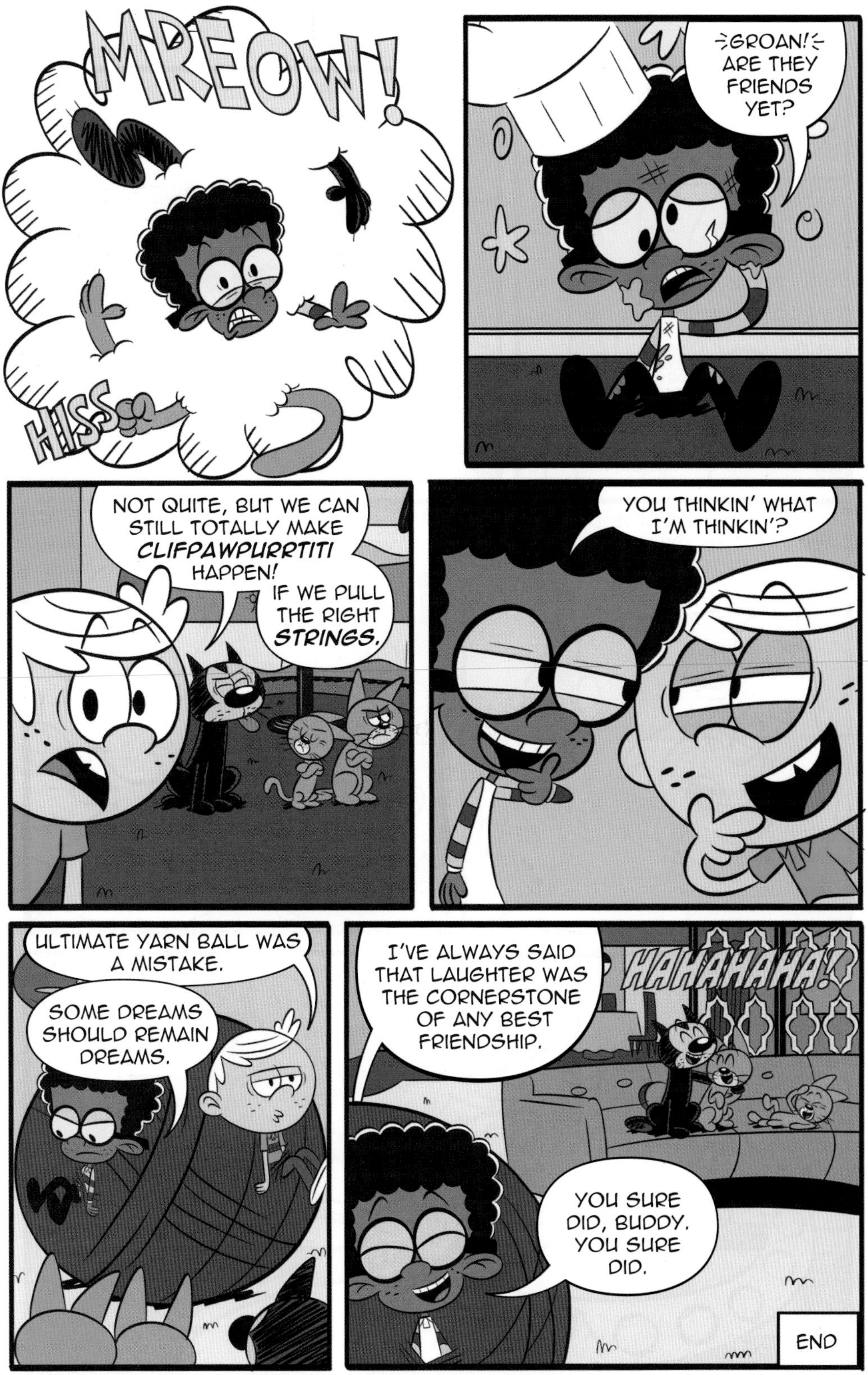
MREOW!
HISS
GROAN!
ARE THEY FRIENDS YET?
NOT QUITE, BUT WE CAN STILL TOTALLY MAKE CLIFPAWPURRTITI HAPPEN!
IF WE PULL THE RIGHT STRINGS.
YOU THINKIN' WHAT I'M THINKIN'?
ULTIMATE YARN BALL WAS A MISTAKE.
SOME DREAMS SHOULD REMAIN DREAMS.
I'VE ALWAYS SAID THAT LAUGHTER WAS THE CORNERSTONE OF ANY BEST FRIENDSHIP.
HAHAHAHA!
YOU SURE DID, BUDDY. YOU SURE DID.
END

"PURRSONAL HYGIENE"

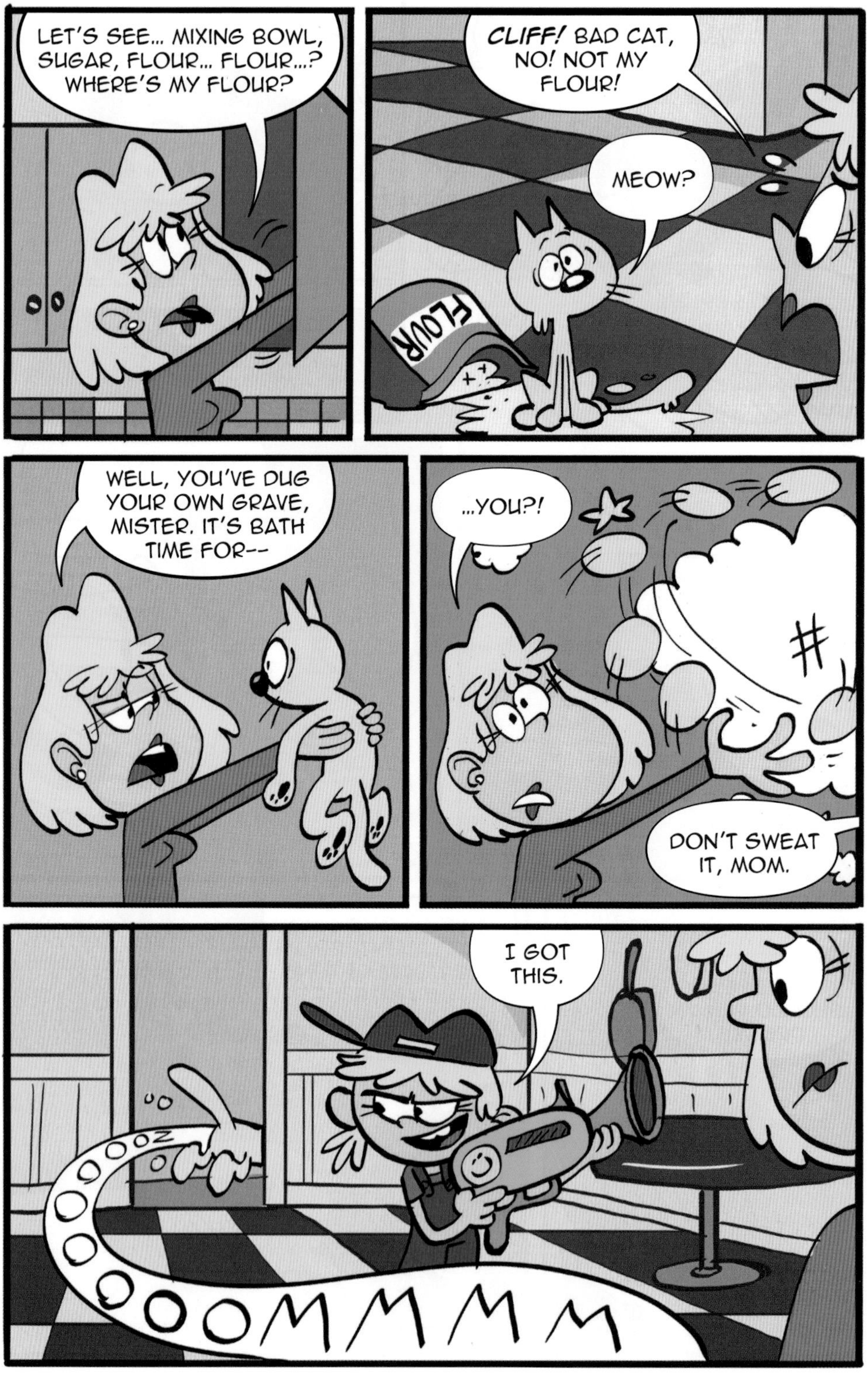
LET'S SEE... MIXING BOWL, SUGAR, FLOUR... FLOUR...? WHERE'S MY FLOUR?
CLIFF! BAD CAT, NO! NOT MY FLOUR!
MEOW?
FLOUR
WELL, YOU'VE DUG YOUR OWN GRAVE, MISTER. IT'S BATH TIME FOR--
...YOU?!
DON'T SWEAT IT, MOM.
I GOT THIS.
OOOOOOOOOOOMMMMM

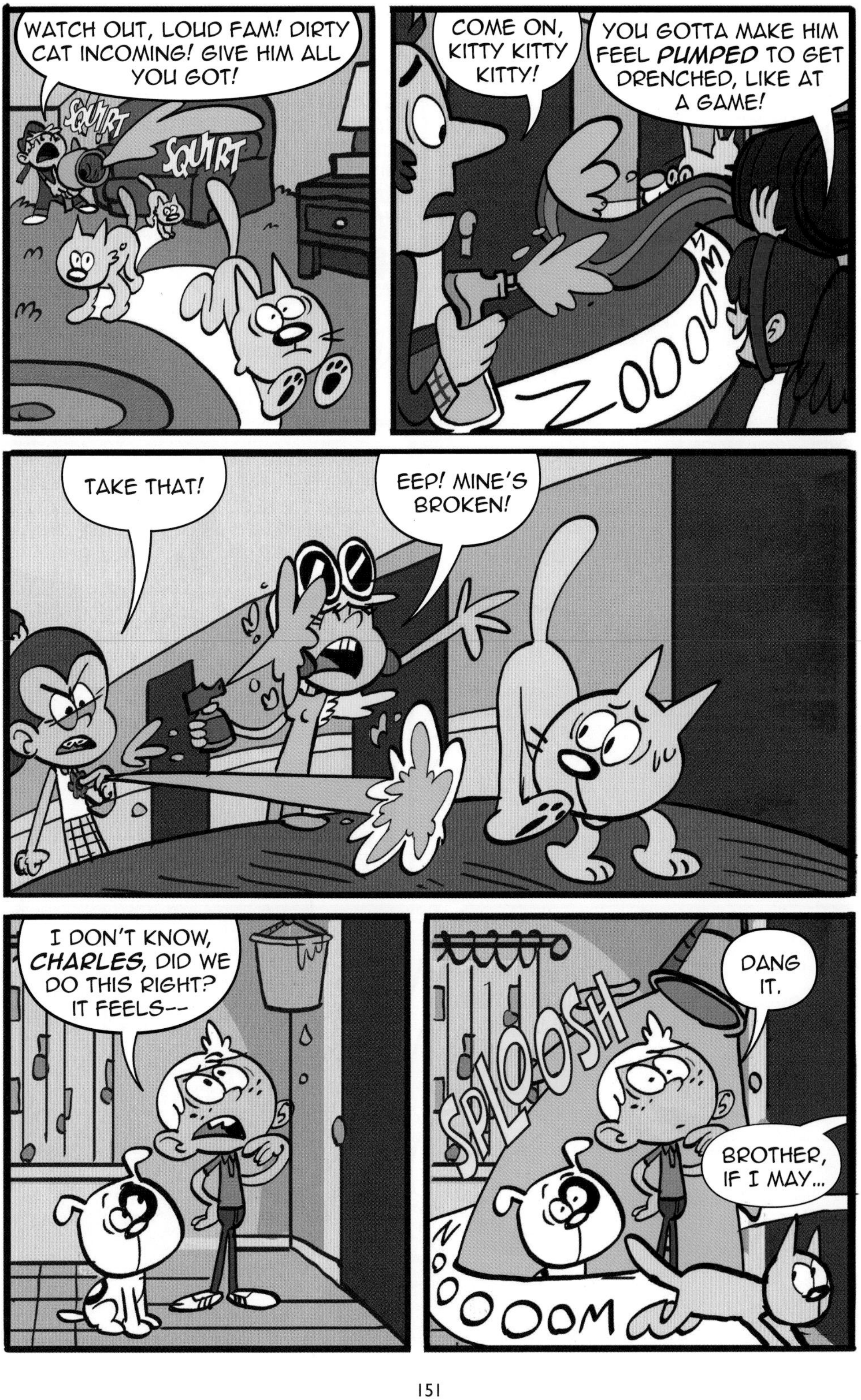
WATCH OUT, LOUD FAM! DIRTY CAT INCOMING! GIVE HIM ALL YOU GOT!
SQUIRT
SQUIRT
COME ON, KITTY KITTY KITTY!
YOU GOTTA MAKE HIM FEEL **PUMPED** TO GET DRENCHED, LIKE AT A GAME!
ZOOOOOM
TAKE THAT!
EEP! MINE'S BROKEN!
I DON'T KNOW, **CHARLES**, DID WE DO THIS RIGHT? IT FEELS--
SPLOOSH
DANG IT.
BROTHER, IF I MAY...
NOOOOOM

THERE'S NO WAY YOU'LL BE ABLE TO BATHE THE CAT THAT EASILY... IT'S PART OF THE LIQUID-TO-CAT VARIABLE. NO MATTER HOW DIRTY THE CAT, THEY WILL ALWAYS REJECT LIQUID.

UNLESS...

BY ALTERING THE DNA RESPONSIBLE FOR THE UBIQUITOUS LIQUID-TO-CAT VARIABLE, IT'S POSSIBLE TO MAKE A CAT TOLERATE WATER- OR EVEN BETTER, LEARN TO ENJOY IT. ALL WE NEED TO DO IS A SIMPLE PROCEDURE, WITH A SIMPLE MACHINE, ... TIMEFRAME. IT SH... ... IN A PINCH. ... ER OF ... WI... ...IN THE AMY... ...THOUT F... ...CUP

OR, IN OTHER WORDS, JUST USE MY NEW MACHINE, THE AMYGDALA CHURNER! A TOTALLY ANIMAL TESTED AND EFFECTIVE WAY TO MAKE CATS NATURALLY HYDROPHILIC.

UHH... LISA, ARE YOU SURE THAT'S, Y'KNOW, SAFE?

MY DEAR, DEAR SIBLING, HAVE I EVER DONE YOU WRONG?

WELL--

IN JUST A MOMENT, YOU'LL SEE JUST HOW EFFECTIVE THIS WILL BE!

LET'S FIND THAT DIRTY CAT, AND--

WHAT! CLIFF CLEANED HIMSELF?!

HAH, I GUESS WE WON'T NEED TO USE YOUR MACHINE AFTER ALL!

SLURP

YES, I SUPPOSE WE WON'T...

THIS TIME...

END

"ONE GOOD PUSH"

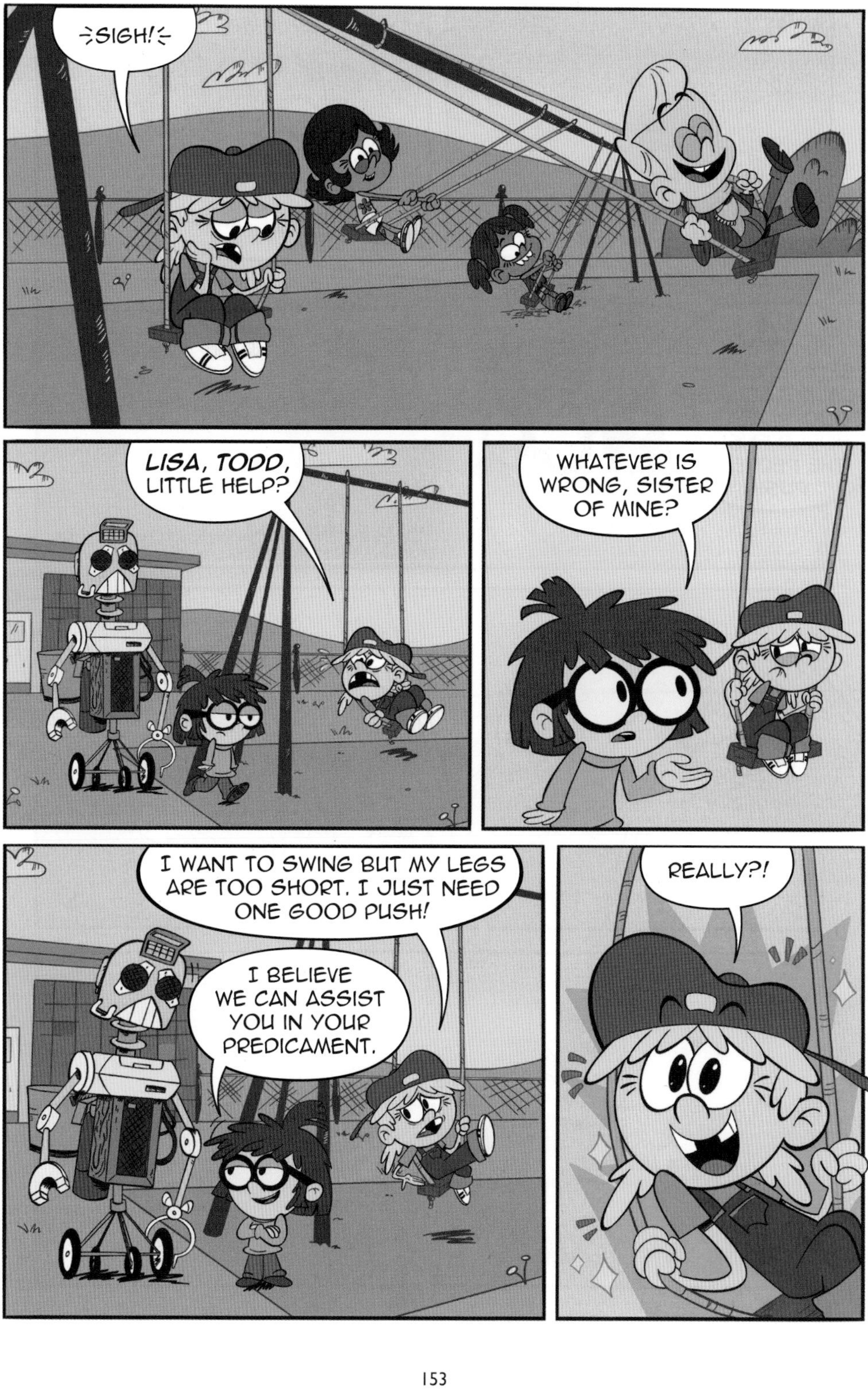

SIGH!
LISA, TODD, LITTLE HELP?
WHATEVER IS WRONG, SISTER OF MINE?
I WANT TO SWING BUT MY LEGS ARE TOO SHORT. I JUST NEED ONE GOOD PUSH!
I BELIEVE WE CAN ASSIST YOU IN YOUR PREDICAMENT.
REALLY?!

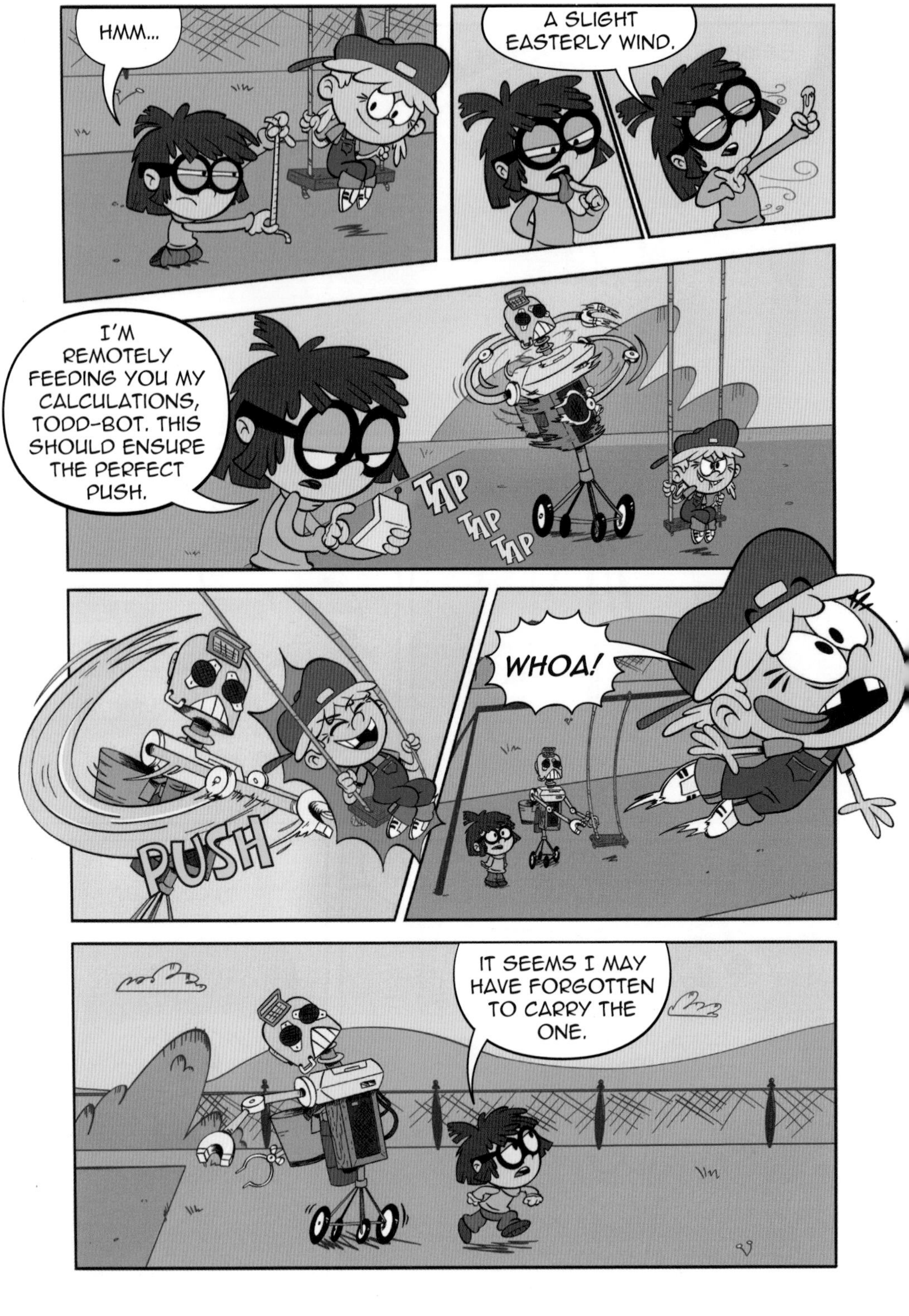
HMM...
A SLIGHT EASTERLY WIND.
I'M REMOTELY FEEDING YOU MY CALCULATIONS, TODD-BOT. THIS SHOULD ENSURE THE PERFECT PUSH.
TAP
TAP
TAP
PUSH
WHOA!
IT SEEMS I MAY HAVE FORGOTTEN TO CARRY THE ONE.

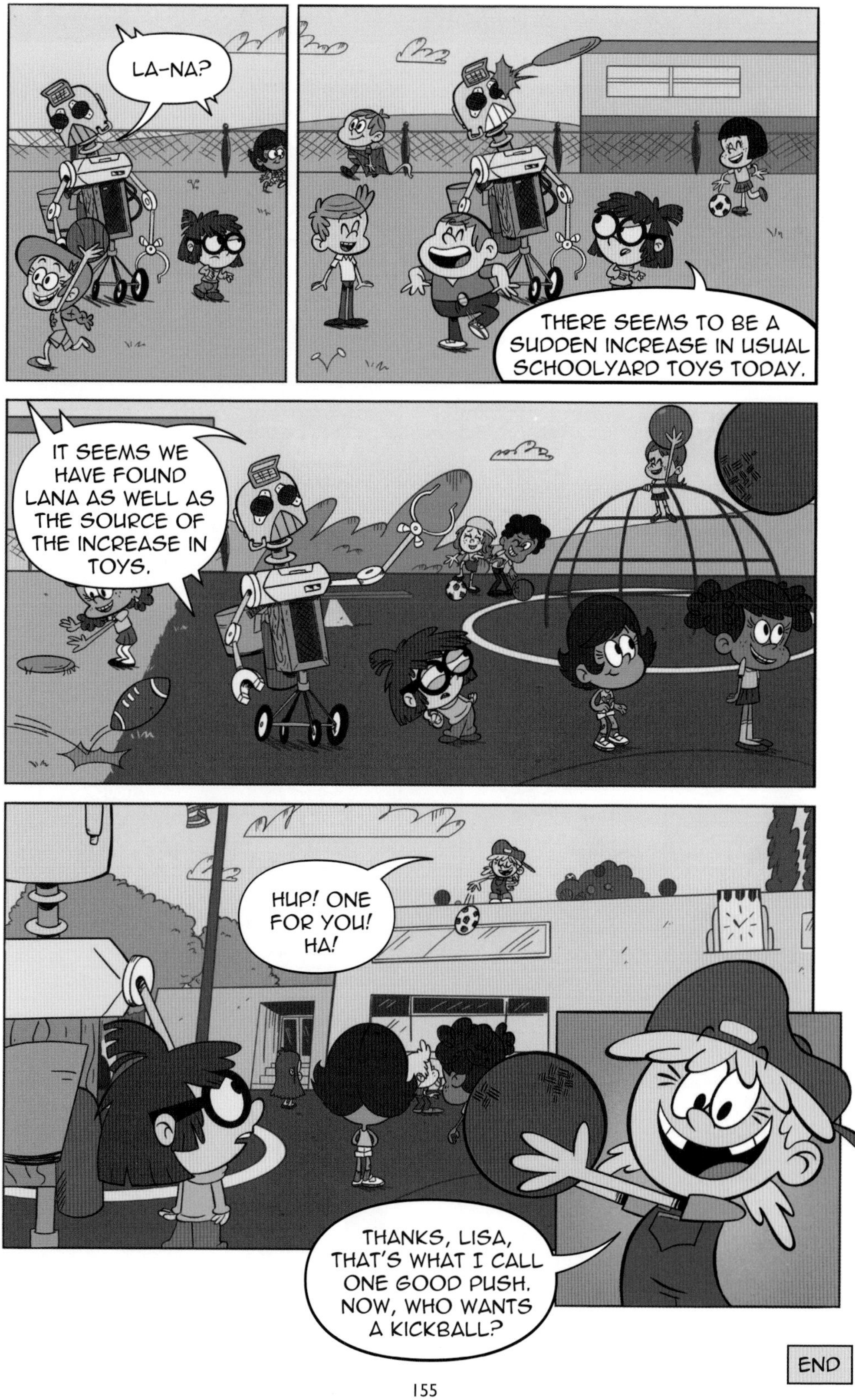
LA-NA?
THERE SEEMS TO BE A SUDDEN INCREASE IN USUAL SCHOOLYARD TOYS TODAY.
IT SEEMS WE HAVE FOUND LANA AS WELL AS THE SOURCE OF THE INCREASE IN TOYS.
HUP! ONE FOR YOU! HA!
THANKS, LISA, THAT'S WHAT I CALL ONE GOOD PUSH. NOW, WHO WANTS A KICKBALL?
END

nickelodeon GRAPHIC NOVELS AVAILABLE FROM PAPERCUTZ

nickelodeon
NICKELODEON'S HIT NEW ANIMATED SHOW
THE LOUD HOUSE
THERE WILL BE CHAOS
PAPERCUTZ

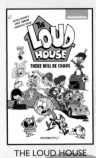

THE LOUD HOUSE
#1
"There Will Be Chaos"

nickelodeon
THE LOUD HOUSE
THERE WILL BE CHAOS

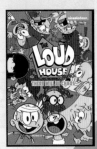

THE LOUD HOUSE
#2
"There Will Be More Chaos"

nickelodeon
THE LOUD HOUSE
LIVE LIFE LOUD!

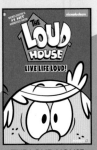

THE LOUD HOUSE
#3
"Live Life Loud!"

nickelodeon
THE LOUD HOUSE
FAMILY TREE
KEEP OUT!

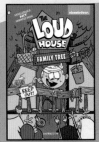

THE LOUD HOUSE
#4
"Family Tree"

nickelodeon
NICKELODEON'S HIT ANIMATED SHOW
THE LOUD HOUSE
AFTER DARK

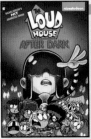

THE LOUD HOUSE
#5
"After Dark"

nickelodeon
NICKELODEON'S HIT SHOW
THE LOUD HOUSE
LOUD & PROUD
PAPERCUTZ

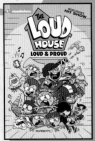

THE LOUD HOUSE
#6
"Loud and Proud"

nickelodeon
THE LOUD HOUSE
THE STRUGGLE IS REAL

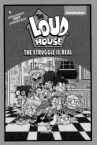

THE LOUD HOUSE
#7
"The Struggle is Real"

nickelodeon
THE LOUD HOUSE
Livin' La Casa Loud!
PAPERCUTZ

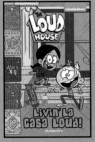

THE LOUD HOUSE
#8
"Livin' La Casa Loud"

nickelodeon
FROM NICKELODEON'S HIT ANIMATED SHOW
THE LOUD HOUSE
ULTIMATE HANGOUT
PAPERCUTZ

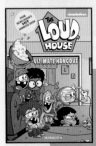

THE LOUD HOUSE
#9
"Ultimate Hangout"

nickelodeon
THE LOUD HOUSE
THE MANY FACES OF LINCOLN LOUD
PAPERCUTZ

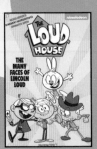

THE LOUD HOUSE
#10
"The Many Faces of
Lincoln Loud"

nickelodeon
THE LOUD HOUSE
WHO'S THE LOUDEST?
PAPERCUTZ

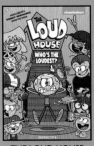

THE LOUD HOUSE
#11
"Who's the Loudest?"

nickelodeon
THE LOUD HOUSE
THE CASE OF THE STOLEN DRAWERS
PAPERCUTZ

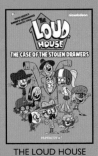

THE LOUD HOUSE
#12
"The Case of the Stolen
Drawers"

nickelodeon
NICKELODEON'S HIT ANIMATED SHOW
THE LOUD HOUSE
LUCY ROLLS THE DICE
PAPERCUTZ

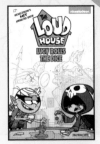

THE LOUD HOUSE
#13
"Lucy Rolls the Dice"

nickelodeon
NICKELODEON'S HIT ANIMATED SHOW
THE LOUD HOUSE
GUESSING GAMES
PAPERCUTZ

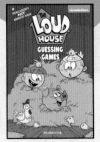

THE LOUD HOUSE
#14
"Guessing Games"

nickelodeon
THE LOUD HOUSE
THE MISSING LINC
PAPERCUTZ

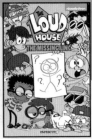

THE LOUD HOUSE
#15
"The Missing Linc"

COMING SOON

nickelodeon
THE LOUD HOUSE
LOUD AND CLEAR
PAPERCUTZ

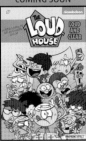

THE LOUD HOUSE
#16
"Loud and Clear"

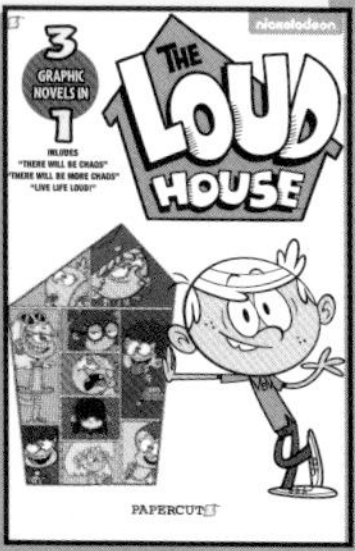
nickelodeon
3 GRAPHIC NOVELS IN 1
THE LOUD HOUSE
PAPERCUTZ

THE LOUD HOUSE
3 IN 1
#1

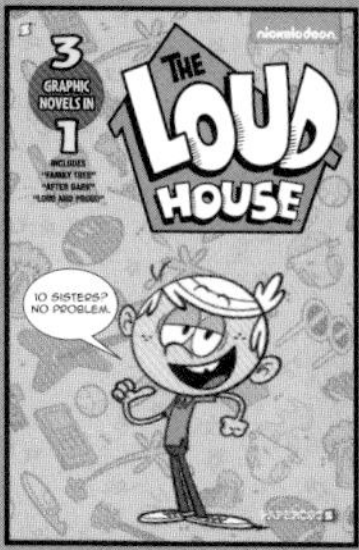
nickelodeon
3 GRAPHIC NOVELS IN 1
THE LOUD HOUSE
10 SISTERS? NO PROBLEM.
PAPERCUTZ

THE LOUD HOUSE
3 IN 1
#2

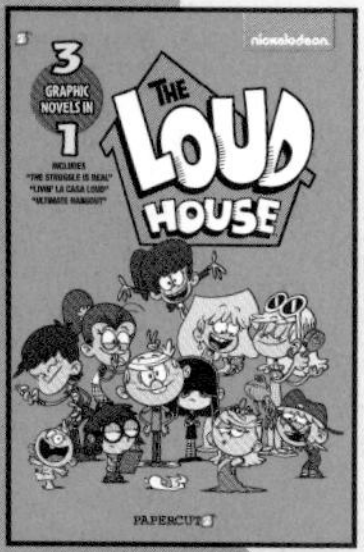
nickelodeon
3 GRAPHIC NOVELS IN 1
THE LOUD HOUSE
PAPERCUTZ

THE LOUD HOUSE
3 IN 1
#3

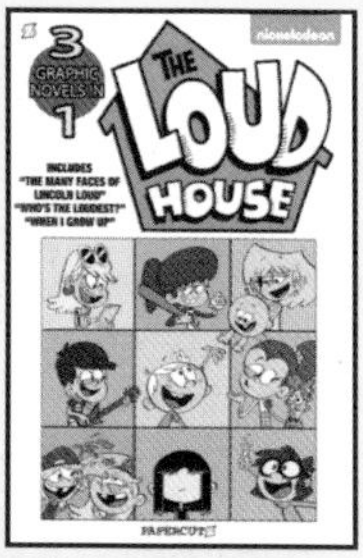
nickelodeon
3 GRAPHIC NOVELS IN 1
THE LOUD HOUSE
PAPERCUTZ

THE LOUD HOUSE
3 IN 1
#4

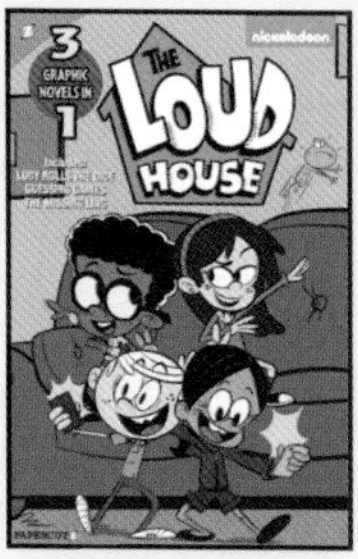
nickelodeon
3 GRAPHIC NOVELS IN 1
THE LOUD HOUSE
PAPERCUTZ

THE LOUD HOUSE
3 IN 1
#5

COMING SOON

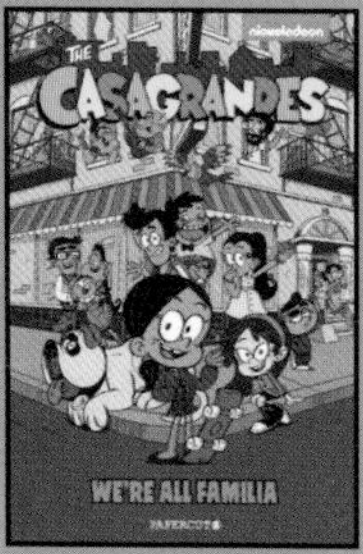
nickelodeon
THE CASAGRANDES
WE'RE ALL FAMILIA
PAPERCUTZ

THE CASAGRANDES
#1
"We're All Familia"

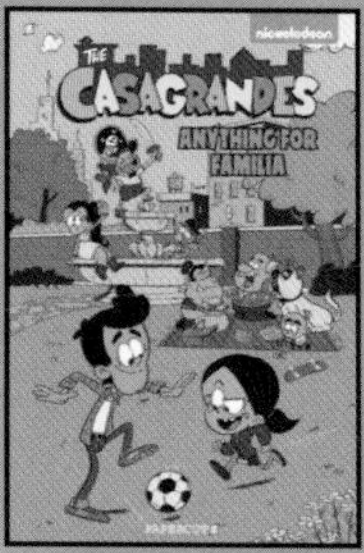
nickelodeon
THE CASAGRANDES
ANYTHING FOR FAMILIA
PAPERCUTZ

THE CASAGRANDES
#2
"Anything for Familia"

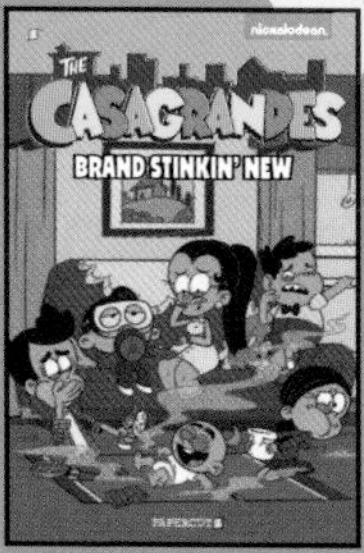
nickelodeon
THE CASAGRANDES
BRAND STINKIN' NEW
PAPERCUTZ

THE CASAGRANDES
#3
"Brand Stinkin' New"

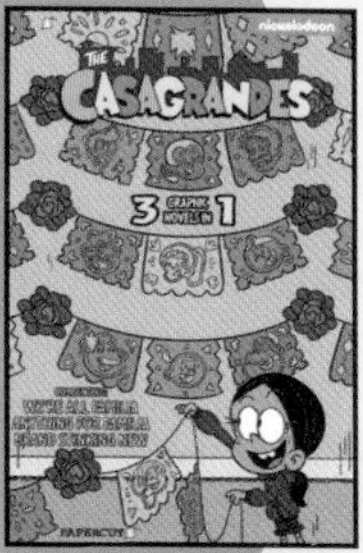
nickelodeon
THE CASAGRANDES
3 GRAPHIC NOVELS IN 1
PAPERCUTZ

THE CASAGRANDES
3 IN 1
#1

COMING SOON

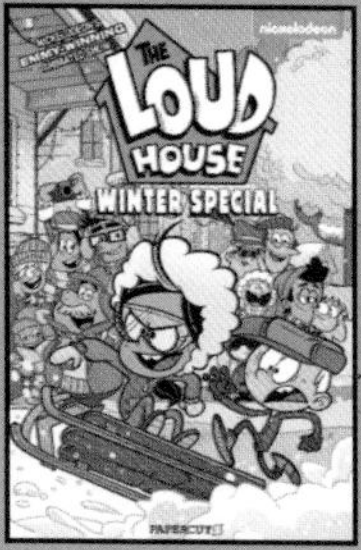
nickelodeon
THE LOUD HOUSE
WINTER SPECIAL
PAPERCUTZ

THE LOUD HOUSE
WINTER SPECIAL

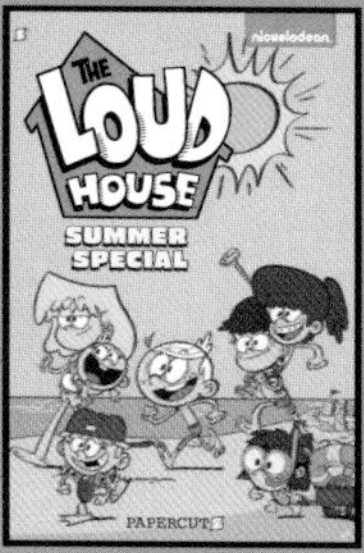
nickelodeon
THE LOUD HOUSE
SUMMER SPECIAL
PAPERCUTZ

THE LOUD HOUSE
SUMMER SPECIAL

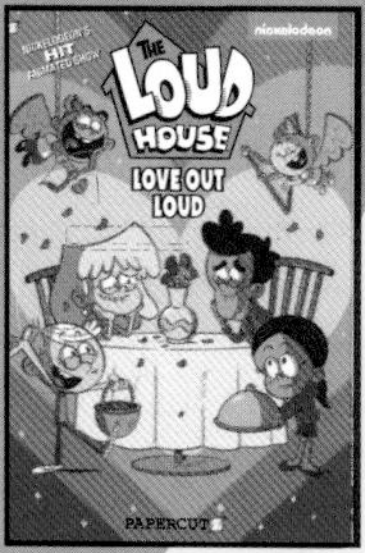
nickelodeon
THE LOUD HOUSE
LOVE OUT LOUD
PAPERCUTZ

THE LOUD HOUSE
LOVE OUT LOUD
SPECIAL

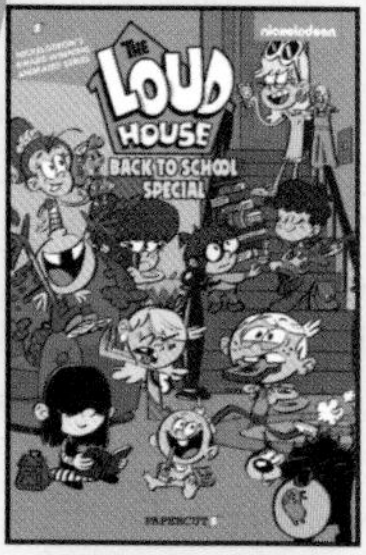
nickelodeon
THE LOUD HOUSE
BACK TO SCHOOL SPECIAL
PAPERCUTZ

THE LOUD HOUSE
BACK TO SCHOOL
SPECIAL

WATCH OUT FOR PAPERCUTZ

Welcome to the fast and furriest, fifth THE LOUD HOUSE 3 IN 1 graphic novel from Papercutz—those pop culture purr-veyors dedicated to publishing great graphic novels for all ages. I'm Jim Salicrup, Editor-in-Chief and Critter Cleaner-upper, here to offer a peak at what exciting new projects featuring the stars from THE LOUD HOUSE are coming your way from Papercutz…

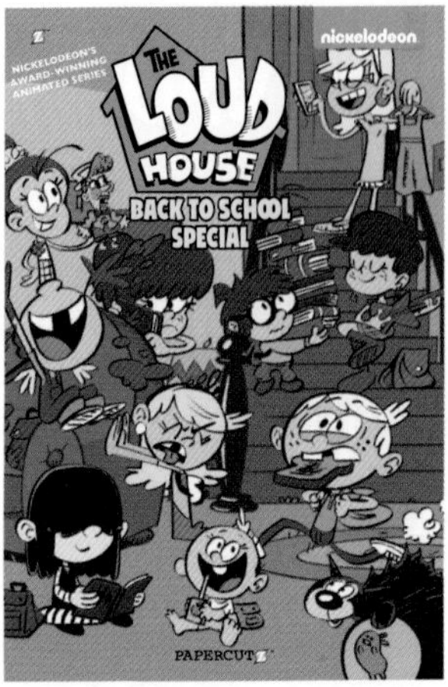
nickelodeon
NICKELODEON'S AWARD-WINNING ANIMATED SERIES
THE LOUD HOUSE
BACK TO SCHOOL SPECIAL
PAPERCUTZ

First, if you enjoyed such stories from this very book such as "I Believe," "Lisa's Paper View," and "One Good Push," then you're going to love THE LOUD HOUSE BACK TO SCHOOL SPECIAL. Lincoln and his sisters Lori, Leni, Luna, Lynn, Luan, Lucy, Lola, Lana, Lisa, and even Lily, are ready to hit the books as they search for the secrets of the universe and hope that can help them survive school. Ah, yes, school. Love it or hate, you still have to go to school. Lincoln's new challenge is going from being the Man with the Plan in elementary school to now being the new kid without a hall pass in middle school. Things have certainly changed for Lincoln and best friend, Clyde McBride. But the biggest change of all is Lori starting college–and what a very strange golf-oriented college it is–while still trying to maintain her long-distance relationship with her boo boo bear, Bobby Santiago. And Bobby's sister, Ronnie Anne, goes to prep school! That's got to be more entertaining than a last period lecture on a Friday right before vacation. Well, the vacation's over for the Louds, and they all have new challenges to face.

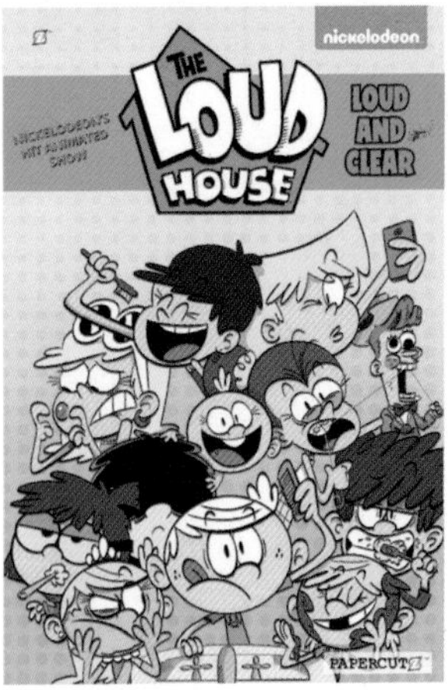
nickelodeon
THE LOUD HOUSE
LOUD AND CLEAR
PAPERCUTZ

Speaking of school, we sort of sprung a little Pop Quiz on you starting back on page 4. Can you identify all the characters from THE LOUD HOUSE and THE CASAGRANDES just from their silhouette? Give it a try! Don't worry, this won't have any impact on your overall grade point average! Answers are on pages 159-160, but no peeking!

Then of course, there's the sweet 16th volume of our regular ongoing series of THE LOUD HOUSE graphic novels, "Loud and Clear." Despite the title, sometimes things aren't all that they seem… Lori is beyond bored in her dorm, until she enters a uniform contest and calls on the best fashion designer she knows, her sister Leni, of course. But is this plan bursting at the seams? Speaking of fashion, Lincoln is rocking a new look. He's feeling confident and looking great, but things sometimes don't go as planned for the Man with the Plan. Find Lincoln and his sisters in a game of Hide-and-Seek where Lincoln ups the stakes with a tempting prize.

All we know is that we're having more fun than ever working with the creative talent of THE LOUD HOUSE and THE CASAGRANDES to bring you all-new stories that we hope you enjoy as much as we enjoy creating them. And based on some of our upcoming sales figures, we must be doing something right. The sales of the Papercutz graphic novels of THE LOUD HOUSE and THE CASAGRANDES are simply sky-rocketing! Just as the Louds are ascending to their next educational level, our sales are climbing ever higher–for which we thank you!

So, do I even have to say don't miss any of the upcoming graphic novels of THE LOUD HOUSE or THE CASAGRANDES?

Thanks, Jim

STAY IN TOUCH!

EMAIL:	salicrup@papercutz.com
WEB:	papercutz.com
TWITTER:	@papercutzgn
INSTAGRAM:	@papercutzgn
FACEBOOK:	PAPERCUTZGRAPHICNOVELS
FANMAIL:	Papercutz, 160 Broadway, Suite 700, East Wing, New York, NY 10038

Go to papercutz.com and sign up for the free Papercutz e-newsletter!

GUESS WHO?! Answers

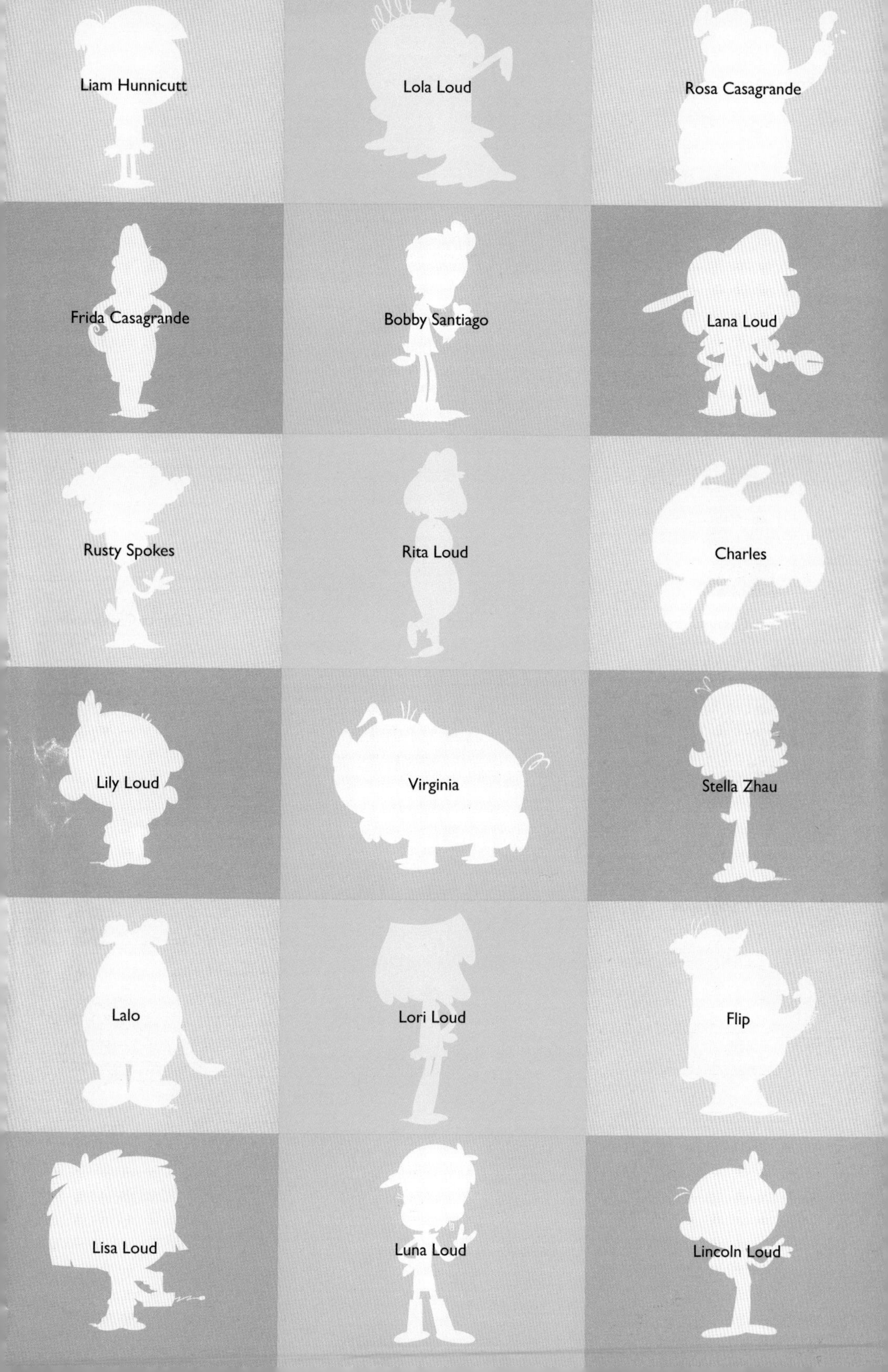
Liam Hunnicutt
Lola Loud
Rosa Casagrande
Frida Casagrande
Bobby Santiago
Lana Loud
Rusty Spokes
Rita Loud
Charles
Lily Loud
Virginia
Stella Zhau
Lalo
Lori Loud
Flip
Lisa Loud
Luna Loud
Lincoln Loud

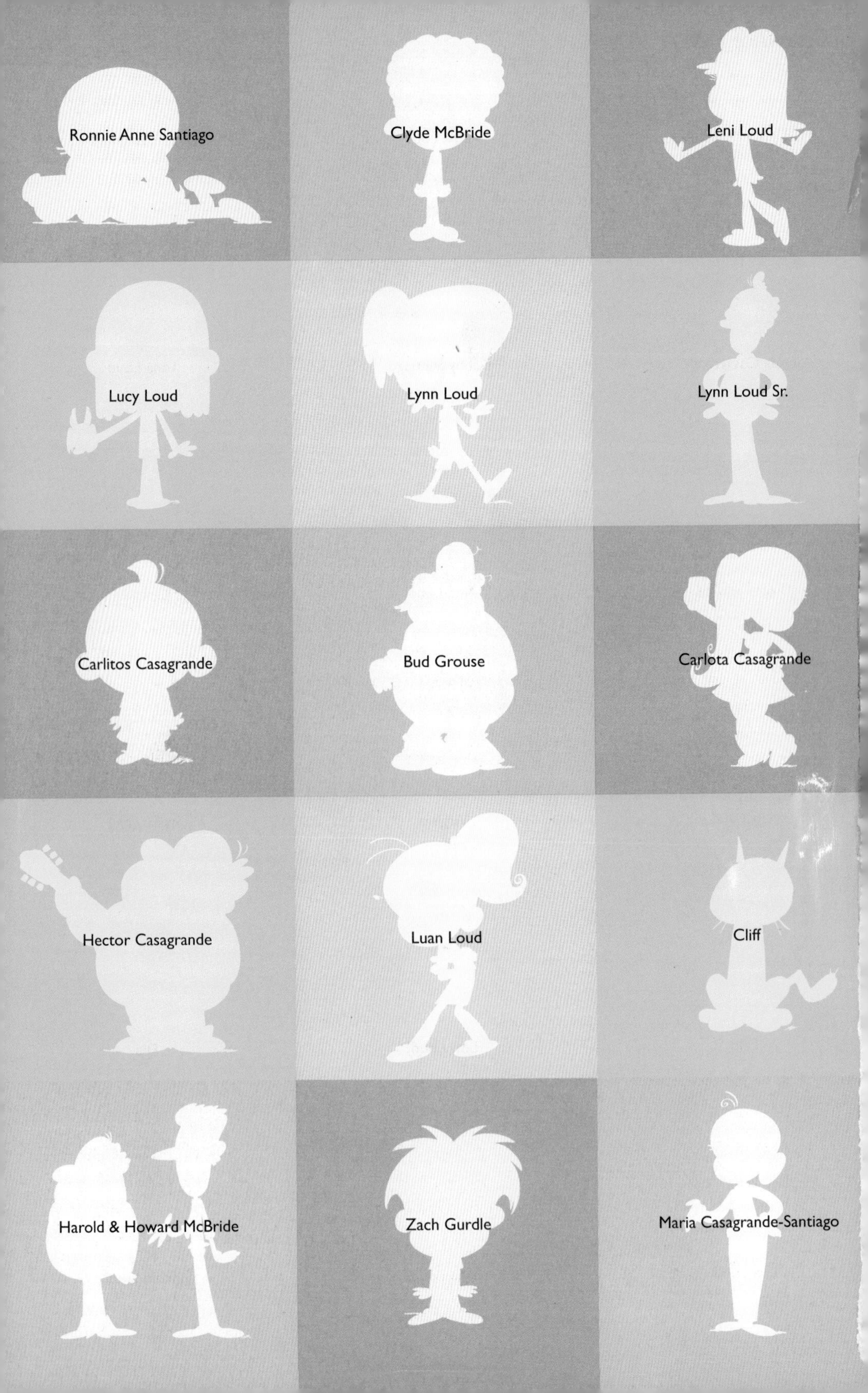
Ronnie Anne Santiago
Clyde McBride
Leni Loud
Lucy Loud
Lynn Loud
Lynn Loud Sr.
Carlitos Casagrande
Bud Grouse
Carlota Casagrande
Hector Casagrande
Luan Loud
Cliff
Harold & Howard McBride
Zach Gurdle
Maria Casagrande-Santiago